D0487824

The Household Guide to Dying

DEBRA ADELAIDE

The Household Guide to Dying

HarperCollins*Publishers*

HarperCollins*Publishers*
77–85 Fulham Palace Road,
Hammersmith, London W6 8JB

www.harpercollins.co.uk

Published by HarperCollins*Publishers* 2008

1

A catalogue record for this book
is available from the British Library

ISBN: 978-0-00-727470-3

Set in Sabon by Thomson Digital, India

Printed and bound in Great Britain by
Clays Ltd, St Ives plc

Dedicated with love to the memory of
Adam Wilton and Alison McCallum

Death, you're more successful than America,
even if we don't choose to join you, we do

John Forbes 'Death, an Ode'

One

The first thing I did this morning was visit the chickens. Archie had already given them the kitchen scraps, so I leaned over the fence and scattered handfuls of layer pellets. As always, they fussed and squabbled as if they'd never been fed before and never would be again. Then I opened the gate and went to the laying boxes, where they still crowded into one corner, even though there was plenty of room. There were three clean eggs: two brown, one white. Not so long ago I could tell which chicken had laid which egg. Now sometimes I couldn't remember their names. I picked the eggs up carefully. One was still warm. But touch is extraordinary, how it triggers memory, and so then I did remember that the tea-coloured ones were from the brown chickens, and the smaller white one was Jane's. I held it to my cheek for a moment, savouring its warmth, its wholesomeness. I wondered if this was something that poets would ever write about, because it was an experience I treasured. The comforting shape, the startling freshness. The idea that this egg, white and perfect in the palm of my hand, was a potential new life, requiring of the world nothing but warmth.

Ripeness is all. That was something a poet once said. Eliot, I think. Or Shakespeare. Perhaps both – it's hard to remember now.

With the eggs in my pocket I made my way back up the garden. Inside the house, the phone was ringing again, but I didn't bother rushing to answer it. It stopped after five rings. It had been doing that a bit lately. The air was rinsed clean from the rain earlier. I could hear the clipping of hand shears. That would be Mr Lambert next door at work maintaining his lawn, Mr Lambert for whom a heavy dew, rain, or even a snowfall – if such a thing were possible here in the temperate suburbs – never inhibited his devotion to the task. As if in his latter years, all his focus could only be directed down. I realised Mr Lambert had avoided my eye for years. I wondered if he thought about returning to the earth, now that retirement had gripped him and even his grandchildren no longer visited. Or was that just me, thinking about my own future?

Did I say future? I really wish there was the right word for all this, because *irony* doesn't come close, is completely inadequate. For a start, I discovered that Eliot was right about the cruellest month – except for me it wasn't April, but October. Spring was mocking me with its glorious signals that summer was on the way. The wisteria outside my window making the most splendid mess of the verandah. The driveway littered with papery blossoms. My car confettied with them. If I'd been driving this morning it would have been annoying, but instead I was free to admire the way the flowers had been tossed across the windscreen. The shabby old car was as radiant as a bride. And now the sun was out and the wind was warm, I could smell the wisteria. Or perhaps it was the jasmine, which was along the front fence, just out of sight. My sense of smell was becoming muffled.

What is it about mauve and purple flowers? I remembered now that Mr Eliot (my high school English teacher always referred to him with respect) also had a thing about them – lilacs and hyacinths – but for me it was wisteria, and now irises. Archie planted irises in an old concrete laundry tub he'd turned into a pond, and each year they were more crowded and abundant. I'd been watching them over the past week or two. Their great long spears. The subtle swell of the buds on the stems. On the way back from the chicken shed, I noticed that the first one was out. It was bent over – perhaps the rain earlier was stronger than I thought – but the bloom was unharmed. I cut it and placed it in a vase on the kitchen bench. It was beautiful in a frankly genital way. Dark purple with a lick of yellow up each petal. And no scent at all. I think the scent of lilacs would make me retch now.

I'd always thought that this soft margin between winter and summer could never be cruel. But here, although the hemisphere is inverted, I was as bitten by cruelty as the poet was. Spring is the time of hope. Of inspiring songs and rousing actions. Of possibility, of anticipation, of plans. People emerge from winter, after tolerating autumn's capricious start to the season, and know that if spring has arrived then summer isn't far away. Every spring our local community has a picnic in the park nearby. Children have outdoor birthday parties. Spring is the time of action, of cleaning, of revolution.

Revolution. I thought a lot about the precise meaning of words now. And their sounds. Revolution is like the word revulsion. Disgust. Rejection. This morning I hadn't yet faced breakfast, which would only be half a slice of toast, no butter, (there was no question of eating one of those eggs in my pocket). The poets were right about one thing, ripeness is all, but I'd like to tell Mr T.S. Eliot at least that his spring represented an insipid kind of cruelty, compared to mine. A laughable cruelty. It didn't get more cruel than this: the season of expectation, of hope, of growth; the season of the future, when there was none at all.

It was spring when I'd had the first operation, giving me just long enough to recover by the end of the year and face my Christmas responsibilities, instead of languishing in bed as I'd have liked. Spring again when I discovered the operation hadn't arrested the cancer. Further removal of body parts and intensive chemical treatment represented a Scylla and Charybdis between which I was pounded for another six months or so. Really, I would have preferred to row backwards, but Archie begged me to keep trying, my mother persuaded me, the fact of my two young daughters reproached me, and so I pushed on. And up until the last operation, when my body was sliced, sawn and prised open (the head this time), I still retained a scrap of hope.

But now the cruellest season had arrived again with an unmistakable finality. At least Mr Eliot had his dry stones and handful of dust to look forward to.

Two

Dear Delia
Can you settle an argument I am having with my friend (we play golf together)? She says you should only do your grocery shopping with a list. That I waste time and spend more money without one. I always take my time and think about it, and it's true I sometimes come home and forget that I needed light bulbs or rice flour. But then so does she.
Unsure.
PS We are both sixty-five years old.

Dear Unsure
I'm sure that the incomparable Mrs Isabella Beeton would have maintained that the efficient housewife should never undertake her grocery shopping without a list. It is said that impulse buying is curbed by taking a list. That a list prevents the unscrupulous vendor forcing unwanted goods on the customer. However life is short. There's a lot to be said for spontaneity. You might occasionally forget the light bulbs but I bet you buy those dark chocolate cream biscuits when they're

on special, or extra tins of salmon when you already have stacks in the pantry. I bet your list-carrying friend does too. PS Mrs Beeton was only twenty-eight when she died. Your friend might want to think about that next time she's writing her list.

Home Economics was promoted to a science some time in the 1970s. I never took the subject myself, already being domestically taught by my mother and grandmother. Both believed in the Deep-End School of home training. And so my grandmother, who cared for me when I was a preschooler, simply pointed me in the right direction and I started to scrub, soak, mop and sweep along with her. When I was a bit older, my mother, Jean, whose speciality was the kitchen, took over. I had to whip, fold and poach (later stir-fry) with barely a lesson. Their theory was that I'd simply pick it all up, that as a female I would learn all this by osmosis. A ludicrous idea, one might think, but there must have been something in the osmosis theory, for I learned without blinking. I understood sewing, cooking, cleaning and knitting. By the time I reached high school and was forced to take a term of cookery, I realised there was nothing more to discover. Learning a subject like domestic science seemed as elementary as learning how to catch a bus or post a letter. Didn't everyone just do these things? And by then I liked movies, books and music and couldn't see much scope for that down in Mrs Lord's austere kitchens or Miss Grover's sewing class.

Thirty years later, it was different. We women of the early twenty-first century knew we were poised somewhere between domestic freedom or servitude. The home was ripe for reinvention. Even the theorists were claiming it. Angels were out, they'd been expelled years back. Now you could be a goddess, a beautiful producer of lavish meals in magnificent kitchen temples. Or a domestic whore, audaciously serving store-bought risottos and oversized oysters and leaving the cleaning to others. Goddess or whore, both were acceptable.

For Isabella Beeton, on the other hand, home management was a matter of martial discipline and political strategy, with the mistress of the house both the commander of an army and leader of an enterprise. By the early twentieth century housework was a matter of economics. The housewife was the linchpin of an autonomous economic unit. Then it became a science, and all that occurred within the home was accountable to clear logic and linear process. Making a batch of cupcakes was the same as distilling a chemical formula. Children given the right quantities of affection and punishment could be raised as successfully as a batch of scones at exactly 170 degrees centigrade for fifteen minutes. Not that domestic science meant a woman was a domestic scientist. That could never be entered on forms under Occupation.

Finally the home became a *site*. Housework, like everything else from surfing to jelly wrestling, has now been hijacked by theory. Whatever the present name for the subject is in the secondary school system, I bet it doesn't include the word *home*. No doubt there are numerous research projects and dissertations underway right now on the house as locus, the discourses of vacuuming and the multimodality of the food processor.

Though perhaps not. It is women's work, after all.

One morning, I was contemplating a list which I'd retrieved from the kitchen bench. I was still in bed, the same bed in which I had cavorted with my husband for the last dozen or so years and had the most tender and exciting sex of my life though, I now realised, not nearly enough of it; conceived two children and borne one of them (the other came close, but stubbornly exerted her right to enter the world via hospital intervention); read innumerable books, many of them excellent, a lot of them trashy but wonderfully so; drunk countless cups of tea every Sunday morning while skimming the tabloid papers with an equal mix of cynicism and delight; and made notes on all sorts of things, including writing lists.

Lists were not essential to my life. Nothing would change now if I never wrote another and I suspected that without them I might still have got things done. But this particular morning's list was not for me, and I'd written it late the night before.

Put on washing
Feed scraps to chickens
Feed fish/mice (pond & tank)
Get girls up
Make lunches (not peanut butter for E)
Feed girls (don't let D have chocolate milk on cereal again)
Remind E re homework sheet
Check D has reader, library bag
Hang out washing
Empty/fill dishwasher
Girls to school half hr early (choir practice)

And also:
Have shower (if poss!)
Make coffee, drink while hot (ha!)

I had only been writing this sort of list for the last year or so, since it became clear that certain tasks would need to be delegated. Until things were *sorted out*. That was the term we adopted to describe the future that yawned like crocodile jaws, deep and daunting. Compiling it was hard because it represented things I had been doing intuitively for years. What to put in and leave out? I'd placed it strategically under the pepper grinder late in the night. When the girls came in to kiss me goodbye the next morning, I was too groggy to tell if their hair was properly tied up, teeth cleaned. I murmured goodbye and raised my head to brush their cheeks with my lips. When I woke later there was a feather on the sheet, a dark brown one. I presumed they didn't take their chickens to school.

As I reread the list I considered how Archie must have felt earlier that morning: was he insulted or bemused, offended or grateful? I wondered if I should have stipulated the girls be dressed in their school uniforms, or reminded him about their hats. Then I wondered why I felt all that was so important. I got out of bed and threw it into the wastepaper bin. Archie probably hadn't even noticed it.

I generally wake early, before the light has fully hatched. Just the day before, I had made a small pot of tea and taken a cup out into the garden. Some of the chickens were already quietly burbling to themselves. I went and sat in the cane chair under the umbrella tree nursing my tea and listening. I'd always found the sounds of chickens to be immensely pleasurable. The five of them fussed and bickered on their way out of the shed as the light grew. Lizzie – Elizabeth – the smallest and most beautiful, was the first out, leading the foray into the sun. She was a Light Sussex, wearing black feathers over her white plumage like a lacy shawl, and she was bossy, instructing the others on the order they should leave the shed. The last to emerge was Kitty, dark brown to almost black on the tips of her wings. As far as I knew, every morning Kitty greeted the day the same way: a pause at the shed door, scratching the earth, a quick dart out a foot or two, a retreat to the door, another few feet, another retreat, before finally making a line for the feed tray on the other side of the run. Halfway there, Lizzie would always turn and peck her back, whereupon the ritual began again until something distracted either of them. Kitty was the last I acquired, though not the youngest, and poultry protocol insisted that, no matter what, this chain of authority remained.

I decided that if I had another life I could just study chickens. Only that morning sitting there, and throwing the dregs of my tea over the fence (they all rushed to investigate: they were incorrigibly curious) I realised despite having chickens for several years, I knew very little about them. The problem was that they were so easy, so compliant, required minimal care. I had, I saw, taken them completely for granted. There were aspects of them I would never understand. Why, for instance, did Jane, an Australorp with magnificent black plumage, glossy and iridescent green in the sunlight, lay white eggs? Why, when I had reared most of them from chicks, did they still hesitate or even protest at being caught? Kitty would once cuddle contentedly in bed with Daisy, but then after five minutes struggle to be free. Realising that the hen preferred to roost at night, I finally had to coax Daisy into returning her to the rest of the flock, after which Kitty became pathologically timid. (And, as was the way with children, Daisy's fierce desire to sleep with the hen every night evaporated. Some other animal obsession materialised. First the goldfish, and then, when she finally accepted that they weren't amenable to cuddling, the mice: India, Africa and China. A few months back, Daisy was insisting that if she didn't take China, her favourite, to school in her pocket every day, she or it would die.)

I tasted the smallest atoms of life in those few quiet minutes. Drinking tea and waiting by chickens before the rest of the world raised its head. I tossed them a handful of layer pellets. Kitty approached the fence and ate from my hand. The gentle prod of her beak in my palm. The contented cackling. Lizzie darted across and shoved her aside. I was gripped by a sudden urge to protect the smallest of my flock. I entered the shed. Despite the dust, the earthy pungency of the chicken manure, the remains of bones and shells and everything else they unearthed in their endless, restless scratching for vermicular treats, the shed and the run was a pleasant place. It offered tender moments that couldn't be found anywhere else. The angled poles of light capturing swirls of golden dust. The feathers rising and settling on the ground. The clucking that sounded equally contented and distressed. Above all, the air of expectancy that emanated from every hen, no matter how silly. The pure optimism that kept her laying an egg day after day, when day after day that egg was taken away. Some might regard that as stupid, but I thought it almost unbearably generous. A laying hen was so full of integrity, with all that devotion and focus in her life. And then, the egg itself, sitting sometimes in dirt, sometimes crusted with chicken shit, sometimes as clean and unblemished as a new cake of soap. But inside, more than complete; stuffed, entirely, with possibilities.

It struck me that morning how I should have taken the opportunity more often to regard and wonder fully at this corner of the garden, this ordinary aspect of backyard life. Too late now.

In fact, it was too early, but I went in to Estelle and Daisy anyway. In sleep their forms assumed a softness and delicacy that would dissipate once they woke. For a minute or two I drank in their innocence and purity. Then I placed the chickens carefully beside each of them. Estelle's hands curled automatically around Lizzie, Daisy sat up with a start when she felt the tickling warmth of Kitty on her cheek.

What's up? she said.

It wasn't much past six o'clock, but I figured my daughters would have to cope with a lot worse than being dragged early from their beds.

I need to show you something very important, I said.

Cuddling their chickens, they followed me into the kitchen where I made them a chocolate milk each and sat them on their stools at the opposite side of the bench. The chickens settled into each lap with a few muted chirps. Switching the kettle on again and taking down the tea canister, I began.

Making the perfect cup of tea is not something you're necessarily going to learn by accident, I said. Although, as Mrs Beeton says, there is very little art in making good tea. *If the water is boiling and there is no sparing of the fragrant leaf, the beverage will almost invariably be good.*

Who's Mrs Beeton? Daisy said.

Never mind, said Estelle, sensing the importance of the occasion.

I made the tea while talking them through the entire process, streamlined for the twenty-first century, and taking into account local conditions. I used the small brown pot which was perfect for two cups, Irish Breakfast tea, and one of the white cups. I explained they would hear of things like warming the pot and the milk-first-versus-milk-later debate, and the metal-versus-ceramic-pot argument, which divided purists into polarised camps of Swiftian proportions.

Swiftian? What's that mean? Estelle asked.

Jonathan Swift. Wrote *Gulliver's Travels*, remember?

She nodded. We'd read a children's version of it together a couple of years back, when she was nine.

He wrote about people called Big-Endians and Little-Endians, I said. All about which end you sliced your boiled egg open. Or something like that. Don't worry about that now. We'll do eggs later.

They would only need to heat the pot on the coldest of days, I went on. Not much of a problem here, especially with global warming. Nor, I explained, did they need to worry about the one-for-each-person-and-one-for-the pot rule. It would all depend on how strong you liked your tea, and, as they knew, I happened to like mine quite weak (they nodded, yes, they knew this), whereas others, especially those who took their tea with milk (Jean, their grandmother) might like it strong.

When the tea was made and poured, I placed it under their noses and told them to inhale deeply. I knew they wouldn't want to take a sip. They sniffed and nodded when I asked them if they could detect the malty aroma.

In my opinion, I added, Irish Breakfast is still the best tea to start the day. Failing that, a brand containing an Assam leaf. And you can forget about Billy Tea, these days it's nothing like it used to be.

Then I poured it all away and started again, to be sure they'd got it. They drank the last of their chocolate milks and watched until their attention span expired and they wandered back to bed still holding their chickens.

Nowadays, I focused on small but significant things. These days, my daughters indulged me quite a lot. A year ago they would have resisted, whingeing. Refused to see the point of cups of tea, which only ancient people drank. Now they were more tolerant of my eccentric demands. Sometimes they looked at me quizzically, assessing if it was really me. I have, I thought, at least taught my daughters to make a perfect cup of tea. They might otherwise go through life thinking it was always done with teabags. Though I couldn't explain to myself, really, why I felt this would be a bad thing.

Alone in the kitchen, I raised the cup to my mouth but the perfect cup of tea now tasted bitter and my throat tightened in resistance. I went back to bed, where Archie was just stirring awake.

Three

Dear Delia
My kids won't eat vegetables apart from potato chips. And my husband hates salad. Do you have any hints to get them eating greens and other vegetables? I get sick of cooking meals they hardly eat.
Fed Up.

Dear Fed Up
Mrs Beeton declared, 'As with the COMMANDER OF AN ARMY, or the leader of any enterprise, so it is with the mistress of a house. Her spirit will be seen through the whole establishment.' Assert yourself, Fed Up . You're the cook, so take command and cook what you *think they should eat. In fact, you should cook what you want to eat, even if your favourite dish is sardines on toast or tripe curry. Take your meals alone if you have to. Let them sort it out. Remember, you're the boss.*

What are the cockles of the heart anyway?

The oddest thoughts come to you when you're standing at a graveside. And at a graveside a dictionary is probably the last thing you have to hand. I knew all about the heart, but when I got home I would have to look up the cockles.

Meanwhile, it was a chilly but clear late winter day, and I was roaming through Rookwood cemetery searching for a grave. The one I was standing before, in that silent city, had a leaning tombstone that said:

Arthur Edward Proudfoot
Late of the Parish

Underneath which had been added:

Also Alice Elizabeth
Wife of the Above

And in smaller lettering the saddest inscription of them all:

Henry James Proudfoot
Stillborn.

And then, under all that:

Died 1875
Gone but Never Forgotten
Always in the Cockles of Our Heart

An entire family history, in one brief and savage year, captured on one tombstone, erected by a family member now probably themselves unknown. There was something inescapably Dickensian about it. Especially when the largest and blackest crow I had ever seen alighted on the headstone two rows down and fixed me with a challenging look.

Let's check the map, I said to the girls, still thinking about the cockles of the heart.

Archie had walked way ahead, taking photos of the enormous monuments to the dead built by the Italians. There were vaults out here larger than inner-city flats, and probably more expensive. Entire streets devoted to housing the dead. It wouldn't have surprised me to see some black-scarfed woman emerge from a vault doorway and start sweeping down the pathway in front, or a few old men sitting at a corner smoking and playing cards.

There was nothing extraordinary about the dead, I had already accepted that. But it *was* extraordinary that I had lived most of my life without visiting them. Now I was doing research for my book. And I was also looking for my father, Frank, who died after a sudden heart attack some thirty-five years ago. His grave was a place I'd never visited. Now that I knew I was dying I needed to come.

I'm bored. This is so boring. When are we leaving?

I told you to bring a book or something.

But Daisy's complaint was fair. It was tedious for a child of eight to be trailing behind an adult around a cemetery. I knew that Estelle was bored too but she understood why it was important for us to come to Rookwood, and anyway she'd brought her Nintendo DS.

I, on the other hand, was delighted. I hadn't found my father yet, despite the maps posted all around as well as my mother's directions, but was happy to wander past the rows and rows of family vaults. We had seen vaults perched like caravans on temporary-looking bases. Maybe they were temporary, maybe some families planned to take their dead relatives with them if they ever moved interstate or overseas. I'd gazed at the Lithuanian monument and peered closely at the sample of Lithuanian soil preserved behind a panel of glass. It looked more like something from a biology experiment than a handful of dirt.

Over here, called Archie, and so I followed and finally came to the place where my father was buried. The headstone was plain, as I knew it would be, Jean being the practical person that she was. It was grey granite, low and modest, with a brass plate inscribed with his name. It said:

Frank (Francis) Bennet

(not even In Loving Memory Of: that wasn't Jean's style)

Husband of Jean
Father of Delia
Sadly Missed

And that was it. No other details. No date. At the foot of the grave, Jean had planted some sort of groundcover which required maintenance once every five years, which was about all she visited now.

Hibbertia, said Archie. It'll outlast a nuclear war.

I leaned over and examined it more closely. This end of winter, the weather was mild and buds were just forming. Soon it would be covered in flat yellow flowers.

I was five when my father died and I wasn't taken to the funeral. Those were the days when everything to do with death was silenced, hidden and guarded, like a rabid beast that a family was still obliged to keep. Children especially were kept well away, even from their dead parents, as if the bite of that beast would infect them forever. In the first few years after my father died, Jean would visit occasionally with a tin of Brasso and a fresh bunch of fake flowers, but she would never take me, and I don't remember wanting to go. Now it was so different, it seemed normal that I was bringing my daughters here – complaining though they were – just as it was normal to be discussing with them aspects of the dying process, which, after all, they were watching month by month, week by week.

Had enough? Archie said after I'd stood for a bit longer at the grave of Frank Bennet. I barely remembered him. He was not much more than a tall shape from the past. I remembered him mainly in the study in the house where I grew up, which contained books that he would take from the shelves with such reverence they seemed to be fragile things. I was rarely allowed to touch them. He had a garden shed full of tools also forbidden to me. He would make me watch from a safe distance as he planed a piece of timber or sharpened the lawnmower blades. The strongest memories of my father involved images of me running to his study or shed with messages from my mother about phone calls or dinners, and the powerful sense of importance that gave me.

I had thought the moment might have been more emotionally charged, but it was not like that. I felt nothing much at all, standing there. But I was glad I came, to see him, and to say goodbye in a way. My father's only heart attack had been sudden and final. He was in his study at his desk one minute, on the floor the next. I wondered what had happened to the cockles of his heart, if they'd just shattered or closed off, or if they'd been faulty all along.

As we drove out of Rookwood cemetery I noticed a huge warehouse on the left, with loading docks down one side. Surely there wasn't that volume of the dead to be stored or processed like airline cargo. At the end of the building was a red and white sign. Australia Post.

It must be the mail processing centre, I said. Strange place to have it.

Maybe it's the dead letter office, said Estelle after a second. Then we both screeched with laughter.

I don't get it, said Daisy, looking aggrieved.

Never mind, sweetie, Archie said as he turned back onto the highway. Do you still want to go to Waverley?

I looked at my watch. It was just after midday.

Yeah, why not? Maybe we can get some lunch around there too.

It'll still be boring, Daisy said. Why can't we go on a different excursion, why can't we go to the beach?

It is near the beach. We could go to Bondi afterwards and get an ice cream.

But I want to go swimming! I want to go to Manly beach.

No, I said, slipping a CD into the player, it's not nearly warm enough to go swimming at the beach, or anywhere. Besides, I get to choose the excursions from now on.

The opening notes of 'Heartbreak Hotel' filled the car.

Eww, not him again, Estelle said. Can't we listen to something else?

No, I said. I get to choose the music from now on too.

Four

A few months before our visit to the cemetery, I had left on another excursion on my own, and I'd found it was also a matter of the right music.

There was a place I had to revisit before it was too late. Way up north, a place where I once lived. Where we'd both lived. But I knew if I told Archie, he would stop me. I knew if I tried to say goodbye to my daughters, I wouldn't be able to leave. I had to choose the day carefully, a school day, a work day, a quiet suburban sort of day, when a drive to the local shops could casually extend into a long trip. I just had to get in the car and go. And of all the things I should have been attending to, the only thing I cared for was the accompaniment to my long drive north. Get the background music right, and everything else would slip into place. It was a soundtrack, this road movie of my life, this one-shot-at-it adventure to end all adventures, where my ears would become the organs I'd rely on more than any other, more than, at times, it seemed, my very heart.

So, I forgot checking under the bonnet for oil and water levels, forgot the spare tyre. Forgot phoning ahead to see which places had motels and which didn't, which places were indeed places, not just dots on the map, specks with only a petrol station, cafe and general store all in one, a pit stop for the loneliest drivers, the emptiest of tanks, a ten-minute stop surrounded by bitumen and disappointment, and on a Sunday afternoon always shut.

I didn't fill a Thermos, or even check I had sunglasses, packets of nuts and dried fruit, two bottles of water, one for me, one for the radiator. Just walked out that door with the barest of essentials in a small bag, a couple of books, and drove off leaving the house to its own rhythms and noises. The beds were roughly made, the dishes rinsed and left in the sink, the note was on the bench.

The screen door was still swinging as I departed. Around me the birds were chirruping in their trees as if it was just another morning in May with the post delivery revving its way from up the road, with the honeysuckle still in need of trimming down by the letterbox and the white dog shit there on the nature strip along with the flattened drink can and the sodden pulp of the week before's local paper which I'd clean away. One day.

Just not that day. Because that particular day I needed to leave while there was no one around to hold me back or ask why or talk sensibly or remind me of all that needed to be done in the next few weeks or months. Or tell me the most logical thing of all: that what I was rushing towards couldn't be found. It was a journey I'd been putting off for years, yet now I was racing off as if it were an emergency.

As I swung out of the driveway in reverse, smooth and swift as a handshake, I waved to my neighbour over the road sweeping her front path, nodded to the postie as she puttered past, then accelerated up the street, which turned into the main street, and then into the highway, the one that would take me all the way north.

Music would be my companion. It would be so vital a presence it would almost drive the car itself. But mostly it would wash through my head, drowning the sound of my own thoughts and the details, the remorse, the despair, the pain that would persist in accompanying me on this escape. The soundtrack would charm the memories up, the ones I didn't want but could no longer ignore. The ones that I had to take with me as I travelled back, and north. The memories, which were a soundtrack of their own.

I chose carefully. Nothing too gloomy. No Tom Waits, or I'd be driving off the road straight into the nearest tree that offered certain and complete annihilation. Bach was good but only for long unbroken stretches: the complex fugal pieces were incompatible with negotiating tricky routes or traffic in unfamiliar towns. I sorted through my box of music, most of them cassettes in cracked covers collected for car trips over the last fifteen years, most of them telling some sort of story, though none with any logic. The Willie Nelson tape with his version of 'Graceland' that I currently favoured (there was definitely a whole story in that). Tapes of assorted unrelated artists: Dusty Springfield, Georgie Fame, the Andrews Sisters, the Glenn Miller Band. The mindlessly cheeky George Formby, now so obscure a performer, I wondered how he ever made the transition from record to tape. Mahalia Jackson, if I was in the mood for august serenity. Country, all types. Hank Williams. Yodelling songs. Gillian Welch. Lyle Lovett. (Asleep at the Wheel I'd avoid, for obvious reasons.) It was a big collection, enough for my needs.

And there was always Elvis. I'd not played his albums for nearly fifteen years, never listened to a single song, if I could help it. But now I'd included the old cassettes in the box I was taking with me. It was time to start listening to Elvis again. But I'd wait a little longer before putting him into the player. It was going to be a long journey, and there was plenty of time for that.

So I drove north with songs like 'Graceland' urging me on, into the lush steamy warmth, to a place remote yet accessible, elusive yet as solid and immovable as a pyramid. There was chance here, a chance that had to be taken or it would slip away faster than a southern sunset. What was it exactly that I was taking a chance on?

I really didn't know, even though I was bursting to get there, my heart accelerating ahead of my thoughts, and, while empty of understanding at that stage, I was still ripe with anticipation. The same feelings that had struck me when first I arrived, all those years back.

The town of Amethyst was off the map, but it was there all right, bordered by thick margins of rainforest and mountains that slowly narrowed out, stretching northward until they began to merge into the long triangle that eventually led to Cape York. The town was situated in the middle of the middle, about halfway north of the New South Wales border, and halfway west of the coast. I could get away from the south and head north without a map – anyone could, there were plenty of signs. But at a certain point, to get near the right place, I needed the map, though the name wasn't marked. I read other names signposting the direction, and they were names that beckoned: Emerald, Sapphire, Ruby. Legendary riches.

Somewhere before the surfing nirvanas and the other lures of the coast I turned west. At some stage I turned off the soundtrack, let Hank and Frank and Mahalia and all the rest lie in their box on the floor of the car along with the tissues and takeaway wrappers and the mobile phone that I'd turn back on again when I could bear to. The cloud that had collected and settled like smog on my memories began to thin out, then lift altogether. And then I didn't need the map. I knew without looking that a place in the middle of places with names like jewels was near where I needed to be. It wasn't that far from Emerald, and not so far from the highway either.

Late in the afternoon on the fourth day of the journey, I glanced to my left and saw the signs and the three roadside businesses: a service station, a timber yard and, most oddly of all, a garden art place with gnomes in rows along the front fence, that indicated the turnoff to the last town on the route, Garnet, the last place before my destination. I was travelling on a rise when I saw jutting out of the trees beside the road the sign advertising Lazarus's trailer and campervan business, three kilometres ahead. A sign about fifty years old, flaked and faded, and pitted with the usual rifle shots. After two kilometres I slowed down, keeping my eye out. There wasn't another vehicle in sight, and I couldn't remember passing one since the last town.

I knew I was in the right place, or near enough. The sign had said nothing about where, exactly, but I drove slowly forward again until I spotted a break in the trees to my left, and I took the turnoff past Lazarus's collection of elderly vehicles, knowing it was the right place to go. The road wound down for a bit then started to rise. Somewhere on the very outer reaches of the range I knew I'd entered that large section of valleys and hills and sluggish little creeks posing as rivers situated between Clermont, not far ahead of me, Emerald to the south, where I'd been, and Alpha to the west, where I didn't intend to go. The road twisted pleasantly. The sun, low and intense, pokered my eyes. I had already dropped the map on the floor of the car.

When I'd first come here over twenty years ago, a bus had dropped me at the side of the road by Lazarus's sign. I'd walked along the road towards Amethyst, not caring how long it would take. And there was barely another car, none that I recalled. It was like entering another time frame. Maybe it was the impression of the gums shooting so high they seemed like anchors for the sky. Maybe it was the cooler air, or the spotty variable light, light that also appeared partly dark. Maybe it was the leaves that drifted down from that dense canopy, slower and more dreamily than leaves normally drop. Or maybe the bird calls far above, musical and hidden. It was timeless, other worldly. It was uncharted, and so it seemed to be invested with a corresponding fairytale quality.

Of course, I was young then, I would think that. I was a walking cliché. Seventeen, pregnant, alone. I had fought with my mother yet again. I had not fought with my boyfriend, Van, since I'd been denied the opportunity when he simply disappeared, justifying all the doubts about him my mother had had ever since she first met him. The more she had tried to talk me into an abortion the more I resisted. She was motivated, I understood eventually, only by concern, and distress that I was throwing away my educational opportunities to strap down my life with a baby before I was barely grown myself. I was motivated instead by my ideals, my dreams, adoring Van and falling easily into his older, larger world of music and poetry and inner-city sophistication.

The morning I had woken in Van's room in Newtown and noticed his romantically meagre belongings were gone, I had felt a sick stab of suspicion, soon confirmed when after days I heard and found out nothing. By then it was too late for an abortion, and definitely too late to admit my mother was right about him.

I couldn't say at what point I became convinced that Van had returned north to the town where he grew up and where his talented performing family still lived. All I remembered was the aching conviction that north in Amethyst was where I would find him. Or he would find me, and our baby.

Five

Dear Delia
I've been reading your column for some years now and I reckon I could do just as well. Who needs to be qualified to write about dirty shirt collars and poultry stuffing anyway?
Yours
Cynical.

Dear Cynical
Perhaps you are unaware that books of household advice form an integral part of our literary heritage. They are cherished by readers the world over and have been particularly sought in times of distress and hardship. Mrs Beeton's Book of Household Management *was beloved by the most unlikely of readers: the conquerors of Mount Everest, the trench soldiers on the battlefields of France. Members of many journeys and expeditions have all drawn comfort from its practical advice and general historical knowledge infused with moral ardour and homely goodness. The members of Scott's Antarctic expedition might have perished, but they did so with copies of* Mrs Beeton *in their hands.*

The fact that generations of women managed without a single self-help guide is admirable and humbling. Now the number of books available on domestic advice, from specialist titles devoted entirely to stain removal to baby care books and handy manuals taking a novice through simple family meals step by step, is enormous. More than enough to stock several shelves in the average bookstore. A hundred and fifty years back there were approximately none. *Mrs Beeton's Book of Household Management* was the first, and that did not appear until 1861. How ever did women manage before the likes of Mrs Beeton?

Unlike Isabella Beeton's, my career as a household expert was accidental. The series of *Household Guides* had become mine and made my reputation, but the original idea belonged to Nancy Costello, a commercial publisher and my employer – if freelancers had employers – and also a friend, though in a limited sense. Nancy and I enjoyed a warily pleasant relationship, one in which neither of us was committed to remembering the other's birthday or socialising regularly, but in which we could ring each other up any time about almost anything. There was no sense of obligation, and no occasion for confusion, resentment or hurt. I doubted I'd ever tell Nancy my best secrets or discuss with her my worst fears, but on the other hand I was always able to count on things like frank gossip, her best recipes (she was a great cook), or the loan of her car should I ever need it.

Nancy was pragmatic, efficient, opportunistic, ahead of her time. She understood, then knew how to address, the crises of confidence that saw intelligent people confounded by the prospect of hanging a painting, replacing a boot heel, or boiling a perfect soft egg. Her first great success was getting a free household magazine into millions of households. Her second was to develop a series of specialist self-help titles that even the vast self-help title industry had not yet thought of.

Nancy decided that the home was diminishing as the site of traditional folklore and knowledge, of mainly female authority. Whereas women had once known almost instinctively how to polish furniture or remove wine stains, now they were more likely to understand how to program a digital set top box, or complete their quarterly tax statement. While it was true that fewer men could now trim hedges or degrease driveways, the deficiency was more obvious in women, who were so traditionally bound to the home. Too many homes were now empty places, physically, psychically but also culturally, lacking the memories, knowledge and wisdom formerly accumulated like cherished crockery and handed down from generation to generation. Like an indigenous language that was no longer spoken, the lore of household life was rapidly becoming extinct, from descaling kettles to preserving peaches, from the uses for naphthalene to the best method for beer-battering fish.

At least, that was Nancy's view and in some ways she was right. Although my own home, and the home that Jean maintained when I was growing up, was filled with the making of food, of clothes, of messes then of cleanliness, over and over, so regularly you almost never noticed it was there, Nancy represented another type of contemporary woman altogether: a woman who was prepared to acknowledge the importance of the household, but wasn't personally interested in it. Nancy's home was a lean and austere place, so tidy that it barely needed cleaning. I knew, without ever having opened any of her cupboards, that she didn't possess a single bag of fabric scraps and wool oddments, nor a collection of reused Christmas wrapping paper, nor a drawer filled with old corks, bent skewers, rubber bands, chopsticks, stained tea strainers, undisposed disposable plastic spoons and an incomplete set of tin cookie cutters like other households, including mine, did.

Archie and I were starting out when I first met Nancy. Or here, in the city, we were starting out again. He was slowly lawnmowing his way into something we had begun to call a business, and I was working as an editorial assistant. Archie had supported my desire to take up the university place I'd rejected years before thanks to my unplanned pregnancy and naïve ideals. Always a devoted reader, I found myself surprisingly ahead when I commenced the arts degree. I finished under time to discover I was brilliantly unqualified for anything. I understood later the degree was more void-filling than vocationally satisfying. It was the wrapping, layers of it, around my grief. But I was happy enough to take on the only job I was qualified for – if being a good reader qualified you for anything – copyediting and proofreading for Academic Press. We published books by obscure academics, books as faded and dull as the authors themselves. They may as well have been bound in brown corduroy. Soon after I met Nancy, in her capacity as book marketing consultant, Academic Press closed its squeaking doors for good. By then I had Estelle, who was followed three years later by Daisy. After that I only freelanced, an arrangement that suited me with two small children.

When Nancy began the household guides I wasn't her first choice of author. That was a man by the name of Wesley Andrews, an enterprising person who was known as a bright spark, someone who had great contacts, who got things done. Who seemed to have a hand in all sorts of books and literary ventures. Who'd written perfectly competent novels as well as ghostwritten mediocre but best-selling memoirs of sporting personalities. He had seemed in every way the right person to put his name and imprimatur on the inaugural guide: *The Household Guide to Home Maintenance*. Correctly understanding that the first book in the series should capture both male and female readers, Nancy felt a male author was necessary. But until the writing ground to a halt somewhere between chapter eight (Roofing and Guttering) and chapter nine (Windows and Flyscreens), no one had any idea that Wesley's chief literary driving force, if not navigator and mechanic, had been his wife – who, by chapter seven (Patching and Painting) had left him for good. Which perhaps explained why the opinions and recommendations on Simple Plumbing Repairs and Basic Electrics in chapters five and six were so very simple and basic. That is where I came in.

I had already been working for Nancy, first as a casual proofreader, then writing the advice column that appeared in her free publication – advertisements and advertorials disguised as a magazine – which she called *Household Words*, a joke that I suspected only she and I shared. Her idea for the column had arrived one afternoon when she was looking at a blank space on page five of *Household Words* and facing a deadline the next day. She phoned me, interrupting a dull editing job, or whatever it was I did then as a freelancer fitting in work between supermarket visits and nappy changes.

I need a dummy column for this issue, then we'll get real letters. Can you knock something up quickly, on polishing silver, or whatever?

Nancy, no one polishes silver these days. They don't even use it.

What about stains, then? You've got two kids, you'd know a lot about stains.

I guess I do.

I'll set up the layout now, she said, and you can email me the copy later. I'll call it Dear Delia. Lucky you've got the right name for it.

Nancy paid promptly and generously for a few hundred words of tame advice which I extracted from my non-creative side between the hours of nine and eleven on a Sunday evening while Archie was watching the Channel Ten movie and the girls were in bed. For months I doubted anyone read it, as *Household Words* was pushed into letter-boxes all over the suburbs along with advertising brochures for Coles Liquor, Woolworths supermarket specials and the Good Guys Electrics catalogue and was hardly distinguishable in content from them anyway. But evidence of its readership emerged when my advice column started to receive more and more emails.

They came regularly, forwarded to me by Nancy's assistant, and for a while I responded easily enough. Nancy seemed happy, and the extra income helped with the mortgage. But then one day, bored for some reason, I amused myself by winding up the reader. It was such fun, I did it again, then again, never intending to send the replies off, until accidentally and in haste (a dish overcooking? a child left too long in the bath?) I attached the wrong file, hit the send key. If I'd assumed my copy was checked, I was proven wrong a week or two later when my mother rang to say she'd been amused by my unusual responses in that week's issue. I sat around waiting for Nancy to phone and complain. Instead I was flooded with letters, and more requests than I could deal with. Nancy congratulated me on the initiative, and insisted I go in a bit harder. As a result the advice column developed a cult following.

Dear Delia was only a version of me, a slightly feral one. A more fearless one. But readers seemed to like being insulted, treated with disdain or having their requests dismissed, and so the column continued.

> *Dear Delia*
> *Last night I had several people over to dinner, including my old friend who is still single despite her divorce coming through a good year ago, and my husband's new assistant. During the dinner my husband managed to fling his arm across the table and knock over a carafe of red wine onto my best cotton lace tablecloth. He was arguing with Don, our neighbour, and they both got a bit carried away. If I bleach it, it might fall apart, or go white or patchy. What should I do?*
> *Uncertain.*
>
> *Dear Uncertain*
> *What I will advise you, Uncertain, is to examine your guilt about your relationship with Don. Are you sure your feelings for him are as hidden as you believe? For you can be sure if I worked it out from just one letter, your unnamed husband will have worked it out by now too. Don't fool yourself for a minute that your attempt to introduce Don to your divorced and still-single friend will work as a cover for your real feelings about him and the relationship you two are conducting on the sly. In fact this will almost certainly backfire: your friend and Don will end up hitting*

it off in all sorts of ways. They might even be out at a matinee screening of the latest Hugh Grant movie right now. I'd suggest that next time you want to have dinners where arguments occur you use a more appropriate tablecloth. Perhaps seersucker. Or one of those wipe-down vinyl ones.

Six

But before I reached Amethyst there was the Garnet turnoff. And this took me back to where it all started. Back to McDonald's. How appropriate. McDonald's, that temple which was the meeting point of modern consumerism, efficiency and cleanliness. Those cold disinfected surfaces, those quickly dispensed drinks, those tightly wrapped parcels of burgers and cardboard-clad chips (for Australians still, after thirty years' indoctrination, called them chips, not 'fries'). All that order and control, all those precisely measured, weighed and timed burgers, buns, nuggets, fillets. All those smug rows of junior burgers, Big Macs and apple pies, slipping hygienically down their stainless steel chutes. All those obligingly happy Happy Meals.

The McDonald's in Garnet had changed. The playground had been rebuilt, and was bigger, brighter. There was now a drive-through facility. The palms were taller but still didn't obscure the all-important signs. After I parked I thought about going in, but then I might have had to eat something, and even for Sonny's sake I couldn't do that. It was enough just to sit in the car, thinking.

When I was last here, Sonny was eight. I thought he would have grown out of the place. But eight was a deceptive age, especially for a boy who also happened to be tall. Eight was past little-kid stage. Eight was when you attained a certain level of coolness, when style began to assert itself. You were no longer in the infants' department at school, you did Real Sport (in Sonny's case, soccer), and you were allowed the heady freedom of using a pen instead of a pencil in class.

Eight was the beginning of the end of things like favourite cuddly toys at night, ritual comfort foods like hot chocolate before bed, special plastic cartoon cups, flotation aids in the swimming pool (becoming contemptible) or vests (despicable, even in the middle of winter, none of your friends wore them...). But eight was also, still, a McDonald's Happy Meal.

There was no McDonald's in Amethyst. For some reason the town had banned all chain stores, franchises and commercial fast food outlets. But there was television. And therefore advertisements. And a neighbouring town twenty minutes away by bus, less if we got a lift with someone. I was a young single mother, equal parts guilt and indulgence, prepared to stand on my principles for only so long. So there we were, sitting over our Happy Meal. And Sonny was happy – I admit it – happy fiddling with the purple and green toy monster. Happy chewing his cardboard chips. Happy alternately sucking then blowing into his Coke, with furtive glances at me.

It was possible that within three or four years he'd come either to hate the food or be bored by it. By the age of twelve he'd probably be into something cool and trendy, like only eating at places offering noisy electronic games, places with names like Radical Zone or the Shooting Arrow. Or he'd simply be able to go out on his own, or with friends. That is, without me. Without his mother. And at twelve, he could be left safely at home for hours at a time. Then I could consider Going Out. Like a date, a real date, as opposed to spending the odd evening after work at Mitchell's bar, listening to the drifters and dreamers sucking up the oxygen while I parried their vague boozy requests for sex.

Sonny looked up at me, cutting into my thoughts. He dropped the goofy toy, frowned, and asked me what was wrong.

Nothing, I said. Why?

You look sad.

Sad?

Or angry. This last was in a plaintive sort of tone. Maybe I was still angry, maybe just a bit resentful, after what had happened earlier.

My heart twisted. Vital to bury your frustration, to put it behind you, to live in the moment, which is what children generally did. I told him I wasn't angry, or sad, patted his free hand, the one that wasn't now fiddling with the toy again, then took it in mine. A bold move. Eight was also when holding hands with your mother in a public place became pretty well verboten.

Then it was my turn to pay attention. He looked pale. Was I just imagining a touch of grey under his eyes? Then I noticed he hadn't eaten his burger, apart from one bite, and was only halfway through the chips.

Hey, I said, are *you* feeling okay?

He shrugged. That could mean anything in eight-year-old code. Really good or exceptionally bad. I already knew that kids weren't always aware of feeling sick, somehow just didn't have the words to articulate what, exactly, was wrong. Could be nearly comatose with something or other but drive their mothers up the wall with unrelieved whingeing or, even more bizarrely, excessive hyperactivity.

Do you feel sick?

No.

Open your mouth and stick out your tongue.

He snatched his hand back. No way!

Go on, open your mouth, I'll see if your tonsils are up.

He folded his arms and sat back, glancing around as if every single member of his class was waiting to leap from the corners and tease him. Being sick was not cool. Being seen to be sick, less cool. Being seen to submit to a mother's ministrations, downright fiery.

I asked what was wrong then. That shrug again. I asked if he wasn't hungry after all. He shook his head, pushed the food aside, looked at me, then away, then said,

Are you sure Archie isn't my dad? Can't he be?

Oh, that. That little big question. Guilt. Dismay. Bitterness. Helplessness. And the thousand other negative emotions the single mother was so familiar with, the reason she gave in and took her kid to McDonald's, though it went against every principle she had.

I risked a prod at his burger. It didn't respond. Typical. It sulked dumpily on the tray, not a bit happy. The bright orange cheese that dribbled out one side had already set into a hard blob. Just out of spite, since I was wound up and guilty over Sonny's undeniable lack of a father, I decided to mutilate it.

He got into the spirit of the act. Children are great like that, adaptable, prone to quick changes in mood. Together we poured scorn on the thing, prising apart the dry yoyo halves of the bun, extracting the lone slice of pickled cucumber to deride it in the time-honoured tradition of every single Australian child – perhaps every child on the planet – and sniffing with exaggerated suspicion at the remaining contents, which by now bore less resemblance to a real burger than the gimmicky magnet I used to attach his latest drawings to the fridge. He suggested we take it home and glue a magnet to it and use that instead. I agreed. And it wouldn't go mouldy, not with all the preservatives.

Our laughter lightened things, but by the time Sonny picked up the burger between thumb and forefinger and minced over to the bin with his other hand holding his nose, we were attracting dark looks from the staff, and I knew it was time to leave.

But there are worse things than McDonald's. Had I known what was to come I would have stayed. I would have eaten there every day. I would have turned away from the dusty afternoon light in my eyes as we pushed through the door onto the highway, as sluggishly crowded as it got at what passed for peak hour in these parts, and marched straight back to the counter and ordered dozens of Big Macs, litres of Coke. And ten kilos of cardboard chips.

Seven

Dear Delia
I've consulted numerous cookbooks but despite many attempts I still can't manage to boil a soft egg. Can you help? I wonder if I should Google it?
A Bachelor.

Dear A Bachelor
You are asking me to impart one of my best secrets. Go Google all you like. I worked it out, I'm sure you can too.

I'd started another list. I should have been concentrating on the real work, but I felt an irrational urgency about this. I would finish it then put it in one of the boxes I was preparing for the girls.

Guests (needs separate list: obviously can't be done now)
Invitations: suggest professional printers
Cake: refer to recipe (but maybe Jean?)
Dress: David Jones's best?

Photographer: god knows. Maybe digital cameras will be obsolete by now?
Catering: Benny's the obvious choice. But Cater Queen if not poss.
Venue: depends on time of year. Back garden perfect if summer/spring.
Musicians: string trio (students from college?)

Ideally this list wouldn't be needed for another twenty years. Ideally, if it were entirely up to me, it would never be needed, since I was beginning to sense the redundancy of marriage. But as I didn't feel it was right to impose my views on anyone else, even my own daughters – especially my own daughters – then it would be better than no list.

Along with everything else it offers (a chance for relatives to catch up, a good excuse for a booze-up), a wedding is a means for a certain level of bonding between mother and daughter. Fraught bonding at times (I remembered it well), but a rite of passage that should not be denied at any cost, no matter the jaded views of the older generation. No matter that the mother would not be there.

That my daughters would not need this list for many years was irrelevant. All that mattered was that they'd know I'd made the effort. And if by then they happened to be capable of organising a wedding without my assistance, then even better. In fact, I'd regard it as a significant sign that the mothering I'd managed to squeeze into the years available was successful.

Archie had recently called me a control freak. I think it was the day after I'd written that late-night list to help him get the girls to school. As I sat at my desk with the preliminary list for the wedding of my youngest daughter, who was just eight, a wedding that might never occur, and which I certainly wouldn't be attending, I confronted this accusation. If all this wasn't the work of a control freak, then what was? I tapped my lips with the pen and gazed out the window at the wisteria. I decided that Estelle was probably in no need of any such list, being supremely organised herself. Also of firm opinions, already, regarding matrimony. It was Daisy I was planning for, though with built-in flexibility if Estelle should turn out to surprise us all.

Them all.

I wondered if these lists said more about me or Archie. I'd spent too many mornings, more than I cared to remember, explaining to him what needed to be done: instructing, directing, losing my temper, becoming impatient, before finally doing it all myself. As if I'd been at the control centre of a military exercise, a full-scale war, instead of a partner in a marriage that included two young children. Occasionally, the children had been dressed and fed (if you counted crisps as food) and otherwise organised out of the house and off to childcare, lately school, without my help. But the fallout had never been worth it:

> Daisy: I didn't get a merit star today because I forgot my home reader.
> Estelle: Miss Blake says if I don't take my permission note back I won't get to see the Dreamtime storyteller.
> D: I was cold, why didn't you pack my jumper?
> E: You know I hate blueberry muffins!

And so on. I tried every method available to the reasonable woman. Pointing out the lapses in a kind way ('Darling, don't you think Daisy should have her shoelaces tied?'). Barking out orders like a sergeant-major ('If you don't take them NOW they'll be marked late!'). Saying nothing. Saying everything. Standing by pretending to be preoccupied with another task but internally writhing as Archie tried to brush hair that was still plaited or failed to understand that children needed reminding to wear sweaters even in the middle of winter. Writing lists. Not writing lists. Doing none of the tasks. Doing half the tasks, like lining up the contents of a lunchbox so that he only had to place them inside, close the lid and grab the juice bottle from the fridge. *Daddy packed my lunch today*.

Nothing worked. Now I was playing my very last card. It was a mean trick, I knew. I felt its meanness myself. How cruel, how unfair, how totally unsporting, how unlike the stout mothers of public life, the mothers of fiction. You could never imagine Mrs Gandhi or Mrs Micawber or Mrs Thatcher or Mrs Weasley dying before their time and leaving their children unmothered. The prime minister's wife – any prime minister's wife – Nicole Kidman's mother, Mrs Jellyby, Angelina Jolie, the Queen, Lady Jane Franklin, Mrs George Bush senior and junior ... they would never have died young and left motherless children. They might have been doubtful, dominating or dysfunctional – all Dickens' mothers were – but they stayed around. Even Lady Dedlock hung in there. Jane Austen's Mrs Bennet would never have left five young daughters weeping over a coffin. The mother dying was a disgraceful breaking of every single rule and if I were Archie, I would have been outraged too. But that wasn't going to change, and it certainly wasn't my idea.

I wondered if my absence would make any real difference to the running of the household. *As with the commander of an army, or the leader of any enterprise, so it is with the mistress of a house.* Like Mrs Isabella Beeton I had applied a strategic approach to the household, its contents, its routines, and its warm and breathing occupants. And how had I forgotten that Isabella Beeton, that wise, visionary, well-read, innovative woman, that *young* woman, had died far too early? Isabella Beeton had left her two children – one just a baby – motherless. *She ought always to remember that she is the first and the last, the Alpha and the Omega in the government of her establishment.*

But what once infuriated me about Archie I now admired. It hadn't been his tendency to dally in flirtatious territory at dinners or parties featuring women with more impressive cleavage than I – and of course, more recently, with cleavage at all. Nor had it been his need to bond with members of the same gender and subspecies (semi-professional, rugby-loving) at the pub once a week. Nor his regular forgetting of birthdays and anniversaries. If this marriage were to have unravelled it would have been over something as trivial and tangible as a misplaced sock, or a forgotten school lunchbox. That indifference to the knitted fabric of the household. It might have been misshapen over time and ill-fitting but still, thanks to the one thread that was me, it all held together: the shopping, the bill-paying, the girls' activities, their dental appointments, their swimming lessons, their need to dawdle in the park doing nothing at all.

However, I now saw a quality that I almost craved. Maybe Archie's indifference to the household was restraint, a capacity for self-control and wide-gazing detachment. Something I couldn't do, being forever focused on the crumbs on the kitchen bench in front of me, the emptying milk carton in the fridge, the multiplying dirty clothes in the basket.

I once heard a famous actor being interviewed on the radio about the breakdown of her marriage. When pressed to name its cause she replied succinctly: shirts. I knew instantly what she meant. The symbol of a married woman's unscripted yet unavoidable role in the relationship. No clause in the contract stipulating the care and maintenance of the male shirt, yet somehow they took over, with their demands to be soaked, ironed, fresh and alert on hangers ready for the next excursion into the working world. It took a stout feminist to withstand the onslaught of the shirt.

My particular argument had never been with shirts, since Archie's work gear was casual. And even if it had been, I would never have left him over a shirt because, despite his domestic blindness, Archie had given me more than I deserved. But there had been times when I could see how it might have been possible to leave. I doubted he had ever understood how tight a thread I had been all these years. And now that one thread was about to be snipped. And if on the very edge of that scission, I was still unable to fall back, stop being the commander of the household, what did that say about me? Control freak, I guessed. Yet I suspected there was something more to it than that. Yet another thing for which I could not find the right words.

I wondered what happened when women disappeared from a family. Another woman enlisted to take their place? A paid housekeeper, or a wife? Despite his occasional flirtatiousness I couldn't see Archie rushing into anything. That didn't fit with the father in him. I knew he would be assisted by his mother and my mother, who between them would probably make life easier for him than I ever had. Then, after a while, depending on how Estelle and Daisy reacted, a new partner would come, followed possibly by marriage. Secretly I was hoping for Charlotte, Archie's part-time bookkeeper, which seemed logical to me, although I'd tried and failed to discuss the subject with him. I liked Charlotte, I admired her. She was a serene young woman who was completing a diploma in business management. She worked with percentages and bottom lines and, I suspected, had never made a sponge cake or done French knitting in her life. She came one day a week and worked in the corner of Archie's shed which was also his office, sending out invoices and settling accounts with suppliers, decoding then dispensing all the paperwork of the tax system that Archie found so mystifying. Estelle and Daisy adored her and only ever wanted her to mind them if Archie and I went out. If she married Archie it would be almost perfect.

Oh, and it would be cruel. Another woman to usher the girls into their teenage years, into their adulthood. To be there for their first period, to buy the most expensive hair products, to offer advice on skin care, to tolerate teenage-girl cravings for Nutella or obsessions with vegan diets. To pretend to understand how vital MySpace was. To be there when their boyfriends abandoned them. Gasp at their mobile phone bills. Shake a head over their newest piercing. Tell them, every day, how beautiful they were. And how much they were loved.

Cruelty. What exactly did Eliot say again? I found my undergraduate copy of the *Selected Poems*, and prepared to torment myself further with his gloomy words. But when I read 'The Wasteland' again I had to admit that Mr Eliot was right: it was winter that had kept me warm, in a strange sort of way. Muffled me in its state of suspended animation, kept me from the cold steel of memory and desire before they sliced through my soul in the expectant warmth of spring.

An attack of wind shook the wisteria so furiously the petals rained onto the verandah. Opening the office window wide I took in its scent. I heard the clicking of Mr Lambert's wheelbarrow next door. This time of year, he was more than particular about his garden: he was obsessive. He would be sweeping up the leaves and blown petals as they dropped, cursing my messy flowering vines and clipping every tendril that sneaked its way past the fence. Instead of shaving his front lawn today, he was probably pruning, the mock orange hedge being his chief target. I never smelled the mock orange during the day, but some nights the entire atmosphere was saturated with it. It could not be just from Mr Lambert's abject specimens, which he trimmed into order every week in the warmer months.

Winter would soon be just a chill memory. The scent on the wind told me that. It might have been the freesias, planted around the letterbox. The fragrance always filled me with a strange distracted yearning, a restless and aching expectation. Perhaps because it contained the promise of summer, the season I loved the most. I remembered the freesias which grew along the railway embankments and in vacant lots all the way down the south coast. The ones that filled a room with a scent at once wild and comforting. They brought suggestions of many things: memories of rough childhood holidays on the south coast beaches; weekends away in holiday shacks with friends; the evidence of the first garden I ever helped plan, plant and nurture into life, when we first came to live here. The garden hadn't existed then: the house perched disdainfully at the front of a long narrow stretch of buffalo grass. There was a Hills hoist rotary washing line, immobilised by age, and nothing else. We brought clumps of the wild freesias and, after hacking away at the grass to uncover cracked but serviceable paths and the faint outlines of former garden beds, planted them here and there.

For all the years I caught their first scent each spring, I experienced a small stab deep within. A distinct physical ache, and one that always made me feel momentarily emotional, though whether on the verge of tears or shouts or laughter, I could never say. This seasonal feeling was so common I had always registered it unthinkingly. Until now. For I would no longer smell these flowers, and it seemed important to define accurately what the scent meant. And it wasn't only the freesias. All the spring flowers taunted me in their postcard perfection, as unwelcome as the memory and desire that now encroached on the day. They all seemed to have come out of the dead land, the garden that I once revelled in.

On the desk beside me the phone rang.

Hello?

There was no one at the other end but I sensed a presence. I suspected it was the same person who also hung up after a few rings, before I could answer it.

Hello? I repeated more loudly, but the presence was not to be provoked by shouting. I slammed the phone down. I had no idea who it was. The caller ID function told me it was a private number.

I closed Mr Eliot, more carefully than I otherwise might, adding him to the collection of books on the bedside table. They probably wouldn't make their way back to the bookshelves in the hall.

Dear Delia
Don has been very good to me, and my husband has neglected me for years for his work. You still didn't advise if I should bleach my lace tablecloth or not. And as well as the red wine it is smeared with green stains where Don knocked over his avocado and prawn entrée.
Uncertain.

Dear Uncertain
Don, Don, Don. It's all about Don, isn't it? And why is it that you are attracted to such clumsy men? I advise you to sever relations with Don and concentrate on your husband. Maybe he works too hard because you are the sort of person who uses lace cloths and makes avocado and prawn cocktails. What were you thinking? It's not 1975 any more. Of course soaking an antique lace cloth in bleach would be crazy. Try lots of salt, cold water, then hang it out in the sun for a day. Let me know how you go.

Eight

By the time it was nearly dark and the families had come and gone in the late afternoon rush with their Happy Meals and movie-deal specials, I felt ready to drive off again.

I'd see if I could find Mitchell. If he was still around he would be at one of three places. The first was the café on the way back to Amethyst. It had a new name, and when I pulled up and saw the sign I assumed it was a facetious one. But when the waiter, dreadlocks flying, rollerbladed to my table with the menu, I understood it really *was* the Roadkill Café. She explained that they were out of wallaby.

We've got python instead, chargrilled. And the specials are rabbit casserole – or rat, if you like. In one movement she yawned slightly and shifted her chewing gum across to the other side of her mouth.

Rat?

Both types. Native and rattus rattus.

Oh.

I wondered if there was a difference. Only in price, she told me, scanning the rest of the room and chewing her gum. The native rat, antechinus, was five dollars more, and it wasn't written down because Parks and Wildlife might be alerted and even though it was genuine roadkill, guaranteed one hundred per cent fresh …

Look, could you come back in a few minutes?

It had been a long day's drive, and I had barely eaten, and should have been hungry. But the whole place and menu had changed. It used to be called Mitchell's café, just like his place in town was Mitchell's bar, though neither had a sign to explain that. People just knew. But it didn't surprise me to find a marginal sort of dining experience here, this strange diner that fed its patrons off the very road that brought them to its doors. Amethyst had always been like that. Nothing ever conformed. It was one reason why I chose to stay all those years back.

I studied the menu again, hoping to spot a salad or soup. Apart from the thought of eating any rat, the threat of the Parks and Wildlife department was off-putting. Would they raid the café and confiscate my meal between mouthfuls, prosecute me for eating a national or state emblem? Or worse, a sports mascot? I thought about taking out my mobile phone and turning it on. It had been four days and I expected the message I'd written for Archie and the girls was by now insufficient. I took the phone out of my bag, stared at the blank unlit screen for a few moments, then replaced it. Not yet. Not until I was really there.

The waiter was getting annoyed.

Is Mitchell around? I asked. A foolish question. She was probably two years old when I was last here.

Mitchell? Never heard of him. Steve might know, he's in charge.

Could you ask him?

Sure. Steve! She yelled so loudly I thought the gum would shoot from her mouth.

A man appeared through the fly strip curtain, wiping what looked like fresh blood from his hands onto a tea towel.

Hi. I was wondering if Mitchell was still around. I used to work for him.

I took over the place from him, Steve said. But that was over ten years ago. Not sure where he is now. I'm from Garnet, back down the highway. But he could still be in that bar in town.

Sure, I said. Thanks.

Are you ready to order yet? the waiter said.

No thanks, I said, getting up. Sorry, I've changed my mind.

I passed Lazarus's Vehicles again. It had barely changed. The same collection of shabby trailers and caravans sitting at angles, having been left by their previous owners without the bricks to prop them up. Peeling reminders of holiday aspirations, plans and dreams that were never realised.

When the bus had dropped me off some twenty years ago, it wasn't a scheduled stop. The driver had said he couldn't take me any farther, but that I could get to where I wanted to go if I waited here by the side of the road. Someone would soon drive past and give me a lift for the final few kilometres into town. He'd seemed very confident of that.

I waited for an hour, then, hot and thirsty, started to walk. I eventually came to Lazarus's yard. He agreed to take me into town when he shut up shop at five. He dropped me at the Kingfisher Boarding House, a block from the main shops and just shabby enough for someone of limited means.

Early the next morning I started looking for Van. Three days later I checked out and returned to Lazarus's. This time I had a proper look, walking around the whole site, investigating cluttered corners of the yard and peering into vans and trailers I doubt he remembered he had. I spotted the most endearing caravan I had ever seen. A comic book caravan. Curved, aluminium, a dull sky blue. It was perched on tufts of grass amid the graveyard of vehicles, most of them decrepit. This was old, but it looked sound enough.

How much? I asked him.

That? Not much use to you, he said. It won't travel, not far anyway.

What about into town?

Well. He scratched under his bandanna. There is a caravan and camping park, a few people live there. Some holiday units, a couple of old-timers in vans. A guy called Mitchell runs it.

I'm staying on for a while, I said. I'll need a place to live.

He looked from me to the caravan, then back to me again.

He's a decent guy, he said, I reckon he wouldn't charge you too much to rent a site.

I gazed at the van. The modest curves, the unrelieved shabbiness, the air of simple hope. I asked him again how much, and it was a matter of moments before he told me I could have it for one hundred dollars. I'd be doing him a favour.

I could tow it in for you, he said.

So, that very evening, I had become a caravan owner. For one hundred dollars it was empty, apart from a thin mattress on the bed, but I made do without a blanket or towel until the next day. Inside it was not nearly as dirty as I'd expected, having been shut up tightly for years. The stale air vanished soon after I opened the door and prised apart the doll's house windows on each side. Over the following weekend I walked into the centre of town and back, gradually stocking up on the essentials, which, I discovered, were few when you stripped life down to the most important things. What I needed, more than anything, were books, and by the time I was ready to have the baby, the second-hand bookshops had supplied enough to line the caravan. It was like living inside a cubby house. Surrounded by books, I felt safe, secure.

Nine

Dear Delia
Do you have a good recipe for a wedding cake? I've tried several but found them dry and tasteless.
Mother of the Bride.

Dear Mother of the Bride
Dried fruit, obviously. Raisins, sultanas, mixed peel. Preserved ginger if you like. Brown sugar, flour, spices ... Oh, for god's sake, do I need to list everything? Surely you can work it out. And don't ask for weights and measurements. That is tedious in the extreme. In fact it's probably why your cakes have always failed. By the way, several *cakes? How many weddings have you had?*

Modern mothering was a snap.

Here I was agonising over my daughter's wedding at least twenty years too early and trying to decide between linen napkins (more stylish, but more laundering) or paper ones in shades matching her outfit (it would be palest pink, more cream than pink, like the flesh of a white peach) that would be much less stylish but more efficient (no ironing), and then I recalled Jane Austen's Mrs Bennet.

I often thought of Mrs Bennet when the going got tough in the blood sport that the game of raising daughters had become. Mrs Bennet's daughters might have displayed more respect for their mama, might not have spent hours in their bedrooms plastering their faces with gooey make-up, rereading the same *Girlfriend* or *Total Girl* magazines over and over, or listening to obscure punk bands; they might not have insisted on dressing like child prostitutes from the moment they could do up buttons on their own, refused to eat meat from the age of eight and made prepubescent demands to have their navels pierced. But I had to admit there was a plus side to my experiences.

First, she had five daughters, and I only had two. And poor Mrs Bennet's entire commission in life was, after raising them, to marry them off to suitable husbands. I might have been planning a wedding, but it was in an age where husband hunting had long dropped off the agenda. Daisy could get married or not as she pleased. Not so Jane, Elizabeth, Mary, Kitty and silly little Lydia. Oh yes, Jane and Elizabeth might have had an element of choice, and Elizabeth may well have exercised her right to reject the absurd advances of Mr Collins and the first astonishing proposal of Mr Darcy without a single reference to her mother's wishes, but neither she nor any other Austen heroine was going to slum it with the love of her life in an artist's studio in the East End of London (a place of such unredeemed vulgarity it was, I suspected, never once mentioned in the entire Austen oeuvre), or marry a man she'd met on the bus or down the pub on a Friday night.

True, Mrs Bennet had household help, and I had none. But Mrs Bennet's obligations far outstripped mine. I didn't have to run our lives to a rigid social and domestic schedule. We didn't have to make tedious calls upon parish spinsters or endure visits from patronising social superiors. We could, and did, spend our evenings lingering over any book we wanted, reading *The Wind in the Willows* or *Where The Wild Things Are*, again and again whether they or I had grown out of them or not. True, it was important to feed my daughters with nutritionally balanced foods, monitor their homework, supply a few extracurricular activities, such as Estelle's netball or Daisy's recorder lessons, and ensure they didn't watch too much television. When the time came, caution them against the more unsanitary forms of body piercing and advise on the use of condoms (if I were there, but perhaps I could expect Charlotte to do that – they wouldn't listen to Jean).

But poor Mrs Bennet had the responsibility of making all her daughters proficient in dancing, card games and needlework. At least one – Mary – had a workable grasp of pianoforte, Italian songs and Scottish airs. They all had to demonstrate parlour and drawing-room etiquette, and have a familiarity with the historical epic poems of Sir Walter Scott. She had to ensure that every daughter's complexion remained clear and fine and fair, that the circumferences of their waists remained within an acceptable twenty-four inches, that their hair stayed dressed in coils and ringlets (Lydia, for sure, would have wanted to shave, spike, streak or do all three to hers). Mrs Bennet was responsible for their deportment, posture, manners when in church or at table, behaviour while strolling down to the village haberdashery (Lydia would have had tattoos, and belly piercings too). She had to foster polite and appropriate discourse in a variety of contexts from the vicar to the scullery maid. She had to teach them about bowel movements (without stooping to vulgar terms), menstruation (without so much as mentioning blood), sexual relations between husbands and wives (without being able to refer to the intimate physical act, let alone uttering, let alone *thinking of*, words like penis or vagina), and then initiate and oversee the vast, all-consuming business of finding the appropriate man attached to the end of the unmentionable organ – the whole reason, culmination, justification, of a woman's life. Poor Mrs Bennet. The task was gargantuan. And she did indeed fail in many of her duties. I don't think even Jane, of all the daughters, managed decent piano playing (though I imagined Lydia taking up drums). Not one of the Bennet girls was schooled and, as there had never been a governess, the level of education had clearly been hit and miss. But Mrs Bennet did her absolute best, and one of the worst difficulties she encountered was the benign indifference and sarcastic humour of her library-closeted husband.

When she was discontented she fancied herself nervous. The business of her life was to get her daughters married; its solace was visiting and news.

I honestly couldn't claim that taking Daisy to recorder lessons for half an hour once a week was onerous, compared with Mrs Bennet's commitments. Readers might have been tricked into thinking that she was a silly shallow woman and that her husband, with all his dry sarcasm. was a self-effacing, long-suffering man, but Mrs Bennet was a champion among women, among mothers, a pearl of great price. I was going dizzy at the thought of linen versus paper napkins, but she – strong, determined and single-minded – was faced with the entire box of dice from the cradle on. Times five.

So why was I thinking about marriage? Did I really desire that my daughters had husbands? My present obsession with Daisy's wedding no doubt had a lot to do with my own. Archie and I were married, certainly, but in the austere political and secular correctness of a registry office. Here we banished all suggestion of offensive sexist symbolism such as white veils or floral bouquets. There were no demeaning vows involving words like obedience. And yet, without an audience beyond our witnesses, there were no obligations to quote mystical Lebanese poets or play chamber music.

I began to question if I was not unhealthily fixated on an entirely imaginary husband, the sort of husband who, if he existed, you wouldn't want for a husband anyway. I could admit now that the perfect husband resembled a wife. I often yearned for a wife. I yearned for one right at that moment, a wife who would bring me a cup of tea, then go and hang out the washing that I knew would be creasing itself after the centrifugal force of the washing machine had plastered it to the insides of the drum. A wife who was me. That person who was, right now, tired. And, I admitted, weary of the housework, which had never really bothered me, which I'd never found difficult or mysterious.

But whether or not it was now too many years of loads put on or hung out or gathered in, wrinkled and all, or if it was an increasing resentment that flowed like the toxic chemicals that I tried to flush out of my system, or just a simple matter of being too tired and too busy all at once, I could no longer tell. All I knew was, today I would be leaving the washing there in the machine while I wrote my list.

Dear Delia
About the wedding cake. I'm afraid I need more precise ingredients than that. And how long would you recommend I cook it for? Hopefully you will be able to help me.
Mother of the Bride.

Dear Mother of the Bride
As with the wedding itself, hope is the chief ingredient of a wedding cake. You are right to be hopeful. Hope will keep a marriage going for a long, long time. Have a go. I'm sure you can manage it.

Ten

The centre of Amethyst was in a hollow, streets angling down towards the main roads, the clusters of shops. The streets were full of enormous trees and then, on the west of town, there were large open spaces like natural parklands along which sauntered a lazy river, bordered with willows and reeds. In autumn, the place was enchanting. In the cooler months it was perfect, and in summer it was shady enough to give the illusion of coolness. Along the main street into town the palms were enormous, dense, and in the late afternoon crammed with brightly coloured parakeets monstering the fruits in a cacophony of greed. They shot back and forth across the road boldly, forcing me to steer the car from side to side to avoid them.

The Paradise Reach Motel, a small family business, was still there. It had quiet, spacious rooms, a palm-crowded front garden with a pool, and a friendly watchdog, whom I noticed as soon as I pulled up. Surely it wasn't the same one from years back – he'd have been well over sixteen by now: did labradors live that long? The woman at the desk wasn't familiar, but she told me the motel was still in the same hands.

You're from Sydney?

Somehow, up north, people always knew.

Yes, I said. But I lived here once, years ago.

Oh, and are you on holidays now? Visiting relatives?

Something like that.

I checked into my room, threw my bag in the corner and myself on the bed. I lay there for a long time, resting, thinking. Until it became dark enough that I had to get up and turn on the lights.

I found Mitchell upstairs in his bar. He appeared to be interviewing a new pianist. I started to tiptoe out again when I realised what was going on, but he waved to me to stay, and without asking what I wanted, fixed me a drink.

This is Chris. He nodded to the man sitting at the bar. He might be playing here.

Chris held out his hand and shook mine. In profile he revealed a lean tanned face, but as he turned, I glimpsed the other side, a mottled mess of dark birthmark, more raspberry than strawberry, spreading from his nose to his ear and disappearing under his hair, which was black and curly. He continued talking.

I'll do requests, but there are certain tunes I won't play.

Fair enough, Mitchell said.

'You Must Remember This'.

Okay.

'Candle in the Wind'.

Yep, fine.

And especially 'Piano Man'. Come to think of it, nothing by Billy Joel. Not a note. Or I walk out that door right there and never come back.

Sure. Okay.

I glanced at Mitchell, who was sounding oddly acquiescent, though he didn't look it. He looked, with his sleeves rolled to the elbows, polishing wineglasses which he periodically held up to the light for exaggerated inspection, like a man with more important matters on his mind than what a temperamental pianist might condescend to play.

Chris seemed to relax. He paused, took a sip of his drink, then added,

Beyond that, I'll play just about anything. Swing, jazz, honky tonk, country, blues, you name it. Bach, Liberace, Mrs Mills, anyone you like.

Mitchell stopped polishing to ask, Trucking songs?

Sure, why not? I'll work any nights you like, within reason of course. Might want the occasional night off for Christmas or something. But no days.

I don't open much before four or five anyway, Mitchell said. Except for functions.

Yeah, well, that's the other thing. No weddings, no engagements, no twenty-firsts, you know? I can't stand those crowds. They expect you to know every tune on the planet and get the shits when you won't play those Burt Bacharach numbers for hours at a time.

Mitchell shrugged and said, They usually bring their own sound. What about funerals, though? I get the occasional one. Usually small crowds. Except the Irish and Islander funerals tend to go on for a while.

Now, funerals I can do. Chopin, no problem. Drunken Irish songs, 'Danny Boy', that's all fine by me. I love funerals. Chris rose, glancing at his watch. He eased into his jacket then held out his hand to Mitchell.

Tomorrow night, see you about ... Mitchell began.

Around seven. Might manage it by then. Chris said goodbye to me and departed.

I raised my drink while gazing at Mitchell. A direct or indirect question to him was a certain way to complete and eternal ignorance. The only way people could find anything out was by waiting, listening, watching. Unfortunately, Mitchell being such a generous host, that also meant hours spent drinking many drinks, all of them pretty potent. I could sit on one of his margaritas for an hour now and then, but I couldn't sustain the pace over the length of a night. If he noticed you drinking too slowly he simply reached out for the remains of your drink, tossed it into the sink, and made you something different and more solvent. A pineapple daiquiri, three times the normal strength. The only advantage was that these sessions had the effect of making your tongue numb but his loose, as if he was the one drinking, though I never saw him with anything other than a bitter lemon. So you got to hear information about all sorts of people, in and out of town. Fascinating, if you could remember any of it the next day.

It was a quiet evening, only half a dozen patrons clustered at a few tables over by the windows. On the bar a canary fluted sleepily in his cage. Behind Mitchell, on the back wall, the row of mirrors reflected the semi-precious gem colours of the exotic and rarely dispensed liqueurs and mixers – crème de menthe, grenadine, Galliano – while behind me on the open windows the gauzy curtains waved in the warm breeze, sucking and billowing out to embrace the potted palms then gently and noiselessly dropping again.

At times like this I could understand what had kept generations of men seated at bars sipping beers with only the drone of a television in the background. It was a sanctuary, where nothing was required of you, nothing asked. An enclosed and protective place that was also a public space with company and conversation should you require it. A place that made few demands, allowed a person to float without care or deadline, timetable or commitment. And drove their women mad with frustration.

I remained quiet, briefly catching Mitchell's eye in the bar mirror as he turned to the shelf to stack glasses or smooth out towels. Then, after he served a beer to someone, I spoke.

So, what's Chris's story, where's he from?

But Mitchell reached down to one of the fridges, then slowly stood up again before asking,

What brings you back after all these years?

He asked it in a way that implied he wasn't interested in the answer, didn't need an answer. He knew why I was back.

Have you been to the caravan? he continued.

Not yet. Going there tomorrow, I said.

About time, don't you think?

I know that.

His curls had greyed beneath the Greek fisherman's cap, and the lines in his face were deeper, but I still would have known him in an instant, anywhere.

Apart from sending on those boxes of yours, I haven't known what to do about the place for bloody years. By the way, he added, you look like shit.

I know, I said. Bilateral mastectomy tends to do that to you. Especially followed up by secondaries. Liver. Tumours. The works, really. I'm just in the queue now for the upsized deal, the mega meal. You know, the one you can never finish eating.

Mitchell finally registered surprise. He put down the glass he was polishing, tossed aside the towel.

Oh, Delia. I always knew you'd return. Not with that, though.

Who would?

He gazed at me for a few moments, as if drawing out all the years in between.

And you've still never found Sonny's father, I suppose?

No, never.

I became entranced by Van the night I first met him. He was playing guitar in a three-man band, singing and entertaining the small gathering with extemporised anecdotes and jokes. It was just an undergraduate trio – on reflection more audacious than sophisticated, making up in energy what it lacked in polish – but then, I was sixteen and suburban. He was twenty-two, and so much more charming and confident than the teenage boys I knew, who functioned via grunts and jerky movements, and who, if you went out with them, thought it was generous to buy you a bottle of Island Cooler then ignore you for the rest of the night.

It was a café and bar, where I shouldn't have been, but I'd escaped from an evening football match that my school's team was playing at the university grounds, and wandered up to Newtown. The venue was a dark place, with lava lamps on the bar and candles on the tables. I listened to the music for a set then ventured to the bar. I was ordering a glass of wine and handing over a dollar to the barman, who looked stoned, when someone whispered into my ear from behind,

Are you *sure* you're eighteen?

I turned to see the guitarist. Up close he was all silky locks and neat beard: his eyes seemed to burn brighter among the dark blond hair. My first thought was that he looked like Jesus Christ, my second thought was how stupid that was, since no one knew how Jesus looked.

Of course, I lied.

I was delighted at the attention. He followed me back to my table with a drink and sat down uninvited while a thrill travelled through me. He introduced himself.

Van, I said. That's an unusual name.

Oh, I changed it.

Changed it? Could one *change* one's own name? Awesome.

My parents called me Ivan, so I just changed it to Van a few years ago. After Van Morrison. It reflects my personality more, you know.

Oh. Yeah, I said, pretending to know who Van Morrison was.

What are you drinking? he asked, although it was obvious.

Moselle. I took a sip. It was too sweet, but Jean drank Lindemans Ben Ean at home and it was all I could think of to order.

Old ladies' drink, he said. You should try some of this.

He was drinking Jack Daniel's and Coke. I watched him as he chatted, envious and far too admiring to notice that he talked only about himself. When he told me that he was a music student but had been dragging out his degree for several years, that he found the lecturers conservative and boring, the work a complete pain, and the program designed to stifle real talent, and when he confided that playing his own style of music was so much more *creatively fulfilling*, I couldn't have agreed more.

I returned the next Friday night, and afterwards we went back to the terrace house he shared near the university. I didn't go home for the rest of the weekend. Jean was furious.

Van's mystique only deepened. He laughed at her job as a hairdresser, my vague ideas about becoming a teacher or librarian when I left school. His parents were circus performers, living up north in a town that had a personality of its own, a town that was famous for its circus. That sounded exotic to me, but he insisted that the place was just another small town. And he felt confined by the circus: he was a musician and singer, not a novelty performer. He'd left when he was sixteen.

My dull sense of inferiority, of having missed out – on something, I wasn't sure what – only sharpened. I began to spend more time with him. I was too keen to be his girl. Too eager to embrace his creatively fulfilling world.

It took me years to understand that it had all been veils and mirrors, the stuff of tinsel and papier-mâché and smoke machines. What he'd come from, a circus background. What he did, pretending to be an artist of the calibre of Van Morrison. Illusions that were necessary for performing, dangerous in real life.

In Amethyst, his home town, nothing was imaginary. Young motherhood was palpable, at times painfully real. From time to time I'd thought about moving south, back to the inner city, where it was common for children to have no fathers, no mothers, serial fathers or even two mothers. Or back to the suburbs, to be near my mother. But although I had written to Jean to let her know where I was, and again after Sonny was born, I made it clear I wanted nothing from her. Jean being right about Van made it harder. As Sonny grew I sent her the occasional photo along with a note. I was independent and capable, and yet so painfully young. The truth was I didn't know what I wanted from Jean, didn't feel I owed her any apology, yet knew in my heart she didn't owe me one either. She and Van had met rarely, as he hated coming to my place, and the first time I invited her to the bar to see him perform she left early and refused to come again. She hated his recreational drug use, his vague ambitions, his nocturnal lifestyle, even his diet. She was suspicious of his past, contemptuous of his unconventional family, scathing about his musical talents. At sixteen, seventeen, I embraced everything my mother loathed.

I left Sydney and travelled north, towards the town from which Van had come. There had been no fight, no scene, nothing to suggest he was going to leave. And so I didn't believe it. He would have gone back home to Amethyst. I believed that. I needed to. He was from the circus, and circus stays in the blood, calls you back home. That's what he'd told me. And it was getting on for winter then. I would go north too, it would be warm there. I would find Van and convince him we were meant to be together and to have this baby. When I arrived I found that the place was stamped with his absence, the circus empty of him and all his family, probably the only circus family ever to leave for good. But after some weeks, after settling into the caravan, I felt like staying. And was unwilling to go back and face my failures, which were several. My friends going on to university without me. Jean being right again, then being too reasonable, to make me feel better for being so wrong. Me being scoured by my own gratitude when she helped me out, as she would. Me being bitten raw by my pride.

Once I'd settled in Amethyst, I discovered I had no real attachment to the city where I'd lived my short life, and I was still ripe for adventure, burning with a thirst for independence that I felt would sustain me wherever I would go, whatever I did. In a few months I would give birth, and I would be the best mother ever. I would more than make up for my baby's lack of a father. My child would be born there, and it would belong there and if its father never returned at least it would be in its home.

For a long time I was filled with that arrogant confidence of youth, the conviction that you are desired as much as you desire: Van would want me and his child sooner or later, and would find the prospect of coming home irresistible. For years, part of me believed that, though there was not the slightest scrap of evidence for it. Van's parents had moved further north, and his great-aunt had recently gone to a convalescent hospital by the coast. The only remains of his family in town were underground. All I had were Sonny and a fierce determination to make everything as right as I could.

Eleven

Dear Delia
Okay, I'll forget about the wedding cake, but I'd like your advice on another matter. My daughter will wear my old white silk veil, edged in lace. But it is spotted with brown stains and has yellowed around the creases. Should I bleach it?
Mother of the Bride.

Dear Mother of the Bride
Never use bleach on silk! Buy some old-fashioned yellow laundry soap. Wash the veil in a tub, preferably outdoors one fine day. Rinse it with half a cup of white vinegar in the water, and roll it up in a towel. Spread it on the lawn to dry, where it will look beautiful as it soaks up the day. Let the light do the rest.

Spring meant that Mr Lambert next door commenced a rigorous routine of lawn maintenance. He devoted every Monday morning to front-lawn weeding. I didn't need to go out and look over the fence to know what he would be doing: lying prone on the lawn and digging out feral vegetation with an old paring knife. Dandelions, bindi-eyes and other unidentified weeds were ritually extracted this way. Mr Lambert was a retired tax accountant, and I was sure he treated his lawn with the same humourless precision as he would have a column of figures. The lawn remained the blue-green shade of the fairest couch all summer until it turned brown in winter. He must have had his reasons, but I did wonder why he selected wintergreen couch for his front lawn, with its tendency to fade in the cooler months. Maybe because it was a more compliant grass, less inclined to provide asylum to refugee weeds that drifted in with the birds and the breezes. Soon after Mr Lambert moved here several years ago, he embarked on a clearing of the property environs that allowed no resistance. Palms, prone to messy explosions of seeds that banked in drifts and rotted odorously. Fence-hugging vines: morning glory, star jasmine and potato. Shrubs and grevilleas. The one large camphor laurel tree out the back. All were hewn, chopped away, chipped, mulched, removed.

A Mrs Lambert once existed but had passed away. He was never inclined to tell me more than that, except to mention that there was a son, and grandchildren, and I knew visits were few. I wondered if, had his wife not died some years before, his attitude towards the garden might have been more benevolent. But knowing nothing about her, it was impossible to say. Over the years Mr Lambert and I had only a few conversations, and in recent times none. But at one point he told me that he disliked trees. Too untidy. He replaced the front wattle tree with the murraya, and permitted a lone clump of agapanthus to loiter meekly by his front doorstep. His final act of garden cleansing was to dig up the front lawn and replace it with the wintergreen couch. He lovingly sowed it by hand and watered it obsessively, first with a fine mist spray gun so as not to disturb the seeds, then with a watering can. Within weeks it grew into a grey-green velvet carpet.

Archie, the lawn specialist, observed all this with a mixture of envy and disbelief. Lawn was a fine thing if you intended making use of it. Finer if you had the water resources to maintain it – but who had these days? Children playing, summer backyard meals, or just sitting by gazing at something soothingly green. But Mr Lambert's lawn, huge in proportion to his small house, barely received a passing glance from its owner, except of course when he was tending it. The front window roller shutters remained securely shut most of the time. He never sat on the tiny front porch, never rested on his lawn. And yet he was forever watering it – by hand, during restrictions, making endless trips to the tap and back to drench every centimetre. He fed it liquid fertiliser. He aerated it with a fancy rolling spike. He lay on it and dug out every suspect growth. He rolled it as if it were a bowling green. It was seven by nine metres of perhaps the most perfect lawn Archie and I had ever seen, but which the owner otherwise ignored. I never saw anything so necessary, but so irrelevant, to a person's life.

I assumed Mr Lambert's backyard was still a small wasteland of pebblecrete punctuated by a set of plastic furniture, which he kept tilted forward and covered in plastic sheeting. I wasn't certain, as it was no longer possible to see over the fence since he'd attached sheets of Colorbond steel to frustrate voyeurs. He even uprooted the rotary washing line, replacing it with a fence line that could be neatly folded down. Recently he sliced the necks of all our monstera deliciosa leaves that perched audaciously above the fence. Archie found them thrown onto our side and I pleaded with him not to throw them back. He couldn't contain his anger at this outrage inflicted upon an innocent plant, and not so long ago I would have flung them over myself, with fury directing my swing. He settled for sticking the stalks back up against the fence so that their withering leaves would at least reproach our neighbour.

It was a beautiful day to be outside idling in the garden instead of trying to remember how to make a fruit cake I once could have made in my sleep. To write it down I needed to remember the ingredients and the method, which was hard when I had always made it from instinct. Never before had I written the recipe down, let alone thought about exact weights and measurements. I had made this cake so many times, but how many kilos of dried fruit did I use? What proportion of raisins, currants, peel and nuts? Did I include cherries? Two bottles of brandy, or one of brandy and one of rum? The thinking would be exhausting even for a well person. Putting off work I tidied my office instead, then walked over to the window, and opened it as wide as it would go. I breathed in the glorious scent. My lungs swelled with the delicate warmth of new jasmine frothing along the side fence and the peppery odour of the council's wattle, already well into bloom. The wisteria pouring copiously from the vine.

Wisteria. Of course. I found the writing pad on which I'd been jotting down ideas for the wedding, and under Venue added Botanical Gardens. The wisteria would be glorious there. Daisy would look like an angel. Her Botticelli hair against a pale frock – pink or lemon or lavender. The lawn alive with colour, the sky a sharp blue, the whole a brilliant contrast for her Renaissance beauty.

I was fantasising on a grand scale. Daisy at twenty-five or so would probably have her hair cropped short and dyed indigo and wear nothing but black cargo pants and strategically ripped shirts. My sweet darling youngest daughter who was forever preoccupied with dolls and pets and everything fluffy, who would sleep with Kitty if I still let her, who played happy families with her three mice and kept one of them all day in her pocket, who begged for real ducklings but settled for the collection of floating ones she still kept for the bath. Doubtless by then she would have found her true sexuality and be in love with an Irish woman, sharing her passion for body piercing, dog shows and one-day cricket. The more the list burgeoned with details of table decorations and seating arrangements, the more I felt convinced this event was never going to happen. It was more likely to be a commitment ceremony, probably in an ironic location like the old Mortuary Station, or Hungry Jack's at Darling Harbour, with the dogs (they'd be staffies) wearing purple bows. But if a wedding did take place, there'd be the rudiments of a list to follow. On the off-chance that Daisy would want one, I would have done my bit.

I considered making the cake (and then I remembered, it was half a bottle each of brandy and rum), which would last the years. But apart from the effort involved in shopping for the ingredients, then mixing and icing the thing, I thought doing so would actually confirm Archie's view of me as a control freak. I would instead leave them the wedding fruit cake recipe, draw it somehow out of my head and write it up properly. I might even give it to Mother of the Bride.

I put the list aside and got on with the real work. Apart from Mother of the Bride's request, there were ten more emails waiting for replies.

Dear Delia
Remember I wrote some time back inquiring about shopping lists? My golfing friend and I consulted that Mrs Beeton *book you mentioned, and now we are wondering if it would be a good idea to write inventories of our households. Linen and crockery, plus our jewellery and stuff. For the children, and grandchildren. And insurance too, of course.*
Unsure.

Dear Unsure
If I remember rightly, you also told me you were both sixty-five. At this age do you really want to clutter up your lives with more paperwork?

Twelve

On the second day in Amethyst I stayed in the motel room. Outside, the day was sweet and inviting, the far north autumn being so kind. But I spent a long time having a bath, using up the inadequate mini-bottles of shampoo and body wash. I dried off with two of the bathtowels, draping the third around me instead of a robe. I lay down on the bed to read through the local brochures and leaflets for drycleaners, Chinese takeaways and day trips to gemstone mines. I raided the mini-bar for its mini-chocolates and made a cup of teabag tea, then a cup of instant coffee with long-life milk, pouring each down the bathroom sink when they tasted as bad as I expected. Finally I got dressed and took a mineral water out to the balcony, which overlooked a lily pond and the fenced-in pool. Close by was the run and kennel of the sleepy labrador.

I had to think about returning to my old caravan in Mitchell's camping park, but I could only do it step by step. Sitting there, I mentally traced through the route to the home I'd lived in for eight years but not seen for fourteen. I would drive out of this motel, turn left, then right, then left again. Straight up, it would take less than five minutes to get there. There would be a sign, Amethyst Caravan Park, probably faded now. Then past the front fence, along the gravel path, past the shed that Mitchell once used as an office, I'd skirt the stand of palms to pass the laundry.

I kept getting to the laundry. No further.

I fetched another drink and the two-pack of chocolate chip biscuits. I ate one and tossed the other down to the dog.

When I lived there I loved that laundry, ancient though it was. The other residents included an elderly couple who had installed a Hoover twin tub behind their van, a retired council worker who took his washing into the town laundromat every fortnight, and an ever-circulating collection of young men who spilled over from the circus, and who slept at the caravan park but tended to use the circus's facilities. So apart from the visitors and tourists, I was the only person to use the laundry regularly and I made it my domain. I would soak my clothes and linen in one of the tubs, poke it all about with the old wooden spoon, then rinse and squeeze it out by hand. For really dirty things, I would light the copper, feeding it with scraps of timber and wads of old newspaper until the place took on the feel and smell of some sort of laboratory, bubbling with potent liquids and thick with a chemical mist. I was the sorcerer's apprentice. Left to my own devices, who knew what I would produce?

Nothing more than clean clothes, of course. After Sonny came along I would settle him in his basket by the doorway so he could have his face kissed by the sun while I stirred and rubbed and squeezed. Back then I could spend hours washing if I wanted, pegging sheets and baby blankets out on the old rope line propped behind the laundry, gathering in the loads of sweet-smelling clothes before the sun started to go down, setting out the ironing board in the annexe and performing the unnecessary task of ironing sheets and tea towels. I knew it was pointless – as if a baby cared how well-ironed his things were – but I always did it. I pressed Sonny's cotton bibs and lawn wraps with more care than I'd ever ironed a silk shirt or a pair of trousers. Somehow it seemed important to do this. Just as later it became vital not to let him go out barefoot. I was never going to be mistaken for trailer trash and no one was ever going to pity me or my circumstances. Maybe it was observing this dedication to the task that made Mitchell offer me the job of cleaner and manager and all-round caretaker, as he'd started up a new business in town which was keeping him away for long hours. Or maybe he was more observant than that.

It must be hard, managing on a single mother's pension, he'd said a few months after the birth.

The payments had only just started coming through, thanks to my recent move interstate and the usual bureaucratic inertia. By that stage I was waiting at the post office in town every second Thursday, was first in the queue at the bank. I didn't dare to think what it would cost when Sonny needed more than breast milk and baby clothes.

I could do with the help, he said, allowing us both to pretend it wasn't charity.

Mitchell didn't tell me there was a man contracted to mow the caravan park grounds. One morning I was on my knees by the front gate, Sonny parked in his pram beside me, and hacking at runners of grass that had snaked across the path almost overnight in the warm moist weather. I was using a pair of stiff secateurs I'd found in the laundry, and after ten minutes I was already sweaty and hand sore, when a man pulled up in a utility. He got out and looked at me for a moment, then brought out a pair of long-handled shears.

These'll do a much better job, he said, offering them to me.

Fine, I said, tossing the old secateurs onto the grass. Feel free to take over. Turning my back on him, I wheeled the baby away.

Nice to meet you too, he called after me. The name's Archie, by the way.

My rudeness didn't seem to have bothered him, for the times I saw him after that he just waved or said hello and continued mowing or clipping. Mitchell only wanted me to keep things in order, so I retreated to the back of the grounds. I could tidy the gardens there and leave Archie to do the more professional jobs around the front. One steaming afternoon I wheeled the pram in from the street, hot and tired, aching for a cold beer, one luxury I kept in my tiny fridge. I found Archie dripping with the effort of lopping the huge fig that grew at the front gate. It was too hot for hostilities. I fetched us both a beer and we sat in the shade admiring his work. After that it became a bit of a ritual. Soon I started to look forward to it, in a wary sort of way. He never mentioned a girlfriend. In fact, while we chatted amiably enough, neither of us discussed personal matters, not then. Later on he told me about a woman he sort of saw, but that it was difficult, on again and off again. Really difficult.

How do you mean, difficult? I asked.

Put it this way, he said. There's competition.

You mean she has someone else?

Something like that.

So why doesn't she make a choice, him or you?

When Archie laughed I first thought that her other person might have been a woman. And how obtuse and small-minded I must have sounded.

Well, that's not really possible. She's in love with a dead man, as far as I can tell. And I'm getting a bit sick of it.

He sat back in his chair, closed his eyes and sighed. I felt like poking him to explain more, until he started to hum tunelessly, Love me tender, love me blue ...

Not Pearl? I said.

Do you know her?

Of course. Mitchell sent me to her soon after I arrived. Half the books I've got are from her place.

Pearl was dark, beautiful, dreadlocked. Her book exchange shop – her day job – was in the front room of her house, which was a mini Graceland. Her night job was president of the Amethyst and District Elvis Fan Club, and the district was so vast it took her away a lot, organising talent quests and commemorative shows and memorabilia swap meets and whatever else Elvis fans did. I felt I owed Pearl a great deal, since she gave me complete freedom with her odd collection of books – mostly picked up from country town fêtes, street markets and car boot sales – and charged me almost nothing. If she and Archie ... well, if it came to that, it would not even be a competition.

That was when I told him about Van – though, as Van was something of a notorious figure, he already knew most of what there was to know – and that was also when I made it clear that no man was ever going to get into the pores of my soul like that again.

Much later, when Sonny grew so fond of Archie, it became harder. I seesawed for a few years between thinking Archie and I could be a real couple, and thinking that maybe I only thought that because it would make it easier for me and Sonny. Thinking that if I agreed to move in with Archie it might only be because it would suit me, with Sonny growing and the caravan becoming increasingly impossible, not because I wanted him for his sake alone. Thinking that I didn't really know what I was thinking. The thinking revolved around and around in my mind like a mouse on a wheel. Strangely, it didn't seem to bother Archie. Which was why I read so much. Easier to enter someone else's dilemmas or questions or nightmares than confront or solve my own.

I told Sonny only what I judged he needed to know, since complete honesty, I'd found, was not always the best option with children. One day, his goldfish, the best pet a caravan-living mother could manage for a child, floated to the top of its bowl and commenced putrefying. Sonny seemed to cope with the fact of Jaffa dying, but the idea that the fish's body then laid solemnly in the good earth – in a patch adjacent to the caravan and marked by a banana tree I had recently planted – would be prone to worms, bacteria and other elemental onslaughts made him sob for hours.

So I told him only the selective truth about his father. The edited story. The Reader's Digest version. And it had always sufficed, except now Sonny was eight and noticing more and more the fact that most families tended to be storybook. And that boys without fathers were almost non-existent. I guessed his question came from a playground taunt, or perhaps an innocently cruel question or suggestion that the teachers were prone to put from time to time. Usually at project time, when fathers were meant to be enlisted to help build the model solar system, or fête days when they were requested to turn sausages.

It wasn't Fathers' Day that had provoked the question at McDonald's that afternoon. It wasn't anything in particular except that we had fought earlier and although Sonny was in the wrong and my anger was justified, I still felt guilty. He had run off that morning while I was in the laundry. He had wanted to visit his friends at the circus and I had told him I had things to do, and couldn't take him until later. I was cleaning up the grounds, emptying the garbage bins, doing a few other chores that were part of my job. After I'd hung out the washing I was going to get him to help me and then we would walk to town to return some library books, and then visit the circus. Tara and some other friends were having a party. But when I went back to the caravan, Sonny had gone. By the time I got to the circus my anger had cooled considerably, but not enough. I dragged him away from his friends while he cried and screamed and called me the worst mother in the world, told me he hated me. When we got back I was so fed up and exhausted I almost threw him through the caravan door.

All the time I was wondering what these moments would be like with a father around. Would Sonny be better behaved? Would I be less angry? I slammed my way through the rest of the cleaning and by the time I'd swept around the barbeque area and finished hosing down the shower block, I was calm. When I looked in, Sonny was sitting in the caravan playing solitaire with a deck of cards. I'd expected he'd still be in a rage, or sullen, or in the process of giving me the silent treatment for the rest of the day. Instead he smiled at me, as if all that anger had been nothing more than a sudden breeze, there and gone before you're barely aware of the change in the air, and guilt and love churned in my heart in equal doses, as it always did at such times. I remembered that he hadn't had lunch.

Want to go to McDonald's? I said. As a treat?

As we headed home that afternoon, Sonny was looking sulky again, and I realised that I hadn't answered his question. But by then I'd finally made up my mind. I had a surprise planned for that very evening, when the sun was dying and we were sitting outside, Archie and me in the fold-up aluminium chairs, Sonny circling us on his scooter. With cool drinks to hand, the lukewarm air stirring and the parakeets daring each other in the palms above, squealing and shooting their way into the growing night, it would be as perfect as it could be for me to tell both of them what they wanted to hear. Sonny would get the father he wanted. And Archie, whom I'd resisted for too long, would get me.

Before entering town, we got off the bus at the left turn just before the main street, out along a straight stretch of road where the trees were taller and thinner and somehow lonely, out to where the cemetery spread like a rash on a dry and flat part of the landscape. It had no fences, this cemetery, and little order, sprawling around trees and shrubs and the occasional boulder as if it had been part of the land forever. I had always thought it was large for a place with a population of around twenty thousand. Did people come here to die, I wondered, did they stake out the land for the dead along with the living when they first established Amethyst over a hundred years ago?

We walked along the road for five minutes before we met the gravel track that poked its way through drunken tombstones and dull corroded plaques. Dry and rather bare though the place was, it was not a bleak cemetery by any means. There were enough stands of trees and clusters of rocks and shrubs to make it seem only partly contrived, almost totally natural. The graves tended to nestle into the ground as if they had always belonged there. I took Sonny's hand as we turned down a fork in a path and continued to its end. Here were three graves marked by granite slabs, one of them a rosy pink, with simple gilt lettering announcing the lives and deaths of his great-grandparents, Ivy and Arthur, and Ivy's mother, Constance. His closest relatives in town, apart from me.

I told him then, simply and clearly, about his father and the past, and explained that the people lying under us were his father's grandparents and his great-grandmother. Confessed that I had fought with my mother when I was pregnant with him, had not seen her since, and refused to let her visit me – us – even though she regularly sent him presents and I sent her his drawings and handmade cards.

I followed your father, I said, or I thought I did. I was very silly.

How did you get here? he asked after a pause during which I thought he was going to become upset, or angry, or demand to go and see Jean straightaway.

I got the bus.

What sort?

I smiled. It was a coach, actually. A Volvo B59. White, with green trim.

After that there was nothing more to say. More words seemed unnecessary, and he didn't seem to want them. So we just stood there for a while, holding hands and feeling the afternoon sun on the backs of our necks, gazing at the graves that marked the only family of his father he would probably ever meet.

We'll visit Jean, I said, your grandma. As soon as I can manage it.

And the rest of my news I would save until that night.

Thirteen

Dear Delia
My aunt has given me her old crock pot, however no recipe book. I am not sure if it is worth keeping. I understand you're meant to cook meals overnight in it. Is this possible?
Curious.

Dear Curious
You have two options. Either regard slow cooking as an opportunity to slow down everything. Stop racing to work each morning. Stop work altogether. Sit outside and enjoy the twilights. Take walks around the biggest park you can find. Or you can toss the crock pot out and enjoy the moment. Eat oysters. See three movies every week. Kiss your lover.

Home was a haven. But at the same time, not necessarily peaceful, not with children. I'd long since learned to cope with the noises outside – and sometimes inside – my office while I plugged away at the weekly column or researched my books. I was always pathetically grateful for email, since it let you attend to enquiries or make ones of your own while your children wailed and fought and called out from the bathroom, or listened to 'The Wiggles' yet again, without the embarrassment of all that drifting over the phone. It was no wonder I'd never secured what I once would have called a real job. No one took a woman seriously whose kid was in the background throwing Duplo at the fridge or falling off a shelf they'd wilfully decided to climb.

Peace was what a dying person craved. Yet in a way I wasn't dying. I was *going* to die. A big difference to my daughters, for whom the future was mostly an abstraction, if it even existed. They could see that I was still well enough to work, to run the house, to travel. They knew that I was not going to be alive for much longer, but that was not the same as understanding that I was dying. And that was the way I preferred it. But sometimes I just wanted to sit around and do nothing but listen to the leaves whispering. Sometimes I wanted to sit in the back yard and hold the girls on my lap, as big as they were, and gaze down past the ponds, the lawn, to the chicken shed. To do and say nothing at all. Just to feel them breathing against me.

And sometimes I really, really didn't want to hear Daisy practising her recorder, especially when it was right in my ear. That most irritating of all instruments, it seemed to shatter my senses. The doctor had explained this was normal. Sounds, smells, even colours, could become repellent, possibly distressing, during and after treatment. I hadn't believed her until one afternoon I realised I desperately wanted to grab the recorder and break it in half.

I sat there in my office with the door closed and my head in my hands.

Daisy opened the door and came in. Mummy, you weren't listening.

Course I was.

I can't practise unless you listen to me.

Okay then. I clenched my jaws and listened to yet another nerve-scratching version of 'Merrily We Roll Along'. I doubted even Jane Rutter could make an instrument like the recorder sound harmonious.

Lovely, really lovely, I said.

That sucks, Estelle called out.

You shut up!

No *you* shut up!

Then Daisy blew into the instrument as loudly as she could, producing such angry sounds that my nerves felt not so much scratched as serrated, all the way through.

And then it was on. Shut up, you moron. I hate you. You're a pig (Daisy). Why don't you play the triangle, that's all you're good at (Estelle). Leave me alone, you bitch (Daisy). Hey, such language! (me). You've ruined my life (Estelle). She *is* a bitch (Daisy). *You're* a bitch (Estelle). I'm warning you both (me again). Oh, just go die in a hole (Estelle). Then the chorus again: Shut up, you moron, I hate you ...

It was a well-rehearsed script, give or take a few improvisations. Retard. Bumhead. You stink. Get out of my room. Loser. It's my room too. Make her stop.

Pushing and whacking. Screaming and tears. Falling down. Kicking.

And it went on and on, right outside my office, despite my pleas. But that day I was so worn down by it. Not completely without energy, though. I leaped up from the desk and, instead of grabbing them both by the hair and dragging them out the front door and throwing them into the street as I felt like doing, I hissed right into their faces,

Be quiet! I'm trying to work in here you know!

And when that didn't stop them, I yelled as loudly as I could,

Actually I'm dying in here! Not that you two care.

They both turned and looked at me. The sudden silence bit hard into my next words.

And at least when I'm dead I'll have some fucking peace! I won't have to listen to this bullshit any more!

I sat on the back verandah with a gin and lime that I didn't even want. I didn't care what they were doing. All I cared was that now it was quiet inside. Quiet enough to hear the remorse grinding through me like a rusty tool. Already I'd done what I swore to myself I never would, use my impending death to make them feel guilty.

What's up? said Archie.

I hadn't heard him come home.

What's up is that I'm the worst mother. I can't cope with them fighting. I just about told them I'd prefer to be dead.

What are you talking about?

I suppose they're in their beds crying under the covers. Well, maybe not Estelle. She's probably sticking pins into a Delia doll.

I took a mouthful of the gin. It tasted awful.

No they're not. Come on inside – it's getting chilly out here, anyway.

I sighed and got up. It was an effort.

After it had all died down, sitting out the back, I realised that what ate me up about having more than one child was that I hated each of them when they were attacking the other, because I loved each of them when they were being attacked. It was like being torn in half and then having both parts fed to the flames. Even if you were well, it would be exhausting.

And I said fuck in front of them.

Come on, Archie said, putting an arm around me.

Daisy was sitting at the dining table in a mess of crayons, paper, marshmallows, buttered bread and hundreds of hundreds and thousands, on the table, on the floor, in the butter dish, a few actually on the bread. Charlotte was by the computer desk next to Estelle. I hadn't realised she'd come back with Archie too.

Hi, she said. How are you feeling?

Oh, okay.

Daisy was hungry, I got her something to eat, said Estelle, not taking her eyes from the screen.

Hey, Mum, look at this drawing I did of China.

For a while out there I'd forgotten about that. Mortal enemies one minute, companionable the next. That capacity for forgetting. The forgiveness that came so swiftly and naturally it wasn't even forgiveness. Living in the moment. I needed a bit more of that.

I thought we could go out tonight, Archie said. Charlotte's offered to stay with the girls.

Thanks, Arch. It was a nice idea. But I don't feel up to it.

So Charlotte sat with Estelle and helped her finish Photoshopping pictures of herself and her friends into gothic street waifs, and I helped Daisy with her colouring in while Archie heated up some soup. And after they had gone to bed, I got down on my knees with the dust pan and broom and swept up every last tiny coloured hundred and thousand.

Dear Delia
I've prepared a sample cake but am not happy with it. Are you sure you gave me all the ingredients?
Mother of the Bride.

Dear Mother of the Bride
Life is short. Take risks. How much brandy did you use?

Fourteen

Thanks to Mitchell's itinerant and sometimes shifty visitors, I was able to equip the caravan comfortably. He had a shed full of abandoned belongings that I was welcome to pick over. The next day, I selected sheets, a blanket, several towels, two pillows and an assortment of kitchen things, nothing matching, everything serviceable. I washed the linen and by the time I'd aired and cleaned the caravan, replaced its curtains and made up the bed it looked and smelled like it belonged to me. A few days later when all my supplies of food had gone, I walked downtown. Things like toothpaste, shampoo, toilet rolls and books were also on my mind. I walked up the slight hill towards the river, turned south, and then strolled all the length of the street, taking in the modestly grand houses that half-hid behind layers of greenery – palms, mainly, of all varieties, and glossy creepers and banana groves and frangipani by the score – punctuated by startling splashes of colour: hibiscus, bougainvillea, Brazilian jasmines and all sorts of other flowers I couldn't name. I saw no one on this walk into town, although it was mid-morning on a weekday and you'd expect some activity:

postal workers, gardeners, women sweeping front porches, children skipping along paths, old men in cardigans reaching down for newspapers on doormats. I saw open windows and wooden slat blinds languidly slapping in the breeze, sprinklers slowly revolving on lawns. I saw open doorways and cats on cane chairs on verandahs, and I heard the dim echoing sounds from inside these houses that said people were home. But otherwise it could have been me all alone in the town, on a beautiful late winter morning.

A block from the main shops all that changed. A car zoomed towards me and turned right, then it was like a director on a film set had yelled Action!, the clapperboard had slammed down and all was alive and bustling again. Someone starting up a mower somewhere to my left, a woman with a child in a stroller turning into the street just in front, a line of schoolkids holding hands further ahead, towels over their shoulders, off to the pool for swimming lessons, and a steady thrum of traffic cruising past: a normal town doing everyday things.

Except, as I saw that day, it was slightly abnormal. Amethyst was a mellow place, a place that would absorb you without protest, and receive you with a passivity that meant you felt held, contained. Almost suspended, like an egg in its shell. And it wasn't as simple and as glib as walking back in time, thirty or forty years, to the days before the tyranny of fast food outlets and retail franchises that grabbed every single town in the country and stamped them with their own unmistakable pattern, elevating them into permanent twenty-four-hour plastic and neon advertisements. There was the computer and electric typewriter shop, the video hire store, the health food shop with its glitzy purple and silver new age window display, and the rack of paperbacks on special outside the newsagent's – confirming that whatever had captured and moulded Amethyst into something so unique, it certainly wasn't a time warp.

In Oasis Street was a shop called Cliff's Handy Mart, a small grocery store with a mere two aisles of neatly arranged goods. The burden of choice, one of the late twentieth century's most insidious, was lifted. I wanted toothpaste and here were just two types: Colgate Fluorigard (red box) or Macleans Freshmint (white box). Standing there weighing up the choice, I felt grateful for the simplicity of it all. Yet it also took a kind of courage to step into a small and dimly lit store to shop for the unknown. You could vanish in the gleaming bright abundance of a city supermarket, but you couldn't hide in a place like Cliff's.

Which is how I came to have my first real conversation with Mitchell Pearson, all that time back, though we'd met a few days before when Lazarus had taken me and my new old caravan into town. It was just on dusk then and Mitchell, preoccupied with getting to his bar for that evening, had barely taken any notice of me. After checking me into the park and taking a deposit, he'd left Lazarus to set up my site and connect the electricity. Late the next morning he came over and told me where I'd find the discarded towels and sheets, if I needed them, before racing off again. And since then I'd only glimpsed him from a distance as he came and went from his bar back to the caravan park. But standing with my toothpaste (I opted for the Macleans) and enjoying the mixed pleasures of relief and regret that little moment of epiphany gave me regarding shopping, my life, and the late twentieth century generally, I must have attracted his attention. Or maybe I just stood out because I was the only pregnant teenager in the store.

Mitchell was wearing his Greek fisherman's cap over brown curls (though underneath he could have been bald; no one would have known because he wore the cap everywhere).

Hey, he said, not too friendly, not too cautiously, at Cliff's checkout, after glancing at the few items I'd selected. It was okay, I'd already looked at his: a packet of Redhead matches, two tins of John West smoked oysters, a roll of alfoil, a rose-scented toilet deodoriser, a block of dark chocolate and a carton of low-fat milk (like handbags, you can tell a lot about people from what they put in their shopping baskets). He apologised for not seeing me around the place, told me more about the bar, which meant that the people in the caravan park were just about left to themselves, but that this was how they liked it, and he'd presumed I was no different.

Come and have a drink, he said, I'm there more than at the park. On my own a lot too. I can tell you all about the town. I've got a café back near the highway too, but someone else runs that for me now the bar's going.

Did he think I was of legal drinking age (though I nearly was, I knew I didn't look it)? Did he think I would drink, in my condition? Did he just not notice, or not give a toss? He dug around in the pocket of his denim jacket and handed me a card.

The bar's just down the road here, next block, upstairs. You can tell by the neon light.

I might not end up staying long.

Sure, he said, nodding emphatically in the way that people do when they don't believe a word of what you're saying. Anyway, it'd be a pleasure to see you.

He couldn't have been trying to come onto me, I thought, not with that kind of frank invitation. Surely.

The front of his card read: Mitchell's Bar tel (07) 42 8282. On the back was Mitchell's Café, with another number. No address, no opening times, nothing else. But as I looked at his figure – thin, average height, navy blue cap tilted back, twin shopping bags dangling from each arm – and thought about the prospect of a night out, just a quiet one, and back to the caravan early enough, the state of my mind hit me. It took a casual invitation out to make me realise how lonely I was, how I was making things like a simple trip to the shops a long, momentous event, to fill up the spaces between the hours, when the hours themselves were becoming longer than days. And this was just a few days into my stay. The next few weeks and months were already starting to crack open to reveal something larger and emptier than I had imagined.

As he walked off I called out,

Mitchell? Is there a second-hand bookshop in town?

He looked at me as if taking in the whole picture for the first time. I was wearing a wraparound batik skirt and an old purple T-shirt. I had twisted my hair up and around my head, but it was falling down in strands that on someone else might have looked casually elegant, but on me was just messy. I wore sandals and held a large woven bag sagging with groceries. I looked like what I was: a careless, glamourless unsophisticate with no money and no prospects beyond that of the obvious in a couple of months.

Two, he said. But also a private lending library, like a book exchange. You might be interested in that. But if you go to her place be prepared: the woman who runs it is a mad Elvis fan.

Fifteen

Dear Delia
My girlfriend says my bathroom is disgusting and she won't stay at my place until I fix it. There is a bit of brown staining in places but it seems clean enough to me. I've tried various products but the ones that say spray and rinse clean don't seem to satisfy her. If the bathroom isn't clean by the weekend I don't know what I'm going to do. Please advise.
Desperate.

Dear Desperate
It is said that ninety-five per cent of men suffer from Selective Ocular Deficiency, also sometimes known as Kitchen-Bathroom Blindness. This condition enables a man to shave skilfully, locate beer in a fridge and tinned beans in a cupboard, but not to see shower mould and piles of takeaway containers in the kitchen. The naked human eye is a remarkable organ, capable of identifying all the separate small components of a pizza within microseconds. Nor is there any proven difference in ocular functioning between the genders. It's the twenty-first century, Desperate, and about time men like you snapped out of this nonsense.

After the second operation and the third diagnosis, as I resigned myself to the fact that the latest *Household Guide* I'd written would be my last, and as I was adding up how many more columns I could manage in the time I had left, I conceived in a flash the best idea ever. I didn't have to abandon the *Household Guide*s at all. I rang Nancy and left a message. Two hours later she was on the phone, pleading with me to relax, to forget about work, to can the idea.

You just don't want to give a contract to a person who'll be dead in a year, I said. It was only half a joke. Nancy was kind but she was also a business person. What would her accountant say about signing a contract with a near corpse?

Why don't you just enjoy the time left to you? she said.

This *is* my idea of enjoyment, I said. I love my work. And I'm the perfect person to write this book, I reminded her. How many other people did she know with the expertise of writing these sorts of books combined with the first-hand experience of dying?

Think of the title, I said. How catchy does *The Household Guide to Dying* sound?

Catchy? Nancy said. Don't you mean confronting? Not to mention weird? Who on earth would pick up a book with that title?

It's original. And everyone dies, Nancy. Think of the potential readership.

There was silence on her end of the line. Leaping into the moment, I compounded my reasons: impeccable research, personal expertise, the gap in the market (I heard a flutter of breath at the magic words), my track record of never missing a deadline. I did not joke about the word deadline, tempting though it was, as Nancy had an unpredictable sense of humour and a corresponding horror of those who refused to take their own mortality seriously. I polished up the gap in the market aspect a bit more. Who else of her competitors had published such a book? Of all the self-help titles and practical guides around, whoever had produced anything like a guide to dying? Not death. Not grieving. But dying. A how-to book, from an insider's perspective. A practitioner's perspective. From a professional.

I could almost hear the sparking of cells, Nancy's brain already warming up with possibilities of large print runs, point of sale advertising, dump bins and excerpts in the glossy magazines.

Nancy, it'll take me two, three months maximum.

I'll need a written proposal, she said.

Commercial publishers are strange beasts. They lived, breathed, thought and handled books. They probably took them to bed. They made vast amounts of money from them. But they didn't read. The magazine publishing basis of Nancy's business meant that words – whole pages of them, entire books of them – slipped through the system like sly fish. They were just a means for inventing needs or selling products, about as creative and inspiring to Nancy's team as feral carp. They'd be eradicated if they could. Nancy was different – she liked books and reading – but she was still primarily head of a business in which bottom lines were just as important as lines of text. She was always reminding me that most of our readers didn't read either: they looked at the words instead. So a book proposal, which she could take to her marketing manager (whose previous position was in the rugby industry), her financial adviser (a former doughnut franchiser) and her publicist (cosmetics), had to be punchy. One page. Less than. Half a page. Ditto the chapter outlines.

Publishing proposal

Death and taxes: the two certainties in life. But while there are plenty of guides to doing your tax, and plenty of professionals to assist you, how many readers can find practical written help for the process of dying? We will all die. That's an inescapable fact. Yet death is such a taboo topic that, when it comes to dying, we've lost the art (if we ever had it).

In practical, compassionate and witty ways, *The Household Guide to Dying* will cater for all those people who find death confronting and frightening. In the same vein as the hugely popular and much-loved *Household Guide* series, this book will demystify the process of dying.

From the first moment of confronting the idea of death to dealing with the family's responses, from practicalities such as palliative care in the home to planning a funeral, *The Household Guide to Dying* will take readers through every aspect of dying in the modern household.

In other circumstances I would have blushed to produce such a glib marketing pitch, but I was running out of time and didn't want to waste it writing up a more imaginative proposal when I could be concentrating on the book itself. And Nancy's marketing manager, her publicist, and various others with the concentration span of a budgerigar, would be persuaded in less than two hundred words, or not at all.

The marketing department would want to know about the target readership, and the trick would be to convince them that it would not only be dying people (although that was theoretically everyone on the planet: surely a marketing manager's dream) who would buy this book. Carers of dying people. Family members, lovers, sisters, mothers, friends ... the possibilities were endless but I did have to be careful to articulate that targeted band of the market with as much precision as possible. They would be asking me to define my demographic. Merely nominating families or dying people wouldn't be enough.

With my other titles, Nancy had either asked me to write on a specific subject, or agreed to my suggestion on the spot, yet here she demanded a written proposal. I suspected that some other element was at play. Perhaps she felt the idea was foolish. Asking for a proposal may have been her way of stalling me, whose condition rendered me pitiable, in need of more gentle handling than would normally be required.

Dear Delia
You think you're so damn clever but I'm writing to tell you that Don and I are still together. It's my old recently divorced friend who went off with my husband instead, not the new assistant, like I'd thought. God, I never saw that one coming. But neither did you, huh?
Uncertain (as I was then).
PS The tablecloth cleaned up nicely by the way. Thanks.

Dear Uncertain
Touché.
PS Congratulations.

Sixteen

Over the eight years I knew and worked for Mitchell, I waited for him to tell me his own story, but I never learned anything much about his past. He was a repository, and in that sense the perfect person to run a bar. But we tended to talk at the caravan park more often, usually on a Monday afternoon or Sunday morning, when he took a breather from the bar. He would open wide the door of his caravan (a deluxe Jayco model, which had its own bathroom) and, to the songs of Gram Parsons or Marianne Faithfull or Emmylou Harris, would sit on his step, smoking, drinking black coffee and gazing at his domain.

If I was walking into town and Mitchell was too busy or stuck in the bar, he would ask me to stop by and pick up essentials, like toilet rolls for the shower block, or stuffed olives for the martinis. Once he sent me to the hardware store for a roll of porous rubber matting for behind the bar, to oblige the health and safety inspector who was arriving that afternoon.

The hardware store proved fascinating, like my father's old shed that Jean had never cleared out. It was full of mystifying items which I couldn't identify, and perfectly ordinary objects with the oddest names. Rolls of fabric were called scrim. Things called nibs had nothing to do with pens and ink, but were essential for roof tiling. Clearly the world of home repairs had another language, and it was a male one. When an annoying drip developed in the caravan's kitchen sink tap, ominously just before the baby was due, I returned to ask for something to fix it.

A washer, said the man at the counter, when I explained the problem.

Washer? Yes, that's it.

Is your tap a capstan-head or a shrouded-head?

Um, I dunno.

Well, how old is it, twenty years or more?

Oh, it's old, it's in my caravan, and that's really old.

Your caravan? Did you buy that from Lazarus?

Yes.

That figures, he snorted, one of those comments that said a great deal. Like how half his customers were probably owners of vans from Lazarus. Like how my repairs would be endless. Like how I'd be back again and again.

Capstan-head, then. The Boston washers might do it. But probably your Delaware washer set would be the best thing. He took down a yellow packet from a stand.

Boston? Delaware? What was the connection between American place names and plumbing? The mysteries of hardware were complex as well as masculine.

Do you want the one with the bonus O rings? he said.

Oh yeah. Definitely. I guess.

Somehow I managed to fix it myself. When I returned to buy a new fastener for the pivoting window over the bed at the back of the caravan, I took the broken one off and showed the hardware man, whose name was Doug, rather than reveal my ignorance by asking for the wrong thing.

A cockspur handle, he said. Might have one out the back.

By the time I'd fitted the cockspur handle and learned what a countersunk screw was I felt remarkably competent. Given the caravan's age I was often at the hardware store getting tools or paint or seals or hinges, and with Doug's casual way of tossing new technical words into our conversations, I became quite confident at talking, and doing, basic DIY. When Mitchell asked me to take on the general care and maintenance of the park, I learned more. The difference between Phillips head and single slot screwdrivers. What a crowsfoot spanner was, and what to do with it. Fixing things became easier, even pleasurable. But it was also the language that made it so appealing. The beguiling, baffling words themselves. I learned about breast drills, ceiling roses, bedding washers, bevel edges, long-nosed and alligator pliers. So much of it sounded fun, creative, even salacious. Flashing, Allen keys and wiggle nails. Not to mention stud finders and butt gauges. I made sure to keep a straight face when terms like that came up in conversations with Doug. I learned why pointing a brick wall was not a grammatical lapse but an important technique to repair damage from weathering and stress. Which I also learned about. And which all meant that years later, when I was writing the household guides, I understood so much about home repairs, even the strangely poetic, blokey terminology.

Seventeen

Dear Delia
I guess I can see what you mean by those brown stains and the mould, but what should I use to clean the bathroom? I went to the supermarket but there was a whole shelf of products and I just got confused and went home again. Desperate.

Dear Desperate
Here is the secret: you remain in the bathroom armed with some abrasive cleaner, a bottle of bleach and a packet of scouring pads. If you emerge in under an hour you'll know the job is not done. Try listening to George Formby tapes to help the time go by. That might remind you to clean the windows as well. Remember that in his day Formby was a bit of a superstar and if cleaning windows was good enough for him it's good enough for you. And don't forget to ventilate the room. No good if your girlfriend arrives one evening to find a sparkling clean bathroom (an unlikely prospect, I know) but an asphyxiated you. Good luck. I shudder to consider the state of your kitchen.

Everyone who has trivialised and dismissed domesticity has done generations of women a profound disservice. Men, of course, have minimised to a gap in their culture the vital nature of domestic endeavour. When Archie left home following an argument (the usual fight over money or sex or something, I can't quite remember now) six months after the birth of Daisy, he was back a week later, forlorn, unwashed and undernourished. I felt sorry for him. I took him back, welcomed him (I didn't really want to be on my own, not with two tiny children), restored his body, washed his clothes. And, to be quite frank, I was pleased to be able to assert myself so competently, to be able to care for him, show him that I was a woman of endless skills, with a capacity for dealing with the slightest and the greatest of household duties. Generations of breeding meant that, like many other women, I undervalued these skills myself, and took them for granted almost as much as he.

Mortality is wonderfully mind-cleansing. Writing the books had also helped. Take the washing line, for instance. Here is a site of profound wisdom, generally ignored, by men and women alike, despite its centrality in daily life. Design-wise, the Hills hoist rotary washing line is an icon. There was Lin Onus's washing line with fruit bats. But beyond that the reinvention ends. There has never been an investigation into the true meaning and function of the Hills hoist planted, at one stage, in almost every backyard in the country. Yet there are certain rules regarding washing-line culture and the laundry that suggest an assertion and independence on the part of women frequently denied to men. Men can be unnerved by a washing machine and its inscrutable instructions. They can drive a car. They can fix a car. But the art of ironing remains mystifying. They can change a tap washer but can't locate the other sock.

Or couldn't. For the rules of washing-line culture have relaxed over the generations. By my childhood they were shifting, but in my mother's day they were still strict, codified and thoroughly gendered. The washing always went out early in the day. Only a disreputable woman would hang out washing later than nine o'clock. Around lunchtime would indicate grave moral lapses like sleeping in or spending the morning glued to the television.

And there was a code of practice determining the correct order of hanging. Socks, underpants, vests went on the innermost lines, then the children's clothes, followed by the men's shirts and trousers. Men's clothes occupied an entire row of their own, signifying their importance in the strict hierarchy of the laundering process and the household.

The code also covered pegs. Only a dysfunctional household left pegs on the line. A sloppy housewife did this, a woman with no scruples, who never bothered to sort whites from coloureds and who even unhygienically washed tea towels in with the underwear. Jean once told me that in her childhood you could actually sum up a woman's entire character from her habit of leaving pegs on the line. She was probably as sloppy and lazy inside the house as she was on the outside, leaving food in tins in the fridge rather than transferring it to plastic containers, and only changing the bedsheets once a fortnight. This would be the type whose children went to bed unwashed, and who bought frozen pies for dinner on Friday nights. She probably also wore nylon underpants instead of cotton, and ate chocolate in bed. All this could be ascertained by one glance at the washing line. Pegs, fading, festooned with spiderwebs, sitting forlornly like abandoned fledglings ... well, that sort of woman would not be invited to weekly tennis or to Tupperware parties. You would not be allowed to play with the children of such a household.

The code also extended to technique. You shook and smoothed out every item, releasing it from the tormented cycle of the spin dryer, and pegging it out intelligently to maximise access to sun and breeze. Towels were stretched and hung by the edges, not allowed to sag in the middle and thus produce misshapen results when dry. Underpants were pegged by the sides and never the crotch (so the sun could penetrate to perform its hygienic function), and men's underpants were always attached with two pegs on the waist. Men abhorred peg marks in their Y-fronts.

And then, in the suburbs, washing left on the line overnight indicated a serious lapse in domestic care. Probably outright immorality: where *was* that woman? Off in the ladies' lounge having a shandy, no doubt. It was also a clear invitation to thieves and perverts to jump over your fence and steal your lace bras or frilly underpants, should you be silly and vain enough to own them.

Finally, you never used dryers. These were for lazy and wasteful people, or those unfortunates who had to live in flats. But out in the suburbs, where the sun was generous and a fresh breeze was free, it was a crime not to hang your washing out. Everyone knew sunshine and fresh air killed germs and acted as a natural bleach. And if it rained, too bad: you triumphed over the elements like a lieutenant on the battlefield, and draped the washing around the living room, in front of the heater (if it was winter), on wooden horses or, if your laundry was big enough, on makeshift lines or frames hanging from the ceiling. If it still didn't dry, you ironed it dry. Because you always did the ironing anyway.

It might have been the washing that made me fall in love with Archie completely. The first time we ever took a bath together was the night we moved into a rented flat, introducing our separate boxes of possessions and odd bits of furniture to each other for the first time. He massaged my toes, then sucked them, and other parts of my body. We drank red wine from mismatched glasses, one formerly a honey jar, the other the surviving member of a second-hand shop quartet of rippled amber. Afterwards, with a pleasure so sensual I almost swooned in my cooling skin, I watched him scoop our hastily discarded clothes and wet towels and toss them into the open mouth of his tiny washing machine. It was a confident and seemingly practised gesture. I felt in my marrow that here was a man who would go on to fill this machine with more soiled clothes, switch it on, add powder, and proceed to make it function. To do a load of washing. Lots of loads. That one gesture, nonchalant, executed while clad only in the remains of our bubbles, spoke of many loads. Possibly done more than once a week.

And on one of those evenings, after another voluptuous bath, when he said to me, You go in and read your book, I'll hang these things up to dry then make us an Irish coffee, I almost thought I'd died and gone to heaven. I was on the last chapter of *Madame Bovary* at the time.

So when Nancy suggested an entire book devoted to the laundry, I immediately understood what she meant, having thought long and hard about the subject. Amid the truckloads of guides and handy hints books and DIYs published, it was an inspiration. Anyone could – and did – produce compendia of household hints, from sauces to shoe mending, but only a visionary would conceive a complete book on just one function of the contemporary household. Nancy was clearly such a visionary.

Before I'd even completed *The Household Guide to Home Maintenance*, after Wesley Andrews's desertion, Nancy had asked me to come up with some suggestions for the next in the series. After all, *Household Words* was distributed to hundreds and thousands of households and so Nancy reasoned that there was a vast potential readership for the guides. Those readers, she thought, could be pushed that bit further, encouraged to specialise. And I could earn some respectable extra income.

And so I wrote *The Household Guide to the Kitchen*, and then, with Archie's help, *The Household Guide to the Garden*. But successful as these were, *The Household Guide to the Laundry*, my last title, pushed the idea further than Nancy could have imagined. No one had yet produced books that eroticised and poeticised such dull tasks as washing, and I only did it by accident. One reviewer called it laundry-porn, intending to be unkind: sales of the book trebled in the following weeks. I had tackled the project with single-minded devotion. I first described the Ideal Laundry, advising readers on location, insulation, ventilation, drainage, convenience of access and the possibility of potential flooding from wayward appliances. I weighed the pros and cons of internal as opposed to external laundries, keeping my own preferences (large, internal, but with separate egress to the backyard) in check.

I wanted everyone who read this book, male or female, to spend their last dollar on a small room they'd hitherto considered irrelevant. Into it I poured all my memories of how seductive I had found the image of Archie doing the laundry, depositing our dirty clothes and towels in the washing machine while I lay back in the bath as the bubbles fizzled around me. I made the laundry thrilling, irresistible, even naughty. In short, I made it sexy. It wasn't porn but I certainly gave it grunt, passion, desirability. I endowed it with narrative. By the time they'd finished reading my *Household Guide to the Laundry* readers would be aroused by the sight of their ironing boards and have hardcore experiences crouched against their washing machines. Which would be gently humming and vibrating (Chapter 2: Choosing Appliances). With plenty of warm fluffy towels to hand (Chapter 5: Towelling and Other Household Linen) their bliss would be complete. In fact, the guide recommended that the laundry, which generally contained a second toilet, also be equipped with a small bar fridge. Thus, and perhaps with a source of music (e.g. portable CD player, but well away from taps, *vide* Chapter 9: Safety in the Laundry), it could be a haven they need never leave.

After emailing Nancy a draft of chapter one, I had experienced doubts. What if she found it stupid and fanciful, entirely inappropriate for her target readership? Dismayed by such thoughts, and confused by her silence, I ploughed on with the research side of the book, beginning the legwork at a huge whitegoods warehouse in Croydon, my first stop on a selective round of product assessment. Like many modern retail venues, it consisted of vast spaces crammed with stock, and almost no staff. So I was free for an entire morning to wander among the rows of washing machines and dryers, collecting the literature and assessing for myself the relative merits of each brand and model. To get to the laundry whitegoods, a customer first had to traverse the ground-floor display of kitchen appliances. This was an experience of exquisite and unparalleled torment and delight, such were the siren calls of the huge gleaming stainless-steel cooktops and ovens, or the enigmatic smoky magic of the black marble benchtops, all so cool, lean and contemporary as to make my chapter on the topic in *The Household Guide to the Kitchen* already seem dated. I strapped myself to the mast of resolution and sailed forth, willing myself on towards the gleaming laundry sinks, the super-efficient front loaders and the thrilling new water-evaporation dryers that left the air entirely lint free, but promising myself another visit to submit to the wicked delights of kitchen goods for a new edition of *The Household Guide to the Kitchen*. Except that commission would not be forthcoming unless the laundry guide succeeded.

My doubts vanished when Nancy rang shortly after to tell me that sales of the previous title, and the third in the series, *The Household Guide to the Garden*, had gone sky high. It was on the non-fiction bestseller list, where it was to remain for an unprecedented eight months. I could make the laundry as naughty as I wanted – the series was well and truly on its way.

Eighteen

Why have you really come back? Mitchell was asking me now.

I had returned to the bar the next afternoon after spending most of the day in the Paradise Reach Motel doing nothing much but developing a larger ache in my stomach. No one made cocktails like Mitchell. Even his gin and tonics were the best. Mine were weak these days, the taste for alcohol being incompatible with the cocktail of chemotherapy. Not that I was taking much of that any more.

I shrugged. You know, Mitch. I never sorted out what to do with the caravan. You must have wanted to let that space plenty of times over the years.

Not really.

Some things in there I need to fetch, Sonny's things. See a few people ...

I placed my drink carefully on the bar, lining up the base with the coaster, then poked at the ice with the straw.

She's not here, you know, he said.

He knew that I would be looking for someone in particular, someone whom I'd never met but who had been part of my life.

I said quietly, You can't be sure.

Mitchell reached out across the bar and pressed his hand onto mine, a rare gesture. You won't find her, he said, not after all this time.

But I have to now. Don't you understand?

What does Archie think?

I picked up my drink again. He doesn't know.

You mean he doesn't know you're here? He must be out of his mind with worry.

I've rung him, I said. Told him I'm okay. I'll be going back soon. I just need a bit of time.

How did you manage to drive up here anyway, if it's that bad?

Calm before the storm, I said.

Come on, Delia, what's the real story?

The real story is that I'm feeling okay, though I get tired occasionally. I'm now onto two-monthly doses of chemo, some radiation. Just recovered from treatment when I decided to come up here. And when I go back I think that'll be it. It might be worth it, might not. It might buy me more weeks, more months. Or nothing. Can I have another drink, please?

So, it's ... ?

Spreading. Metastasis. Had a small tumour removed last year, and was good for six months. Now there's another. Even though they dose me with chemotherapy I know it's growing. Like I said, it's the full deal.

And there's nothing more they can do?

I've had three operations, two years of chemo on and off, enough radiation to power a third world country for a year. Archie and the girls have had to watch me go through all that. I think they'll cope better by watching me die in peace.

As he fixed me another gin and tonic, the phone at the end of the bar rang. He ignored it and when the place was quiet came back and handed over my drink.

And this girl, he said. If you find her, have you thought about what you're going to do? What you'll say? Do you think she'll want to have anything to do with you?

My eyes were filling up by then. I shook my head. I don't know, Mitch, I just want to see her – I just need to see her.

What makes you think she's even in town?

Only that I know her family decided to settle here after her operation, they liked it so much. Some of us were like that, you remember.

Despite his aloofness, Mitchell had helped me in many ways. He'd arrived at the hospital the day after the birth bearing a bunch of pink carnations. Safe, neutral, old lady flowers. The sort of flowers that men like Mitchell, unaccustomed to giving them, bought for young women like me, unaccustomed to receiving them. I think we were both more embarrassed by those carnations than by the sight of me in bed, in a too-tight T-shirt, which I'd thought would do for a nightgown, with my suddenly mountainous breasts blossoming with wet patches. Mitchell gazed instead at the football of tender flesh and fuzzy hair wrapped tightly in a cotton waffle-weave blanket. To the point, as ever, he asked me what I was going to name him. I had thought about it for a long time but still couldn't decide. Girls' names came easily. I could have chosen from a long list beginning with

Abigail and ending with Zenya. Mitchell picked the bundle up and cradled him.

Well, sonny jim, we have to think of a name for you.

That's a good name, I said.

What? Jim?

No. Sunny, as in Sunday. Except I'll have to spell it Sonny.

It was a Monday morning. My baby had been born the night before.

Nineteen

Dear Delia
Desperate here again. That hour I spent in the bathroom almost killed me but it worked. Now my girlfriend stays in there for longer than thirty seconds and has stopped holding her nose. And you were right about the kitchen. I have to admit it is a mess. Maybe I'm just a slob, I don't know. Anyway, I've thrown out all the empty food containers and dishes and put the garbage out. She still says it smells and that at night there are more cockroaches than in the entire third rike, whatever that is.

Dear Desperate
It's not a question of maybe – you are *a slob. Also a profoundly ignorant one. It is the Third Reich your girlfriend is referring to, the government led by Adolf Hitler up to and including the second world war, by which she obviously means your kitchen is infested by the smaller brown species of beetle known as the German cockroach. So if you want to retain this relationship you had better apply yourself to the kitchen with some dedication. Two hours, this time. You'll*

need at least an hour for the stove alone. As for the fridge, my guess is you'd be better off dragging it outside and blasting it with the garden hose, if not getting a new one. The cockroaches will go crazy at this, fridges being their favourite hiding spot. Spray first.

Given her initial reluctance, Nancy's acceptance of my proposal for a book about dying was obscenely swift. And then she started on the publicity campaign, briefing her marketing people well in advance. It was amazing how publishers like her could do that, wake up one morning and switch over into commercial mode, putting their efforts into selling an idea that the day before they might have disdained. She asked if I could finish in time for a release date of the following October. I wondered about the wisdom of aiming for the Christmas list, as despite my own optimism it seemed a curious market to be chasing, but I left that to her.

Over the next few weeks I wrote a detailed outline, roughed out the chapters and compiled a list of further reading. As it was the last guide I would be writing I decided to take a more creative approach. I collected epigraphs for openers. It was lucky that I hadn't embarked on tidying the poetry books, sorting and culling, and so there was plenty of material to hand. Sylvia Plath was an obvious choice with her sly Lady Lazarus claiming that *Dying is an art*, one that she did exceptionally well. And there was John Donne with his magnificent cheek: *Death, be not proud, though some have called thee Mighty and dreadful.* How was it that Donne had believed that death was really a feeble, unworthy antagonist, long before he'd confronted it himself? That death, in fact, was mortal too? *Death, thou shalt die.*

I had discovered Donne in a volume of poetry in Pearl's book exchange in Amethyst. Her collection, like those of other second hand bookshops, was full of old high school texts: tattered, stained and reluctantly read books all of a certain type. It was as if one person in the world had decided that schoolkids should eternally read *Hamlet*, *To Kill a Mockingbird*, Herodotus's *Histories*, *The Catcher in the Rye*, and something called *The Metaphysical Poets*. I discovered what a metaphysical poet was about the time I was getting to know Archie. I remember telling him I'd discovered there was a poet called Andrew Marvell who wrote about gardens, even about mowing.

Mowing? Archie had said. Give me a look.

I showed him the poem about the man mowing and lamenting that his cruel lover would do to him what he did to the grass.

And thus, ye meadows, read Archie, *Which have been Companions of my thoughts more green, Shall now the heraldry become With which I will adorn my tomb*. What do you think that means?

I don't know. That his lover will kill him then bury him under the lawn?

Archie handed back the book. Meadows fresh and gay? Unthankful meadows? This Marvell bloke, he obviously never mowed a lawn in his life.

But I always remembered that bit about the mower's green thoughts adorning his tomb. Not that I pretended to understand what it meant.

Fortunately many poets approached death with sanguine attitudes. Keats's gentle welcoming of the experience captured much of the mood of the volume I was planning. *For many a time I have been half in love with easeful Death*.

Rereading those lines, I felt death could be desirable. It might indeed *seem rich to die*. Something to aspire to, eagerly, fondly, rather than submit to with reluctance. I glanced through *In Memoriam* then put it aside: I would avoid Tennyson, even eschew the Victorian poets altogether. No dreary or gloomy sentiments for my book. Plath's Lady Lazarus was so appealing I considered using her words for the title. *The Art of Dying* had a ring to it. It was balanced, grave, literary. But already used.

I worked on *The Household Guide to Dying* in a pleasant fever of anxiety, amused by the idea that for the first time in years of deadlines I was really and truly working towards one. Knowing I was making something useful of my own death. Death, inevitable, meaningless, it confounded us all. I never wanted anyone to be carrying on trying to salvage meaning, hope or comfort from my premature demise. To go on about triumphing in an afterlife somewhere, about finding solace in unexpected places. I couldn't agree with Donne. Death was death. Death could not die itself. The final score would be Delia: nil, Death: one. But I could leave my guide to dying, to show others the way through it. I hoped it would be on sale at my funeral, that Nancy would have a dump bin or some display at the wake, although I hadn't yet raised this with her as I knew she, along with everyone else, would find it tasteless.

My guide to dying wouldn't be speculating on the afterlife or advising the bereaved about the process of grieving – that was best left to the psychologists and counsellors. Instead I determined to concentrate on the practical: choosing your own coffin, stocking the freezer for when you were gone. Cancelling your credit cards. Finalising your tax return. Palliative constipation. Erasing your hard drive. Food for the dying. Cancelling the newspapers. Planning your daughter's wedding. Finding a new home for the cat. Selecting the right outfit to wear at your funeral and for the rest of your death. Organ donation. Embalmment. Burial or cremation. Mrs Beeton died at just twenty-eight and I felt sure her comprehensive book would have included advice for the care of the dying, except that for such a healthy, active and well-informed woman in her twenties, the prospect of death was like a fabled land, a place of griffins and hydras, too bizarre and remote to be seriously considered. Not so long ago, I would have felt the same.

Under my health care scheme, things were as grim as a Russian co-op store. In a not quite public but not quite private system either, 'clients' like me (patients were being linguistically phased out) scored doctors who believed their main mission in life was to improve your vocabulary. My oncologist, Dr Lee, enlivened our consultations by the casual introduction of numerous polysyllabic specialist words. I visited her, clutching blood and urine samples in one hand, a pocket medical dictionary in the other (I really didn't mind – you never knew when a word like desquamation or neoplasm would be useful; it even gave me a small frisson of pleasure to know that I could pull out a word like thermoanesthesia and apply it if needed).

After my last visit I decided that, apart from prescriptions for drugs, I didn't need her at all. There was no advice she could offer, and not much comfort. Her bedside manner combined formality with a strange timidity. A diminutive, greying woman, she cowered like a guinea pig behind her oversized desk, and always had trouble meeting my eyes, as if the sheer weight of her responsibility was slowly but inexorably dawning on her, that, as an oncologist, she was inevitably going to be treating the dying, a monstrously unfair burden to be bearing. And I could only agree with that. But, to be fair, Dr Lee explained my condition and outlined my future months with impressive clarity (when I remembered to take the dictionary, our sessions were almost enjoyable). And after several postoperative visits I was in no doubt as to the progress of my illness.

Just as she predicted, I had good weeks and bad weeks during treatment. Weeks where I felt more ill and wretched than ever, and despairing of recovering, where I had no appetite, vomited continually, and found the very effort of rising from bed unthinkable. Then the course of drugs altered, or stopped, and the cells had a chance to bounce back. Then I had a period of good health, where I could eat and walk and shower and otherwise function. Even consider going out to lunch. The good weeks were so blissfully free of the symptoms of the bad, that I was energised beyond myself. So relieved not to feel pain, not to be vomiting, not to feel as though every drop of blood in my veins had been siphoned out and replaced with molten lead, that I felt far better than I was. For I was fooling everyone but myself: I wasn't buying back my life, only extending the lease by a matter of months. Still, in these weeks I felt I could do almost anything. After the girls left for school I always went straight to my desk.

As I drafted the chapters I focused on creating a book that Nancy's team would find irresistible to promote. With marketing, you always had to focus on select key terms, to remember that the very word *key* was a key term, which had nothing to do with locks, everything to do with outcomes – another key term. So I would not, for example, mention quoting the poets at this stage. Although Nancy was amenable to poetry, I'd have to slip it in surreptitiously. Poets were not key indicators of anything much. Poetry was not a key term. In fact, poetry was almost unmentionable. Suggestive of obscurity and paranoia as well as negative financial returns. So it would not do to highlight poetry in the proposal and sample chapters. But soon, with the safely dead poets sidelined for the moment, I put together the skeleton of what I felt might be a worthy, perhaps inspiring sort of book, as well as a frankly utilitarian one.

I wrote about diet, leisure activities, the need for a soothing environment, but also for enough stimulation. I wrote about discussing death with family and friends, about winding matters up at work, about tossing out all the detritus of your life – not for yourself, but to save your family the chore after you were gone. I wrote of plans and lists, the importance of them. I wrote of books and songs, writers and singers, things you'd want to be read or performed while you were dying, or at your funeral.

I kept writing. About being in control when everything – sickness, drugs, procedures, doctors – was threatening to control you. About walking away from the last resort that would always be offered, the last chance treatment, the other cure they always had up their sleeves. About how empowering it could be to tell them no, that the few extra months or minutes the treatment might give you weren't worth it. About the illusion of cure, the imminence of mortality, about embracing it, not resisting it ... I was writing all that because I'd done it, I knew what it was like. I wrote and I wrote and I had it all covered, or so I thought, because I'd been there, I was the expert. Until one day I could write no more, because one day I woke up and realised there was much more to taking control than I thought.

One day I knew that I'd been deceiving myself, and that if I was going to write about tying up loose ends then first I had to do that myself. One day I just had to get in the car and leave.

Twenty

The shadow on the curtain was shaped like a four-pointed star: two arms, two legs. It revolved slowly, then rapidly, then slowly again, in time to the beat of the music. The curtain was midnight blue, but lit from a spotlight far away across the other side of the tent to a luminous shade, and the shadow on it was black as ink.

Then another spotlight illuminated the revolving figure and the audience, though small, breathed a loud collective gasp of wonder. She was dressed in a glittering pink leotard and spun and circled and twisted and turned with such ease and grace it was like a dancer pirouetting on a floor, except she was fifteen metres up on a slinky rope that descended from the centre of the tent roof, and seemed to be hanging on by nothing more than the toenails of her bare feet. At the end, she leaped off the rope, bowed, and ran towards the curtain and vanished. It was as if the lid of a music box had shut. The light on the curtain dissolved to nothing and when the ringmaster reappeared with three clowns rolling behind him, the glittering pink figure so high on the rope performing the impossible might just have been a dream.

Afterwards, I sought her out. By then the late afternoon was cloud-fractured, and I found her brushing one of the ponies in the enclosure behind the big top, shafted in light that vanished as she moved.

Tara?

She turned around quickly, registering momentary surprise like everyone else here.

Hey. She came up to me and held me tightly for a few moments, then stepped back, eyes locked onto mine. How long has it been?

About fourteen years, I said.

Oh, it's good to see you. We each caught the glint of tears in of the other's eyes.

I knew I'd see you again, I just knew you'd be back one day. How are you?

I'm okay, Tara. Okay.

She was just a teenager when first I met her, and from a distance still looked about sixteen. The same trim body. The long ponytail. She'd grown no taller, was no leaner, only close up her muscles were more defined, tighter. Back then she was the youngest of the family of trapeze artists and acrobats that remained the core of the circus.

She first performed with her mother. They had the safety net below but her mother had developed an act where she threw Tara to her older sister, who was wearing a blindfold. The sister caught her, tossed her up in the air once, then threw her back to their mother on the third swing of the trapeze. They were still performing it when I first met Tara, although one of the young men had taken the place of the sister, who'd left the circus and town by then, and Tara was looking around for a younger child to take her own place in the act while she took on the role of her mother. Who'd also left town. A story best left untold, then and maybe even still.

Remember the blindfold act?

Yeah. She dug around in her back pocket and drew out a crumpled packet of Drum. It was never a big deal, you know, she said. Just timing. If you could count, you could do trapeze, wearing a blindfold or not. And we never did it without the net, not then, only when I was older. Anyway, it was nothing compared to Danny.

Who's Danny?

He was one of the Continis, she told me, the family that left the circus years back, when she was still a child. At the age of four Danny was part of an act with his older brothers. They would jump off the springboard and land on each other's shoulders, biggest to smallest; he was the third and the last. They practised it hundreds of times over and it was perfect, the family of circus boys like Russian dolls opened up and placed on top of each other. Except the very first time they performed it in public, something went wrong, and instead of landing right on top of his brother like he had every other time, Danny went flying out to the side.

She took a long, slow, infuriating drag at her cigarette, expelled the smoke with a sigh.

What happened? I asked.

He flew way over, she said, landed on one of the mats behind, rolled over and then stood up. We were all terrified, including me and I was only six and hated his guts, but the audience loved it, thought it was all part of the act. The little bastard actually took a bow.

She rolled another skinny smoke and, having lit it, lounged back in her chair looking, in her sleeveless shirt and with her tanned, muscular arms, like an old stockman or a veteran shearer reminiscing at afternoon smoko. Tara and I became friends when Sonny's increasing interest in the circus developed into a fascination, then a desire to participate. Tara was happy to have him around, joining the gang of circus kids, some of whom were training for performance, some of whom were just there because that was where they belonged.

We sat in the last of the afternoon sun sharing a bottle of Diet Coke. I couldn't see any kids around the circus now and it was much quieter than I remembered it.

After all these years, she said, some of the families are moving on. Leaving the business for good. Taking their kids somewhere better, or so they reckon.

And what about you?

Me? She paused then said, I'm never having kids.

That's not what I meant.

I know, she said. Sorry.

Twenty-One

Dear Delia
I notice you go on and on in your columns about cleaning, especially to men. It seems like you have a problem. I put my empties in the bin, tidy up the newspapers and that sort of thing. What is it with women and cleaning?
Puzzled.

Dear Puzzled
It is not just women. Cleaning is a verb. And as one male author has so cleverly expressed it, 'There is always something brave about a verb'. Verbs, in case you're unaware, are doing *words. Tossing a few things into a recycling bin every now and then doesn't compare with the effort of getting brave and bold with mopping, scouring and polishing in the face of mould, grease, rust, dust, and all the other active forms of dirt.*

Mr Lambert was enraged when he discovered cockatoos in his backyard. More precisely, they were on his roof, the only place a bird could roost. They arrived each afternoon to shatter his postprandial peace with their noisy screeching. He let it be known that he held me personally responsible for this. In a way he was right, since I'd chosen most of the flowering trees that attracted birds. However, I think he meant (at least, this was recently put to Archie; he no longer talked to me) that my leaving out of dishes of water in the backyard was an irresponsible act. Worse than that, it was done deliberately to upset him. This was grossly compounding the insult of the chickens, which, he claimed, the last time we spoke over the side fence a couple of years ago, had destroyed his life.

What life, Estelle had muttered, ripe with nine-year-old cynicism.

And your children are the rudest I have ever met, he threw at me before his bald head disappeared below the fence. It was not long after that the casuarinas, those most indestructible of natives, turned yellow and died. Then Archie's bamboo plantings in the back corner followed. After that I knew there had been some surreptitious late-night applications of weedkiller. I did nothing, fearing for my chickens, and more: he had already shooed the girls away from his spotless white Corolla when they were rollerblading out the front.

I understood that Mr Lambert's resentment of the cockatoos was displaced anger. Something I'd unintentionally inflamed when, after our side fence encounter, I left half a dozen eggs on his front porch as a peace offering. The result was a visit three days later from the local council's health inspector, an apologetic young man who explained that Mr Lambert had written a long letter complaining that I was exceeding the number of domestic fowl that could be legally kept in a suburban backyard (he'd decided the number was three); that I was keeping a rooster, which disturbed him every morning; that the smell was putrid, making it impossible for him to go out into his own back yard; that the entire area was a haven for vermin, namely rats; that my chicken shed was too close (by one point five metres) to his side fence and my back fence, again in contravention of laws no one seemed to have heard of; and finally that the entire neighbourhood was against the chickens.

Did he say anything about the eggs? I asked.

Eggs?

I gave him some. Beautiful brown ones.

Oh yes, that. He consulted his documents again. There is something in here about food being left in unhygienic conditions. Something about having to dispose of eggs into his own garbage bin.

They were fresh! I only left them at his front door.

The young inspector sighed. I'm sorry, he said, but I'm obliged to report this to you, that's all. I can see your chickens are fine.

Do you want to come into the shed and do a proper inspection?

That's not necessary. Thanks.

Frustrated by the health inspector's refusal to order me to get rid of the chickens, Mr Lambert then fired off another letter to the council, repeating the same objections and adding some new grievances: the tree stump that Archie decided not to grind out but incorporate into a display of ferns and epiphytes (it was apparently harbouring white ants); the pond Archie had laboured over for months and was, rightfully, so proud of (it was infested with mosquito larvae, deeper than the regulation eighteen inches, and unfenced); and the illegal back verandah Archie had allegedly built not long after we moved here. Since Mr Lambert had never been in our back yard, no one knew how he could be so sure that the pond was too deep (it was, I thought, not deep enough: the waterlilies weren't doing so well, but I didn't mention that to Archie) or how he spotted mosquito larvae from such a distance and with a tall fence in between.

The next time the health inspector arrived he apologised again, and said this time he would have to inspect the back yard. He complimented me on the chickens, noted the lack of smell, and explained I could keep as many as I liked, provided the area remained clean. He agreed that none of the hens was a rooster, then confirmed from my description of the so-called vermin that the native rat, antechinus, was prevalent in this area, close to the nature reserve, and that to kill one would incur a one-thousand-dollar fine. Turning his attention to the remainder of Mr Lambert's list, he decided that not a single mosquito larva could survive in a pond full of hungry carp and black moors; that the alleged illegal verandah appeared to be a minor renovation, a rebuilding of the existing one that fell down shortly after we moved in (but that he could get his colleague, the building inspector, to confirm that in writing if I wanted – and by that stage I did); and that the stump near its corner was not infested and never would be, being the remains of a eucalyptus citriodora that white ants rejected as too resinous for their taste.

Surveying the entire back garden, taking in the abundance of trees (not on Mr Lambert's list: he knew that would have been pushing it), the red-roofed chicken shed and the black, white and brown hens contentedly bickering as they scratched the earth, the shady corners, the water features, the piles of sandstone rocks left to weather over the years, the clumps of irises and lilies, the central lawn like a smooth and comforting apron around which all the other features clustered like a family of unruly, charming infants, the whole cool and fertile passivity of the place, the inspector said to me,

It's a wonder you don't have frogs. Ideal conditions for them.

That's an idea, I said.

Meanwhile, most afternoons the cockatoos came unannounced and noisily to the neighbourhood, like a gang of hoodlums squealing brakes and burning rubber. It would have killed me to let Mr Lambert know this, but I wasn't so fond of them either. And Archie hated them. They stripped grevilleas and shredded flowering gums with the same lack of discrimination with which they reduced fascia boards and pine fence trims to splinters. However, I was glad that Mr Lambert's focus on them meant he relaxed his efforts on the chickens, the trees, and our children. I only wondered what he would adopt as his new mission when the cockatoos departed; for depart I was sure they would, in their typically capricious way.

One day I was amusing myself watching them perch on Mr Lambert's television antenna, a ridiculously elaborate affair – and for what, I wondered, as I was sure he never watched television – while he danced around trying to dislodge the birds with a long pole, or propped an old wooden ladder against the side of the house and wobbled about in a fluster of helpless yelling and waving. The cockatoos just barked at him. After one several frustrating minutes, in which he scored a large white dropping in the very middle of his head (it would have been such an irresistible target) and I, seated on the back verandah drinking tea and reading, smirked, Mr Lambert scowled at me and actually raised his fist, then dropped it quickly to clutch at the guttering as the ladder swayed. I wondered if he was really as harmless as I'd thought. If his manic devotion to sawing and uprooting and poisoning most forms of life from his and my back yard could go further. Would he ease up after I'd gone? I wondered. If there was a core to him that contained a small streak of kindness then it was inaccessible. So far my illness hadn't exposed it – Archie had told him, after the second diagnosis, but he'd merely nodded and continued with his watering – so I doubted my dying would.

Watching him that afternoon, his white hot anger against simple cockatoos, the helpless fury of his attempts to control nature, I confronted the depth of my own resentment and anger, feelings that had sustained me all through his ridiculous depredations. And I realised that I didn't want to take those feelings to my grave. I'd never had any impact on him, and never would. My dying would not change the way he acted. But I could make something of that. I could have my revenge, but in an innocent way. I would upset him, but in the most benign manner. Somehow I would stamp myself on him, indelibly.

I was having trouble finding the right way to start the guide. Not the research; I had plenty of fat folders on my desk. Not the contents; they were well in hand. But the beginning. I was having trouble finding the right words to describe certain things. Like the state of imminent death. There was the one word: to die. I die. A brave and simple verb. I am about to die. I will die. I am dead (if that were possible). Or she is dead. And there was an equally brave word in our language to describe the other end of life's journey, the beginning. I was born. I am born. Yet for the woman giving birth it was verbally more complex. Yes, one could birth a child, but no one ever said that. It was always a matter of *giving* birth.

At one time Nancy had wanted a household guide to childbirth. Birth, birthing, ante-natal, post-natal, babies, children ... Like many non-mothers she tended to lump all the stages and experiences together. She decided that the next in the series, after the success of the guides to the laundry, the kitchen and the garden, the logical one to do – the one that if not done would be considered a vast hiatus in the entire series – would be birth. She had thought that, with my experience of mothering, I was qualified to write it. In a way I was glad to repudiate her plans with an entirely different suggestion, to trump her with the ultimate guide, the guide that would end all guides. I was no expert on children. I knew little about mothering. Giving birth a couple of times only made you realise how bad you were at it. And mothering itself was a vast hole, on the edge of which I was merely standing, uncertainly peering way down into the endless dark.

Maybe it's the title? she suggested at one point. Maybe if we called it something other than *The Household Guide to Childbirth*? Then readers won't make the mistake of thinking you're a medical expert, a midwife or whatever.

What should we call it, then? I asked.

The Household Guide to Mothering?

Sounds like something from the fifties.

The Household Guide to Motherlove?

Motherlove? You're joking. (I hoped she was joking.)

Well, she complained, it has to be a marketable title. And it has to fit in with the series.

I didn't want to tell Nancy about my troubles with the latest guide, the one I'd insisted on writing. There was no way to describe the waiting for death. Pre-mortal? *Dying* was not good enough. It was both too broad and too precise. For a start we were all dying, all our lives, from the moment of birth. And we were dying most specifically when we were laid on our beds entubed, respirated, catheterised, in the final days or weeks when the body began to shut down for good and the relatives gathered around. But what about now? What word could describe my exact condition, active and alert, feeling well for the most part, yet facing the unambiguous end of life within months?

The irony of this gripped me tightly, though yet again irony was such a feeble, inadequate, contemptible word for it. There had to be something else, but my great collection of dictionaries and thesauruses, my passionate regard for words in any context, or none at all, my logophilia, my love of neologisms, of cryptic crosswords and arcane word books, failed me on this one. Me, of all people. A professional proofreader, someone who read dictionaries for fun. Who, when she was a lonely new mother in a caravan, read every book she could and so began to feel like a goddess, as if words had become life itself. Who knew what words like nidification and gelogenic meant. Who could come across words like afflatus, ephetic and sciolism and never confuse them with affluence, mephitic and scoliosis. Who had words like deliquescence and sesquipedalian at her beck and call. Used such words without a hint of shame. Been totally lexiphanic and proud of the fact. If it existed, I couldn't find the word to capture the process when dying actually felt like living, when decay, corruption and disease focused one so smartly and keenly it was as if you were living every day left to you balanced on the blade of a carving knife.

The author of a guide to dying had a responsibility to find that right word, I felt. I would have liked to commence this book with some positive thoughts about the activity of death and in this instance one brave verb would have been helpful. Also helpful would have been a good noun. One was not a patient. Nor a resident. Customer, client, applicant. All were relevant, I supposed, but none quite right.

Arthur Stace found the right word. This elusive homeless man mystified Sydneysiders for decades by writing the perfect word wherever he could. Eternity. The perfect word, his gift to a young city perched on the edge of an ancient continent, came to him like a ringing call one day when he was in a church. He said the word was the only one that got the message across, that made people stop and think.

It was still there, on the headstone of his grave, as I had discovered when we visited Waverley cemetery. Arthur Stace was almost illiterate and yet he achieved literary perfection. Eternity contained everything he needed to say. In one word he had written an entire poem, an unforgettable one. He chalked it on the footpaths and hoardings of the city over fifty times a day for thirty years. As you would, having found the perfect word.

Twenty-Two

I was leafing through the Paradise Reach Motel's local telephone directory, looking up names from long ago, when my mobile phone rang. It was Jean. I handed the book back to the receptionist and went up to my room to talk to my mother in private.

Thanks for going over to help out, I said. I guess everything's okay?

Okay enough. If you manage to ring the girls every day I'm sure they'll be fine.

I thought maybe it would be better if I didn't, I said. You know, get them used to the idea ...

Delia, don't be ridiculous. As if anything could get them used to the idea.

Perhaps.

Charlotte's been helping too, she said. She's got her final exams soon but she's been going over there some afternoons. She was there on Sunday night. They're really fond of her, you know.

Yes, I know.

She seems to understand all that computer stuff Estelle's into, My Room or blobbing or whatever it's called.

It's called lots of things. But she's twenty-eight, she's into all that.

And she'll sit down with Daisy and share a plate of those dreadful cocktail thingies.

I could almost hear Jean shaking her head. The first time she confronted a cocktail frankfurter was at Estelle's fifth birthday party. You'd have thought it was a cockroach.

By the way, she said, do you realise how much tomato sauce that child gets through in a week?

Yeah, I know.

It seems to be her chief source of vitamin C.

Look, I know Daisy doesn't eat much fruit. But I can't be bothered about that at the moment. Anyway, she's healthier than me.

You ate so well when you were little.

Jean was right: I barely ate a thing that wasn't natural, homemade and unprocessed, until I was corrupted by high school canteens.

Yes, and look at me now, hardly evidence that cancer's based on poor diet.

Oh, my darling, she said. I knew exactly how she was feeling. She understood my silence on the other end of the line, hundreds of kilometres away.

You're tormenting yourself with this. Why don't you leave it alone? Come home.

The silence swelled out, then burst.

You were there, Mum, I said, crying. You remember what happened. Did I do the wrong thing?

You did exactly the right thing. You know that.

So why is it eating me up like this? Why did I have to come back?

You should try to rest, she said, then think about coming home. I can keep ducking over to help out and mind the girls for Archie, but it's you they need.

I know that. But right now, I need her. I need to find her. It won't be forever. It'll only be a few more days.

Maybe you finding her isn't really what this is all about.

What do you mean? I said, rubbing my eyes.

Maybe she's the one who needs to find you. When she's ready.

And maybe by then, I said, it'll be too late.

But Archie needs you too, don't forget.

As Archie and I settled into a cautious kind of love, there were still questions in my mind. But when I finally asked him, he insisted he and Pearl were finished.

Pearl, she's a great person, he said. But we have nothing in common. It's over, she knows that.

Do *we* have much in common?

At least we're compatible.

And weren't you and Pearl? You must have been.

What would be the female equivalent of Elvis? he asked.

I dunno. Marilyn Monroe?

Right. So imagine spending the rest of your life hearing her voice, seeing her photos everywhere you look. Even over the bloody bed, while you're having sex. What would it be like, living with that kind of man?

Painful.

See what I mean? It's sad, but despite what she says, Pearl's never going to commit, to me or anyone. She's got

Elvis and that's too much competition for me. And anyway, I love you.

There. He'd said it. He loved me.

Archie, I love you too. But …

Why, he said, taking my hand, does there always have to be a *but* with you?

If Tara took Sonny to sleep over with the other circus kids I occasionally stayed the night at Archie's place. But I'd resisted his offer to move in with him. My stubborn core that kept me independent when I had a baby and no one and nothing else. My scorched ego that said I didn't need a man. I was hanging onto them, with pride. I would never be disappointed, abandoned, denied again.

But never is a foolish word when you are young, and one day I finally woke up and realised I'd recovered from Van. That if he hadn't left when he did, he would have later. I was always happy being still. I was a reader. Home was something permanent, even if it was just a caravan. But Van was a performer, a musician and singer, and I would never have been enough of an audience for him. He would have always been moving on. Probably was right now. I pictured him doing late-night gigs in Irish pubs one month, busking on the Bund the next, and ending up running a bar on a beach in Costa Rica where the local girls would be kinder than I as he grew old and leathery.

What was I doing saying no all the time to a man like Archie? I would say yes, but I wanted to include Sonny. Archie would meet us before dinner, and I would surprise them both.

Twenty-Three

Dear Delia
It's me again. Thanks for all the advice, and the kitchen's looking pretty good now. My girlfriend and I cooked in it last Friday night. Spaghetti bolognese, and a salad. Can you explain to me how to use an iron properly? Also there seems to be some problem with the washing machine, all my clothes are turning a funny grey colour.
Yours
Not-So-Desperate.

Dear Desperate
You are wrong, you are still Desperate. Don't you have a single role model in your life, someone you can turn to for basic domestic advice? I can't explain how to use an iron, Desperate, that is something that has to be demonstrated, but I'm sure you can get a video of it somewhere. YouTube has to be good for something. As for your washing, the problem is not with the machine but you. Like every male the world over you wouldn't think to sort your clothes and I'm not talking shirts from pants. I mean whites from coloureds.

Yes, good old segregation, vital to harmony in the laundry. And stop washing the tea towels with your underwear.

I was watching the neon yellow fluid travel through the tube into my arm. It was such a poisonous shade one could believe in its ability to kill anything. Two more hours, then another two to be flushed out with saline. But it wasn't killing the cancer cells, not enough of them. It was the last treatment, I'd decided. And since I'd decided, I wasn't entirely sure why I didn't just pull the cannula out of my arm and walk out of there forever. Would another five hundred millilitres of methotrexate make any difference now?

I lay back in the chemotherapy chair and tried to relax as the drugs assaulted my system, but it was hard. In a day or two I would be vomiting up water. The small fuzz of hair I had cultivated since the last treatment would thin out yet again and I would be wasted, pale, wretched beyond words. Though exhausted I wouldn't be able to sleep. I would hate to be bothered, and upset if left alone. I wouldn't be able to read. The smell of soap, of coffee, of flowers would be repellent. Certain colours, like orange and purple, would be intolerable. People would bring me beautiful roses and I would not be able to bear having them in the room. My mouth would taste like metal. There would be ulcers, some of them all the way through my alimentary system. And then, when I stopped feeling sick, I would want to eat food that at ordinary times wouldn't interest me – snack foods, fast foods – while the dishes I loved best would taste disgusting. I would be a bloated, bald, grumpy, slit-eyed monster consuming takeaway pizza and sweet fizzy drinks. And after all that I would still have cancer cells merrily reproducing by the minute, dividing and conquering the parts that were left: what remained of my unPromethean liver, my brain, my spinal cord, my throat.

So yes, it was going to be the last treatment.

The chair was luxurious, well padded, capacious. Here in the oncology clinic, we were the ambulant patients, obediently hooked up to our monitors and IV machines, cheerfully waiting with magazines while the toxic fluids trickled into our veins. Eating our sandwiches before the drugs kicked in, after which the thought of food would be agony. Except today I was not having a measure of vincristine or a nip of carmustine to cut the straight dose of methotrexate. Today I was having my cocktail neat, unadorned. No olive, no perky parasol. Lately, instead of reading or doing the daily cryptic crossword, I'd been bringing my notebook and making the most of the experience, getting down the whole authentic feel of the place for the benefit of the guide, making sure I got the details right, before it was too late, and I was out of here for good. Now that I was paying close attention, it struck me how self-sufficient we all were in the oncology clinic. Up to a dozen patients at a time were plugged in, quietly being dosed, barely a nurse to be seen. Left to ourselves, we kept an eye on the machines, made sure we drank enough fluids, kept samples of our urine when we wheeled our IV trolleys out to the toilet. We even managed to adjust the monitors when they beeped at us. I'd driven myself here, though Archie had offered, and would drive home again, and pay a hefty parking fee for the privilege. If we could have taken our own blood samples and injected ourselves with the intramuscular drugs, I'm sure they would have let us do that too. I peeled a banana and turned another page in my notebook.

Just at that point, Dr Lee walked in. She rarely appeared in the clinic, preferring to handle her patients at the comfortable arm's length provided by her very large desk. Stripped of her office furnishings, she looked almost naked.

She examined me as she always did, with faint surprise. I'd been her patient for nearly three years and had primaries, secondaries and now tertiaries, yet she still reacted as if I was intruding on her professional territory. I generally felt that she'd have been an excellent doctor if she didn't have to encounter real people. She stared at the methotrexate in the bag as if it were a reptile. Warily, she asked me how I was.

Fine, thanks.

Good, good, she said, smiling now, as if the most relaxing thing in the world was to be sitting in the chemotherapy ward of an oncology clinic having doses of poison, for a disease that would kill you anyway. Yet, in a curious way, it *was* normal. It had become quite normal for me at least, so that I felt that waiting here for hours, surrounded by strangers, attached to machines, holding a half-eaten banana, represented a level of reality I could accept.

We'll get your bloods done now, she said. Then book you in for the next treatment.

No, I said. I'm not coming back.

On the way out I passed the paediatric clinic. Usually I rushed past, unwilling to encounter the bald toddlers, the babies in their clear plastic cots, the gaunt teenagers, all eyes and lips, features exaggerated by the sculpted nakedness of their heads. In one bed a baby was sitting up, sucking a fist, her cheeks blooming from steroids. She was attached to her IV pump through a catheter implanted in her chest. Her peach vest emphasised the rounded chubbiness of her arms. I stared at her through the window. She stared back, taking the fist from her mouth and dribbling slightly. Her eyes hooked into mine, frank and unselfconscious. She was probably eight or ten months old. I expected she was having drugs similar to mine, though for what disease I could not be sure. Acute leukaemia, perhaps, the commonest form of childhood cancer. All of it an outrage in such a tender body, a new life barely unfurled in its world. I walked on, out of the ward.

How pure and wholesome my babies had been to me. I imagined what a violation the mother of that baby felt when she saw the catheters going in, as she watched week after week the blood being drawn. How every general anaesthetic for the lumbar punctures, the aspirates, the biopsies, would be like small deaths for her, again and again. How she would lie close to her sick sleeping child to breathe with her, in and out, to cherish the feel and the smell for as long as she could.

Did I now remember the smell of a newborn baby? Did I know a word for it?

I thought I was remembering my babies, and although it seemed impossible, since my nose and mouth were dominated by the metallic flavours of the drugs, the smell came back to me as they travelled further away from babyhood and as I rattled on towards the end of my life. As babies, their heads had seemed engulfed by an invisible nimbus of something altogether holy. In particular, there was a spot on the back of the neck, where the smell of fresh human life was exquisite. It smelled wholesome, warm, faintly sweet. Slightly earthy, yet pure and heavenly at the same time. It was a new smell but a familiar one. A smell you may never have breathed in before your baby was placed into your arms, but one you recognised at once, as if it was imprinted in your DNA, and had been there all your life just waiting to be found. Each baby had a different smell, yet each was equally fragrant and soothing. You picked your baby up and drew deeply through your nostrils, again and again over months and years, before finally exhaling in utter satisfaction. No other perfume, no drug, nothing ever had the smell of a baby. Fresh-cut grass, a coffee bean, a glass of aged port, a lemon leaf crushed in the hand, a drop of Chanel No 5, a new book. All the smells in life that we savoured, treasured, the ordinary and the rare things that made us glad we came equipped with noses and so miserable when they were stuffed with colds and flu.

My body would be starting on its gradual ascent into death. Or perhaps that was *descent*, since the process was more like the preparation for a landing, the pilot switching off instruments, shutting down systems, pulling back on the throttle, dimming then killing the cabin lights. And so I thought more about the smells of life because I suspected that death would bring its own new smells, none of them welcome.

I thought about this late one night when I sneaked outside. A few weeks earlier, I had decided how to leave my unique mark for my neighbour, and had begun the preparations. It took a long time, these brief visits spread out when I could manage them, for I needed the conditions to be right. I needed to feel up to it. I couldn't be confined to bed by exhaustion or immobilised by nausea or in the grip of a drug haze that made me weak or dizzy or unable to focus. Then there had to be no moon, of course. And everyone else had to be asleep, including Mr Lambert who, for an elderly widower, kept some late hours.

I read for hours, putting my book down and peeking out the front to see if his lights were off. Small chinks were visible through the otherwise blank sheets of his roller shutters. But eventually they too dissolved into the darkness. Barefoot, in dark track pants and T-shirt, I stepped lightly across the front verandah, avoiding the squeaky board, and padded down the steps for all the world like a burglar. Except for the fact that I would be putting something in, not taking it away, I might have felt a bit of guilt. Instead, I felt a thrill of achievement each time I made my night time excursions.

The silence was confirmed when I pressed close to his front fence and listened. No radio (he favoured the insomniac stations and, to his credit, I never heard any shock jocks coming from his kitchen window). His front gate was so ridiculously low I didn't need to open it (it would not squeak, though, he surely oiled it). The mock orange smelled so strong it was like a drug, and yet he never came out to sniff the air. I just stepped over it and then I was onto his concrete side path, which shot straight down beside his front lawn, past the house, up to the gate into his back yard. His front lawn was virginal. No path, and apart from the mock orange along the front fence clipped into submission, no shrubs. No stepping stones leading to the front porch either. Just the perfect empty lawn.

I was put off by the chilly winter nights, but then the job was done, and all it needed was to wait. A night here, a night there, and the only tool I required was an empty biro case. Lying there on Mr Lambert's lawn, adding my own special touch to his couch grass, making my own statement in a way, for those few nights it took, I almost felt that this would be a lovely place to die. There would be the satisfaction of having Mr Lambert find a corpse despoiling his perfect front lawn, leaking cytotoxically from various orifices as well, then the tramping boots of the paramedics who'd have to be called in to remove me – that would be a perfect revenge for his poisoning of our casuarinas, his slicing of the leaves of the monstera deliciosa, his attacks on the bamboo. His tossing those beautiful eggs into the bin.

And his couch lawn was a pleasant place to rest. Soft, fragrant. A most soothing shade of green. Devoid of a single bindi-eye, naturally. Very comfortable to the bare foot. And the smell, of course, a very fine one. One of the best nature has to offer. As I poked into the soil (organically enriched, I was sure) with my biro case filled with seeds, the grass and the damp dirt smell rose up to greet me in a way that could only be called inviting. Earth to earth, that I would be soon.

Meanwhile, wishing I could at the very least find one word to describe the scent of a baby (I'd given up trying to find the word that captured the dying condition) I turned my mind to the smells of death. I had become a bit obsessed lately with the smells around me: not the chemotherapy gas, the putrid odour of shit and wind that blasted out of me when I was in the full swing of it. I regarded that, undignified as it was, as totally *unnatural*. And after the chemotherapy ended, it was all natural. Just the body doing what it was meant to do, maybe what it did best after the years of growth were over: turn around and begin the descent, slower for most people, back down the mountainside, back to the earth.

The smell of death, I was thinking, was not the same as the smell of a dead and decomposing body. That foul, curiously sweetish smell was something I knew. I had dealt with enough dead rats and the odd dead chicken to know the smell of decaying flesh. What would happen, and what I was not looking forward to, was the stale odour that clung to the sick and dying person. I had examined the medical illustrations and the state of the art electronic photographs of cancer-riddled organs. You surely didn't get that kind of decay without a smell. And yet I had heard and read stories of the dying whose bodies, as they slid towards the end of life, took on a sort of innocence again, a freshness. I was prepared to abandon my quest for single words, and write up some proper material for the chapter in the guide. Soon.

Twenty-Four

The circus had come to Amethyst during the Depression and stayed, eventually becoming the base for its satellites travelling across the top of the country, year after year. People like Tara spent more than half their time on the road, but when they were back in town they were happy to perform a couple of times a week for the meagre audience the place attracted thanks to the circus's longstanding reputation. Some of the families were destined to move around forever, but over the years they returned so regularly that the circus gradually became more permanent. A few never left, surviving on minimal living expenses and dedication to the most creative way of maintaining their unemployment, disability, single parent or any other benefits they could coax out of the government. But mobile or not, the circus families continued to live in caravans, though the site had its own washing and bathing facilities, and a large communal kitchen. Gardens adjoined each caravan and surrounded the circus. Tara's caravan was parked next to her older sister's on one side and her mother's on the other, both shuttered and sprouting grassy skirts, as if they were slowly turning into great mushrooms. They were relics of the sixties or seventies, a bit younger than mine, shabby but not really dilapidated, the sort of caravan that retirees would once have taken away on slow fishing trips, before abandoning them in their back yards. Tara had painted the outside of hers bright pink, the inside yellow. Climbing into it was like entering a seashell.

Hers was also from Lazarus, as everyone's caravan was, and the circus and his odd business had enjoyed a symbiotic relationship. As the caravans deteriorated they were replaced, not by new caravans, just slightly less old ones, all bought from Lazarus on the highway south of town. But this wasn't how he made his money. That occurred in a unique manner that was a marvel of recycling and a model of supply and demand. It began chiefly with the hundreds of pensioners who perennially set off from Melbourne determined to escape the cold and visit places they'd read about or seen on getaway television shows. Inevitably, they were sick of it well before they reached the northern parts of Queensland, and by the time they arrived at the outskirts of Amethyst and Lazarus's welcoming sign – TRAILERS VANS KOMBIS BOUGHT FOR CASH INSTANT DEALS NAME YOUR PRICE (not entirely true, though meant in the spirit rather than the letter) RETIRED PEOPLE ESPECIALLY WELCOME 3 KM AHEAD – they were mentally shifting their belongings into the rear of their station wagons and wondering how far it was to the next train station or airport.

When they reached Lazarus's yard, they were nine-tenths of the way there, emotionally as well as mentally. Financially, Lazarus would quickly take care of the remaining one-tenth of doubt. He indeed paid cash, shaking his head and sighing and muttering about the wisdom of taking the caravans and the doubtful chances of reselling them, but he was feeling generous that day, and he'd like to do them a favour, and he could see they were desperate ... He would point them in the direction of the next motel and within a day or two would make a profit selling the caravans on to the young tourists hitchhiking down from the north, tired of dossing down in cockroachy youth hostels reeking of dirty shoes, and sick of carting their possessions around and looking like off-balance tortoises.

Lazarus was shameless, rarely giving the caravans a clean-out and frequently not even stepping inside them, between buying from pensioners one day and selling the next to the first pair of footsore and fed-up youngsters who spotted his other sign, this one a few kilometres north of the town, advertising CHEAP QUALITY CARAVANS FOR SALE, VEHICLES ALSO AVAILABLE BACKPACKERS WELCOME, as if they were a couple of Galahads and this was the grail of some long and weary quest.

Scores of young men and women towing caravans fitted out by retired people, equipped with hot-water bottles and foldaway shopping trolleys, collections of large-print historical romances and decks of worn playing cards. Kitchenettes with tins of diet jam, Steradent, instant soups and cartons of long-life milk. And then what if the new owners lived out their lives down south in Bexley or Ballarat but then followed a dream to travel north when they retired, and decided by the time they reached Amethyst, they were sick of it? Something like this had once happened, and Tara knew because it had involved her grandparents, who'd decided in a fit of youthful rebellion to leave the circus and the town, and had disappeared south for a dozen years or so, only to return unexpectedly one day, towing the very same caravan. They traded it in for a larger model and continued into Amethyst, where they found their original site still vacant and, apart from being more weed-ridden, awaiting their return as if they'd just gone off for a few weeks' holiday.

A lot of the circus people's stories were taller than the big top, and Tara was one of the worst, but this was one story I knew to be true: I had bought Tara's grandparents' van from Lazarus in my first week in town.

Twenty-Five

A recent Blair & Sons survey has discovered that nearly 65 per cent of respondents enjoy the task of lawn mowing. More than 55 per cent of respondents admitted to feelings of pleasure and tranquillity while mowing the lawn. And approximately 50 per cent agreed the task was an opportunity to transcend the moment, reduce stress and even meditate. Somewhat less than 50 per cent admitted the task provided a valuable chance for solitude; for them the engine noise was like a musical accompaniment, repelling in a legitimate way the need for interaction with partners, children, neighbours and pets.

'The Art of Lawn Mowing'
The Household Guide to the Garden (2004)

One afternoon I woke from a nap to the regular tick-tick-tick of the rotary lawnmower. Archie no longer used the noisy motor mower. The girls were absorbed in the afternoon television shows, a ration I'd shamefully increased over the months in order to claim more time in bed. But this day I felt refreshed, and quite well. I moved to the back verandah and sat in the shade with a soda water to indulge in the harmless spectacle of a man tending his lawn.

I had thought that Archie's competence with the washing was what made me fall in love with him, but now I wondered if it might have been the gardening all along. There was some inexpressible allure in the sight of a man tending a garden, taking charge of a lawn, striding across and claiming it for his own. The man mowing and the woman ironing were archetypal domestic images, polarised, irreconcilable. But what really was the difference? Turning grass into lawn, or crumpled linen into smooth sheets? Maybe the so-called domestic oppositions, the traditional roles, were much more compatible; maybe they existed because they were so fundamental, powerful, and even erotic.

And maybe someone else could work all that out. I was too tired for theory.

Here we were in post-middle-aged positions and yet we were not into our middle years. I was sitting on the verandah and Archie was propelling self and machine across the back yard in smooth assertive strides. Beyond him the shed. His shed. Filled with mysterious male items that looked foreign, even to me, and I knew my hardware. To him they were indispensable. Rusted grates and lengths of black and silver cladding. Huge drill-like bits for which, surely, no drill large enough existed. Coils and coils of wire, hose, rope and conduit. Junk, I believed, all of it, yet the tidiest junk ever, everything in its place. Beyond Archie's shed was a vegetable patch and then the chicken run, four-foot-high wire decorated with a choko vine.

I was dressed in the oversized T-shirt and stretch pants I favoured now for lying about; he was wearing his weather-beaten King Gees, elastic-sided boots, and a naked torso. His body was muscular, golden with sun and a thin sheen of moisture. Even grimy and sweaty, Archie smelled divine, like the fresh mown grass and the earth of his occupation.

Mowing for a living meant he did not always appreciate the romantic possibilities of the lawn. When we moved here he ripped out the buffalo grass and landscaped. The back yard became a project, representing his transition from gardener and mower into landscape designer. Sandstock brick pavers laid in herringbone pattern. Raised garden beds, judiciously placed palms, and a water feature: a black urn gently dribbling water down its sides. It was beautiful, it was peaceful, it was unpretentious. And it was functional. The washing line down one side of the fence, permanent but discreet. The shed at the back. But after a few years I would catch Archie gazing out at the back yard longingly. I knew what he was seeing: a soft carpet of blue-grey. Or a lush rectangle of bright green. He never would have thought it, but he missed the chore of mowing. He realised it was in fact no chore, but an opportunity for self-expression as well as meditative stillness. That was when he embraced the zen of lawnmowing and began again. The sandstock pavers went. He dug, ploughed and aerated, fertilised and fed and sowed a new hybrid grass. When it was all done and grown, and mowed again and again to achieve the right kind of stubbly toughness, we would sit out there like children, feeling the lawn under our palms, getting green stains on our clothes. We would sit there with the girls as well, and neither developed grass rashes.

Archie's lawn was the most beautiful creation. Not so soft you were afraid of treading on it, not so bristly you felt uncomfortable in bare feet. In the dry periods he would water it by hand with the waste water that we siphoned out of the laundry. In heavy rain he would aerate it with a pole to which he'd attached a special kind of garden fork, with long thin tines that broke up the soil without disturbing the surface. When he mowed, the smell was that of all your childhood holidays, birthdays, Christmases and every single treat rushing towards you in a warm breeze. The wholesomeness of that smell was hard to identify, impossible to resist. I breathed in that scent the afternoon I sat there on the verandah. If only it could be bottled.

Idling the afternoon away again, eh? Archie said.

The mower came to rest after the final square of lawn exactly in the middle. Sometimes there was a sharp edge to Archie's teasing.

All right, I'll do some chores then, I said, getting up and stamping down the verandah steps, walking harder than necessary past where he was now raking. I went to the chicken shed. Fetching eggs was one of the few things I could usefully do. But although there'd been a lot of crowing and boasting earlier in the day, there was only the one egg in the laying boxes.

The chickens must be going off the lay, I sang out.

Wrong time of year, he said, bending over to scoop up a pile of clippings. He brought them down and tossed them over the fence. Instantly the five hens raced across to investigate for the possibilities of bugs. He was right; the chickens should have been laying more in early spring, not less.

I handed him the egg. I'll just clean up a bit in here, I said.

My contribution to our garden had been the chickens, although my plan to have them roaming freely created tension until Archie installed a proper wire fence and secured the shed door. As much as I adored the sight of a brown, black or white chicken against an emerald green lawn, I accepted they needed to be cooped up. If I'd ever had any doubts, the state of their run after just a few days of occupation enlightened me. Every last blade of anything green, weedy, noxious or not, ended up pecked to oblivion. I knew they could reduce an entire lawn to dust and rubble within weeks. For some reason, though, the image of a chicken on a lawn persisted, as representative of some sort of domestic perfection, some ideal harmony of nature, so that occasionally I just took Jane and placed her on the lawn for a while and sat back to admire her iridescent plumage contrasting with the chlorophyll rich grass. She was as resplendent as an emblem on a herald.

I scraped away with the spade and laid some fresh straw. The hens were as flustered as usual, behaviour which was for display only. There was nothing about me to fluster them; I was their owner, their feeder, the one who'd raised them from chicks. It was more a matter of principle. A signal that whatever lowly status they might have, they still had their pride. The scruffiest hen, I had noticed, had her dignity. Perhaps it was because of their ability to lay eggs, which after all wasn't something that just anyone could do. I discovered another one under Kitty, who pecked me gently, then gathered up her feathers and hopped down from the laying box. She darted off almost with relief. Devotion to the task of hatching was all so pragmatic in the end. If someone relieved you of the chore, you registered a protest, but then busily got on with the next task in hand, which in her case was scratching away beside the feed tray on the chance that any pellets had survived the day so far, or perhaps a worm. Such optimism.

The lawn was where I would soon end up. More precisely, under one. The possibilities of the lawn came into their fullest with death. All the world over, lawn meant death. Green mounds. Barrows of the ancients. Those fields of white crosses, once mud and guts, across France. The cemeteries and crematoriums, lush and warm, fragrant and restful. All the memorials to the dead, in parks and gardens throughout the world. In my local park. Lawns all lovingly tended and cropped and fertilised and weeded and watered and mown, endlessly mown, in tribute to the dead past. No one could repair the damage of death, especially death in battle, but every slice of the mower blade, every drop of the sprinkler, was someone trying to show they cared. The lawn wasn't really a lawn, but a blanket of sorrow and hope, something we all cast over the past, hoping the past wouldn't return.

I knew I couldn't be buried under my own lawn – even if the family could have lived with that, it was against the law. But I thought about how beautiful a picture of our lawn would be for the cover of the book. If I could just tie that into the theme I would be happy. A picture of a coffin on a lawn would, I guessed, be too confronting. And then there was the matter of branding. It would be unwise to break with brand recognition. I supposed the guide would have to conform to all our others, the same terracotta red and sand yellow border and spine design. I considered further details. *The Household Guide to the Laundry* had featured a shot of white linen napkins flapping gently on a washing line against a backdrop of bright grass and serene blue sky. Familiar images, though no one ever used linen any more. But they invested the book with a reassurance of quality, and of a small aspect of household life that householders would never use themselves, yet also never be alienated from. This sort of detail was important, in the books as well as on the covers. Not many people would consider this, but Nancy and I knew that this subtle layering of images – crisp clean sky, free and familiar to all, along with refined napkins, with the purity of white linen too, a touch of holiness – were all vital to the product we were promoting, because we weren't simply selling household hints, but something larger: the ideal of the household. The concept of family wholeness and permanence and security that all these household books implied.

Similarly, the cover of *The Household Guide to the Kitchen* featured a row of utensils on a rack above an elegantly austere stainless-steel stove, a chequered tea towel tossed across a corner for ironic effect. Few could afford that sort of stove (six thousand dollars approximately, not including the rangehood ventilator fan and stainless-steel splashback) but everyone could and probably did have a check cotton tea towel, which were less than two dollars from the two-dollar shops. If you had that tea towel then you could by association, at least in your fantasies, have the Miele stove too. That you couldn't really have it was ameliorated by the fact that you still had the tea towel. Trying to explain the significance of all these levels of meaning to Archie was beyond me, which was why I had given up discussing cover designs with him. Nancy and I had been at one on this. She understood exactly why these details were important without needing to discuss them. Maybe it was a gender thing after all. But I could still see Archie scratching his head and telling me that lacy red undies or black bras would look much better on that washing line than a row of plain white napkins.

Nevertheless I doubted Nancy would agree to a lawn and a coffin for this cover, in fact anything that suggested burial. Despite the title of the book, she would insist the images promote the idea of life, of hope, of renewal. Maybe the lawn without the coffin? As it was more than likely I wouldn't be around to have a final say (*control freak*) I had to think hard about this. How to persuade Nancy? The idea of a quirky cover persisted. Someone once sent me a brilliant postcard of a desiccated corpse in an open coffin from Mexico. Despite looking decayed and shrivelled, the body was peaceful, almost prosaic in its grinning repose. It possessed an air of such quiet ordinariness as to suggest that dried-out corpses on display in simple coffins were on every street corner in Mexico. As indeed they may well have been, for all I knew. It – male or female, hard to tell – was holding a small book, probably a prayer book, in one hand, and what appeared to be a dried trumpet lily in the other.

Then it hit me – a most brilliant idea for the cover. I would pose as my own corpse in an open coffin. Plenty of authors had their photos gracing the front covers of their books. It was egotistical, but so what? I was never going to become a celebrity, so why not pretend, just the once? I intended to buy my own coffin anyway. This would just accelerate the process. It would make it more fun. Already I fancied the idea of wearing a red and purple linen apron. The minor domestic goddess laid to rest. That sort of theme.

At this point, somewhere in the back of my mind I sensed Archie cringing. He was already ill at ease with the idea of his wife using her experience of dying for expedient and mercantile ends. I wanted him to see that it was much more than that, and especially had nothing to do with the money. But he still resisted. I knew he couldn't understand how I could be occupied with writing a book about dying when I should just be dying as peacefully and as comfortably as I could.

But that was it. There wasn't anything comfortable about dying, not that I had found. Lying around waiting and cultivating a peaceful attitude was the worst way to die. And when you thought about all the cupboards you needed to tidy, the books you wanted to read, the places you had never visited, the papers you should throw out, the favourite movies you wanted to watch again, the list became endless. The adventures you might have long fantasised over, like bungy-jumping off a bridge or hot-air ballooning or whatever thrilling experience you had never tried, or all the special indulgences – dining just once at Maxim's in Paris, wearing only silk underwear, bathing every day in Coco Chanel's private scent, or opening the Grange Hermitage you wanted to taste before you left the world forever – in the end made no sense. It was all meaningless. What made sense was to keep doing what I was good at. And more than that, to keep doing it because I believed Estelle and Daisy needed life to carry on normally, as much as it could. Already they'd had to experience wretched illness, absences in hospital, my tendency to slow down and rest. If I started disappearing to line-dancing classes or taking up the piano accordion they'd think I'd become completely unhinged.

And I was not writing about my own death. Perhaps I needed to show Archie some of the chapters to reassure him of that. In the company of others, friends or his business mates, he would ask me not to be too specific about the nature of the book. Just tell them you're working on something with a family theme, he would advise. They can assume it's anything then – lots of books are about families, aren't they? Amongst Archie's friends especially, like the builders and developers whom he'd collected during the transition years from gardener to landscaper, or his rugby teammates, I had actually taken great pleasure in playing the housewife. Although I'd never dared hijack a pre-roast conversation about fibre-reinforced concrete or rapid ball recycling by asking for opinions of Omo versus Radiant, I didn't mind inspiring an occasional dinner-table silence by announcing I was currently researching plastic pegs or sandwich toasters. And I didn't regret this as my condition worsened and some of these acquaintances gradually drifted away.

I wondered, briefly, if the narrative of my life had become so claustrophobic that it was devoid of characters. I decided (and noted this for chapter six in the guide to dying) that it was because all but your very closest friends would desert you in your hour of terminal illness. The rest would be so overcome with horror, guilt, fear (was it catching?) or just so immobilised by helplessness that they would not want to remember you existed, let alone were once their friend.

Meanwhile, the image of Archie cringing at my idea for the cover image remained. I decided to work on it incrementally. I would have to get the coffin, and as this constituted perfectly relevant research for the guide I didn't anticipate a problem. After it arrived I would work on Archie. Then one fine softly lit day I would drag the coffin out the back onto the lawn and prop it up at the head end with a few bricks. I'd line it with some cushions and maybe scatter a few blankets around for casual effect. Perhaps I would wear the frilly 1950s hostess apron, not the red and purple one with hibiscus all over it, and I could be holding an egg beater in one hand and a cheerful cocktail in the other. I could be reclining in the coffin, rather than reposing, and I'd keep my eyes open. I would be smiling, very brightly.

Dear Delia
Bathroom, check (though I do have to keep an eye on the mould in the shower recess). Kitchen, check (we've been eating out most of the time anyway). Laundry, check. No real problems there (do you think cockroaches are keen on washing machines too?). But my bedroom seems a bit musty, even I'm noticing it. I keep the window open and everything.
Thanks
Desperate (I've kind of got used to the name).

Dear Desperate
I've definitely got used to it. Have you considered changing your bedsheets?

Twenty-Six

In Amethyst Archie spent most of his time mowing. Clearing, clipping but mainly mowing. It was during the years when he would work alone for days, just him and his utility and a block of lantana to clear for a developer, or him and the mower with parkland to trim. On one particular day it was the swathe of land on the east side of the river, not cultivated enough to be a park, but a popular place for families on weekends, and the occasional itinerant worker camping out before the authorities moved them on. Archie was doing what he loved best then, imposing the minimum of order and skill upon the land, cultivating and shaping almost nothing out where *the sweet fields do lie forgot*. After I thought about it more, Marvell did make sense to me, though Archie disagreed. Mowing was the least and most a man could do upon nature: all else was unnatural, a vice, grotesque, adulterated.

He was mowing that afternoon, when Sonny and I were returning from McDonald's via the cemetery; mowing some place way across town on the edge of the new developments. Though it was getting late and the shadows were moving swiftly across the grass, he stayed on to finish off the job rather than have to return the next day. We had arranged that he would drop by the caravan after work, we would share a beer while Sonny had an iceblock and played on his scooter or jumped through the caravan park's sprinkler. Eight wasn't too old for that sort of fun, apparently.

Sonny and I walked home from the cemetery via the main street to hire a video, and had just crossed the road. He was a lively boy, always on the move. A sudden whim made him pull away and dart back onto the road. Not far onto it, but far enough. What had blinded his vision or attracted his attention for that crucial second? A special type of car he'd spotted (BMWs were the current obsession)? The parakeets shooting above us from date palm to date palm, low and bold, as if they were daring each other? Someone he thought he recognised? It was enough to mean he was in the wrong place when the blue Ford, also in the wrong place, travelling too fast for the main street, swerved too close to the kerb. The driver braked quickly, but not quickly enough. Sonny, caught on the front left-hand side, was tossed high into the air before landing head down in the middle of the road.

People gathered around us. I was sucked into another zone of time and place where it seemed Sonny was about to jump up and say, Tricked you! but where nothing happened. I heard no breath, saw no movement. Not even the voices shouting seemed real as I stared at him lying still on the road in front of me. Believing and disbelieving my eyes until, when the emergency ambulance arrived, the spell finally shattered. Fifteen minutes later he was on a trolley in intensive care and by then no ICU specialist had to tell me: I could see for myself the pulpy mess at the back of my son's curly blond head, feel when I reached out to him, his limp body, before they tethered him to a row of machines.

Doug from the hardware store raced off in his delivery van to fetch Archie. It seemed like in no time, though it was half an hour later – for I was watching the sun vanish behind the trees from the hospital window – that Archie appeared. He smelled of grass and sweat, and when he walked over to me and held me without saying the words he knew wouldn't work, not at that moment, I understood why Sonny loved him so much, and wondered why I had taken so long to make up my mind, and why, now that I had, it was all too cruel, too late.

Later, I wondered if it was the light. The shadows. The beguiling effect when afternoon descended into twilight, when shapes distorted, images blurred. Maybe the driver was not travelling too fast or was not too close at all. Maybe Sonny was at fault, and the low intense sun had stopped him from seeing the car. Or maybe the light had refracted off the dust on the vehicle's windscreen, making the driver sun blind for long enough to mistake a boy for a mere shadow, or for nothing at all. I could ask neither of them, and there were no witnesses for although plenty of people were around, it had happened so quickly there was no one who could confidently say what had occurred. The police interviewed a dozen people and got a dozen different versions. The driver was from out of town, and had an otherwise unblemished driving record. There was no sentence. And what did it matter?

In those last days in Amethyst, when everything was tidied up and there was nothing more to do but leave, I would return to that place in the street again and again in the late afternoon, looking each way, every way, imagining I was that Ford driver or that boy, trying to work it all out. There *had* been something intense about the light, something golden, I was sure. And the twilight afterwards went on for much longer than usual. This is what it did in October, way up north. But then everything was mixed up that day, and I smelled and heard things that I knew didn't exist, and so it made sense I would have seen things afterwards that were not there, in the end, to be seen.

Twenty-Seven

Tips for those intending to purchase their own coffins: allow for ample time, take supplies, be prepared for surprises. Better still, remember the advantages of online shopping and throw caution to the wind: one is unlikely to get carried away and order several coffins, as happens when buying film posters, novelty cufflinks, cleanskin wines or all the other bargains offered on eBay.

'Pre funeral preparations'
The Household Guide to Dying (forthcoming)

The first thing I learned was that the *coffin* no longer existed. It was now called the casket. An important distinction in the mythology of the funeral business. Quite logical too. Never use a blunt, prosaic and utilitarian word or phrase in this industry if you could replace it with a more poetic, dignified and abstracted version. Thus *dead* or *died* was *passed away*, or the increasingly popular *passed on*, which implied Another Side, and hence offered the illusion of another world, comforting to the bereaved. More recent still was the Americanisation, *passed*. So succinct, dignified, poetic. *Passed*. Evoking the life of the deceased moving by like a mysterious wind.

A coffin implied the very corporeal aspects of death. A corpse, obviously, being dead was therefore in a state of decay: not a pleasant thing for the bereaved to have to think about. A coffin raised uncompromising images of plain wood – probably cheap – a basic design. It had a grim and inescapable purpose. It was all too suggestive of the smells and vapours of death, so mouldy, rank and repellent. Coffins held bones of the unwanted and unloved. Corpses of the dispossessed. Dressed in austere clothing or wrapped in calico shrouds. Coffins were for paupers. And people whose souls were endlessly circulating the cosmos in abject misery, unable to find proper repose.

On the other hand, a casket invited imagery that was not only palatable but soothing: adornments, carvings, raised panels on the box itself, gilded handles, concealed hinges, white satin linings, pleats and folds and quilting. Like a fine musical instrument, it smelled only of beeswax polish and rosewood. A casket held the final remains (not body, not corpse) of one who had definitely found repose. It was possible to believe that the soul of a person reclining peacefully on satin cushions within a dark timber casket was already gaining admittance at the pearly gates of another existence altogether, where death was so foreign there was not even the word for it.

I learned all this at the Serenity Funeral Parlour, in a neighbouring suburb. There were three local funeral businesses, but for now Serenity Funerals offered a fascinating window into the business of death. Of passing away. It was in many ways all that I expected. Discreet atmosphere combined with tasteless furnishings, soft fluting music from concealed speakers. Ingratiating staff. Not a sign of the purpose of the place – much like a brothel. And if the lighting was more dim, the décor more dark, and the music a little livelier, there would not be much difference, at least not in the reception area.

But I had expected some evidence of the business side of the business. Disappointingly, there were no caskets on view. I was standing at the reception desk, above which rose a fake stained-glass window of contemporary design illuminated from behind. Upon the desk was an impressive display of native flowers. No lilies: was that a good or a bad sign? A person glided into the room. He slid shut the opaque glass doors behind him, concealing the departing backs of a small number of people, evidently being ushered out of a funeral by a side door. He was surprisingly young, dressed in a pale grey suit and wearing painfully neat hair. A small black tag pinned to his left lapel told me his name: James.

How may I help you, madam?

I'm interested in buying a coffin.

There was no virtue in not coming straight to the point. Funeral staff were well known for their suave unflappability, but this tender example of the species was visibly taken aback. Only momentarily, however. Whatever training existed in the trade evidently placed customer handling high on the list. James blinked twice, opened and shut his mouth once, then opened it again.

Um … yes. A casket. He emphasised the word significantly enough to indicate that at this point in the relationship he could only correct the customer – or client, I supposed that would be – by implication.

May I ask, he continued, specifically, for .... ? He raised his eyebrows and gestured meaningfully. It must be improper to ask outright for whom.

I decided not to be helpful. A coffin, I repeated, for a body, of course. A dead one.

He swallowed, making his Adam's apple dance noticeably. Then he glanced around. I had uttered the D word within the hallowed precincts of repose. Would a superior come and reprimand him for a clear breach of etiquette? A contravention of the industry code?

He swallowed again, then briefly smiled.

Yes, of course, a ... casket ...(more emphasis, I could tell he was down but not out) for a ... a ... deceased person. He smiled again, as if reassuring himself that although uttering the word had been unavoidable he wouldn't be struck by lightning, or fired from his job. But were we talking about someone in particular? Or ...?

Again I was meant to help him out.

Absolutely. And that particular someone is me. I want to buy a coffin, for me, for when I'm dead.

His eyes were a particularly intense shade of blue, but maybe that was because they were wide and open, as was his mouth. I saw deep inside his mouth, which was so endearing, pink and innocent, containing small perfect teeth. I began to feel sorry for him. He closed his mouth and swallowed visibly for a third time, his Adam's apple now shooting up and down like a yoyo.

But you're ... you're ...

Not dead? No, I'm quite alive, as you can see. This time it was my turn to smile. But I will be, soon. You see, I'm dying of cancer and I want to organise my funeral in advance. And buying a coffin is the first step.

Despite my persistent use of the wrong term, the awkward atmosphere was transformed somewhat. Latching onto the phrase *funeral in advance*, like a shipwrecked sailor to a floating piece of timber, James recovered some of his poise. His professional self took over.

Well, madam, of course we can help you there. Many people come to us to plan their funerals in advance – it makes it far less stressful for the bereaved family when the time, sadly, comes.

Ah, you misunderstand me. At this point I'm only interested in buying a coffin.

Casket, he murmured, as if sensing this was a battle already lost but that there were some points that should never be conceded.

I will of course be planning my funeral, but not just yet. At the moment I only want to buy the coffin – (I would not, I could not, yield, not just yet) – and so I'd like to look at what you have available.

It was then that I discovered that Serenity Funerals, like most other funeral parlours, did not have a showroom. Maybe it was the result of researching too many *Household Guides*, legging it across the city from warehouse to megastore to showroom, but I had expected to be able to walk into any reasonably sized funeral business and stroll around the floor display. Or maybe it was because Serenity was situated between a budget furniture store on one side, stocked with cheap unvarnished pine goods, and a second-hand car dealership on the other, where under bright flapping bunting and behind outsized day-glo signs which all included the numerals 999, clean and shiny vehicles awaited purchase. Or maybe I just had an unrealistic idea of the funeral business.

For there was no hardware to be seen. All the products were of the service variety. And James could only offer a catalogue. Shuffling through the various brochures available behind the desk gave him time to regain his composure. Meanwhile I surrendered my consumerist fantasies of stalking the aisles and running my hands across the polished surfaces of coffins in all their variety. Had I done so I might have been persuaded into calling them caskets. I examined the brochures he handed over. He pointed out that there were several styles of casket available, and in a variety of price ranges to suit a budget. He explained that they didn't sell caskets as such. They were a funeral service, and the purchase of one of their quality caskets was just part of an overall service.

One colour brochure contained a number of attractive-looking coffins in various timber finishes. But there were no prices, and the coffins were all made by the same coffin maker, Quality Caskets, from way out west. James seemed reluctant to reveal any prices, yet this was fundamental to the research. Finally he admitted that while there were at least five other casket manufacturers in the city, Serenity Funerals only used the services of one. And that the prices varied between about five and eight thousand dollars. Too late, I realised I gaped, just for a moment.

So for the price of a decent second-hand car I can get a basic sort of coffin?

Well, I wouldn't know about that. His tone implied that he rarely associated with second-hand cars. I can assure you these are quality caskets. And that no one ever complains about the cost. Indeed, the more expensive caskets are among our best sellers. People want to give their loved ones the best send off they can.

Well, I'm buying this, and it would be my business if it were cheap.

No one would complain if I wanted to have a budget coffin. I was getting fed up with James. I wouldn't have been surprised if there was some kind of kickback involved. So if I wanted another type of coffin, or something cheaper, I would have to hunt one down. Which probably meant finding the coffin makers myself.

I decided to visit two more parlours before going home to continue research via the Yellow Pages or the internet. Federation Funerals was on the other side of the suburb, a bit further south down the highway. Cleverly worked into the cement render above the rising sun emblem of Federation architecture were the numerals 1901, underneath the inscription A FAMILY BUSINESS. I doubted that was still the case. Most funeral businesses were owned by multinationals. Banks mainly, US in origin. Federation Funerals offered a more comprehensive range of coffins, but still had nothing on display, only brochures. They were very nice brochures too, but the consumer in me was still wanting satiation. After Federation Funerals I visited W.B. Small & Co. The same story here too. Each place offered the experience of muted pipe music, soft light, golden-coloured furnishings, and the absence of anything relating to the containment or conveyance of a corpse. At W.B. Small there was also a young man in a dark suit and grey tie, named John. They seemed to be a particular species.

I'm dying, I said. In a few months. And I want to choose my coffin. Can you help me? Fatigue and irritation made me blunt.

John seemed as alarmed by the mention of death as James had been. I almost began to admire this industry's ability to conduct business without any reference to the actual subject. The euphemisms were endless. Instead of answering straightaway, John produced a handful of brochures from under the counter. One was for Small's business itself, which seemed redundant seeing I was already there. But as I leafed through it while John tapped at his computer, skimming through pictures of roses and crucifixes on lace cloths, all blurry around the edges, accompanied by small paragraphs in large type which featured phrases like *everlasting repose* and *final resting place* and *loved one in peace*, it occurred to me that perhaps this business could have the answers.

Do you have a good word for dying? I asked. I mean the *right* word, for someone like me? I gestured to myself. Dressed in my best jeans, not too baggy despite the weight loss, and a silk knit top, I looked quite normal. I was wearing make-up, a headscarf. No one would guess I was dying.

John opened and closed his mouth.

I mean, look at me, I'm dying, but I'm also living. Still alive. What is the word for it? What would that word be? I fixed him with a desperate gaze.

Umm ... he shook his head. Umm, I really don't know.

Don't you think in this business you should know?

In this business we always refer to the deceased with respect, he said, sounding like he was quoting from his first class in Mortician Theory 101. And our clients are the bereaved.

People, I said.

I'm sorry?

People. The deceased. The bereaved. There's no need for formal nouns. We're ordinary people, you know, we dying. Just people.

So it was without a word, but a handful of brochures instead, that I returned home for the next phase of the research, but after trawling the internet and finding some fascinating information about the last piece of furniture a person ever needed, I just felt exhausted. Down to Earth coffin makers, who produced eco-friendly coffins guaranteed to decompose bio-organically within two years, didn't ship to Australia. The Dig It Yourself company provided stylish coffins in kit form but advised that a professional cabinet-maker would be needed to assemble the kit, and I didn't want that. The Cardboard Casket, situated in the western suburbs, manufactured cheap and environmentally responsible coffins from recycled boxes, but the coffins on their website looked about as attractive as a supermarket aisle display. And the Bush Burial company, based in Mudgee, was idiosyncratic and vulgar in the extreme: I couldn't imagine what clientele opted for their gum-leaf shaped coffins and faux-leather plaited coffins and other samples fashioned from rough stripped branches and bark slabs. They even offered a Henry Lawson deluxe featuring scenes from the author's best-known poems in mulga panels down each side.

Then, after all that, I found the name of someone I knew, someone I'd never wanted to remember.

Twenty-Eight

There are times when, despite all the arguments and the swelling resentment, despite years of cold silences, you desperately want your mother. I had so wanted Jean when I was giving birth but I bit down on that desire and refused to let it burst through.

And when my son was dying I was also crying from the loss of my mother after that final fight when she told me Van was worthless, that I was wasting my time going north for him, that I should have had that abortion, and that I would be ruining my life. I told her then how I hated her and her plans and her perfectly successful life, and slammed her front door so hard I heard the ornaments rattle behind me.

After I had sent the first peace offering of news about Sonny's birth, we'd contacted each other irregularly, and I'd assumed Jean only remembered him at birthdays and Christmas as an obligation. But when I phoned from Sonny's bedside to tell her about the accident, as the machines murmured and the nursing staff pattered in and out, the first sound of her voice scorched my throat, making me unable to say anything more than just, Oh Mum,

Mum, and crying through the words, because I understood then just how much she loved me, how, no matter what, she could never stop loving me. How the pain of your child suffering felt like a rock had lodged in your chest. That was her, when I left. And it was me now, watching Sonny.

The next morning, Jean appeared like a magician's dove at the hospital. And after we cried more and said sorry then told each other there was no need to say sorry, she began to do the things she was so good at. She took care of the practicalities, like my clothes, my hair and the coffin. His casket, which would be plain, functional and distressingly small, but necessary.

And so we were standing in the yard of Vittaro and Sons, which abutted the southernmost edge of the circus. Jean had taken me there knowing what I didn't yet realise, that I would want to choose Sonny's coffin myself. I was sedated by the diazepam a doctor pressed upon me, numbed by the shock and gagged by the magnitude of what I had just allowed to be done to my only child. I was a zombie, a non being. A liminal thing inhabiting a twilight zone between living and non-living. Jean's remedy was action. Confrontation. Besides, a small coffin needed to be custom made with some urgency.

Vittaro's place was fronted by a low cyclone wire fence and a sagging gate that looked permanently held open by clusters of weeds. The shed was low and shabby, but there was a cheerful garden of geraniums out the front and a line of banana palms down the side. Apart from the small sign, there wasn't a hint that Vittaro and Sons were in the death industry. The noise of an electric drill drew us around the back. If Jean and I had expected a migrant tradesman with a thick accent, curly hair and three sturdy inarticulate sons, then we couldn't have been further from the truth. A middle-aged man leaning over a long trestle table, Mr Vittaro was tall, slender and curl-, accent-, and son-free.

These are my boys, he gestured towards a trio of indolent dogs – two cattle dogs and a tiny cross something or other with short brown fur – who panted politely then went back to licking their balls.

Bill, Bob, and Peanut, he said. The small dog wagged its tail obligingly when he mentioned its name. And I'm Al, he said, holding out his drill-free hand.

Sounds very Italian, Jean said.

He smiled. Short for Aldo.

Well, I was right, then.

Vittaro and Sons sounds better, he explained, putting down his drill. In this business, especially in this area, family is important. People think if the family is involved then you're respectable, trustworthy.

Al Vittaro had been a real estate agent who branched into household renovations which led him into amateur carpentry, his real love, and cabinetmaking, which he studied at night. Coffins had been a recent sideline. Cupboards, sideboards, tables and beds were his speciality. But before she died peacefully and contentedly at the age of ninety-three his grandmother had asked him to make her something nice for her coffin, and after a few more commissions he decided to add coffins to his catalogues. Few people ever visited the yard, preferring instead the funeral parlours that represented him.

No one ever wants to see the coffins before they're finished, he said, eyeing me.

We want to choose our own, said Jean, coming to my rescue. We need to. And she quickly explained why.

He raised his eyebrows. I remember I was glad about that, glad that he didn't try to console me, try to find words to express things that couldn't be said. Instead he asked short, quiet questions about timber, finish and fittings, asking them of Jean but looking at me, so I felt grateful that he was relieving me of the necessity of making choices that were only going to be painful, yet not excluding me in a way I would have found patronising.

Since Al worked mainly in commissions there was not much stock to survey. Most was consigned to the back of his shed. Some were down the yard propped up against the fence amid weeds. Grey from weathering, with their lids on, bland and faceless, they looked like a silent straggling row of postulants sent out for punishment until vespers. He seemed uninterested in selling, content to resume drilling and hammering while we wandered around. While Jean inspected samples of timber I went back and stood beside Al, watching him work. He finished screwing the last of a short leg then hoisted what turned out to be a small coffee table right side up onto the trestle. Reaching up he swept the top, grainy and rippled and not entirely flat, smooth like a lake ruffled by a breeze. It was a loving, un-selfconscious but regretful gesture all at once. There was a palpable sense of the devotion and hard work that had gone into this simple piece of furniture, almost a sigh of sorrow at the prospect of parting from it.

Customer's coming for it this afternoon, he said. I've been a bit behind.

It's beautiful.

There was a dark stain through the timber, slightly off-centre, almost burnt. It must have been the harder core of the tree, whatever kind it was.

River red gum, he said, reading my thoughts. A bloke I know picks them up from outback – stumps, fallen trees, branches, that sort of thing.

I felt gladdened by the idea that Al worked with nature's discards. I wasn't much of a greenie, but the idea of hewing trees to make coffins left me uneasy.

But what about you? Made a decision?

I couldn't say it. Did it matter? It was just a means to an end that was already thumpingly final. When Jean stood and held me I still couldn't say the words to describe the size of my dead son's body. Instead of words the heaving sobs returned, muted but powerful all the same, sobs that rose like great stones from somewhere in my stomach and blocked my chest, my heart, my throat.

Al stared at his boots, surrounded by fragrant curls of wood shavings fresh from the plane.

What if I come to the hospital and see your little boy? he said. Then I'll make something nice. The right size. Plain, if you like.

I nodded. The stones seemed to shift a little, not enough for me to speak but enough for Al, I thought, to feel my gratitude for that breath of understanding.

Twenty-Nine

Even before the first sod of earth is turned, consideration should be given to the variety and expected lifespan of the plants with which you intend to populate your garden. Some soils will encourage unwelcome growths, others inhibit desired ones. For instance, casuarinas will thrive in sandy conditions to the point of pestilence, while roses will languish without heavy soil. Think carefully about what you want to survive in your garden.

'Planning before Planting'
The Household Guide to the Garden (2004)

After all my research and funeral parlour visits, I could only decide on what I *didn't* want. I wasn't after anything wasteful, garish, vulgar, expensive, decorated, veneered. In other words, I was after what the funeral industry seemed incapable of supplying. But when I came across the name

Vittaro, I realised I may have been wrong. He'd left Amethyst, I knew that. His website showed Al was now in business somewhere in Tasmania. He hadn't retained the 'and sons' part of the business, and I doubted he still had the dogs, at least the same ones.

But when I phoned him I could hear a frantic barking in the distance. He didn't need a reminder of who I was.

You went back there recently, he said.

Yes. How did he know?

He'd just heard. I guessed he'd heard why, too, and that I'd failed.

I came south to be with Marie, he said, my new wife. She's from Devonport.

I heard regret in that sentence, as if he'd never wanted to leave his town up north. I could understand that.

So how can I help you now?

Well, I thought, he didn't know everything, he didn't know I was dying. When I told him, he just said, Oh. I pictured him, on the other end of the line, standing amongst timber offcuts and wood shavings, looking at his boots. I relieved him of the need to try and respond by launching directly into questions about the coffin I wanted.

We discussed materials, and Al explained about the latest fad, the eco-coffin, which he refused to supply. Made from compressed recycled materials and entirely without bleaching agents and using only biodegradable glue, the whole thing – including the plugs and handles instead of metal screws and fittings – was designed to break down completely within two years of burial, leaving no chemical traces in the soil whatsoever.

Guaranteed, Al said. But how did they know? Did people dig up their deceased relatives and check on the progress of decay, and did anyone ever demand a refund? Don't laugh, he said, this is the opposition, they're killing me. Oh, sorry ...

Don't be, I said. With the chemical traces the breakdown of my own body was likely to be leaving, the environmental factor was a small thing. Anyway, I'd already dismissed the idea of an eco-coffin, I told him, that was why I was ringing him.

I said I wanted to decorate the coffin myself and he sounded almost pleased, but when I started to explain why, he interrupted.

You want to feel you belong?

Yes.

Have some say, some control?

Yes.

I bet you want to make some sort of statement too.

Of course. I want it to be ...

Ironic?

Exactly. Witty, and ironic, just like me.

We both laughed. Al was my man. Just as before.

Dear Delia
I wrote a while ago asking about crock pot recipes. You advised me to throw the crock pot out and eat oysters or something. A few weeks after that I met a really lovely man at the RSL club and we've been going out ever since. The funny thing is, he wants us to cook crock pot dinners together, and now I no longer have it.
Curious.

Dear Curious
Normally I would advise also throwing out a man whose idea of fun was cooking crock pot dinners. Now I suggest you go to your nearest charity or second hand shop, where they always have things like crock pots. I expect he'll have the recipes.

Thirty

The world was full of the bruised mass of ordinary lives – lives that would rarely be blessed by the Midas touch of corporate expansion, but which were frequently cursed by it. In this world, it was hard to find a dead end untouched by what once might have been called progress, harder to cherish such a dead end without seeming an embittered old relic of a pre-economic rationalist era. In this world, the circus was a genuine haven. It was the true socialist ideal, still creaking along in its shabby glory, still harbouring lonely misfit lives that the grinding jaws of economic and social progress would otherwise have chewed up and picked dismissively off its teeth.

The circus in Amethyst was where the bits and pieces of humanity left behind by change and development came to rest, and now when development was so rapid it was like a continuous whirlwind, the bits and pieces that fell out the sides to rest in the dust and debris of the wind's wake were more noticeable. The circus accepted and found a place for everyone. It made everyone feel they had something important to do and, briefly, made everyone a star or a hero.

And it looked after its own, sharing the spoils as readily as the hardships. When Sonny was small and friends were few, the circus welcomed us. No one asked about his father, or my past; they didn't need to. I thought that with Van having left his home and family and the circus world, there would be some hostility, along with the small town suspicion of newcomers, especially strangers from a southern city. Instead, the circus people were touched to find that in part it was the idea of the place that had drawn me here, and that I wanted to stay to bring Sonny up. They were glad Amethyst had become our home. In their laconic way this was never exactly stated, but was apparent as I got to know them, as the people there such as Tara and her family, and Monty the clown, quietly opened their lives to my son and me.

It had been a peaceful afternoon, watching the show, with its complement of three audience members, then sitting with Tara for the remainder of the day.

Afterwards I felt ready to return to the caravan, to open it up and start the sorting, packing and, above all, throwing out that needed to be done.

Do you want me to come? Tara asked.

Thanks. But no, I can do it on my own.

And I knew I could, I could go back and complete what I couldn't years ago. I told her I'd see her again soon.

The next morning I left the Paradise Reach Motel and had driven nearly halfway there when I decided to walk. That's how it had always been before. So I parked in Oasis Street outside Cliff's and got out of the car. It was too early for the Handy Mart to be open but as I peered through the window I saw that little had changed. Cliff's displays had always been remade every Sunday night: perfect rows of identical Andy Warhol-like soup cans, rising to a pyramid, packets of cereal or boxes of washing powder stacked like bricks to form neat walls. Now there was a more creative aspect at play. Someone, perhaps a younger member of Cliff's grocery family, had made a mock bathroom display with an old dunny spilling over with toilet rolls trailing out to the corners of the window.

It used to be a good twenty-minute walk. But that was back when I was pregnant, or pushing a stroller, or dawdling with a child for whom arrival was nothing compared with the joys of the journey. Now it took less than fifteen minutes, up Oasis Street past the large timber houses set well back from the road, guarded by palms and shrouded in vines. At the end of the street a turn left, then another right until I reached the caravan park. All the way along I felt that nothing had changed yet everything seemed different. Nothing I could place but an unfamiliarity. A shadowy distance.

By the time I arrived I was tired and out of breath. On a calm day in a peaceful place it was easy to forget you were ill. And I'd brought no water. The front garden tap was tucked behind the clump of pampas grass, so I leaned down and drank deeply, then sat on the front fence, a low rail once painted white and now flaking to expose the grey timber beneath. In the morning, the caravan park belonged to the birds and it was still early enough for them to be fussing in the palms that clustered around the park. Mitchell's trailer was shut, so either he wasn't up or he had spent the night in the bar. There were half a dozen caravans and a couple of campervans on the site, and it was hard to tell how many of them were occupied. I walked over to the laundry and shower block, in the centre of the park. Next to it was the old orange hibiscus that was always neglected, still alive, still draping shockingly bright flowers onto the grass. The laundry was concrete with a corrugated iron roof, and hadn't been used in a long time. The wooden door with its press-down metal latch and perpetual squeak was off its hinges. Inside, it was cool and dark. There were two old coppers and a row of deep tubs, each with its brass tap perched high above. A shelf under the windows once held long bars of yellow soap. Now the atmosphere was dry. It looked like no one had turned on a tap in years. The copper lids were missing, and the coppers themselves were coated in dust, with leaves and dead insects lining the bottoms. On the shelf sat a small piece of soap, cracked like a fossil. Beside it was a stick of thick dowel. I picked it up. It looked like the broken handle of the wooden spoon I used to stir Sonny's nappies with. Beyond the laundry block was my old caravan.

It was right at the back of the park, close by the fence, still decorated in the morning glory which I'd always been cutting back, for fear it would swallow us. The grass was long around the brick stumps but the surrounding lawn was trim. Already ancient when I'd bought it from Lazarus, a dozen or so years later the caravan had sunk further into the ground. The annexe was gone, but it had barely been an annexe, just a stretch of shadecloth where I'd kept a potted ficus benjamina and where we'd left our shoes and Sonny's few outdoor toys. There was nothing around now. The ficus was gone but no one had bothered to remove the pot beside the door.

On the outside the caravan might have been flakier, the paint more dull, if that were possible. The aluminium window and door trims were bleached and pitted, and the windows were coated with dust. But apart from that I might have just been away for a week. The key was in my purse, and the padlock took a bit of wiggling until it released. Opening the door wide, I closed my eyes, prepared to inhale the air of fourteen years of bitter memories, fourteen years of anguish, and guilt, and an emptiness that was often contained, but never filled. But it smelled like nothing at all.

It was tiny inside. With a house in the inner suburbs, with Archie's beautiful generous gardens, with an office of my own, a room for our daughters, a kitchen that was bigger than the caravan I now stood in, it was hard to believe that Sonny and I had lived here for all that time and never felt cramped. It was neat, nothing out of place. Before leaving, Jean had helped me tidy and pack the few things I wanted, and I had made a ritual of packing up all the books with which I'd lined the caravan, to send on after I had gone. Cheap paperbacks and spotted mouldy hardbound classics – garage sale bargains, most of them – they were all that I valued. I placed them tenderly into cardboard boxes, sprinkling them with naphthalene, never once considering that I might have done without a single one. I might not want to read *Ivanhoe* or *Doctor Zhivago* or *Zen and the Art of Motorcycle Maintenance* or all those staples of the second-hand book stores ever again, but nor would I part with them.

Without the books the caravan looked naked and vulnerable. And cheerless. The curtains had faded to a grey blue. The red vinyl bench seat was cracked. The cupboard by the sink still contained our few plates and pans. Blankets and towels were stacked neatly on the shelves above the bed, now just stale dusty reminders. On the bench next to the sink sat my one vase, pressed pink glass. Inside it was coated brown. I must have tossed away the last bunch of flowers but left the dirty water which, over the years had evaporated to a stain.

On the floor, beside the fold-down table, was the old brown suitcase, bought for two dollars from a junk shop to store Sonny's baby things. Later he kept his treasures in there, and I put special things in it from time to time. Kneeling down before it, I flicked open the catches. When I left Amethyst I had intended to return just as soon as I was ready. That readiness never arrived. Not while I was staying with Jean, not after Archie came to claim me, not after we married and made our home.

Estelle was born and those vacant cockles in my heart were filled up for a while. Then Daisy came along, and I still put it off. But now, before I died, the place had tugged me back, and with such urgency I had abandoned them. I had just driven off one day and left Archie and the girls a note, and barely spoken to them since. I had been a bad mother yet again, and all to take in my hands scraps of clothing and toys, books and drawings, to caress them once or twice more in a vain attempt to capture the feel, the smell, the sound of my son, to be close to him one last time, before it was too late.

But now, as I took out his special things one by one – clothes and costumes I'd made for him, a story he had written and illustrated and folded into a book, the McDonald's toys, a miniature pair of cowboy boots which he'd outgrown too quickly – as I took them out and held them up to the light, all I experienced was absence.

I had left my family, neglected my work, driven all this way to recapture my son before I died, to reclaim whatever part of him was left. But he wasn't here. There was a part of Sonny somewhere, the most vital part of him, but it wasn't here, not in this caravan.

I felt a stab of desire for my daughters. Right at that moment, kneeling in front of Sonny's suitcase, I just wanted to catch and hold Estelle and Daisy, push my face into their necks and breathe in their warm children's scent. Feel their hot sticky hands on my cheeks again. I wanted Estelle to be pulling at my hair in the way I found annoying but always allowed, letting her do what she loved, trying out styles and experimenting with clips and bands. I wanted Daisy to be blowing her recorder right into my ear with yet another tuneless attempt at 'Lightly Row'. That painful sound. How I missed it right now.

I folded Sonny's things and packed them away again. The gold suit I had sewn from bargain scraps. The lion tamer's outfit and the whip plaited from vinyl strips. The copies of *Fractured Fairytales* and *Ping the Duck*, the only books he ever wanted to keep. A magic set and a clown's costume. Just about all of it handmade, makeshift, fake but somehow magical. I snapped the lid shut and picked up the suitcase. I knew what I would do with it now. And I would do it as quickly as possible in order to get back to the living.

On my way out I noticed Mitchell's door was open. I called out to him, and he appeared at the doorway. He was still wearing his bar clothes, and his Greek fisherman's cap. He looked at the suitcase.

Got what you needed, then?

You know I came back for more than this. I held the suitcase up.

I told you, you won't find her.

Well, I'm not leaving just yet. Got to keep looking. I'll be seeing you, I said.

What about the caravan? He jerked his head towards it.

I turned and looked back at it. The place I had been afraid to return to for so long. It was humble now, innocent as a pet rabbit, crouching low in the long grass as if trying to hide.

It looks like it's staying, if that's all right with you.

Yeah, he said, that's fine.

Thirty-One

> Remember that, while the style and value of the casket, or coffin, are ultimately irrelevant, this is a focal point for the family members and friends. Many will find expression for their grief in the casket, or coffin. Thus the budget item that you and your dying loved one agree is sensible and practical, may prove impossible in the force of all this expectation. The best way to offset disappointment and conflict is to involve as many people as possible in the preparation of the casket (coffin) before the death.
>
> 'Pre-funeral preparations'
> *The Household Guide to Dying* (forthcoming)

It was raining the day the coffin arrived by courier. I signed for it at the front gate under the curious eyes of Mr Lambert, out checking his letterbox, then dragged the parcel up the path to lay it on the verandah until Archie came home. As agreed, Al had provided a customised flat pack, with easy-to-assemble instructions. I knew that Archie would want a hand in all this, and yet I'd also known that the prospect of him making the entire coffin was a joke. Handy and capable as he was, Archie was useless when it came to timber. He could do many things with surgical ease. Yet I'd seen him split more picture frames, destroy more garden furniture, and reduce more bookshelves to kindling than I cared to remember.

I sat on a stool, listening to Mr Lambert's hand clippers decimating blades of grass trespassing along his path, and reading from the sheet while Archie slotted Side A into End D and lined up the brass Phillips head screws Al had provided. The snipping continued despite the rain that drizzled peacefully. Compared with the computer desk we bought for the girls, the coffin was a pushover. It took less than half an hour. It was not a casket, most definitely a coffin.

Al's promised personal touch was obvious: each panel was an off-cut or leftover piece from some other commission. I would be laid to rest knowing I didn't exploit a forest, not one tree. Plain knotty pine down one side, two-toned Huon pine down another, like butter rippled with honey. The base was some darker reddish timber I couldn't identify. Archie said it was Queensland maple and he might have been right but I also knew he was only pretending. The head was oak, I could tell that from the grain, and the nutty smell, while the end seemed to be off an old packing case.

But the lid gave me a small private joy: a pale silvery sheet of camphorwood, the scent divine to my chemo-soaked senses, a scent that thrust me back through all the winters of my life, all the blankets and woollen clothing, the wardrobes and boxes that stored belongings sprinkled with naphthalene flakes against moths. It sent me back to the camphorwood jewellery box of my childhood, where I kept prized trinkets. To the huge blanket box at the end of my parents' bed, where I would hide in contented solitude. And to all the boxes of my old but treasured books I'd packed up back in Amethyst, and which eventually followed me here. Al could not have known this. Nor that Mr Lambert removed the camphor laurel tree in his backyard, the one tree that stood close by the fence, and how much this upset me. Camphor laurel was a noxious weed – as the wife of a landscape gardener how could I not know that? – but I adored the smell. I smiled to myself. It was nice to take a secret joke to your grave.

The coffin was sanded and bevelled – just like Addie Bundren's but, I hoped, fated for a better end – and lightly finished in Danish oil. Space was a bit limited in the house but the front verandah was free. The tradition of sitting out the front was long gone in the suburbs, but I kept a wicker chair there and a small table for books and a mosquito coil.

The girls surprised me by barely reacting to the coffin's presence, but maybe because they'd watched Archie assembling it while swearing and muttering, there was nothing for them to be shocked about. Within days it was part of the furniture. Estelle started leaving her things on it: exercise books, CDs and bracelets. Daisy brought out her coloured pencils and paper.

Several days later, as I was watering the pot plants and Daisy was drawing, I asked,

Would you like to decorate a side each?

Can we? Hey, Stelly, Mum wants us to draw on her coffin, she called inside.

Estelle appeared at the door. I'm not drawing on that, she said.

Why not? It'll be fun, Daisy said.

Estelle just flicked a glance at me then vanished inside.

You can still do something, Daise, I said. What about getting your paints out and ... ?

They're all dried up.

Your marker pens, then?

I can't find them.

It was going to be one of those conversations, so I left it for the moment.

I decided the top of the coffin would be for Archie. My contribution would be obvious. But when I put it to him, his reaction was much the same as Estelle's.

However, Daisy discovered her art box under her bed, and over the rest of that week she scribbled and painted and erased and painted again until, on the Sunday, Estelle came and told her to make her mind up, that it was driving her crazy.

Just stick to one design, retard, she said.

But it was an affectionate insult because she sat down next to her sister and helped her fill in some of the pictures. Then she went and fetched her own paints. She even let Daisy use them. By the time I went out again she was painting some of her favourite song lyrics on her side, from a band called, appropriately, The Dying Breed, whom I pretended to tolerate, and Daisy was blocking in a set of pictures inspired by *The Saddle Club*. By the time I would be dead the current obsession (each lasted about three months) might have been Bratz Girls or SpongeBob. Or the Ninja Turtles may have made a reappearance. But for now it looked as though I'd be lowered into the good earth sporting lyrics about guitars that killed their owners on the one side, and pink horseshoes on the other. Archie had yet to make a mark on the lid.

Having recovered from the last chemotherapy treatment, I was waiting to feel ill again, from the disease. I felt fine, but knew this wouldn't last long, so I was trying to make everything I did as perfect as possible. Difficult when running a household. Impossible with children. And I felt this apprehension not from within me, but as something captured and reflected in Archie. I would look into his face and catch a glimpse of my own demise. It was not necessarily a bad morning, the day I realised this, but I sensed this sadness and fear from down in the yard.

He was watching me hanging out the washing with my usual colour-coded precision. He would have stepped out of the bathroom with the feeling of optimism always induced by his morning shower. Now he was standing on the back verandah sipping his coffee as he usually did when the morning was kind enough.

I was pegging out the girls' lemon yellow school blouses with matching plastic pegs. The laundry contained an entire cupboard full of sets of plastic pegs, most of them in the primary colours, plus green. There was a manufacturer of heritage-coloured pegs, the evidence right there in my peg basket: Brunswick Green, Federation Cream, Rooftile Red. Archie had stopped believing me when I said I collected them for research.

I had already pegged out his underpants: Jockeys, plain colours, attached patriotically by each side of the waistband with white, blue and red pegs. I did the whites, the pastels and then the coloureds. The very dark coloureds last, if there was any room left on the line. It was amazing how quickly the laundry burgeoned. It was as if it grew like spores under cultivation in a lab overnight. He would be thinking that, and thinking also that this was the second or maybe the third time I'd done the washing this week, and yet there were at least five pairs of his underpants hanging up on the inside of the line. And numerous socks, all his. I'd never worn socks until recently, even in winter, but now my feet were always cold. I'd had to go and buy several pairs of ridiculous thick cotton socks, for feet that would barely use them. Our daughters' socks, pale yellow, pink and white, were perched next to Archie's. You could buy pink pegs. Pale pink.

He sipped his coffee, which he always took black, with two. He drank Lavazza, strong but never bitter, made in the plunger. *We* drank Lavazza. Always. Now the smell of it was repugnant to me. I had shifted the larger coffee maker to the back of the cupboard above the stove along with the crock pot, the serrated electric carving knife, the pasta maker, and the other little-used appliances that constituted a time capsule of our culinary life together. And which would not be used any more.

I had nearly finished the hanging out. His shirts were the easiest of all: a vigorous shake, where the damp fabric gave out a satisfying crack, and then a matching peg at each of the bottom seams. They would dry quickly, and not need ironing. I stood with my back to him, bending and reaching with a fluidity that I no longer took for granted. Two days back I wasn't able to move so smoothly. He was noticing, perhaps wondering why, that first thing in the morning I was completely dressed, apart from my slippers. My wisps of hair drawn up and around my head and bound in a scarf. He would be wondering if I were too thin. I spread my hand against the last shirt. No one could say I ever resented this task, but could I really love it so much? Or was it a gesture directed towards him? I hadn't even acknowledged his presence, standing there up at the house sipping his coffee. Making the most of the opportunity to scratch gently and thoroughly around his genitals under the bath towel before dressing. When I did turn around, collecting the peg basket and the empty laundry basket together – I never left them out at the line to endure the elements – I smiled and frowned at the same time. It could also have been the sun in my eyes.

He smiled back, drained his cup. His face had the telltale after effect of someone who'd been staring when they felt they shouldn't. He would want to appear to have been scrutinising the lawn or something, not me and the washing. But the uncompromising patterns on the line would have suggested to him things were on the downslide. And he wouldn't know what to do. And I'd want him to do nothing but the essentials. Things that might become difficult as I became too tired.

As I passed him on the steps up to the verandah he leaned across and gave me a kiss on the cheek. The evidence of some slight desperation all spread before him, flapping merrily and brightly in the rising breeze, above his smooth lawn. This week's pattern was chequerboard, with two garden gnomes facing each other across the battlefield: Daisy's contribution, I thought.

Had I spoken to him that morning? I suspected my first response of the day was that frown I offered when I saw him on the back verandah. And his kiss on my cool cheek was about as sensual as a fly brushing past.

Dear Delia
You mean like all of the sheets? And how often?
Desperate.

Dear Desperate
If I were your girlfriend and those were the sheets you expected me to repose and do other things on ... Just the thought of what your sheets might contain summons up bacterial images too gross for words. Please don't write to me again, you are a lost cause. If your girlfriend sticks around after all this I'd be surprised.

Thirty-Two

A circus is a dismal place in the rain, muddy and cheerless, as if all the glitter and the magic has been washed away, exposing the acts and the people as their fake and fallible selves. Rain had prevented much of a crowd the Saturday afternoon I returned to see Tara. Members of the acrobat team sat sullenly at the entrance to the big top, smoking and not talking. A few people stood just inside the door of their trailers. Tara's door was open, as if she was hopeful for a change in the weather, and I approached to see her sitting back reading the local paper.

Come in. She glanced at the suitcase in my hand. She knew what was in it.

I've got a few things for you, I said.

Are you sure?

Oh yes.

I opened the suitcase and took out the clown suit, the lion tamer's outfit, the bamboo hoop and the whip. The black acrobat's leotard. Down the bottom of the suitcase were a red plastic nose and a large plastic daisy, attached to which was a tube and bulb.

I think that's it, I said.

She picked up the lion tamer's outfit and laughed quietly.

Poor Sonny, he never understood why we didn't have real lions.

Or many real animals at all, I said. Remember the stuffed dogs?

Monty, one of the adult clowns, had an act in which he pretended to train a collection of stuffed dogs. How he did it was impossible to work out, since you never saw the strings or fishing lines attached to them, but the toys would flop and jerk and move around, sit up and beg, so that by the end of the act the audience would be convinced they'd been seeing real animals: chihuahuas, terriers and poodles.

Sonny had been an incorrigible play actor and when Tara had wanted another small child for her act Sonny had begged and begged. He was four, and I could only let him do it if all the nets were under him. And luckily they were, because despite his persistence and devotion, the child was completely uncoordinated. After months of training, Tara just shook her head and redirected his attention towards the other acts.

Sorry, she told me, I can't use him. He's bloody hopeless.

Maybe because he's so little?

Maybe it's because he's not circus, she said.

But she was wrong there. Van wasn't an acrobat, but he was still from a circus family. Tara got Sonny interested in the clowns and then the lion taming. He used a stuffed lion and pushed it around the ring, then when he was a bit older, six or so, enlisted one of the circus toddlers, who occasionally agreed to fall through a hoop for him.

Now I tidied the collection of costumes into a neat pile, placing the red nose on the top.

You might find another kid who can use all this, I said.

She picked up the nose and the daisy.

How about you keep just these? Take them back with you?

I'm not going back just yet, I said. I've got something else I need to do. But I will keep them.

I replaced the red plastic nose and the water-squirting daisy in the suitcase, and left.

Thirty-Three

There are many reasons why an autopsy would be performed: sudden death, violent death, suspicious death, suicide, industrial accident; death in the event of no medical attendance in the previous month. Bereaved relatives can avoid confusion, uncertainty or distress by confronting this fact prior to the death. Be prepared for the autopsy report, and for what it implies.

'The Postmortal Condition'
The Household Guide to Dying (forthcoming)

Any comprehensive guide to dying would have a chapter describing an autopsy. In my case I doubted my body would be autopsied; however, there was always a chance. If, for instance, I decided to overdose on morphine and hasten matters, then any suspicious circumstances would require an autopsy. If that were the case, I would feel sorry if Dr Lee were implicated, as she would only be doing what doctors all over the country did: easing an inevitably painful death, just privately, discreetly.

But my brief was to produce a professional text, and therefore professional research needed to be done. Nancy was onto this of course, pressing a contact in the department of forensic medicine to allow me to observe an autopsy. She had no success. A mass of voyeurs, perverts and the more primitive species of sensationalistic journalist in recent years had led to a tightening of regulations and only those authorised could view an autopsy. When she rang to advise of developments, I decided to help her out.

There's someone I know, I said. A doctor I met years back.

Who?

Roger Salmon.

Never heard of him. But you know I could ...

He's a heart surgeon, I said, interrupting her.

Yeah?

He could get me in. I'll give him a call.

Viewing Room A was indicated by a laminated sign Blu-tacked onto the door. It was a small partitioned-off section of the dissection room. On one wall a separate doorway led out to the corridor, and on the opposite wall a window came down to waist level. The floor was lino, the fluorescent lights above were cold. There were six orange plastic chairs, a wastepaper bin in one corner and, high on the wall, a small speaker. There seemed to be no Viewing Room B.

Although Dr Salmon's influence had worked this small miracle, the department of forensic medicine still would not admit me to view the procedure without a guide. It was policy for all non-medical professional personnel. Clare, the guide, seemed extremely young, yet at ease in the place. I wondered how many times you had to see it before it seemed normal, before it felt like something possible to face in the everyday course of events. It was hard to believe that someone of her age not only had the stomach for witnessing the procedure, but the stamina to come back time after time.

The first one is the worst, she explained. After that it's routine. Except for children.

I could not ask how many children.

Do you know what the word *autopsy* literally means? she asked. It means seeing with one's own eyes. I learned that the first day I worked here. Now you'll see with your own eyes, see what you won't be able to after you're dead.

Dr Gordon MacConachie, the facility's most senior pathologist, met every one of my television-fed expectations about the profession by being obligingly Scottish. He was a flamboyant figure, in a bow tie and with wavy hair swept back from his forehead. He also bore an unfortunate resemblance to Andrew Lloyd Webber. When he spoke it was almost reassuring to hear a twang behind the accent, though not so much nasal as rasping. No Smoking signs perched everywhere around the morgue, but he stubbed out a cigarette the minute he walked in the door, then lit up another straight off. Soon it was clear that Gordon was an artist, and a performance was imminent. He cracked his knuckles, snapped on his latex gloves, and flourished instruments from the sterile tray. I made a note in my book. Why sterile? Sterility seemed superfluous in the circumstances, especially when it became apparent that, despite the gloves, Gordon was going to continue to dart over to a small table in the corner and light up throughout the autopsy. He held his hands above the body in an ostentatious display of inspecting it for imaginary surprises, before advancing on it with a black marker pen to make a series of marks down the middle.

It's all show, of course, Clare reminded me, for our benefit. Normally Eric would do this.

Eric was the assistant, a dumpy, balding fellow, wearing thick glasses. Unlike Gordon with his prancing movements, Eric seemed to shuffle. Clearly he was more Igor to Gordon's Dr Frankenstein than Mephistopheles to his Dr Faust.

Gordon commenced his monologue, which wasn't only to entertain. Every autopsy had an accompanying taped description for legal purposes. The difference with Gordon was that he included entirely superfluous information and details, probably designed to impress his small audience.

At first I could only glance at the body. Staring seemed rude. You wouldn't stare at a naked person on the beach, or anywhere else, even if you knew them. Especially in such bright lighting. I felt I had to get to know this body first. Just a bit. So I gazed at the top of the head, ignoring the groin, then had a good long look at the feet, before allowing myself to look directly at the rest of him.

Why had I assumed it would be a man?

She was very pale but recognisably Caucasian, though I'd expected something else. Something bloated, or visibly decaying around the edges, like a fungus growing on the hands and toes, or collapsed facial features. I didn't expect her to be pale beige-white. Grey, maybe. Perhaps a purple hue. Or yellow. Something suggested by the word *deathly*, at any rate. This body was five days old. It had undergone enormous changes since the time the heart ceased beating, since there was the irreversible cessation of all the functions of the person's brain, or irreversible cessation of circulation of blood in the body, which I knew, since Clare had quoted it to me on the way in, was the official medical description of death.

By this stage rigor mortis had come (at twelve to eighteen hours after death) and gone again (at thirty-six hours). She had been found within twenty-four hours of her death, and kept in the morgue's refrigerator, so the process of decay had been halted early. The green and purple stains on the torso, the distended appearance, or the marbling of the veins that came with further decomposition, were not apparent. She was not there, I kept telling myself. I wasn't sure if she should still be called a *she* or if she had now transcended to another status. Maybe she was an *it*. Whoever she was, she was long gone, and this was just the casing, the housing of something other that was now departed – spirit, soul, imagination, something that had no name – which was no more to be revered or feared than a carcass in a butcher's shop. Gordon and Eric displayed no reverence or fear, handling her as briskly as if she was a side of pork about to be stripped down to spare ribs, fillets and offal.

Under the harsh lights that exposed every scar, blemish, bristle, the autopsy happened so quickly that, prepared to be horrified, I was actually shocked, then amazed, then admiring of the deft efficiency. I thought it would be a reverential sort of procedure. I imagined hushed voices, subdued lighting in bleak blue-grey tones, cavernous silences pierced by portentous utterances. And overall a quiet, discreet handling of flesh and bone, at this most intimate of human intimacies, the vivisection and frank visual devouring of a body that had given no consent, had no awareness, and no way of expressing modesty or urging restraint.

Shortly after Gordon began dictating details into his recording microphone (the body of a mature woman, known to be fifty-eight years of age, no visible scars, with several identifying blemishes including a pear-shaped pale brown mole, the size of a ten-cent piece, on the right shoulder ...), three students entered the viewing room, making it full and busy in a strangely quiet way. Nursing students, it appeared, all women, dressed in plain blue uniforms. The experience of a private viewing was destroyed. But enhanced instead was the sense of ritual. Now we were definitely a group, fellow worshippers at a small shrine, paying our respects to some unreachable, inscrutable deity. We all now had certain obligations, were mindful of each other's reactions, feelings and beliefs – acutely so, given the size of the room. If the priests attending the ritual didn't feel that way, it didn't matter to these women, especially one, the oldest of them, who was obviously attending her first autopsy. As she stared at the body (or was it now a corpse? or cadaver?) she clasped her hands together and groaned. It was an ambiguous noise signifying something in between distress and pleasure. Awe, maybe. She continued to groan and utter noises and clasp her hands and say occasionally, Oh my god!, so that the actions being performed on the other side of the glass window seemed almost liturgical.

An added factor was the identity of the corpse (patient? specimen?). Privacy prevented us from knowing her name, but, in whispers, Clare supplied the details. She was an ex-nun who had lived by herself. She was found by her niece four days previously, slumped over the kitchen table. A pot of tea was knocked over beside her, and tea had dripped onto the floor. Two crisp pieces of toast were sitting erect in the toaster. The butter and marmalade were laid out neatly on the bench. It appeared she had died of a heart attack or stroke in the few minutes it took for a pot of tea to draw and the toast to cook. How more natural could it get: milk and wholemeal bread in the kitchen, a morning bathed in sunshine? But with no history of either condition, and in the circumstances, with no one discovering the body until an estimated day after the time of death, the medical officer had no option but to order an autopsy.

Gordon attacked the body with gusto, raising his scalpel dramatically. He sliced all the way down from the neck (noticeably pinker than the rest of the body, and crisscrossed with soft wrinkles, as is the neck of someone who spends time outside fully dressed but forgets to protect from the sun) to the dark brown pubic mound. He swiped the blade straight over the first cut and directly under her breasts, which he pushed out of the way, first one, then the other, as if they were just two nuisance speedbumps on an otherwise fast and efficient route. After making a large cross on the body, he then peeled away the top halves from the centre with smooth movements of the blade. Then he stood back while Eric approached with something that looked like an electric carving knife, and began sawing down the centre of the ribcage. Gordon appeared to enjoy watching this, given the comic disproportions of Eric, who was short, labouring over the high dissection table. On his tiptoes, Eric grunted and sawed, while Gordon stood between the viewing window and the body, smoking and providing the running commentary that, for the next half-hour, competed with the radio in the corner next to the digital scales and the ashtray.

It was too horrific to be bizarre, but too matter-of-fact to be horrific. It was, I suppose, pure human comedy, in every sense of the word: the cycle of everything from birth to death, from the bold exuberance of Gordon's pink and yellow spotted bow tie, to the lonely buff-coloured tag attached by a rubber band to the ex-nun's left big toe. It was as ordinary and as meaningful as the half-drunk polystyrene cup of coffee that Gordon placed on the table that held his notebook and recording machine. The stainless-steel ladle that Eric was now using to extract fluids from the cavity was the same as one I had in my kitchen. The one stamped Mermaid Stainless Steel 6 oz/ 175 ml, bought from Johnson's Overalls and that featured on the front cover of *The Household Guide to the Kitchen*. I last used it for bean soup.

Before we can proceed further, Gordon explained, the body fluids must be removed and measured, otherwise it's simply not possible to work efficiently with the organs.

Eric, unconcerned about the splashes landing on him, indeed humming with contentment, ladled vigorously into a clear plastic measuring jug that held two litres. I had one the same brand, half the size. The girls used it for making jelly.

With the ribcage out of the way, lying down in two flaps either side of the body, and the fluids collected, Gordon and Eric set to work with harmony and speed like two comedians in a well-rehearsed slapstick routine. Eric extracted body parts and tossed them to Gordon who threw them on the scales and sang out the weights to be recorded on tape. I was forced again to make the predictable but irresistible comparison to a butcher in a shop. Someone insouciantly slapping down quivering whole rumps or strips of fillet, or slithering mounds of sausage, for weighing, wrapping in white paper and handing over with a wink. There was even some flirting with the customers, as I could see that Gordon's performance was a huge flirtation of sorts, intended to impress his female audience.

He pounced on the heart with palpable satisfaction. Either the heart or the brain would provide the key to the mystery of this sudden death, if Gordon was right, and so far there were no suspicious circumstances to assume he wouldn't be. In the heart, he explained, he would be looking for telltale calcification, a whitening in the muscle, or, more telltale fatty deposits in the arteries, and probably a complete blockage in a vein somewhere (telling tales of what, though? a lifetime's indulgence in alcohol? gross consumption of cigarettes and bacon fat? in someone who was once a nun?). He dissected the heart straight through crossways, exposing left ventricle, right ventricle, left atrium, right atrium, and pointed to the crown of arteries on the top, the ones that earned the name coronary.

Gordon placed the specimen on a small stainless-steel tray and brought it close to the window. The butcher shop image persisted. I saw plastic sticks with prices and strips of artificial parsley.

There, he said, you see a perfectly healthy organ. No fatty deposits, no thickening, no calcification, no clotting, no evidence of heart disease whatsoever. He strolled back to the table. Still, we take a small sample for further analysis. And he chopped off a morsel from each side of the heart, before pushing it aside. He walked over to the ashtray and relit a cigarette, inhaling deeply while Eric finished off his work on the head.

The organs looked so familiar, the liver just like those I had seen countless times in the butcher's. By the time Eric began peeling away the scalp, having first made a sideways incision under the hairline at the back of the neck, the body on the slab had progressed way beyond dead ex-nun, dead woman, or body. It had become a carcass. A dripping, gaping carcass with a wide hole in its centre, ribs and breasts and flaps of skin sticking out at ridiculous angles. Its scalp was turned back inside out to cover the face, with tufts of grey hair poking out from underneath. Eric sawed around the middle of the head, laid the instrument aside, and removed the top half of the skull as if he was just lifting off the lid of a boxed gift. Inside, the brain shivered, wet and glistening, and familiar since in shape and colour it looked exactly like a sheep's brain. Why, I wondered, did we call it grey matter? Maybe because after preservation it discoloured, but this brain was pale pink, almost creamy, and when Gordon sliced it in half, it revealed inner depths of purple, blue and magenta. Mood colours. Colours of the emotions.

The brain was the other main player, the second starring talent in Gordon's little drama that afternoon. With the heart at that stage displaying no sign of clotting or congestion, the other most likely cause of death lay within this organ's rippling soft pink folds.

Because the brain is so soft, he explained, we usually find a preliminary examination inconclusive. What we will have to do is chill it to near freezing point, so that it can be sliced thinly enough for detailed examination. In the meantime – he sliced the two halves into portions about two centimetres thick – we'll have a quick look.

But the gods were with Gordon, for as he laid the last of his neat thick slices down he emitted a satisfied Aha!

Here – he pointed to a dark spot about a centimetre in diameter – you can clearly see the cause of death. He stood there, bow-tie erect, forefinger pointing directly at the reason the ex-nun dropped dead four days ago in her sunny kitchen while waiting for her toast to cook. He was deeply satisfied. The ultimate showman, the perfect performance.

That, he said, with a small pause for effect, represents a massive stroke. It is huge, one of the biggest I've ever seen. There's no question that this caused the death and, you may be interested to know, a death that would have been sudden and painless. The victim would have had no idea it was coming.

Nevertheless, he continued, it is policy to send off all organs for analysis, and so here we continue to take samples of everything, before tidying up.

He and Eric began slicing pieces from the kidneys, liver, intestines and everything else on the table before them, placing the samples of organs in plastic bags and tagging them. Then Eric took a plastic garbage bag and began scooping all the other body parts inside. Intestines slithered out onto the floor before he grabbed them and hauled them back into the bag. When it was done, he tied the bag with a yellow plastic strip, and placed it into the chest cavity, pressing down on any extra air. They folded back the two sides of flapping ribs and finally lifted up the breasts and pressed the skin to meet in the middle. It looked a pretty good fit, considering what had been removed and what had been replaced. Gordon took a huge needle, threaded it with thick, waxy-looking thread, and began stitching up from the groin, the needle arching and diving above the corpse in strong swift strokes. Eric meanwhile was filling the empty skull with grey industrial wadding. He replaced the top half of the skull and folded back the scalp, which settled surprisingly neatly into place. Then he fetched his own needle and thread and began stitching along the incision on the scalp. Since the head had flopped over the edge of the dissection table, supported somewhere just under the neck, and since Eric was so short, this wasn't as hard as it sounded. Surrounded by thread and grey stuffing, the two of them were quiet. Busily stitching away at either ends of the body, they looked like a couple of oversized elves at work in Santa's workshop on some naked floppy toy. Gordon was now nearing the navel, pressing down on a piece of plastic bag that kept poking out of the cut. He made a few knots in the thread and snipped his needle off. Eric, by then at the base of the neck, would soon be meeting his stitches.

Then, Gordon said, the relatives will receive a report detailing weight, size and condition of the vital organs.

Would the relatives, I wondered, have the faintest idea of what an autopsy involved? They simply wouldn't think about the implications.

> Heart, normal, 650 grams.
> Liver, normal, 2.75 kilos.

And so on. Every organ weighed, inspected, its condition described in a word, every last examinable part of the body observed in cold monosyllables and indisputable figures.

> Blood type: O positive; alcohol content nil; drug content nil.
> Estimated time of death: 4 to 5 days previous.

Until the only significant part of the entire procedure, for those uncertain as to how death visited:

> Brain: 2 kilos; ruptured artery in right hemisphere of cerebral cortex.

And then at the end, in the few lines allowed for Observations:

> Cause of death being a large cerebrovascular accident (stroke) occurring in the right side of the brain, resulting in sudden cessation of all functions of the body (death).

It would seem to render Gordon's efforts so slight, having them boiled down to one page. He would complete this and sign it to be sent to the family. If they thought about it, they would have to think this: in order for a brain to be weighed, the organ would have been taken out and placed on a set of scales. No wonder that few did think about it.

We made our way out with that empty, restless feeling you get when you emerge from the movies in daytime. The nursing students were silent and yawning, apart from the prayerful one, who still seemed stunned.

I had entered the morgue, an hour or so before, by the back entrance, where I was instructed to meet Clare. Now we left by the main entrance. It was as if I'd performed some kind of ritual test, and could now be led from shame to triumph. The roar of traffic met me as I exited the tinted glass doors. I crossed the road and passed through the iron fence of the university opposite. Here were lawns studded with flowering gums and Moreton Bay figs. So early in the afternoon, yet already there were lorikeets gorging on the gums' nectar. The air vibrated, the birds screeched energetically in the trees. Everything seemed to be growing visibly. Amid this, the idea of death should only have lingered momentarily. Yet I fancy I had an easy familiarity with my subject now. I could look death in the eye and not flinch, not be the first to look away, but what did this really have to do with the book I was trying to write? How could I convert the scene I'd just witnessed into something useful? Behind me was the squat brown building where deep inside, on that Friday afternoon, when much of the city was contemplating after-work beers and relaxed dinners, Gordon would still be scrubbing his hands and Eric hosing down the remains of a dead ex-nun as if they were tidying up after any old sort of job. Which, of course, they were.

Dear Delia
My local Vietnamese butcher sells strange things like intestines, pig's bladders, spleens and blood. What possible uses can pig's blood have?
Curious.

Dear Curious
Authorities such as Prosper Montagné and Isabella Beeton tell us that black or blood pudding is an ancient dish handed down from the Assyrians, whose pork butchers were the finest in the known world. Black pudding can be made from any blood, but apparently pig's blood produces the best quality sausage. Other blood is considered to be mediocre, with little nutritional value.

Thirty-Four

In an upstairs room of the Amethyst RSL, the meeting was already underway, so I slipped into a seat by the back wall. About two dozen people sat in the first few rows of plastic chairs that faced a small stage. The group of people showed an extraordinary disparity in age. It was just after eight pm and the boy in front of me looked too young to be up that late. And the old man next to him, white-haired and crinkled, looked like he was going to nod off any minute. Very young, teenaged, middle-aged, elderly, both sexes.

The other notable thing was the silence. Then a man who was just leaving the stage inspired a soft round of applause, while out the front the woman who sat at a small table and chair adjacent to the front row so that she partly faced the room and partly faced the stage, tapped the table with a pencil, and then they all rose to their feet and broke into a rousing, unaccompanied and surprisingly harmonious rendition of 'I Saw the Light', at first thought a curious choice to commence a meeting of the local chapter of Elvis Presley fans. But in a secular age, it was probably as valid a religion as anything else. And anything that brought young and old together with such sober unity couldn't have been laughable. It could be desirable. Maybe that was the point. Elvis was a lifelong devotee of gospel music: it made sense to open the meeting with a hymn. Especially a hymn written by a fellow southerner and traveller on the slippery road to musical success.

The meeting went for an hour, as a succession of people spoke and sang and shared experiences, all in the loosely structured way that suggested an Alcoholics or Gamblers Anonymous meeting. When it was over I went up to the woman at the desk.

I wondered when we'd see you, she said.

I hadn't expected a friendly welcome. But we both knew there were things to be tied up.

Do you want to go for a drink? I said.

Not tonight, I'm tired after all this.

Then I might come and see you tomorrow, if that's okay.

Even back when Sonny was alive, statistical evidence showed that the number of Elvis fans was increasing yearly all around the world. Not to mention the impersonators: they existed in every possible shape, size and dimension, so that the world abounded in short, grossly fat, bald, bearded, female, disabled, bespectacled, black and blind Elvis impersonators. There were Elvis impersonators who couldn't sing. Soon there would be ones who were completely mute.

Pearl, the founder and president of the Amethyst and District Elvis Fan Club, epitomised its eccentric yet oddly plausible character. The daughter of several generations of local people who had come from the canefields, Pearl believed she understood Elvis like few others. No one, she once told me, was more marginalised than her: rural, poor, female, black (well, dark). A soul mate for her idol.

She knew Sonny when he was a baby, even before he was born, when I first went to borrow books from her exchange, following Mitchell's recommendation. But it wasn't until Sonny was five or six that she heard him singing one day. I wasn't taking any notice as I was picking through a box of spotted hardbacks seeing if it held anything more exciting than historical romances by Sir Walter Scott.

Listen to that boy, Pearl said.

Sonny was outside on her lawn with his toy mower singing, *One man went to mow, went to mow a meadow …*

I'd been aware that most children couldn't sing much better than a cicada, but even though Sonny's voice was charming to me I'd never realised just how sweet and pure it was.

Hey, Sonny, come in and sing with me, she called out.

She put on a tape and ran him through the first few bars of 'Teddy Bear'.

He's a natural, Pearl told me, but I guess you know that.

I hadn't. With no musical skills of my own, I wasn't good at recognising them in others.

I wish I could sing half as well as that, she sighed. I could have been an impersonator too. But, guess what, I can spot and nurture talent in others without having it myself. Bummer, hey?

Just where Pearl's Elvis obsession might have led if she'd also been an impersonator didn't bear thinking about. I found it strange enough that she spent every other week running a meeting full of misfits, and all her spare time outside the book exchange organising ways to work Elvis into every aspect of the local culture. By now Sonny's fascination with the circus was cooling, and Pearl started taking him around with her, to small gatherings of the club, where he could have fun and sing as much as he liked, and to fêtes and parties where people wanted some novelty. But that was before Archie and I became serious, and after that it was different. Their on-again, off-again relationship was by then definitely off, had been for a long time. Of course there were always two sides to the story, but by then I knew Pearl well enough to see what Archie had meant. I found the huge posters of Elvis around her place intimidating. I thought her devotion was more of a disease. And as Archie had said, it wasn't his fault that he couldn't match up to the King: it was tough competition.

By then Pearl had become far too fond of Sonny to let him down, but with me she became cool and even hostile. I stopped visiting her book exchange. And as much as I delighted in Sonny's singing talents, I worried about this aspect of his personality. Performance was in his blood. I was afraid of what that might mean as he grew older.

Thirty-Five

> The dying person is frequently coddled and patronised, and always discouraged from taking extreme actions or making outrageous demands. But this person has a right to take charge of their death as much as their life, and to resist going gently. They should be allowed instead, as the poet Dylan Thomas said, to *Rage, rage against the dying of the light.*
>
> 'Care and Handling of a Dying Person'
> *The Household Guide to Dying* (forthcoming)

The light was perfect the day I dragged the coffin out onto the back lawn: not too bright, with some cloud to tone the images down. Archie hadn't mowed recently, which I thought looked better, more natural. Dandelions were perching a few inches above the lawn. I propped the head end up and placed the lid lying at an angle on the grass, so it looked like a person was all ready to appear from within. Then I set to work with the digital camera. Half an hour after emailing the images to Nancy, I phoned her.

What do you think?

Incredible.

You mean they're good? You like the idea?

No, I mean it's incredible that you want to do this.

So you won't come and help? What about sending around a professional photographer?

I hadn't asked Archie to photograph me in my coffin. I knew I couldn't ask Jean. But I thought Nancy would do it. And setting up the digital camera with the timer and stand was beyond my technical skills. I needed someone to come and take shots of me lying in my coffin holding a martini.

I didn't say I wouldn't help, she said.

When Nancy arrived an hour later I was ready with the props. I was made up, dressed in the apron, cocktail shaker and egg beater to hand. She aimed the camera at the coffin, while I climbed inside. It was the first time I'd tried it out. Lying there was not as strange as I had expected. I could smell all the different timbers Al had used, even the rough old pine of the packing-case end. I breathed in the faint camphor scent of the lid beside me. Shutting my eyes, I could almost feel myself back in the camphorwood blanket box at the end of my parents' bed. My hiding place.

I opened my eyes and stared straight out at the sky. This is what it would be like. Lying several feet under the earth, if you could look through the clay and rock and crumbled dirt, the grass and granite of the grave above, this was all you'd see, if you could see. Endless sky. Blue fading to the colour of nothing.

The light was behind Nancy and the clouds lifted. Then I was squinting.

Not like that, she said.

How about this?

I sat up instead, holding high the martini, cradling the egg beater in the other hand.

That's better.

After she'd taken a dozen shots I climbed out. I had expected to feel some sort of experience in there. Something meaningful. Frightening. Ominous. But all I felt was how sore my backside was. The unpadded base was so uncomfortable on my bones I thought about lining it for when the time came to use the coffin permanently, until I realised how ridiculous that was.

I handed her the martini glass while I looked at the images.

These are terrible, I said.

I looked dreadful. Worse than a corpse. And I'd tried so hard with the clothes, the scarf, the make-up. They were doubtless the worst photos of me ever taken. Every single one. My cheeks were sunken, my lips were too thin. My eyes seemed to have disappeared. My nose was too big.

I don't understand it, do I really look that bad?

Maybe the camera sees things we don't, she said.

I handed it back to her.

Or maybe everyone has been right, I said. Let's forget about it, then. It's Archie's camera anyway, I'd better delete them.

After she left I sat on the back step gazing out over the empty coffin, the discarded props. The light had been so perfect. I thought it had been such a good idea. I finished off the martini then went down to the chicken shed and fetched Jane. When Archie came home with Estelle and Daisy I was still taking shots of her perched serenely on the head of my coffin.

Dear Delia
Sorry for writing again, but there's something I wanted to let you know. My girlfriend and I have broken up. I didn't want to tell you before because I thought she'd change her mind. Do you have any advice to help me?
Desperate.

Dear Desperate
No.

Thirty-Six

Pearl's home doubled as the office of the Elvis club, and had been a dilapidated weatherboard on stilts, badly in need of renovation when she bought it. After removing the verandahs, replacing the windows, creating a small upstairs balcony with a balustrade, adding a couple of fake marble columns at the front, and painting the entire structure white, Pearl had a creditable miniature replica of Graceland on her hands, from the outside at least. The work had paid off, with tourists diverting to Amethyst just to view the house. For a set fee, a club member would pose for photos in a costume of the buyer's choice (invariably the white satin flares and caped version, Las Vegas circa 1975) on the front lawn. Pearl was also a registered marriage celebrant, the only one in the far north specialising in Elvis ceremonies. In these cases the guests were treated to a ceremony using words taken from Elvis's own life or lyrics. His sweetest love songs were played in the background.

The inside of the house made no attempt to replicate the original. Matters of cost, practicality and taste came into play here. Pearl – when we were on speaking terms – had told me that the outside was one thing, but that she had to live with the interior. So no midnight blue shag pile carpets creeping halfway up the walls, no mirrors on the bedroom ceiling. She maintained there was a difference between being a serious proponent of the Elvis ethos, and being a mere slobbering fan obsessed with memorabilia. Hers was a more intellectual, even spiritual, commitment, she claimed, which had inaugurated the club and kept it apart from any old Elvis fan club. She only collected music, posters, books and videos, spread over several rooms, and made a virtue of the fact that all else was ephemeral rubbish.

The place was the same as when I'd last been here. The lawns were still trim, the surrounding trees higher, but the house itself was fresh and white as if recently painted. The only difference was in the front room, which had once been the book exchange. It was now stacked with records, CDs, recording and sound equipment.

You don't have the books any more, I said, walking into the shop; behind the counter a television was playing an amateur video recording.

Packed them all away a few years ago, she said. Now I just deal in the music.

She was waiting for me to say something more but I just stared at the screen.

It's from the annual Elvis Impersonators Convention, she said. Parkes. Last year.

One fellow was sitting on a fence rail in front of a small red-brick house. He wasn't terribly fat, but he carried an enormous beer gut that stretched the limits of his blue T-shirt and spilled way over the front of his shorts. He had a full-length beard, dark glasses and was cradling a guitar.

Yeah, he said, I have a lot of trouble getting shows. I try every year but never get a look in. I dunno, people say I don't look like Elvis much, but I reckon I do, a bit anyway. I've got the dark hair, and I wear me sunglasses. See? He took them off and held them towards the camera. They're gold-rimmed, just like Elvis's. He replaced them and stared back at the lens, an amorphous mass of glasses, beard and stomach.

But people say I don't look the part, he said. They say it's the beard, but I say that's not the point, I'm getting into the essential Elvis, myself, I don't think the surface is so important, it's the essence that matters.

And as if to prove this he balanced the guitar on his ponderous stomach and strummed the opening chords of 'I Can't Help Falling in Love With You'. When he began to sing the sound was truly execrable. I'd never heard such bad Elvis impersonating before. I'd never heard such bad singing before. After a few lines he stared back at the camera, almost in implacable defiance, as if daring it, the person filming him, or anyone else, to contradict the stunning incorrectness of what he'd just said.

Despite the tension of this visit, we both started to laugh. She switched it off, shaking her head. Here's a guy whose only resemblance to Elvis is that he's a man, she said. Who can't sing a note, but is convinced he's got it, convinced the rest of us are wrong.

But that guy is one hundred per cent genuine, she continued. He'll go to Parkes and every other convention and talent quest he can year after year, and despite the knockbacks and the ridicule, he'll still think he's captured the essential Elvis. Because he has, in a sense. He's a complete nobody with nothing going for him, no talent, no good looks, but when he's Elvis he's someone important and glamorous and famous, who's still completely true to himself.

I've never seen a more un-Elvis-looking Elvis, I said.

And I've got hundreds of hours of recordings of people just like him. Because that's the greatest ambition for many people. You can transcend your life but remain true to yourself, just like this guy. Elvis saves.

Sometimes.

I wondered if her idol had saved her. It seemed to me an empty sort of religion, if you could live all those years and still resent the woman who had what you once desired.

Do you want a coffee?

I shook my head, then sat down on a sofa and put the suitcase on my lap. She looked around the room, as if deciding what to do, then sat down too. But she wasn't giving me an inch. She waited for me to speak again. When I did, the room sounded hollow, cavernous, and I felt as if I was disappearing into the sofa. My words echoed too loudly in my head.

Pearl, at least Archie was honest with you. And it was his choice, breaking up with you. I never forced him into anything. You have to stop blaming me.

Why? To make you feel good before you die?

I raised my eyebrows, wondering how she knew. I didn't think Mitchell had told anyone.

She went on:

I've heard all about it, and I know I'm not meant to say that. But I loved Archie and wanted him and there's been no one else since.

No one except the obvious, I thought, looking around the room.

If Pearl imagined I'd come seeking forgiveness, she was wrong. And if she thought references to my impending death would upset me, she was wrong about that too. When I had left town all those years ago Pearl was like a woman with an invisible illness, one she could never talk about or seek treatment for, a disease of bitterness and guilt. She resented a woman whose son had just been killed. And she had loved Sonny, I knew that, she had loved him very much. She had been good to him, indulging his little obsessions, playing along with his fantasies. The complexities of her feelings must have been immense, but back then I wasn't in a state to pity anyone except myself.

Now I found compassion for her, but not for anything in the past. She lived in a shrine. She was devoted to a man who, after all, was just a glorious voice. The most moving song by Elvis or any of his imitators could never seal the fissures in her life.

I know you loved Archie, Pearl, I said quietly, but I just can't do anything about that. I never could, you know. But look, I've brought something.

I opened the suitcase, took out the gold suit and held it up. The comical size of it, the lace gold trim that was all but plastic, the shiny folds of the cheap synthetic fabric that still never creased despite all the years it was packed away.

She reached over and took it. Then I handed her the toy that went with it.

'Teddy Bear', she said.

Yes.

It was the wrong outfit for it, but Sonny loved singing 'Teddy Bear'. He clutched the plastic mike in one hand and a little bear in the other, which at the end he would wave around his head then fling into his audience, whether that was just Pearl and me, his classmates, if they were in the mood, or Tara and Monty at the circus, and anyone else he could round up for an informal performance.

She folded the suit over and over in her lap, placing the bear on top, staring down at it as she spoke.

You've got other kids?

Two daughters.

What are they like? How old?

They are the most beautiful children in the world. Estelle is dark, eleven. Daisy is eight, and she's got red-gold hair. Neither of them has much musical talent, just like their mother. And I miss them so much I'm not sure what I'm even doing here.

And so, how is Archie?

He's great.

Her face was as blank as she could make it. She wasn't going to let me see the envy for the children I'd had that she hadn't, for the man she'd wanted but hadn't worked out how to keep, for the child I had for just eight years, which to her would have still been better than none at all.

Archie is the best father, I said. Ever. He loved Sonny too.

She said nothing. Finally she looked me square in the eyes and asked,

Did you know I could never have children?

No. I didn't.

Archie knew, she said.

The moments while I digested this seemed to go on forever. I saw Archie, years and years ago, sitting down beside me outside the caravan, telling me it would never work out with Pearl. I saw Sonny, playing on the lawn right in front of us. Archie and I watching him fondly. Archie, watching.

Somehow there just weren't the words to reply to this. Saying sorry would be inadequate. Insulting.

Look, Pearl, I said, I'm dying – I could be gone in a few months.

Her face was set.

Do you know what that means?

She shook her head.

It means, I said, that only the most important things matter now. I've come here to say how much I appreciated everything you did for Sonny. He loved hanging out with you. He just loved it. I think sometimes he lived for it.

I reached into my bag and took out three books.

I wanted to give these back, too, I said. Remember I borrowed them before he died?

How would I remember that?

Well, I always have, I'm like that with my books. So I thought I'd return them but now I suppose you don't want them, if you've given up the exchange.

I handed her the copies of the three Alice Walker titles I'd taken with me when I left Amethyst. *To Hell With Dying. You Can't Keep a Good Woman Down. Possessing the Secret of Joy.*

She examined them and then, for the first time since I'd seen her last night, she smiled.

Don't you think you'd better keep this one? She handed me back the first. It's obviously your kind of book. In fact, keep them all, they all sound like they're you. And I'll never read them.

Okay, I will. And I want you to keep Sonny's suit.

Thanks. There was a scrap of gratitude in her voice. I'd like to, she said.

Thirty-Seven

> No one should assume they are too old or unhealthy to donate organs. Even those people who know they are dying may qualify, as successful transplants have been performed from all sorts of donors. The heart, kidneys, lungs, pancreas and liver might be debilitated by treatment or disease, but eye, bone and skin tissue may all be suitable for grafting and transplantation.
>
> 'The Postmortal Condition'
> *The Household Guide to Dying* (forthcoming)

Sometimes Nancy embraced the concept of the guide to dying so thoroughly I think she forgot its author was about to pass on. Pass over. Cross to the Other Side (see Chapter 9: Euphemisms and the Dying). She became extremely helpful. Verging on the pushy. Several days later she rang to tell me the guide needed to address organ donation.

Organ donation?

Yes. Why, what's wrong?

Oh, nothing.

She talked on about arranging for literature to be sent to me. Meeting with the publicity officer of the Organ Donation Council. Interviewing successful recipients. There was the chance I could witness an operation. The autopsy showed I was the sort of person who could deal with it. Heart transplants were the most common, she could probably get me into one of those.

Heart transplants.

Nancy ... I stopped her.

What?

There's no need. I don't need to attend an operation.

Okay, I trust you. But you'll include the chapter? I think it's important.

It was important, all right. And I was prepared for it. Although not prepared for the way afterwards the whole story came rolling towards me like a huge boulder, gathering layers as it came until it hit me with the full force of its narrative power. That pulsating organ, blood bright, glistening with life.

For I was a step ahead of Nancy. I had already done the research on this. And more than the research: I had done this. Not that Nancy knew, nor did anyone much.

Early on I'd decided I would donate my organs – all of them, any of them – but thought it might not be possible. When I had asked her, Dr Lee fixed me with an uneasy look then cleared her throat before reminding me that despite their devastating toxicity, the cytotoxic drugs were in fact cleaning me out. My insides would be free of germs, bacteria, decay. I'd be polished clean like a rack of dishes. Hence, of course, the susceptibility to every passing disease or ailment. No, what I needed to understand was that a certain ... (a long pause here) ... deterioration ... (she finally got the word out) ... in my body would preclude the chance of organ donation.

Eventually I prised the information out of her. Some doctors are so reluctant to speak the unvarnished facts. But I came to understand that, while the medical profession stoutly maintained the myth that my body would respond to treatment, in the end, she, no one, and now I, believed there would ever be anything but cancer, possibly invading and outright colonising every organ of my body. Imperial forces overtaking and annihilating inferior races. Uniformed and armed soldiers landing on the shores of little islands, shooting the natives dead, erecting flags and boiling the kettle for tea, all before the day was done. By which time it might not have been a good idea to invite others to partake.

I had to confess, there weren't many circumstances in which you could feel this level of rejection. You've had cancer in three different parts of your body, fine. You've had bits and pieces chopped off, sliced away. You have the therapy: chemo and radiation that nearly has to kill you before it can cure you. But it can't cure you, you'll be killed anyway. Not that you'll be killed, it won't be an active verb situation here, it will be a passive one, you will die. Or wait, yes, you will be killed, you will be killed by your disease, by the cancer. And yet you still can't save the situation by offering your body, like an old car wreck that you think might still be salvageable for spare parts: a starter motor here, a side door there, a rear left indicator panel.

The organ, your organs, and all your body parts, will, by the time you die, be potentially so infused with cancerous cells that your body nearing death will be quite worthless. Even at your premature (yes, dying before forty is premature) demise, you can't donate. In a culture that has commodified the body down to the last toenail, you still can't make it a useful product.

I imagined the state of these poor forlorn organs that made up my barely functioning body. The thoroughness of those invading cancer cells, planting the flag way out in the deepest, darkest reaches of my spleen, the more inaccessible folds of my liver. God, even my corneas wouldn't be safe but would be thoroughly overtaken and replaced with the new rulers.

By the time Dr Lee had finally finished explaining all of this – a long process, given her impassive and diffident deskside manner, her tendency to euphemism and polyglot medical jargon to mask, as ever, the plain facts (you will die, it will happen within the next year) – I was sick of the word organ.

Organ, organ, organs. My body sounded like it was stuffed full of musical instruments or genitals. I associated the word with church music, hymns, Bach. Soaring architecture, great steel tubes, elevated keyboards, and dust motes circling in the air. The word summoned up the sound of swelling fugues, triumphant songs all about marching on to war, kings of creation, or angels proclaiming this or that. Or blood washing clean, that oxymoronic image that persists despite every woman's intimate knowledge of blood, which if it washed anything, did so only to stain.

The only body parts I could seriously consider organs were external ones: the ear was an organ, anyone could see that. It looked like one, rather ugly despite its delicate folds, its undeniably organic curving into itself, into a secret hidden chamber. And the male genitals were organs, of course. They were played, for a start. And when I was a child these parts were always referred to euphemistically as the male organs. But everything else – lungs, heart, kidneys, spleen, pancreas, liver and tissue, which included the valves of the heart, bone, skin and eye tissue, such as the corneas – was hard to see as an organ. Not the glistening sometimes pulsating parts I imagined as vital living portions of my body. Pink, red, purple, even creamy white. Why wasn't the brain up for organ donation? Who would care that you'd have someone else's memories and desires, obsessions and fears, if at least you had a brain that functioned? If you were otherwise fit and healthy but your brain had permanently shut down, wouldn't you – aged eight or twenty or thirty-three – and your family welcome the chance of a new life? It would be like sticking a whole new CD into the player, and letting it run. Like rebooting with Linux as your operating system instead of Windows. Why waste a beautiful and especially young body?

Why hadn't I thought of this earlier? I could have done more research into the question and incorporated it into the guide.

Or perhaps my own brain was more affected by treatment or disease or both than I thought and I was allowing imagination to overrule logic. And I was losing sight of the point. Which was that my body was rejecting life, and life was rejecting it. So, no organ donation, no tissue donation. Only top-shelf, Triple-A, Class 1 body parts could be passed on to a patient in line, a liver disease patient, a heart failure victim. Dr Lee made it clear, without ever explicitly stating it (she was skilled at this, I even admired her for it), that just a hint of poor-quality tissue would result in rejection. I'd be foolish to waste my time considering it.

What about my blood, then? Could I at least donate that?

Well, oddly enough, yes, you could, she said. It's probably the healthiest part of you, given how quickly the blood cells are renewed. But of course, she added, you can only donate blood while you're alive.

After this consultation I gathered the collection of feeble, substandard organs and tissues that counted as my body and exited her rooms. I walked confidently for a woman whose every body part had just been rejected as unworthy.

Dear Delia
Do you think if I bought new sheets she'd have me back?
Desperate.

Dear Desperate
I've already told you I have no more advice for you. Although you never know your luck. I understand there is a sale on in the household linen department at David Jones' (I recommend something in pastel, nothing floral).

Thirty-Eight

I awoke from a dream, sweating and finding it hard to breathe. A panic attack, I knew the signs. It could have been a symptom of the comprehensive chemotherapy, except I was well over the last treatment. I hauled the bed-clothes off and sat up in my damp T-shirt, controlling my breathing, until I calmed, could suck down some oxygen. If it hadn't been four in the morning I would have rung Archie, but I couldn't disturb a man who I knew was sleeping badly. If I'd been a smoker I might have lit a cigarette. If coffee and tea weren't so flavourless I would have made a cup. I had no Scotch, Irish, wine, anything. I lay back on the pillows.

The problem was, it wasn't a dream. *It was no dream. I lay broad waking.* The memory had never gone away, but over the years I had smothered the details. Since arriving back in Amethyst I had been waiting for this moment, really, waiting for the vast panorama to unreel before my eyes once again. And as I lay there not drinking, not smoking, not moving, I finally allowed myself to travel over that landscape of the mind, that memory too terrible and powerful to contemplate until now, except in occasional furtive glances.

The only thing I could think of was to get moving. The light was just nudging the low streaked clouds when I pushed through the front door and set off down the driveway of the motel. The Paradise Reach's dog was snoring lightly in his kennel, and high above in the palms the first birds were chirruping awake. After nearly an hour I was calm again. I had half circled the town by then, and seen no one except the milk delivery van and the newsagent from the main street doing their rounds. I sat and rested in the memorial park that looked down towards the river, hidden from view but delineated by the darker green line of willows and casuarinas. I realised I was near one of the places I had been looking up in the phone book. The place where I thought the young woman I needed to find might still be living. I walked through the park, crossed the road, and made my way east, following the slope of the land. Soon I came to the cul-de-sac, Nile Crescent. A cul-de-sac couldn't be a crescent, I thought, looking this way and that, avoiding looking straight ahead to number 3A. Who named this street anyway? I felt strange, light-headed. Perhaps it was all the walking. Should have brought water with me. Should make my way back to the motel, drink and rest. I turned my back on the place, on the feeling that there was something here for me. That was just an illusion. A lie.

Any luck? Archie asked, the next morning when he rang.

Not yet.

Where have you gone?

The police, the hospital, the high school …

She would have left school by now.

I know. I just thought someone might know where she is.

How are you feeling? he asked after a pause.

Okay, a bit tired.

I want you to leave, I want you back here. What about the drive back? You won't be up to it, I think I'd better come and get you.

Please, Archie, no. I'm fine. I'd say so if I wasn't.

And I was fine, just. I felt a creeping fatigue at the end of every day, but otherwise I knew I was well enough. Taking it slowly over several days, I could do it. I needed to do it. I needed to pull up in the drive and get out and walk through our front door, all on my own. I would have Sonny's suitcase in my hand and that gap in my chest through which a cold wind had blown for the past fourteen years would finally be closed over.

Don't worry, Arch. I promise I'll take it slowly. And I'll be leaving in a few days. Give Estelle and Daisy big kisses for me. Tell them I'll see them soon.

How do you know?

How do I know what?

That you'll find her in just a few days? Then he hung up.

After you become a new Subaru owner for the first time you notice Subarus everywhere, wherever you drive. When you are dying you are acutely conscious of deaths all around you. Do you seek them out, or do they adhere to you as if some invisible magnetic force is pulling you and death together at every possible opportunity? It is like being a wallflower at a dance, with a bustling well-meaning do-gooding matron thrusting you together with a lanky pimply two-left-footed youth.

The difference was once I became closer to death in all its manifestations, once I took its sweaty flaccid hand, I was unable to let go. I was unable to resist the total and tormenting recollection of every aspect of that time fourteen years ago. I could only bear to relive it, though, because in my mind there was Archie by my side.

Even when he was a young gardener, Archie was a well-respected, reliable worker. Being a one-man business, he took on any and every job possible. Once every six weeks in the cooler weather, and once a fortnight in summer, he trimmed Mrs Gowing's minuscule front lawn, and pulled out the weeds from her doll's-house bed of roses. The roses she always pruned herself. It was a job that took all of half an hour and for which she paid him five dollars, the same amount she'd been paying him since he was fourteen and had first started knocking on doors in Amethyst to earn money doing odd jobs after school. It never seemed to occur to her that Archie was now a businessman and that inflation might have upped the rates.

The local high school employed him to mow its playing fields, and he also planted and tended the memorial garden in front of the RSL. He trimmed the lawns and tidied the gardens surrounding the bowling greens behind the RSL, though the bowling green itself was kept immaculate by an aged greenkeeper. When the local golf club was busy or lush or too overgrown, Archie often picked up work there, too. He was cheerful and honest, the sort of person who could be entrusted with your best couch lawn or your most temperamental native orchids. Someone whom you could leave working all day around your house and not worry if you had to go off and leave the doors open.

I knew all this from the time I'd first met Archie, back when he came to trim the caravan park lawns. I knew he was a gardener and I knew he was a worthy man but I didn't know how tender he was. He tended plants. He nurtured them. He was capable of giving so much. I failed to understand this, until I needed him. So tender, he could do for me, for Sonny and for a little girl I never even knew and her mother, what in the end I desperately wanted to do but could not.

Thirty-Nine

> Dying is a chance to express some of the most inspiring and creative ideas of your life. Never forget that.
>
> 'Wills and Wishes'
>
> *The Household Guide to Dying* (forthcoming)

It was a bit like the recipes of old. Hang your hare for a fortnight in a cool dry place to tenderise the flesh. Isolate the bird and force feed on rich yellow grains for a month prior to the festive season. Use only the first six eggs of a newly laying hen. Keep the kid tied upon a short rope and feed upon milk and soft cereal.

I had been thinking about this for a long time. They might well find it disgusting, repellent, but for me it was the ultimate gift. I could not stay, and my body would decay and eventually rot, desiccate, vanish into earth and dust in its fine and private place, but before it did I would give them a part of me that would be pure and sweet and something they would not get, could not get, from anyone else.

Except that it would be pure via great effort, and salty, not sweet.

Once I might have thought it strange and repellent myself, but the more I considered it, the more the idea appealed to me as the ultimate expression of devotion, of being the most generous act a cook could give the people she loved. I put myself into this dish, I always said, I made this with love, I said to them. Especially when pleading with the girls not to reject a new dish they, child-wary, refused to try. Sometimes with more than love, with stern annoyance: *Don't toss that lunch away, it may only be a Vegemite sandwich, but I made it with love.*

Now I could give them something with love and with more: with the essential part of me that was unique, irreplaceable, the stuff of sacrifice and devotion, and, if you believed the stories, redemption.

In the back of the freezer I prepared a space. People would bring food, afterwards. They were already bringing food, most of which I could not face. Anything sweet, for instance. Nancy's delicate crème caramel was now wasted on me. Jean's chocolates, even the black bitter chilli ones, which I would normally pick as my favourite, tasted foul. Any food too sweet, too sharp, too strong, most meats. ... Some days I didn't mind, but mostly I preferred to face nothing more complex and fragrant than an egg and bread, a salad and a pot of tea.

Food was the language of grief and suffering. I knew that for months after I'd gone Archie would arrive home to a doorstep bearing chicken casseroles and chocolate cakes, boxes of oranges and plates of muffins. Fruit cakes in tins, jars of pickles, legs of ham, lasagnes, pies: as if death was a feast, a celebration, a thanksgiving, dying a trigger for activity in the kitchen. I understood this. People think there is some special code or language for talking to a bereaved person, and that they don't have that language, so they prepare and offer food instead. They feel unable to wrap their arms around the bereaved and say, *I am so sorry, I am so very sorry, let me hold you for a minute, because there is nothing else I can do*. But they can stand in their kitchen and patiently stir pasta sauce, or hand over trays of mini muffins, anointed with chocolate icing, kissed with hundreds and thousands, because all that says instead, *I know you are suffering, I cannot say that, here is the food that might say it for me instead*. A saucepan of spaghetti bolognese becomes as sacred and as special as the Last Supper.

I had many of these last suppers after Sonny died. I came home from the hospital to a dish of steak and kidney pie. The next day someone brought a hamper containing a pot of the delicatessen's finest pâté. Jean made some wry comment about the insensitivity of food made from offal. Many of these gifts of food were anonymous, left at the step of the caravan. I would feel momentarily sad that I'd missed the bearer, until I realised that most preferred to be anonymous donors, preferred not to encounter the grieving person. What did you say to a young mother who had just had their only child smashed to death? Obviously, the conversations appropriate for these situations had yet to be created, the very words invented. So it was by the plastic microwave-proof containers, the aluminium pots and baking trays, the Corningware dishes that I sometimes identified the giver. Often I simply put the clean dishes out the front where, just as anonymously, they would be collected. And so many wet dishes: bean casserole, curried chicken, beef in red wine, Irish stew, meatballs and gravy. As if sickness, suffering and death required fluid, digestible foods. And soup, soup, soup – chicken predominating. The wetter the dish, the more sympathy. *I cannot speak the sorrow I have for you, but here is my warm, liquid, loving soup, eat it and be comforted, if you can.*

Oh yes, I understood this so much better than I would like.

I considered a diet of fragrant herbs and fruits only, with clear honey-sweetened drinks and apple juices. Maybe some nasturtium- and clover flower-flavoured salads, sweet raw carrots, milky fresh almonds and baby peas. Just like those pigs in northern Italy or France that are raised on nothing but acorns and apples, and whose flesh is consequently so sweet and tender the ham they produce is worth hundreds of dollars per kilo, obtainable only at certain times of the year at a handful of outlets around the world. I would be like a prize-winning product, cosseted and cultivated for an elite consumer.

Dr Lee had told me my blood was clean. She'd assured me.

But the supermarket, just up the road, was all I could manage to reach for grocery shopping, and it was pretty light on nasturtium flowers and fresh almonds. I decided that no drugs, no wine, and plenty of water and fresh food was enough. After a week, one Monday morning when the girls had gone to school and Archie was safely at Zetland supervising the planting of an industrial site with grevilleas, I settled at the kitchen bench with a bowl and a syringe.

She had said I could donate blood, if I wanted.

I admired my skill, I could have been a health professional. I could have been lots of things. And now I had become a dying mother with a book that possibly would never be finished. I didn't want to consider that for too long. Instead, I saw that I had collected plenty for my dish.

She'd said I still had to be alive.

Forty

Machines were keeping Sonny alive. I had to make a decision. Three days after the accident the specialist at the ICU silently propelled me into his office and shut the door. I tried to focus and take note, though the world I saw now was filmy, smeared. Down south was a girl who had been born with a congenital disease. She awaited a new heart.

He showed me photographs: a child, two years younger than mine, also connected to a bank of machines. A sweep of brown hair across the pillow, a face tight and pale, eyes enormous, punched underneath with grey. And there beside her on a chair was the mother, brow knotted and mouth too small for joy, staring at the camera. She looked too old to have a child that young. The specialist murmured something about years and no hope, but if I said yes now they could run the tests and see, and if there was compatibility they could do it probably within two days. I looked away from those photographs, that anxious pieta of mother and a child half-grown but as good as dead, unless she could have my son's heart. I turned away and thought of golden-haired Sonny, except the back of his head was smashed like a broken flagon, the blood staining the pillow, blood darker than wine. How come it wasn't enough that he was being taken from me? Did I have to give even more?

He could live for weeks or years or never, connected to tubes that fed and ventilated him. Or he could recover and be all body, no mind, and I would have to look after him for the rest of my life. Or he could wake up one month or ten years later, and walk out the hospital door as if he'd just been having a long, long sleep. The difference between brain death and a coma was explained again and again by the resident, the neurosurgeon and the paediatric specialist. A coma was a state of unconsciousness where although the brain was injured, it continued to function. It had the chance to heal. It definitely appeared Sonny was brain dead.

Definitely appeared? What's that supposed to mean?

Well, said the neurosurgeon, there are some signs of a state of coma as well.

What signs? I asked.

Small ones, he said.

They were smaller than small. More likely aberrant readings of the tests. Which they would run again, of course. But I had to accept there was no hope. There was the literature. Articles and dissertations which they mentioned, documenting the ninety-eight per cent of cases, like Sonny, who could be kept living but who would never live.

Sonny was alive but not alive. I stared again at the photograph of that child and her mother and forced myself to realise that that mother felt exactly the same way about her child as I felt about mine. I made the decision with a passion of bitterness in my heart. But I could not let just anyone cut into my beautiful boy's chest. I could not let a stranger slice through his perfect skin, warm and toasted from the far north's mild winters, which meant bare-topped escapades in the park, by the river, at the playgrounds. By the time I walked back into that room with its bank of glittering chattering machines, capable of monitoring and maintaining a life but not restoring it, I had decided but with an acid resolve. The girl, whose name was Amber Morgan, could have my son's heart but I would have to do it, I would. I wanted to reach into the tender body of my own child and take that heart out, feel the pulsing muscle beating for myself, then hand it over. Not some surgeon who never knew Sonny. Not anyone else, but the mother who loved him.

And Amber would have to come here. They would have to fly her in from the south and bring her right here to the hospital in Amethyst: no one was taking my son's heart away from the place where he was born.

By the time I expressed this to the medical staff through my tears and groans – all the muffled inarticulateness of a young woman unaccustomed to the demands of grief – I was resolute. It was by then morning, several days after the accident. Jean had been sitting quietly beside Sonny ever since she arrived, holding his hand when I needed to get away. I'd had a shower, changed my stale clothes and was drinking tea in the parents' room. A green uniformed assistant entered and rustled a bin liner. I sat beside it and pretended the noise didn't bother me.

And then Archie arrived, and came to me where I sat at the window gazing out to the new day, seeing nothing of it. The view extended across town to the council property where he had been mowing the week before, when he'd heard the message yelled by Doug from his delivery van, that he was needed at the hospital, that Delia needed him. I had never admitted to needing him before. I thought I'd never needed anyone, just devoted myself to raising a boy whose father, a long way away, had vanished like a shadow. And now all that had ended in a sudden squeal of brakes. I wanted Archie. That afternoon, he'd run like a madman for his utility. And now, this morning, I needed him again. Archie, my friend and occasional lover, who had no children of his own but wanted Sonny, wanted me. Whose suggestions about the future, offers of marriage, of being Sonny's father, I'd not managed to accept because I'd had this idea about timing my answers and then the time was kicked away from under me that afternoon. As Archie walked into the room while the green man was slopping disinfectant across the lino tiles, I realised that he could do what I desperately wanted to do but knew I could not, slice into the body of my child and hand over his heart like the bud from a plant, to be grafted into a new life.

On the trolley in the ICU, at first glance Sonny just looked like a mischievous child who had escaped from another part of the hospital, climbed into the wrong bed and was pretending to be asleep. But he was connected to a respirator and heart monitor, and surrounded by so many blinking murmuring machines. And although he was clean and unmarked, where they'd cut away all his clothes and washed him down in order to attach the tubes and needles and pads, a closer look revealed the large red-brown patch on the back of his hair, which the nurses knew, as they'd always known, would be useless to clean off.

But before the procedure, the hospital authorities stipulated that only a qualified surgeon could perform the operation. Archie or I could be as close as we wanted, we could hold his little body around the chest, we could watch every millimetre of the scalpel's progress, but the extraction of the organ would be done by the state's heart transplant specialist, Dr Roger Salmon, who was flying in from Brisbane that afternoon. To ensure its optimum condition for transplantation, speed would be essential. Words which meant, in effect, that interfering, grieving parents would only hinder the process. The exact wording now lost, though it was repeated to me again and again. There was a stringent code of practice covering such procedures. Various personnel had to be on hand during the operation to ensure it was followed.

Archie had been my voice, my medium. He was intensely focused, as if he had put all but his most vital elements on hold somewhere. Shut down everything except what was absolutely necessary. Cups of tea and white triangles of hospital sandwiches were thrust before us, but he was indifferent. He was preserving his self-control, saving his energy for the task ahead. We barely left the waiting room until the preparations were done. Beside him I wept quietly and constantly. I was still seeing the image that haunted me: my son flying high up like a thrown toy. Still hearing the adrenaline-pumping screech of brakes, the dull thump of his body on metal. Afterwards Archie would have to live with the operation he had scrutinised: cutting out the heart of a child who was not even his. Afterwards, we both had to live with the memory of standing before Sonny's gaping chest, a hole of glistening purple tissue framed by flaps of ribs like the undersides of a bird's wings. Then Dr Salmon holding the heart, which I tried to grasp for a moment, right at the end, and which Archie prevented by closing his hands over mine. He held me so tightly it hurt.

Forty-One

> Consider your shelves first. If there is not at least one shelf in the kitchen devoted to cookbooks then you will need to rectify this immediately. Obviously the selection is vast, but the first rule to remember is that one can never have too many cookbooks.
>
> 'A Cook's Tour'
> *The Household Guide to the Kitchen* (2002)

The problem with recipes is that you never want to follow them to the letter, never have all the right ingredients, never have enough time.

Or maybe the problem was with me. I always consulted recipes, yet could rarely do what they said. And I didn't know why this was the case, I just felt in my bones that I somehow knew better, I always had.

In this case, I felt it in my blood. So when I took down the recipe for black pudding, or blood sausage, which I had made before, though not for years, I was instantly struck with its impracticality, for one, and its utter unappetising description for another. Chopped pig fat, diced onion, salt, pepper, spices, pig's blood and, of all things, fresh cream. This time the problem was not the ingredients, but the fact that I couldn't see how it would all bind together, let alone look palatable. Unless it was properly stirred, fresh blood would congeal and cook into something with the texture of sloppy scrambled eggs, but who would ever eat it? I couldn't imagine myself eating it. So I would have to adapt. These were going to be the finest blood sausages ever.

I fried onion in my best olive oil, until it was clear and sweet smelling. Then, with a gentler heat, I added the garlic, which I had pounded to a paste with rock salt. I added chopped smoked ham along with the fat. Then freshly ground black pepper, and some smoked paprika powder. From the garden I fetched some lemon thyme and two shallots. I crushed the former into the mixture and added a glass of red wine, then not quite a quarter of a glass of balsamic vinegar, then I cooked the mixture for a little while longer, savouring the scented steam in my face.

This would be the last time I ever cooked with lemon thyme. The oils released in these first few seconds of cooking were like the gifts of the Magi. I hoped it hadn't taken imminent death to make me appreciate that. I thought – but I couldn't quite remember now – I'd captured the joy of that first invisible spray of orange peel, the mouthful of coldest pale ale on a summer's afternoon, the warm and acidic anarchy of a cherry tomato picked straight off the vine, begging to be devoured and exploding on the tongue. The smell of freshly brewed coffee and its sly follow up, the cup that tasted nothing like the smell but was perfect in another way altogether. All the everyday smells and tastes of food, most of them now repugnant to a cancer-tainted palate. But I hoped it wasn't too late for all of that.

I added the rice, which I'd already cooked. The traditional English way was with barley or oatmeal, but I preferred rice and nothing about this dish was traditional anyway. Finally I stirred in the chopped shallots and some grated lemon rind before taking it off the heat. The sausage casings were all ready on the bench. The mixture alone would make some splendid sausages, which my family would love. I could have formed them then, and poached them lightly, then frozen them for one of those dinners when Archie would be too tired or busy, when sausages and mashed potato would be the best meal to have.

There was no need to add anything more. The bowl sat on the bench. There was no need to add my blood. I reached for the bowl.

Do eat this meal, it contains one secret ingredient.

I made this with love, my darlings.

The colour was shocking. Deep red, solid and opaque, with the density of paint. The pinky-brown sausage mix was soon purple-black.

I formed the sausages quickly, glad of the adapter on the Magimix which I had hesitated to buy years back. I could never have done this by hand. In just a few minutes, eight smooth fat lengths sat on a plate, glistening with promise and awaiting their fate. They were ready for poaching, although I decided to steam rather than immerse them. This took just ten minutes, while I cleaned up the kitchen and disposed of the evidence. Luckily I seemed not to have spilled a drop. After that I felt that a celebration was in order. From the bottom of the pantry I took a bottle of one of the softer shiraz blends, but after several minutes of futile stabbing with the corkscrew I realised that I simply didn't have the strength.

I suppose it was logical that I should feel as if I'd committed a crime – well, maybe I had, maybe there were health regulations preventing the serving of one's own blood in dishes, just as there were laws against burying one's own dead in the back yard – though I hadn't expected to feel guilt. But when Archie slammed the screen door minutes later I literally jumped.

He took the bottle, deftly extracted the cork and poured me a glass. His hands had that achingly summery smell, of two-stroke fuel and grass, despite the fact that at work he never mowed himself these days. Or maybe I was just imagining it.

He didn't ask why I felt compelled to drink red wine in the early afternoon. Instead he said,

I'll get some bottles that unscrew, Del. Easier for you.

Dinner that evening was a vegetarian pasta, which I picked at half-heartedly, although the girls enjoyed it. Daisy drenched hers in tomato sauce; Estelle, however was prepared to try the garlic cream that I'd prepared to accompany it. Dipping her bread in it she said innocently,

What did you do today, Mum?

Why did she ask this question? Estelle never wanted to know what I did during the day – she was eleven, no one else ever did anything during the day, certainly not boring adults, especially not dinosaur mothers who were meant to be resting anyway. Did she suspect something? Had she smelled something?

Nothing much. Why?

Just asking, she shrugged, already bored with the topic, and pushed her bowl away. Is there any ice cream?

Estelle had recently been asking for coffee sprinkled on her ice cream, which she then mixed to a puree and slowly licked from the spoon. Somewhere she had picked up that the flavour was sophisticated, yet her eleven-year-old tastebuds still craved the childish sensation of mushy ice cream, to be eaten as slowly as possible until the penultimate moment before it melted into oversweet milk. Daisy drenched her ice cream in chocolate sauce. Sometimes I thought all of Daisy's staple foods could be contained in bottles.

Replacing the ice cream bucket in the freezer I pointed to the meat section.

By the way, Archie, I said, with the door ajar at my face, the frosty air delicately wafting out, I've made you all some sausages.

His face lit up, he adored homemade sausages.

They're already poached, I explained. You'll just need to fry them.

He nodded again, contented with the prospect. Until he realised I was referring obliquely to the future. Then his face fell, he glanced at the girls, now TV-bound, and came to my side. I lifted my face to his, feeling too tired for anything more that night than the journey into bed.

Forty-Two

It was early morning, three days after I made up my mind about Sonny. Everything seemed suffused with an air of formality. I was much calmer than I expected to be. And I remember I was dressed in pastel pink, unconsciously but maybe in defiance of the state of mourning I was already expected to be in. The afternoon before, Jean had hauled me out for the one form of therapy she could provide, using the premises of Snip!, whose owner was happy to oblige and who kept me down the back of the salon, away from eyes and questions and clumsy half-spoken condolences. Jean set to work shampooing, massaging, trimming and blowdrying until she was satisfied my head had gone elsewhere for long enough. It worked for a while.

We gathered in a small alcove off the operating theatre. Sonny had been born in this hospital. Since I refused to let him be taken away, conditions were crowded. The heart transplant surgeon from Brisbane had brought his own team. Amber Morgan and her mother waited in another operating theatre. I would not meet them.

There was only one chair. None of us took it, after glancing around at each other and at it, as if by mutual agreement that if anyone were to sit it would be me. The surgeon, his assistant, the anaesthetist, and two nurses materialised in the operating theatre, followed by the blue-clad figure of Archie. We stood in a bubble of silence. Jean was looking at the centre of the room and the white hump on the operating trolley surrounded by its retinue of electrical assistants, all of us, including me, waiting for some sort of cue.

Archie stepped up to the body of my son, as the assistant surgeon drew back the sheet to his waist, stared for a few seconds, then cupped his large hand across the gold curls. Then he turned towards me, summoning me with his eyes. Tight, brittle, frozen as I was, I could have dissolved into a puddle on the floor. I could have fainted, wailed, screamed or vomited. That was why I knew I couldn't stand right there next to Sonny and hold him in his final living moments while his heart was removed. That was why Archie was doing it instead. I stepped over, into the pool of fluorescent light, and kissed the child who would soon be dead, kissed him not for the last time, but for the last time in his life. I kissed him before I allowed him to be killed.

In those few seconds when I bent over I could have gathered him to me, I could have held him forever, thinking he would simply open his eyes and smile at me, as he did, morning after morning of his life. If I had remained close I would never have let go. I turned away, rigid, afraid, wondering if I should leave altogether. Except I owed it to everyone to stay, Sonny, Archie. And to the mother of Amber Morgan, who – I had to believe this, I had to keep telling myself this – felt exactly for her daughter what I felt for my son.

For the whole time, even when Dr Roger Salmon brought the scalpel down and the blood glistened in a sudden streak, Archie remained still and steadfast, as close to Sonny as he could, cradling the lower half of his body as if he was bearing a bowl of fragile glass. The surgeon's back was to me, but I could catch his expression reflected in Archie's eyes, glowing above his mask. When the loud cracks came indicating my son's tiny ribcage had been opened up, Archie's head moved up. I came closer then, still wrapping myself tight in my grief and apprehension, and the surgeon turned and looked straight at me, his eyes asking, *Did you understand it would be like this? Do you still want to stay?*

There was a pause. Then I nodded, and Dr Salmon's shoulders moved forward as he groped deep into Sonny's body. This was when I started to shudder, however I would not, I could not, leave.

No one spoke. The only noise was the clink of a scalpel or scissors tossed into steel dishes, and the general low-key hum of the machines. Surgical theatre staff were notorious for chatting through operations, exchanging stories of weekend capers or telling jokes or listening to music. What would they be doing if this were a routine operation? Jean pressed the play button on the portable tape player we had brought in and the sounds of 'Teddy Bear' filled the room. The percussive reminder of the everyday pleasures of my child was too much and finally, as the operation continued, I sat down in the chair. Even though the procedure was swift and precise, the waiting was forever. The next song was 'Always On My Mind'. Jean moved to turn it off but I held her arm. I wanted to keep his favourite music going.

Suddenly Archie was leaning further forward. The surgeon had released the heart. He cupped it in his hand. I could see it clearly. It startled me. Its glistening rawness was more confronting than I had thought possible. But Archie through his mask kissed the air in the direction of the ripe purple organ, as if blessing it for its new life. Tears that pooled now made tracks down his paper mask. That was when I lunged forwards, crying aloud, my chest jerking, my mouth loose as I tried to reach out for Sonny's heart. I wanted my own sliced out instead, and stopped forever.

Archie held me back as the heart was held up briefly while the surgeon snipped through the final strands anchoring it. Everything told me this was the right thing to do. Yet there was a cold and empty chamber inside me, as if my own heart had been taken out. I sat, rocking on the plastic chair, barely registering the sounds and movements around me. Hands of someone – the grief counsellor, the social worker? – brushing across my back like falling pages. Jean turning down the volume of the tape. Elvis singing something about not holding you, all those lonely, lonely times. Jean taking my hands. Archie standing by the operating table looking undecided, whether to stay there by Sonny or over with me. Then Dr Salmon disappearing, along with the assistant surgeon and the rest of his team.

After that it was over within seconds. The heart was now an organ, wrapped in sterile cloths, placed in a polystyrene box on a trolley, and travelling to the operating theatre next door. The machines were all switched off, the tubes and needles and catheters pulled out. The noises silenced. The remaining surgeon stepped up and repaired the hole in my son's chest, pushing back the bird-wing flaps of his ribcage and stitching up the incision with delicate movements. Gently, one on either side, two nurses commenced washing him and by the time he was dried I was ready and composed. Jean and I dressed him in the clean outfit we had brought along, the ridiculous amateur costume of pale blue satin and silver foil rhinestones, but which was his current favourite. Finally, Jean went to fetch us a drink of water and I stayed there for an hour or a year, combing my fingers through Sonny's angelic curls, stroking his cheeks and kissing his forehead as he slowly descended into the chill of true death, leaving me with the echo of a song that was always on my mind.

Forty-Three

> Your garden will outlive you. This is rarely taken into consideration, especially when trees are planted. Think very carefully about how you will stock this garden. If you want to be remembered by enormous pines that last into the next century, go for it. But do you really want the grandchildren to be cursing you as they spend huge amounts on storm damage or new sewerage pipes?
>
> 'Your Garden's Future'
> *The Household Guide to the Garden* (2004)

Lydia finally laid an egg. Of course, she could have been shamming, claiming another hen's as her own. She'd done it before – most of them had. But there was more than a sly look about her as she sat in the laying box, there was almost a look of contentment. And the egg was smaller than any of the others, as pale as milky tea. I congratulated her and in return she pecked me on the wrist. As I set about collecting the other eggs and scattering the feed it dismayed me to see that she had drawn blood. The chickens' claws had scratched me plenty of times, and with complete justification as over time I'd subjected them to the humiliations of lice-spraying or wing-clipping. But their pecks had never hurt, they'd been more like kisses than jabs. I closed the gate and sat on the garden chair, nursing my wrist and aching with a foolish sort of sorrow. To take so keenly the rejection of a hen – a ridiculous, intractable one at that, the silliest of all the chickens – showed I wasn't doing as well as I had thought. I considered returning to bed for the day. But I spotted Archie up on the back verandah, gazing down, and I could see that crease between his eyes. As I walked back up the yard he sang out.

Phone call for you. He jerked his head towards the house.

But again when I went to the phone the line was silent. Silent yet not empty. I said hello a few times then shouted, Just piss off, will you! and jammed the phone down so hard it jumped back out of its cradle on the wall.

Who was it?

I don't know. Someone keeps ringing then hanging up, or when I answer it there's no one there. What did they say to you?

Nothing. Just someone asking to speak to you.

Who? A man or a woman?

A woman. I think. Hard to tell.

He followed me back outside.

What is it, what's wrong?

I don't know, I said. Can't work it out. Anyway ... beautiful morning. Think I'll go for a walk before I start work on a new chapter.

He rubbed my shoulder briefly as I passed. Did he know how drained I was, did he know I would barely write a word that day? But perhaps it was only the lack of sleep.

After several nocturnal visits to Mr Lambert's front lawn, my project there was complete. But then Daisy brought home a jar of tadpoles from a school excursion, and I thought about what the council inspector had said. I tipped half of them into the shady pond by the clump of golden cane palms, and saved the rest.

Taking my trowel and a two-litre ice cream bucket, I sneaked out again one night, after eleven o'clock. There was a small gap behind his agapanthus clump before the front porch rose a good eighteen inches above. The soil was damp. In no time I dug a hole for the container, which I filled from Mr Lambert's own tap. Several sets of headlights swept past as I crouched there, but fortunately in these suburbs no one cared if a tracksuit-clad woman bearing a silver potting trowel was lurking in a front lawn close to the midnight hour. Folded back, the agapanthus leaves concealed the makeshift pond. After the chlorine evaporated, the water would be ready. Fresh tap water was deadly for tadpoles, I'd learned. Also that in certain conditions, some tadpoles, who might have been nearly dormant for months, would quickly develop into metamorphs. Fully grown frogs, just weeks off.

A week later I returned for an inspection. Now I could see by the torchlight that algae was forming nicely, blossoms of blackish green gathering around the sides of the ice cream bucket. There were also some wriggling things. So I tipped the tadpoles in, brushed back the cold strips of the agapanthus and returned to bed.

Dear Delia
Guess what? It worked! In fact, my girlfriend and I both went shopping and, as well as sheets, we bought new pillows, a quilt, and matching Hers and Hers towels. We also put a set of saucepans and some new plates on lay-by. I've already thrown out all the takeaway containers and plastic forks. We're moving into a new place together!
Desperate.

Dear Desperate
I think you mean His and Hers towels, don't you? Which, by the way, have been out of vogue for thirty years.

Forty-Four

After we left the hospital we went straight to the Paradise Reach Motel, where Jean had checked in when she arrived. Not that she had spent much time there during the last week. She made me tea with brandy and sugar and produced crackers and cheese from somewhere while I sipped and nibbled what I could between sobs that were diminishing from sheer weariness and the sedatives a doctor had prescribed. I wondered where Archie had got to. I presumed he'd returned to his place to sleep.

That night I dreamed I had watched Sonny's chest being opened up and in my half-sleep felt fear and panic until I reminded myself I was asleep and I pushed hard through to the surface of that nightmare until I woke. *It was no dream ...*

Awake, sweating, panting for air, I sat up in bed to find it was not even dawn. Beside me in her bed Jean was also awake.

Are you all right? Do you want a drink of water?

Yes, please. There was a sudden parched feeling in my throat that I hadn't been aware of until she asked. I drank two glasses and still felt thirsty. My head ached. My bones ached. Had I run a marathon the day before?

The days that followed held me in this stupor of confused exhaustion, where I slept for brief periods but felt like I was awake, and where the waking hours were like a hideous dream. Life and death gripped me in some sort of vice, both squeezing hard from either side. And somewhere in the middle was the heart of my son, which I had sent off into another life.

Archie still didn't appear. I thought he'd abandoned me. I drifted about in a daze. Attended to the coffin. The funeral arrangements. Documents and forms, which I signed without reading. Bunches of flowers wilting everywhere, food going off, and Jean taking charge.

After three days of this, I decided it was the sedatives, and so I cut down on them. I had to wake up properly and face whatever awaited me, whether I slept or not. And the future that beckoned, which I was not sure I wanted now that it seemed not to include Archie as well.

Trendy psychobabble was beginning to talk about *closure* then. The importance of the funeral, the mementos, the conversations. Keeping alive the memory but at the same time accepting what had happened. I was told that this was closure, that I needed it, that everyone who'd lost someone did. But I disagreed. I didn't need any more closing off. Another door shut, locked, bolted for good. Archie disappearing was only more of it. I needed opening up, if anything.

But coping ... That was another topic altogether. Coping was what you did when death struck. Coping was what people admired you for. They didn't realise that they would *cope*, just the same as you. *I don't know how you cope.* People said this to me constantly in the ensuing months.

There was nothing admirable about coping, it was almost like a malign spell, one you didn't have the special knowledge to undo.

I coped because there was nothing else. When the world had shifted so dramatically and left me contemplating the yawning space left when one day I was a mother, and suddenly not, I was unable to process my feelings. Overwhelming everything was that hole in my chest, where the grief was funnelling up from some unrelieved and endless source. This was what I was meant to close. But this was what coping was. This was what you did. Fed off your tortured emotions like they were the only nourishment on earth. And while I had lost two people, my mother had finally found me.

Forty-Five

Care of the dying also involves care of the living.

'Final Things'
The Household Guide to Dying (forthcoming)

This is disgusting.

Jean had brought over clear tomato soup, a speciality of hers, and was poking around in the freezer and so I told her what I'd made.

I breastfed them, didn't I?

That's hardly the same thing, she said, peering at the plastic container as if it were full of maggots.

How come my breast milk was okay but not my blood?

I didn't add that Archie had drunk my milk a couple of times, not because he liked the taste, but because he thought it might be erotic (it wasn't).

Delia! For a start there's no goodness in blood, she said.

That's not true. It's full of iron.

Well, feed them iron tablets, if you want. But these? Anyway, pig's blood is nutritious, but why do you think yours would be?

Jean had read the same gastronomic authorities as I had, of course; she'd introduced me to most of them. But she hadn't read as I had about the Aztecs, who made corn tortillas with blood. The Aztecs, who were heavily into the commodity of blood, who ritually bled and sliced their sacrificial victims then skinned them before they were barely dead then wore their skins, still dripping with whatever blood was left after all the savage fun. Corn was a staple of the Aztecs. So, it seemed, was human blood. It must have been logical to combine the two, like elements, making a powerful magic, undoable. The tortillas became sacred food, images of the sun itself, a god who'd sacrificed himself in fire. The idea of blood and corn tortillas had become irresistible until I was on the verge of more ritual purification myself, more bloodletting and saving and cooking – with none of the glorious public display of the Aztecs, though some of its magic – until I realised I could not get the right corn. And that I wouldn't have had the strength to grind or knead it. Still, it was a compelling idea.

When I told Jean about it, she only sighed.

I truly don't know why you get fixated on such ideas. First the coffin, then that photo business, now blood sausages and tortillas, for god's sake. Why can't you just deal with this like any normal person?

Always the mother, Jean, always brisk, authoritative, pragmatic, even with her daughter in the last months of her life.

And then all that stuff you've been talking to Archie about – getting a girlfriend or whatever. How do you think that makes him feel?

So, they'd been talking. I let the comment pass.

It's unnatural, she added.

Yeah, well, so's this. What's natural about all of this? Having your tits sliced off, half your liver out, taking in weedkiller through your veins and still not beating the fucking disease?

I whipped my scarf off. There were a few strands of hair left, making my head look like that of an old doll, pulled to bits by too much possessive love.

It's all in here, the cancer, I said, tapping my head. Is it any wonder I get funny ideas? And I know I'm meant to be writing a book on it, but I don't know what a normal way of dying is any more. All I know is I'm not just going to disappear without a trace.

She said nothing.

It's me, Mum, I said, quietly, sweeping an arm around to indicate the food, the coffin, the house. I want to leave little parts of myself so they'll remember I was here, they'll always know how much I loved them.

And then she began to cry. I could only recall her crying once before, when she first arrived at the hospital before Sonny died. But after that she had remained dry-eyed. Even at the funeral. Which had consoled me immensely. Knowing that Jean was firm, stalwart. That was important to me when everything had broken apart. I loved her more for her lack of tears.

Mum. I grabbed her and held her tight, her tears now suddenly softening me to my stomach.

You know, she murmured into my shoulder, you know more than anyone what it's going to be like for me. You're my only child.

I do, yes, I do. And that's why I want to leave something special, different. I had nothing of Sonny's, you know. I buried it all away for too long. I thought his things would remind me and it would be unbearable over the years, but I was wrong, wasn't I? It was reminding that I needed.

She wiped her eyes and held her head back to look into my face, brushing away a meagre strand of hair from my forehead as if I was three again and she was soothing away a fever.

So what have you left for me? she said.

You'll see. I'm leaving something for you all.

Dear Delia
I've now made fruit cakes from every one of my recipe books (and believe me, I have a lot). None are good enough. The wedding is getting closer and closer and I want this cake to be just perfect. Can you please *give me your recipe?*
Mother of the Bride.

Dear Mother of the Bride
I might.

Forty-Six

Sonny's funeral was a simple affair. The day after the operation I felt I had turned into some ancient swamp creature, a loose mass of pulpy flesh, with no bones, and a primitive brain. Making decisions and taking actions were too hard. Perhaps if Jean hadn't been there someone else might have taken over – Mitchell or even Pearl – but I clung to Jean's calm efficiency. As soon as Al had the coffin ready, the local funeral service gave us a day, a time, placed the advertisement in the paper, drove us there and back. The service was brief. Words were said, and songs were played at the cemetery chapel. Not Sonny's songs: I couldn't bear that. No one had it in them to find a way of expressing hope or comfort from so much sadness, not even the minister whose job it was to find solace where others could not.

And after Sonny was winched into the ground and I threw in a bunch of flowers someone had given me, I turned away to see Archie. He'd jumped out of his utility and was running towards me across the cemetery grounds.

I'm sorry I'm late, he panted. I came as fast as I could. There was an accident on the highway that held me up.

Where have you been? I sobbed.

Long story. I'm here now.

He held me and caught his breath as we stood beside Sonny's grave. He was unshaven, still wearing the clothes I'd last seen him in at the operation. Eventually he explained what he'd been up to.

And I'm sorry, he said again, but I'm going straight back there after this.

Don't be sorry, I said.

The others said their goodbyes and left. Archie and I hugged tightly before I waved him off in the utility. Then Jean and I went to Mitchell's bar, which he had closed for us for the rest of the afternoon. Pearl, Tara, Doug. Monty the clown. Sonny's classmates. His teacher. Others I didn't know. I drank gin and tonics like they were lemonade, accepted the pats and hugs, nibbled at egg sandwiches and cheese on biscuits when they were pressed onto me, and half listened to all the words about Sonny being at peace, about that other little girl having a chance of life, about being able to move on now the funeral was out of the way, until finally I laid my head on the bar and wondered when I would see Archie again.

Come back home with me, Jean said when it was all over. What do you have to keep you here? And you can always return when you want.

If Sonny had been the reason for staying in Amethyst then it seemed Jean was right. At the caravan she gathered up the clothes and other belongings while I fetched empty boxes from Mitchell's bar. They were all liquor boxes, the perfect size for books. I packed them carefully, sprinkling a handful of naphthalene flakes in each box before sealing them with tape. In one dark green box stamped Jameson Irish Whiskey, I placed the titles I would take. Nothing logical or thought out, just ones I instinctively wanted to keep with me for the moment. The set of novels by the Brontë sisters, which I had bought second-hand. *Crime and Punishment*, which I wanted to re-read. *The Metaphysical Poets*, which had so unexpectedly captured my imagination and in which I'd discovered poems about mowing and gardening. *Mrs Beeton's Book of Household Management*. Paperback copies of the three Alice Walker titles which Pearl had found somewhere for me after I'd told her how wonderful *The Color Purple* was. *Lolita*, which I was just beginning to understand. And an illustrated edition of *The Owl and the Pussycat* which I had read many times to Sonny and which I think I had enjoyed more than he.

The caravan was always tidy despite the clutter, but now it looked fresh as if waiting for new occupants to go on holiday. Sonny's things were packed away, and I didn't want to look at it any longer, stay another minute more than I had to. Now I'd made the decision I wanted to go. Holding one box of books I joined Jean outside where she held the bags. I would ask Mitchell to send the rest of the boxes on.

At the door of the taxi back to the Paradise Reach Motel, juggling bags and books, I was about to turn around and speak as I'd been doing several times in the previous days, and say the ordinary things you say to your child, like, Hurry up, we have to leave, or, Have you done your teeth yet?, things said without thinking because your child is like a shadow by then, and these things come automatically from your mouth – when I remembered, and stopped.

Can we go straightaway? I asked Jean. Can we just leave?

I've already booked the seats, she said. First thing in the morning.

Forty-Seven

> The dying person may not wish to remain in their own bedroom. Often there will be a quiet, airy and sunny corner of a room, or one that can be converted to make these final days as pleasant as possible. An outlook is preferable, ideally onto a small water feature or another restful aspect of a garden. Never refer to this room as the sickroom.
>
> 'The Palliative Care Room'
> *The Household Guide to Dying* (forthcoming)

My office, an enclosed end of the back verandah, was gradually becoming a room for resting. Archie decided to paint it. He chose eau-de-nil. I wasn't a particularly green person, inclining more to purples and reds, but I now found the prospect of being surrounded by pale green a soothing one. It was as if I wanted to be washed in the sea. We installed a daybed and I collected from around the house all the green furnishings that I had barely been conscious we owned. Estelle's old cotton baby blanket, milky green. Two sage-coloured cushions from the front room, shabby but serviceable. An ancient satin quilted blanket, the colour of seaweed, that I remembered adorning my parents' double bed when I was a child. And for the timber floor, a small mat that I found in the laundry.

In this room, for the first time ever I found I could banish the children. Archie and I had never once kept our bedroom door shut, nor theirs, and there was nowhere in the house that was forbidden to them. I'd wanted them to feel welcome in every corner because as a child I had often felt like a stranger in my home. I would never forbid them my books, deny them access to the kitchen, stop them from using tools, discourage them from making or cooking or constructing anything at all. Even when I was at work at my desk, my door was open. Even when they were distracting me to the point of desperation.

But after the green room was aired of the new paint smell, the furniture replaced and my books and papers brought back, I felt possessive of it. I found I liked being in there on my own. I wondered if it was because it would be the only private place for me before I died. Maybe I was making the most of the solitude.

Or maybe it was more than that. One of Archie's building contacts was a colour consultant. She had told him some interesting facts about the colour called eau-de-nil. Apparently it was suitable to accompany death. The ancient Egyptians took the business of dying to a rarefied level. They knew death well, they studied all its aspects, accommodated its every requirement. The colour of the Nile was revered, almost sacred. Walls of death chambers were painted in the same shade, to lull the deceased into the afterlife. It would lull me if I wanted, Archie had said to me.

I had argued that there was no point. Why repaint a room, albeit a small one, just for a few months? But he seemed to think it was important, and it did only take him an afternoon. And afterwards, lying on the daybed, I thought I could see why – I thought I could *feel* it. He had painted the ceiling and window and doorframes an aqua green, the walls eau-de-nil. The result was a wash of gentle colour that managed to make me feel warm and cool at the same time. It seemed to hold me, like the breast of a river. I could almost see the feluccas floating downstream.

The Egyptians had got it right. The journey from life to death to afterlife would be as calm and as natural as a lone boat gliding down to the delta.

Dear Delia
I am about to become a mother for the first time, and while I've read a lot of books on the subject I would really value any advice you might have. What do you think I should be prepared for the most?
Expectant.

Dear Expectant
You will have been told that exhaustion, lack of time, lack of sleep, lack of a sex life, and the inability to focus, to finish a meal, a conversation or even a sentence, are all things you should expect to experience in the first months or years of motherhood. None of these comes close to what you will have in abundance and for the rest of your mothering life: guilt.

Forty-Eight

In Sydney, at Jean's home, my childhood home, the climate was drier, cool. I went back to taking the diazepam and disappeared under the feather quilt in my old bed. I slept for three days, Jean coming in to bring me soup and tea, to rub my back and hold my hand, or just sit there, reading or knitting or doing nothing at all.

When I emerged from it and woke up properly I felt calmer. Empty but not quite as hollowed out. My raw grief now made a space for Archie, and I was wondering when I would see him again.

I had taken a shower one morning, dressed properly for the first time in days, in clean jeans and a white cotton sweater, and had even eaten. Jean had gone back to work, and as her salon was nearby she would be returning at lunchtime. I was sitting out the back looking at the changes Jean had made in the garden in the years since I'd left. A new path in herringbone brick now curved down past the washing line to a raised pond. There were several sorts of citrus, including a lime. Beside me on the flagstone patio were pots of fuchsias, all in flower, purple and red, my favourite colours, the blossoms bending down, as fuchsias always did, in mild submission.

Tears were still wandering down my cheeks, but it was better than the flood. My chest had finally stopped heaving. The stone in it felt lighter. I was now just tired, not exhausted. When the doorbell rang I almost couldn't be bothered getting up but I dragged my way back into the house and opened the front door.

We stared at each other for a few seconds until I said,

Archie, you look terrible. And gathered him close.

He had circles around his eyes and hadn't shaved. I was chewed out by guilt and grief, but this was the man who had watched over my son's heart, keeping vigil beside the child who received my reluctantly given gift. Watching over her, for her sake and for mine.

He had followed Sonny's heart and the transplant team to the theatre where Amber lay prepared and waiting. He stayed while the operation proceeded, never leaving for the hours it took. And then learned that there were complications. Amber was taken to the larger teaching hospital down south by emergency helicopter, where the necessary facilities awaited her. Archie just got in his utility and drove for hours, keeping awake with coffee and determination, speeding back to Amethyst for Sonny's funeral, returning to Amber's bedside to see it through to the end.

How is she? I asked.

The morning I left they got her out of bed. She walked a few steps. Her mother told me she's breathing normally for the first time in years.

So it was a success?

Sonny's heart is doing a great job, he said. It looks like she's going to be okay.

We smiled at each other, blurry through our tears.

It was a good heart, I said.

One of the best, he said.

So it was impossible that Archie and I would ever part. Archie, who had shared the most opaque depths of my mothering. Who reached out with a courage and generosity that I couldn't. Who might stick the newspaper up between him and the rest of the household, who might forget our daughters' dinners or baths, but who could mind a dying boy's heart and ensure it was handed over to save another child. Who could watch over that child, barely leaving her side, who could efface himself like that, having no claim, no relationship, no obligation, but who could do it because he knew I would want it.

We have confronted death, Archie and I, and survived. When death came snarling at our heels, we turned around and faced it down. When Archie leaned close to Sonny's heart, the roar of death was silenced. To regard the balance of life like that, small but pulsing tightly, hot and slippery, smelling ferrous and earthy like the ground from which we are meant to have been made, is to vanquish all idea that death might triumph. *Death, be not proud, though some have called thee Mighty and dreadful.* I had disagreed with Donne but deep inside I knew he was right. Death would always come, but it could not always gloat in victory.

Forty-Nine

> The authorities will tell you that despite all the care bestowed on a family – fresh air, clean water, healthy food, sensible clothing and, above all, love, comfort and guidance – disease will invade the protected domain, and death strike in mysterious and arbitrary ways. But what they will never say is that beyond death there is something more. If your dying person is a child, you will need to know this.
>
> 'Confronting Death'
> *The Household Guide to Dying* (forthcoming)

There is nothing exceptional, original or inspiring about wanting to be a good mother. Don't all mothers want to be good?

In my mother's time, between the ages of twenty-five and thirty-five were perfect. Any earlier, and there was the risk of immaturity, of being tied down before you really knew what you wanted in life. Any later, the shame of being mistaken for your child's grandmother at the school gate. Well, they did have babies at twenty-one. Sometimes eighteen. But anyone working hard at rising above their situation, as many in the suburbs were, didn't.

Jean finished her apprenticeship, worked for two years (the house deposit), married my father, then worked for another five years (the house loan) before setting up her own business. After establishing a strong clientele she produced me at twenty-eight, thus enabling her to return to her career full-time before she turned thirty-five and satisfy everyone's requirements that she devote herself to her child in her crucial formative years; that way, she could cultivate her business before it became too late to ascend the greasy pole that was career advancement for women in the 1980s.

If you called hairdressing a *career*. I found out later – when I met university people, creative people, people like Van – that many didn't.

Jean did everything exactly right. She managed her salon and reared me with sleek calm. She was fond and caring. She was not a great deal of fun but back then good mothers weren't meant to be fun: they were serious, restrained, dedicated.

In those days a neighbour collected me the few afternoons each week when Jean couldn't leave the salon early enough. Back to idle sessions of biscuits and chocolate milk and afternoon cartoons until she fetched me at five-thirty sharp, whirling me back home where neat piles of clean washing awaited, folded that morning while she had listened to the news and sung out about teeth and library bags. Home to thawed chops or prepared casseroles which she would never have forgotten to take out of the freezer in the mornings. Afterwards into pyjamas that always matched, hair that was always brushed before bed, and stories that were always, but always, read.

Jean managed all this without going grey, gaining or losing weight, without slapping or ever yelling that I can recall. She sipped wine while stirring the gravy or mixing the salad dressing or grating the cheese, or doing whatever wonderful things she always did for dinner each night. She read books for her own pleasure, knitted, kept up with the latest TV shows, and went to the occasional movie or play with friends, while somehow all the time smoothly managing the quiet personality of my father, whose interests were elsewhere. Such as his study, where his new cassette player and radio deck absorbed his attention. Where he read in privacy. Or the shed, where tools were ritually oiled, sharpened and polished, then used to make odd items like whatnots or doorstops, which somehow never seemed to be to Jean's taste.

From the moment I was conceived, Jean did everything right, without appearing to try. Confident, clever and beautiful. Coped with dignity when Frank suddenly died from heart failure. Resisted the pity that was the right of the younger widowed mother.

My mother was definitely a good mother.

Such a good mother that she saw Van's musical charm, his whimsical manner and his carefree lifestyle for the clouds of coloured smoke they were, long before I did. Such a good mother that she told me he was worthless, begged me to have an abortion and probably even anticipated his cowardly departure before he broke my heart somewhere in the second trimester.

Such a good mother.

My resentment at that boiled inside me, taking up almost as much space as the growing baby. By the time I could see that whimsical verged on wilful, carefree on careless, that Van was probably not rapt in me and obviously not responsible, I also saw that my mother was right. How I hated that.

Of course a good mother plans her children. They don't come too early in life to invoke implications of carelessness, sluttishness or ignorance. A bad mother is definitely a bad planner. Bad at reading calendars, for instance. Bad at counting, especially in units of fourteen or twenty-eight. Bad at making decisions about men. Bad to decide to stick with a man just because they are having a baby together.

I was not a good mother.

A good mother doesn't lose track of dates, for starters.

A good mother doesn't lose her child's father.

And a good mother certainly doesn't lose her child.

The actual words amongst the yells and screams were indistinguishable. I had the radio on in my green room, listening to the evening news, and The Simpsons was on the television down the hall in the lounge room, so I had to get off the daybed to find out what was going on. Before I reached the kitchen there was a crash, and I entered to see a plate shattered on the floor, a mess of red and orange everywhere. Archie was standing at the door looking tense, Estelle was waving her arms around and yelling something about there never being anything to eat, Daisy was sobbing and bending down, trying to pick up the pieces.

I didn't bother asking if it was accidental or not. Archie would surely not have thrown a plate, but even if he had, at either of them, I couldn't have blamed him.

He's burned the pizza again! yelled Estelle. You can't expect me to eat that! And she stamped off to her room and slammed the door.

I don't mind, Daddy, I'll eat it, said Daisy.

Then he shouted at her, or me, Don't be ridiculous, it's all on the floor! before stamping off himself. Daisy commenced crying again.

Even without the dropped – or thrown – plate, the kitchen was a mess. Everything seemed to be smeared red. Was there really that much tomato paste in one small jar? Grated cheese littered the floor, salami wrappers, onion skins and gutted capsicums exposing their insides were strewn across the bench. I didn't need to be told what had happened since it had happened to me often enough. Cooking what you think they'll like. Involving them in the process. Them fighting over who gets to roll the dough or grate the cheese. Telling *you* what to do when you're pretty certain you've done this once or a hundred times more than them. Grabbing for knives you're terrified will slice their fingers. You finally chasing them out of the kitchen. Or feeling like throwing a plate at them.

I wiped Daisy's tears and together we retrieved the intact slices of pizza and put them on a clean plate. I went into the girls' room where Estelle was sitting on her bed with her knees drawn up under her chin.

Come and eat dinner. Dad's made a big effort, you know.

No! He's put capsicum in it too. He *knows* I hate capsicum!

Nonsense. You eat it all the time, you had it last week in that Subway sandwich.

That was red! I hate *green* capsicum.

Ah, colour prejudiced now, are we?

And I hate you too!

She turned and faced the wall and put her pillow on her head. I should have known not to joke. But it was better than doing what I felt: grabbing the pillow, hauling her out of bed, sitting her at the table and prising her mouth open to force every mouthful down. Shards of plate and all.

Fortunately, I didn't have the energy for it.

Back in the kitchen I finished wiping up the mess, and put all the vegetable remains and ruined pizza in the scrap bin.

The chickens will always eat it, I said to Daisy, still snivelling on her chair at the bench. When it was done I went and gave her a hug.

Hungry?

She nodded.

What if I make you a sauce sandwich instead?

She nodded.

Then maybe a bit of ice cream?

Okay.

What if you take Dad in a beer first? I reached into the fridge and took out a Stella, his favourite. Tomato sauce sandwich, ice cream and beer for dinner. Whatever would my mother have thought?

Over the years I might have complained about Archie's minimal domestic involvement, but never once about his cooking. Around the home he wasn't incompetent, not at all, just neglectful, indifferent, content to let me do it. But in the kitchen it was a different matter: Archie was possibly one of the world's worst cooks. He could nurture a skinny shrivelled mandarin graft into astonishing new life or produce the most robust tomatoes grown from nothing but compost, but he was somehow missing that essential piece of wiring that told him how to assemble several basic ingredients to form a meal as simple as pasta with sauce or a roast dinner. Lately I'd stood around almost in a sweat from the effort of saying nothing while watching him put the vegetables in the oven before the joint of meat. Before the meat was even thawed. I'd quietly begged Estelle and Daisy to eat their burnt porridge or their watery mashed potatoes rather than criticise their father. Every cook in the world is a supersensitive human being and a parent cook is no different from the most temperamental culinary genius. Even if you know you've produced a spectacular disaster or something that's barely a cautious success, you feel that failure acutely and no one needs to tell you that, not even your children.

Later on, when I took Daisy to bed I wasn't sure if Estelle was asleep or sulking. I lay down with Daisy for a while until my breaths matched hers, then I pulled the blankets up and tucked her stuffed snake under her arm. I went over to Estelle's bed. Rigid. She was still awake.

Stelly. What's wrong?

She was crying. Such a rare thing for my eleven-year-old daughter, who at times was like a teenager. At other times like a toddler.

I know you don't really hate me, I said.

Yes, I do. I hate you because you're going to die. I hate it, I hate it, I hate it.

She turned around and grabbed me, holding tight and letting the tears flow properly.

This was her moment, and I would not cry. I couldn't let her know the hideous dread inside me. The fear.

I hate me too, I said. I hate it too.

Jean was right. The next day when they were all out I went to the freezer and tossed the blood sausages away. They were worthless. Maybe they had nutritional value, but that was irrelevant. My family would think they had bled me dry and eaten me up, rather than thinking I was leaving them an essential part of myself. There was still plenty of room in the freezer and I spent the rest of the week cooking up everything I could manage. All the ordinary simple dishes that I knew they would eat and that wouldn't insult Archie if left in there. The dishes I cooked and froze anyway, for the times when I was away or out or working. Chicken soup. Lasagne. Even if Estelle was vegetarian in another six months (a very likely prospect), then she would cope. The neapolitan sauce that could go with rice or pasta or couscous. The ratatouille (with red, not green, capsicum), the spinach pie. Then there was the creamy chicken curry that even Daisy liked. The shepherd's pie. And if Estelle went vegan, that would be too bad (I pitied Archie: that would stretch even my culinary patience) but there would still be things she could eat. Lentil burgers. Rice croquettes. Spring rolls. And then, for Archie, some more sausages, ordinary ones with pork and veal, garlic, pepper, chilli and other seasonings and flavours but nothing resembling blood. At the end, it looked as though I had prepared enough for a siege. Maybe in my mind it was. I'd considered involving the girls but the pizza incident made me decide not.

They thought they were in for some sort of feast, so on the Friday evening when they asked what was for dinner I surprised them by telling them I'd prepared nothing.

But you've been cooking all week, Estelle said.

That's right. My night off tonight.

Are we going out? Daisy said hopefully. I think KFC was on her mind.

Nope.

What then?

I hadn't fetched the eggs that day so I sent them down to the chickens while I made myself a cocktail. More of a ritual really, I wasn't sure I even wanted to drink it. I wondered if this was the last time I would feel like a martini. They came back with the eggs. Like a gift, there were four, and all perfectly clean.

Nothing from Lydia again, said Daisy.

That scatty, unreliable chicken. I named her well, didn't I?

I asked them to sit down and watch and listen. When I got the small saucepan out and then the bread, Estelle said,

Is that what we're having for dinner? Boiled eggs and toast?

Not just boiled eggs. The most perfect boiled eggs. My secret recipe.

They looked at each other doubtfully.

Listen, I said, over the years people have asked me in that column for a recipe for the perfect boiled egg and I've never told them my secret. You girls ought to be grateful.

Can I watch? Archie had appeared at the door, just home from work.

Sure.

And so I told them. And showed them. How you first warmed the eggs in a bowl of hot water from the tap. Then placed the saucepan of water on to boil. Then you sliced the bread. When the water was boiling you slid the eggs in with a spoon, and then straightaway put the bread in the toaster. As soon as the bread was toasted and buttered, you lifted the eggs out and placed them in the egg cups. Daisy's duck-shaped cup for her, Estelle's star-shaped one, and the glass ones for me and Archie. I handed a teaspoon to Daisy, who solemnly whacked every egg, then the knife to Estelle, who sliced off the tops. The yolks were like a thick golden sauce. The whites soft and moist.

There, I said, dipping a finger of toast in. That is how you make the perfect boiled egg. Nothing complicated. No timers needed. Nothing but the right sequence. I really don't think I could pass on a better recipe than this, for anything.

It helps, said Archie through a mouthful, having the right egg to begin with. I think mine was laid by Lizzie.

Dear Delia
What is the secret to a soufflé? My attempts are always too soggy and they sink in the middle.
Wondering.

Dear Wondering
I used to believe that the secret was to have eggs as fresh as possible. Which meant taking them from under your hens straight to the kitchen. But now I know differently. The world is divided into two sorts of people, those who can make soufflé and those who cannot.

Fifty

Amber Morgan's mother was a good mother. So good that she shielded her daughter from the celebrity-hunters that tracked down child recipients of donor hearts. So good that she protected her from what she imagined was the wolfish roaming of someone who had lost everything, and then given even more. Perhaps she feared that this other mother would return one day, to look hungrily upon her daughter's face, to place her palm upon her breastbone and feel the heart of her own son throbbing musically there. Feared how greedily she would have drunk in her daughter's life, maybe wanted to snatch it back.

That was the other reason I had taken myself off to Amethyst. The other reason that propelled my hasty preparations and sudden flight. The real reason I abandoned my family at a time when I needed them more than ever. I needed to find that girl who was now a woman, I needed to tell her how willingly I had given up my son's heart, and I needed to know that she was all right, that she had survived.

But Amber's mother could not possibly have known that my return would be fuelled by something different. It was simple desire. A dying woman is not so desperate for reconnection with a dead son. And she could not have known this because I didn't know it myself, not until after I went back to Amethyst and collected all the brittle pieces of my long-held grief and guilt. By that stage I just wanted to look upon the face of the person whose life had been illuminated by my own flesh. For the sake of peace. And yes, if you like, for closure.

How old would she have been by now? Nineteen? Twenty? She was a couple of years younger than Sonny, about six when she received his heart. After the operation, after Amber recovered from the complications, the Morgan family returned to live in Amethyst, which wasn't such a mystery. It was that sort of place, something I'd come to know when it held me to its breast at a lost and lonely time. It was full of people like Mitchell, and Tara and the other circus folk. They cared, but they also left you alone.

But I couldn't be sure if they were still there. Mrs Morgan would have known that I left town soon after Sonny died, and that Archie followed me. And she would have known that we never returned. She was not to know that we had made a whole new life way down south, and that I had two daughters. She was not to know that my desire to gaze upon her own daughter was nothing more than a necessary tying up of a long loose end that had trailed beside me for too many years, tickling my side, which I brushed at from time to time, but could never tear away. Mrs Morgan, Amber, I only wanted to say hello, and then goodbye.

Fifty-One

> Some people have streets, parks, swimming pools and entire cities named after them. Some just have their name on a headstone. What do you think your memorial might be? It is worth considering sooner rather than later, because later is too late.
>
> 'The Postmortal Condition'
> *The Household Guide to Dying* (forthcoming)

It was Mary, of all them. I was in my office when I heard a strange squawking that was nothing like the everyday boasting or bickering that formed the usual backyard chorus. I went outside to see a black and white cat disappearing over the back fence. The chickens were clustered in a corner of the yard, clucking and scolding like a bunch of old ladies harassed by schoolboys. All except Mary, who was high up in the mango tree plaintively calling. I had no idea how she'd got up that high, and neither, it appeared, did she. I tried to coax her down by calling, then I fetched the rake and gave her a few gentle touches with the handle, but still she wouldn't move and still she called.

I gave up and went back inside to work. My plan was to finalise the section about making legal wills by the end of the day, but her calls continued to distract me. She had never done this before. I went back out again and tried hosing her with a fine mist, but she remained stubbornly in place and out of reach.

It was just after two. It was no good ringing Archie. Even if he'd been working nearby he'd have told me not to worry, that she'd be fine and he'd deal with it when he came home. But there was something about her attitude and her calling, quieter now, but like a hopeless plea, that I couldn't ignore. Perhaps she was hurt. Although I felt a bit light-headed and wobbly, there was no helping it – I would have to get the ladder and rescue her myself.

At the highest rung I could manage without feeling I would fall, I was just close enough to reach for her when she screeched loudly in my face, jumped past me on the branch, lifted her wings and flapped gracelessly to the ground. She raced straight over to the others where they all muttered and tsked as if agreeing how outrageous it was, that someone thought she needed rescuing from a tree. Sometimes I wondered why I wasted my affection like that.

I stayed on the ladder for a minute to catch my breath and steady myself. From this height, I could see right over into Mr Lambert's back yard. It had been years since I'd had so much as a glimpse of the place. It had all changed. The plastic-shrouded outdoor furniture, the pebblecrete paths and the ugly brick incinerator were gone. At the very centre of the lawn was a large round garden bed, planted with weeping roses, just coming into bloom. I knew the variety well, the soft classic pink Dorothy Perkins. And right in the centre, surrounded by the mass of pink and green, was an old-fashioned sundial, weathered sandstone. Although I couldn't see them from where I was, I knew that the letters carved around the dial would spell out the words CARPE DIEM.

How long since Mrs Lambert had died? Perhaps it had been just shortly before he moved here and commenced his chopping and pruning. All I had ever seen was his hostility to the garden and now, perhaps, I understood why. He was clearing everything away to start again and make his own memorial. Then I noticed the outline of Mr Lambert standing inside his screen door. I didn't know how long he had been watching me. I descended the ladder slowly and went back to work.

Dear Delia
Do you have a good recipe for cooking stingray flaps?
I can't find one anywhere.
Fish lover.

Dear Fish lover
Stingray flaps? I don't even have a bad recipe for stingray flaps. I don't even know what they are. If you like seafood, why don't you buy the best mudcrabs you can find (currently $75.95 per kilo at the markets). Or Beluga caviar. Better still, both. Make a real meal of it.

Fifty-Two

Fourteen years ago the Morgans had moved into 49 Lark Street. They weren't there now when I knocked. Forty-nine was the home of a young married couple with two dark shiny cars in the driveway and three fair but just as shiny children playing in a painfully neat front room. They'd never heard of the Morgan family, although the husband's brow creased in what I thought was an instance of comprehension when I mentioned the transplant operation. After all, Amber was a local celebrity for some years. But then he explained that his family had only moved from Emerald five years ago, before politely closing the door in a that-is-that manner.

The next Morgans on my list were in a block of units closer to the main shopping strip. Three young women, flatting together. Morgan, the name in the phone book, turned out to be one of the girls' fathers, the owner of the place. Needless to say none of them was an Amber, though they were about the right age.

My last hope was the place in Nile Crescent. It was in the older part of town, which reached down towards the river.

The houses there backed onto lazy parklands of an uncultivated type, the sorts of places Archie was often employed to mow and strip away lantana, but where nature generally had her own way. Nothing much distinguished 3A from the other houses. Perhaps a bit smaller and a bit less surrounded by foliage, but it was the same raised weatherboard residence wrapped in wide verandahs that featured down the length of the state. As I approached I felt a stab of something inside my stomach, the same something I had felt several days before when I stood here in the early morning. Again, it was familiar, and looked to me like the sort of house where Amber Morgan would have lived. The wide wooden steps up to it were silver with age and the verandah boards brittle and shiny with exposure. The front door was open and the screen door was unlocked, and instead of a doorbell there was a wind chime, which rattled tinnily when I shook it.

I shook it again. And again. And after a long two minutes I realised no one was going to answer, so I pushed the door open calling out hello a few times. Inside it was dark and cooler, though there was an air of stuffiness that suggested either the front door wasn't usually left open, or that this was an old person's place. The furnishings seemed to confirm that. They were sparse, clean but shabby. Everything seemed generally faded, but with age, not sunlight. The kitchen was clean and tidy. A teapot wearing a cosy sat on the draining board.

She was out the back, latching the gate on an old chicken run which held three brown chickens. It was dilapidated but intact. She looked up and saw me and I was about to apologise when she gestured me down the stairs with one hand. In the other she was holding an enormous brown egg.

The door was open, I said, I called out ...

That's all right, she said, I'm used to people coming in.

It's a beauty, I said, looking at the egg. And your hens are gorgeous. What are their names?

She smiled. Do you know, dear, hardly anyone asks me that, no one thinks they've got names. Then she turned and pointed. This is Jenny, this is Patch, and this is Mrs Bennet.

I laughed out loud at that, I couldn't help it, and she frowned until I explained.

Well, she said, I named Mrs Bennet after the woman at the co-op. When I had lots of chickens, years back – she waved behind her which indicated a vaster collection of laying hens than the current shed suggested – I'd sell them through the co-op and that woman was the most picky, fussy woman I ever met. Inspect every egg like I was selling diamonds or something. This Mrs Bennet's just the same, always has been. A great fusspot. And how can I help you? she added. I hope you don't want eggs – she held hers up – don't get many for myself these days.

No, no eggs. My name's Delia, and I'm looking for Amber Morgan.

She was walking back up the steps into the kitchen. When she reached the top she turned around.

Well, my name's Margaret, and there's no Amber here.

I followed her in and asked further questions, but she was adamant. She couldn't help me. Didn't know what I was talking about, or who. I thought she was avoiding my eye as she moved about the kitchen, placing the egg in a bowl, getting a glass from a sideboard, putting the kettle under the tap. But, then, her eyesight seemed weak despite her spectacles, as she peered about in an unfocused manner. There seemed to be no way I could ask anything else without insulting her, or implying she was lying.

In her old-fashioned kitchen, with its single cold tap dangling high over a yellow porcelain sink, its table with a vinyl cloth patterned in daisies, its pastel crockery collected on the sideboard and its sad teapot and cosy, I felt out of place, too large.

It was nearly twilight when I went back to the car. I left with a feeling of profound depression in my chest. I apologised to Margaret in case I'd been unintentionally rude or intrusive, and she farewelled me politely enough. As I started the car I could see her standing behind the screen door, and when I glanced back through the rear-view mirror, she was still there.

The pit of depression grew. Short of knocking on every door in town, I had no idea what to do. I had asked at the post office, at the banks, at the newsagencies. I had gone to the community centre. The high school. The technical and agricultural colleges. I'd been to the hospital, knowing how confidential their patient information would be, but just hoping someone would have a lead, or someone would take pity on me, even as I despised myself for desiring pity, of all things.

At the circus, at Mitchell's bar, in the Elvis club meetings, at church, in the parks, in the grocery store, everyone was evading me, deliberately avoiding my question, lying to me outright – or otherwise the truth was that Amber and the Morgan family had gone, and no one had heard of them for years. I was wasting my time in Amethyst. I would not meet my son's heart again.

Hi. It's me.

How are you?

You were right, Arch, it's been a waste of time. Why didn't I listen to you?

Maybe because you just shot off? Without even telling us? Because you didn't even ask me in the first place?

Yeah, I know. I'm sorry.

He sighed into the phone. You would have gone anyway, Del. I know you had to.

You understand, I said, you were there, you did it. You know why I had to try to find her again.

Course. You're just not up to this, not now.

Are you saying I should have done this years ago?

I'm not saying anything like that.

We both breathed audibly for a bit. Archie sounded as tired as I was. After a moment I said,

Arch, I know I didn't find her, but what if I hadn't tried? I still had to come, because otherwise I would have gone on until the end never having known if I could let go of the idea or not.

But have you?

Yes. I have now. I don't have to see Amber Morgan. I can accept that. I'll be leaving first thing in the morning. I'll make it back in a few days. Tell the girls I'll see them soon.

I put the phone down and sat back on the bed. Yes, I was disappointed, deeply. But it was also true, what I told Archie. I accepted it now. It was natural to want to tie up the dangling threads before you died. These threads had tripped me up too often over the years. Long ago I'd accepted that Sonny's father would never reappear, so I'd tried to have something else for my child to go on in later years. But that last day, the day the world stopped then tilted and tried to slide me off its face, I was cheated. I never spoke the words that would have made Sonny so happy, and I held the regret in my chest like a toxin for all those years. Which was why, when I had been diagnosed with bilateral breast cancer two years ago, I was devastated, enraged and bitter – but unsurprised. It made sense that my breasts would have soured with remorse and sorrow over the years.

Chop them off, I'd said, like I was the Red Queen and they were the heads of knaves. Slice them away. I didn't need to consider it for long. What were breasts compared to a heart, a life? If only that was the cure.

Fifty-Three

> The will only takes care of certain things. Other matters can be resolved before death, and some of them are fun as well as practical. Suggestions include throwing a party and inviting all the guests to choose something from among your possessions. Closing your bank accounts yourself and demanding the bank give you cash. Informing the Tax Office in advance and securing an early refund. Handing the car keys over to a special friend or relative.
>
> 'Wills and Wishes'
> *The Household Guide to Dying* (forthcoming)

It had been weeks, and Archie still hadn't decorated his part of the coffin. The girls finished their sides, as far as they could. It still represented a challenge to repaint and redecorate, so every few days one or the other of them took a wide brush and blocked out all the hearts (Daisy) or skulls and crossbones (Estelle), replacing them with stars and arrows, monkey faces and lightning bolts. Estelle seemed to have settled on painting a red satin pillow on the top, while Daisy painted grass and flowers at the end. The lid remained undecorated, apart from a few coffee rings. By now it had become a table top collecting the usual household junk of pens, plastic cups, school newsletters, iceblock sticks, dried out marker pens, colour letterbox catalogues, bobby pins, Post-it notes, muesli bar wrappers and somehow, always, one odd sock. I'd asked Archie to clean it up a few times, and he ignored me. One morning he was drinking his coffee out on the front verandah, feet up on the coffin reading the paper. I took it personally. It was my coffin, after all.

Archie, can't you tidy up just once, for god's sake? Who the hell do you think will be doing this when I'm dead? I started picking up stuff.

He threw the paper down and got up.

Just stop it! Give it a rest, will you?

What?

This. All this. He waved his hands at the coffin, gestured at the rest of the house.

All this matter-of-fact, doing-it-right bullshit. Who gives a fuck if the place is tidy or not? Do you really think it matters? Really?

I stared at him.

Yes. It matters to me.

You're insane. You're ill and dying, and you're telling me all you care about is a clean house? He brushed past me and went inside.

I examined the junk mail I was holding. I did care about leaving the place clean and tidy, it mattered enormously to me to do that. But it wasn't all that mattered. I had always kept a neat and clean house, it went back to the days when I lived in the caravan and had to keep everything in place or otherwise be swamped by mess. And it was more than a matter of pride in leaving my house clean. More than anything, I feared that if I let domestic matters slip, Estelle and Daisy would feel insecure, frightened, that things were out of control. Things *were* out of control. Their mother was dying. But I just didn't want them to feel it, not before they had to.

He opened the screen door behind me again.

And if you think involving the girls by painting it is helping them cope ...

It's not hurting them, though, is it?

He glared at me, then shrugged. Maybe not, he said more quietly. He pulled on his jacket. And by the way, that bloody bastard has done it again, be careful if you go down the yard.

Why?

He jerked his head towards next door. He's chucked something over the fence, right down the back. Probably something noxious. I'm in a hurry, I'll clean it up when I get home.

I drove the girls to school slowly. I drove like a pensioner these days. Partly I was extra cautious in case my driving was starting to suffer without me realising it. Partly I was conscious my passengers were more precious with every passing minute. When I returned home I went down the back to see what Archie was talking about. There was indeed a pile of something tossed over the fence, but when I approached I saw it was nothing noxious. Nothing dead. Not even a weed. My hands almost shaking with the moment, with the implications of it, I bent and picked it up. A large untidy bunch of weeping roses, loosely tied with string.

I pushed my face into the soft mass of the pale pink blooms, still damp from the morning dew. Cut from the garden he had cultivated in secret and made beautiful for no one's eyes except his own. There were thousands of unsayable words in that gift Mr Lambert intended for me. Inside the house I found my widest vase, and arranged the Dorothy Perkins roses in it. They wept over the sides and onto the table.

Then I went back to the front verandah. Archie was wrong. I cared nothing for the clean house, just for what it represented. There was an orderly calmness and security in my house, and it didn't just happen. I made it that way. My daughters deserved everything that a home was supposed to be. Just the word *home* meant profound things to me. Home was where I wanted to be. After being out or at work or away somewhere, home was always where I desired to return. I couldn't help it – and I wouldn't apologise – for wanting to make the place where my family lived as comfortable as it could be, and whether or not Archie understood, keeping it clean was part of that. Cleaning to me was never an ignoble activity. Of course I yelled at the girls dropping chips and wrappers on newly swept floors, dirty clothes and wet towels on their beds. But the act of cleaning, like cooking, suspended from its context – which meant it was instantly unmade or consumed – was a source of simple pleasure. And for a writer, even a hack commercial writer, domestic work provided valuable thinking time. A lot of words had been written in my head while I ironed or mopped. I had often wondered if there was some neurological link between the gentle repetitive action of your arms wielding a broom or your hand stirring a pot and the ideas that filtered through to the front of your mind; some fusion between physical action and creative ignition.

I cleared everything off the coffin, carefully matching lids to pens, returning cups to the kitchen and taking papers to the recycling bin. I swept the verandah and trimmed the dead leaves from the trailing philodendron. I took the cyclamen that had refused to flower from the little planter table and tipped it into a shady spot in the garden. Left to itself, it might just come good in another season or two. I brought out the vase of roses and placed them on the table, where some of the blooms reached down to the floor. Then I fetched an old quilt, a pillow and a fresh pillow case, and my black Chinese slippers, and took them out to the verandah.

I opened the lid of the coffin and saw that I had been wrong. Archie had made his contribution after all. He had painted the inside.

When he returned with the girls that afternoon I was sitting beside it with the lid open. Intent on afternoon cartoons or computer games, Estelle and Daisy said Hi as they ran up the stairs on their way inside but I held my arms out as they passed and they melted into my embrace instead. Archie paused a moment before ascending the steps, as if he needed to assess my response.

I thought you'd like some poetry in the end, he said.

It's perfect.

The girls peered over and started to read aloud the lines Archie had painted in deep purple against a golden background, flowing italics that began with the words, *Had we but world enough and time …*

I was going to do a sonnet or something, he said, I reckon you can't go wrong with a bit of Shakespeare. But then I remembered how much you liked Marvell, all that stuff.

Yeah, that stuff, I agreed.

An age at least to every part, And the last age should show your heart. Estelle read more than Daisy but then stopped too. It wasn't quite as gripping as Philip Pullman, for sure.

That's great, Mum, can we watch the telly now?

They both disappeared inside. Then I said, Archie, Archie. And I was in his arms, and I could say nothing else. He had remembered what I had almost forgotten, how I would chant the lines to myself again and again. One of my most favourite poems, so witty, so wise, so urgent and fluent. And now not at my back but right before me, didn't I hear, didn't I see, time's winged chariot hurrying near? Gaze out, every day, towards the deserts of vast eternity? How much it must have cost him to paint those words, when every minute of every day was another flap of that winged chariot, coming nearer and nearer.

I'm sorry, Del. About this morning.

I held him tighter.

I know how hard it was for you to write that, I said. How hard it is for you.

He shuddered. A man's sort of sob, a tearless one but somehow more awful for that. I didn't want the girls to see this, not yet.

Come on, Arch, I said, we have to keep on. I'm not dead yet. And I've had a good day today. Really. Look at these.

What's that?

What Mr Lambert tossed over the fence this morning.

You're kidding? He examined them more closely. Dorothys, aren't they? Where'd he get them from, do you think?

He has an entire garden of them out in his back yard. I saw them the other day when I was up the ladder.

I sat down and picked up one of the stems, clustered with tiny half-open buds.

Gather ye rosebuds while ye may, I said.

Was that Marvell too?

Don't think so. Can't remember now. I held the stem right up to my nose, but there wasn't much scent. Is it just me, I said, or aren't these supposed to have any perfume?

Can't remember now. Archie smiled.

You know, I bet his wife was called Dorothy.

We sat together looking at the coffin. He pointed to the second stanza on the lid.

It's a bit too close to the bone, isn't it?

Maybe. But my grave will be a fine and private place. There won't be any finer, I said.

Archie. My beautiful, clever, wise gardener. Calm maker and tender of lawns. Calmest of all things, the lawn. Best of all people, a gardener. And then he explained that he thought on the outside of the lid he'd put one of my favourite expressions, along the lines of W.C. Fields: *I'd rather be reading*.

What about you save that for the headstone, I suggested, if it's not too expensive? Then I said, Except I will be.

Will be what?

Reading, of course. I pointed to the flowing purple script, the perfect poem he had transcribed for my eternity of repose.

Dear Delia

No, I did mean Hers and Hers towels. And I don't care if they're old-fashioned, nor does my girlfriend. We chose the same colour too, lavender. What I've been meaning to ask you is, how come you've always assumed I'm a man?

Fifty-Four

The cemetery at Amethyst had become greener over the years. The lawns less dry and patchy, the clusters of frangipani and stands of pampas grass and lines of palms taller, denser. There was more shade, and so the sunlight seemed sharper, if anything.

Beside the three graves of his great-grandparents and his great-great-grandmother, Constance, Sonny's headstone now looked like it belonged. It seemed to have developed a skin, mottled, slightly flaky, with a thin layer of lichen spreading up from the base. It was plain white granite. It stated his name, SONNY BENNET, the dates of his birth and death, and in much smaller lettering at the bottom, *Only child of Delia*. And then: *A heart, a life*. It was the only tribute I could think of at the time.

When I had last looked upon that headstone, the morning before I left Amethyst with Jean, the sight had hurt. A week or so after the funeral, it was still too new, too bright, a blinding signpost to what lay beneath. Now I gazed at it, for a long time, and the pain felt as mild as a cough.

I had wondered why I'd been frightened of this for so long, but sitting there in the grass beside his grave I finally understood. I had grown up, grown old, and now grown towards my own death. Back then I was young, and life stretched out for a frightening and unknowable distance, way into a future I was sure I didn't want. But I had chipped away at those years in short increments, keeping busy and preoccupied for a day or a week or sometimes just an hour at a time. Now it was as if all those years had taken care of themselves while I wasn't really looking.

There was nothing to be done at Sonny's grave. How dead you were when you were dead. How useless for those left living to be bringing flowers, or tokens. To be attaching framed photos or plastic flowers under domes, or installing glassed-in recesses containing the dead one's favourite things. Even if I'd planted a rose or lavender or a hibiscus, and even if they'd survived the years, I doubted I would have bothered to trim a single leaf, for underneath my son still lay as dead as he was the day he was buried.

Only child of Delia.

Goodbye, Sonny, I said as I got up off the grass. I have to get back to your sisters now.

Fifty-Five

> The death of the author is one thing, but the consequences of the death of the reader are yet to be explained. If the reader is dead, where will that leave the book? A good place for it may be as a memorial on your grave. Many fine books carved from white marble adorn cemeteries all over the world.
>
> 'The Postmortal Condition'
> *The Household Guide to Dying* (forthcoming)

Even before I realised I'd be leaving this world prematurely, I had fantasised over what I would be reading at the point of death. Now I was beginning to think I'd plan for it. But as I roamed the house gazing at all the titles, I couldn't settle on anything. All the books I had loved and admired and thought absolutely perfect now seemed to have lost their savour. I took out my most beloved titles, ones I had read and reread endlessly – annotated, underlined, written about in a very undergraduate way – and nothing much seemed to kick in. *Middlemarch* was far too heavy. Witty, yes. Ardent, doubtless. But just too damn heavy. I took *Wuthering Heights* back to bed one day and its fussy trick-box narrative, which I knew was so brilliant, frustrated me to tears. And I wanted to kill Nelly Dean. Or Catherine. Both of them. *Lolita* was too clever. *Pride and Prejudice* was suddenly all so brittle. *Lost Illusions* dreary. *Madame Bovary* far too sly. Even *Mrs Dalloway* struck me as being impossibly pure. Then I realised, when I started rejecting books that I knew were perfect works of literature, that it was not them, and not the authors. It was me, the reader. The reader in me was unwinding, spooling backwards. The reader who was me was now no longer.

If I'd never been able to accept that death was imminent this fact would be enough to convince me. All my life I had read, and reading had been the only place where I felt entirely whole. And now, I couldn't read. Yet, despite that, I couldn't abandon my obsession with finding the perfect deathbed title.

Death in Venice
Death of a Salesman
Death Be Not Proud

Endless trips from my bed back to the bookshelves were made all the more frustrating due to the fact that all my life the only cataloguing system had been in my head, and now my head wasn't functioning the way it once did. All the hundreds of books around the house had been shelved according to no system, except maybe in the last year or so, when the system had simply been to place them in order of acquisition in the one available space – the bookshelf in the far right corner of the living room. No system and yet I knew to the last story collection, the skinniest publisher's sampler, where each and every title rested. Over the years I'd thought about cataloguing them in some sort of order – not the Dewey system, but at least something expressing logic, such as collecting all the Australian fiction in one place, or all the green Virago reprints in another – something sensible and not too anal. But then when I found a little-read book or a title I hadn't touched for many years, I always decided not. Why change something that suited me perfectly? No one else seemed to need my books, so why sort them and perhaps risk never finding many of them again?

Now I wished otherwise. Those well-worn paths in my memories had blurred over, like a sandstorm over tracks in the desert. There were few signposts left now, not much to go on. Whole mornings were taken up with the search for a single novel, and then when I settled back in the green room, starting the first page of *Vanity Fair* or *The Stone Diaries*, it was like tasting ashes instead of pomegranate juice.

Till Death Us Do Part

For Whom the Bell Tolls

I even tried the old Reader's Digest volumes that once were my father's and which Jean had intended throwing out. I had saved them not because I wanted to read them, but because they were connected to the few memories I had of him. Frank only kept hardbacks. According to Jean he would never have handled a paperback in his life: they weren't real books. For the sort of man who'd risen from bank teller to assistant manager, who'd left school at fifteen but always felt he'd missed out on something, the Reader's Digest books that arrived every month were precious. Jean skimmed through paperback historical novels while she watched the television and knitted. Frank sat in his study, with the volumes carefully laid on the desk, turning pages with deliberation. I could remember the solemn anticipation

I felt waiting for him to come home after work when the post had arrived with that month's book, how excited I was to hand it to him, and how slowly he would unwrap the brown paper, fold it and hand it over for me to take to the garbage. That reverence for books. The sense they explained all the mysteries you'd ever need to understand. Their careful placing in the bookshelves when he'd finally finished reading. I could still see myself aged five, not long before he died, lying on the floor at the bottom of the shelves trying to spell out the gilt titles on the dark blue or crimson spines. One title in particular mystified me, because it contained an unfamilar word. I always misread this as *From Here to Enter Nity*, since the word was hyphenated and broken, to fit on the spine. The volume that contained James Jones' novel still sat on my shelves. Of all the books, I wondered if *From Here to Eternity* might be the one to read right now.

What might have been blindingly obvious came to me slowly, but it took weeks of those dead-end journeys around my bookshelves, those dry, sterile tours of a library that I once would have only wanted to live for, until I worked it out. It was when I found a very obvious title, one that I could read, and then another – *As I Lay Dying*, which I finished in a day, slow for me but fast for the new reconstructed dying me, and then *Chronicle of a Death Foretold* – that I finally worked it out. I could only read something very short. A smarter dying person might have seen that weeks or months back. Bad idea to commence fat nineteenth-century novels, especially those you'd never read before. How pissed off would you be shaking hands with the Grim Reaper while with your other hand turning the final chapters of *Jane Eyre* to see if she marries Mr

Rochester? And plenty of contemporary ones would be equally impractical, should the hooded one suddenly pop up at the end of your bed a little earlier than you'd planned. Excuse me, I just have to finish *The Corrections* and see if Enid does get her bloody family together for Christmas after all. Not likely. And the chances of a deathbed companion, a relative or friend having read the book and being able to fill you in as the lights dim and the music fades ... Not much chance of that either.

I'm Dying Laughing

The Loved One

But it was more than the practical consideration. I began to see that it wasn't the length, but the distilled nature of the piece. I needed to reach into the writing and find the essence of it in one hit. This made sense too. Now if I wanted to drink I desired no more than a small glass of medium dry sherry, or a nip of cognac, rather than several glasses of wine. Often after dinner, even if I'd eaten very little, Archie brought me a sherry or something in one of the best crystal glasses. When the girls were in bed, after I'd read another few pages of those boring fantasy stories to Daisy, we sat there for a few minutes in the lounge room with the television low, and he had another beer or two while I sipped. The taste of fortified wine was much better lately. And so with the poems. I knew I'd read them and in some cases known them off by heart – for all the annotations and marks and underlinings and turned down pages were there in the volumes as evidence – but I could peer into those words, some of them just two stanzas on a page, and it was like I was not only reading them for the first time, and that I was their first reader, an Eve in the garden of literature, but that I understood exactly what they were saying without the slightest effort. I knew, though I barely remembered, that I once reread poems like 'To Autumn' again and again to extract their endless juice. Now my insight, my understanding, was so sharp it almost hurt. They spoke to me straight off, with utter completion.

What would I be reading at the moment of death? I didn't know now, for as the moment approached old knowledge became undone, and new things emerged unexpectedly. But if I was reading at all, it would be poetry. Of course, I could be listening to old Johnny Cash records, or Pearl Bailey, or Liberace – death made anything possible – because my eyes might not be working so well. The senses shut down, and hearing is the last to go. I knew that. Which made this speculation on reading matter somewhat redundant. Perhaps I should have been raking through my record collection or seeing if some of my oldest tapes still worked. Or checking if there was actually a cassette player to play them on.

Yet it was hard to relinquish the idea of reading. It had been a persistent idea in my life and thus a persistent one in death. Then I began to notice that the pile beside my bed contained not much more than poetry.

Elegy Written in a Country Churchyard.

Now I understood it. Dying was a distilled experience. Dying was a poetic moment. The ultimate irony. The final drama of one's life. It made sense to be able to read only poetry.

I abandoning all thought of rereading *Love in the Time of Cholera* or *Bleak House*. Not so long ago, if I'd known I'd be dying without the chance of rereading my most beloved books, I might have wept, been desolate at the idea of taking off without a final farewell to such cherished friends. Felt sad that there'd be no more opportunities to read *Catch-22*. Sorry that I'd not be able to understand *Finnegans Wake*. A profound failure for never having come close to solving the Rubik's cube that was *Pale Fire*. But now all that didn't matter. Looking at those titles, piled up against each other on the shelf in the hallway, I felt almost pleased that I could say farewell. All those cherished books, some of them worn and tattered, with pages falling out and stick-on notes littering the edges. I calmly accepted the fact that I would not be rereading them, ever again.

Besides, as I passed them by clutching instead Keats or Plath or Forbes, or the *New Golden Treasury of English Verse*, I thought that it was they who should like to farewell me, not the other way around. Perhaps it was that sharpness, that clarity of insight provided by death again, but now I wondered if they never really existed, all those novels, unless I called them into life?

Or maybe that was death. Making you a touch more arrogant than you were. Making you feel slightly divine.

But I expected that at least I'd be holding a book at the actual moment of death. I hoped I'd be up to holding it. Frank was reading when he died: a copy of Henri Charrière's *Papillon*, which he'd bought after seeing the film. What would my book be? Obvious titles suggested themselves, but I knew it was unlikely to be Keats's *Odes* or *The Odyssey* or *In Memoriam*. It would have to be something postmodern. Something unlikely and unpretentious. If I were the sort of person to attract an obituary this would matter. Posterity would want to record what I was reading in my dying moments.

She was, to her everlasting regret, only halfway through Possession *when death tapped at the door.*

She managed to achieve a lifelong ambition by reading to the end of Remembrance of Things Past *before submitting to the call of death.*

A professional reader to the last, she turned the final page on the latest Booker Prize winner, pronouncing it stylistically overwrought and thin on narrative, before closing her lids forever.

Fortunately, I was not such a person. If there was to be a book involved, my final reading matter needed to be no more challenging than the latest poultry-keepers' newsletter. But obviously the perfect deathbed reading would be *The Household Guide to Dying*. I had better hurry up and finish it.

Dear Delia
I know you keep chickens. My three Red Orpingtons won't lay, even though they have a nice cage with fresh newspaper. There's a mirror in there, and a bell, and I've even got a fake egg to encourage them. I feed them the right pellets. What have I neglected?
Eggless.

Dear Eggless
Nature, I'd say, is what you have neglected. Mrs Beeton expresses it better than anyone when she says that the art of nidification is one of the most wonderful contrivances which

the wide field of Nature can show. In other words, for all your contrivances, your chickens won't lay eggs without making their own nests. Nidification: all it needs is for you to throw in some straw and leave it up to them. You'll be eating omelettes in no time.

Fifty-Six

The next morning, I packed up my things in the Paradise Reach Motel and when I was done checked the cupboards and drawers. No misplaced earrings or lipsticks or forgotten underwear. In the bedside drawer I found the Gideons Bible. In all the times I'd stayed in motels and hotels I had never once opened one. And it was too late to be thinking of religion. My home had been my religion, my family the object of my devotion.

But I wouldn't get another chance to read a Gideons Bible, so I sat down on the bed and opened it up. From my childhood Sunday school days, I remembered there was a beautiful story about a woman called Ruth, gleaning corn amongst strangers in a field far from her home. I turned to the Old Testament, found The Book of Ruth, and read it through until the end. Ruth is determined to belong in a place where she has no ties but one, the mother of her dead husband. She wants comfort and protection, but she does not beg, she has dignity and patience. She merely asks for kindness from her kinsman Boaz and he spreads it over her like a coat. He fills the mantle she holds out with six measures of barley from his harvest. And then he takes her for his wife.

Ruth, it struck me, was every person far from home, exiled from all they knew and loved yet determined to triumph over the aching dislocation of their life. Keats understood this when he wrote about the sad heart of Ruth, standing in tears amid the alien corn. I finished The Book of Ruth feeling something of her sad heart. Ruth was the mother of Obed, the grandmother of Jesse, and the great-grandmother of David, the king of Israel. I too was sick for home, but there were to be no more sad hearts. Closing the Gideons Bible, I left it on the bed and zipped up my bag. It was time I was off.

It was nearly midday when I left, and I'd not eaten that morning. There was one last stop I thought I'd make, so I turned into the Roadkill Café for a late breakfast. It wasn't Mitchell's but I still felt I should try just one meal. There were no other customers and I took my time choosing a dish, before ordering scrambled wild duck eggs on wholemeal toast. With the accompanying native tomato and chilli sauce, the Roadkill's own brand, the eggs tasted much the same as any others, and weren't nearly as good as my chickens' eggs. I followed the meal with an excellent café au lait, and took my time drinking it before I set off.

It wasn't important to eat fried rat or peppercorn wallaby or anything else like that before you died. I did buy a bottle of their tomato and chilli sauce, which I saw at the counter when I paid.

While every hour of the long drive north was imprinted on my mind, while I could remember every place I drove through, every song I listened to, every stop I made, the journey back was just a smudge across time. Failure propelled me. Grief my companion, still, but an amicable one. I was returning with an emptiness but I knew how I would fill it up for good, with what was waiting for me at home. Three days, and I drove without registering anything but the stops I had to make. All I could see lay far ahead of me, and when finally I pulled up at my house in a peaceful kind of exhaustion, I knew that inside there was a mantle waiting to cover me.

Fifty-Seven

> Expert cooks advise keeping in stock what they call the basics, yet their lists include things like vanilla beans and verjuice. The average family represents potential crisis, so the most sensible things to keep on hand are instant noodles, corn chips, tinned beans and lime cordial. The child who won't be satisfied with at least one of these products doesn't exist.
>
> 'Stocking the Pantry'
> *The Household Guide to the Kitchen* (2002)

Inside there was also a household demanding attention. I walked in, expecting the girls to throw themselves into my arms like I wanted to throw myself into theirs. Instead, Daisy rushed up and asked me what was for dinner, and Estelle took her time peeling herself away from the computer before coming over and taking my bag.

I have to go out, Archie said, there's this meeting with the architects at six. I thought you'd be back way before this.

It was hopeless getting over the bridge this time of day, I said.

Can we have takeaway?

I bet you've had takeaway every night I've been away, I said to Daisy.

Not every night, said Estelle. Grandma came over and cooked us real food too. What did you bring us back?

Later, I said.

Archie rushed past me with a kiss and into his jacket all in the same movement. Maybe he was genuinely late. Maybe there was also still some resentment of my being away. I dropped my handbag and keys onto the kitchen bench.

I'm hungry. I want dinner. Can I have a milkshake?

Daisy, I've just walked in, give me a break, please.

She looked cranky.

Give me a hug then, I'll get your milkshake in a minute.

The hug was brief. Hard to compete with evening television. But that night I was glad of it. I went and sat on my bed for a while. I could not have felt more tired. Just the thought of opening the fridge to see what might be there after two weeks away was unbearable. The prospect of assembling anything more complicated than beans on toast impossible. But I had left them. And I had returned with little more than failure packed in my bag.

I had wanted to give them special things of his, his books and toys, but now I was back I knew they wouldn't be interested. And why should they be? How could I expect them to have any interest in a long-dead brother? Half-brother. A non person, who'd lived and died well before they were born. A phantom child. Yet one they were probably jealous of anyway. I pushed his old suitcase into my wardrobe, unpacked my few things onto the bed, threw the dirty clothes into the corner of the room, and took out the Paradise Reach's wrapped soaps and mini shampoos I'd saved for them. Not much, but better than no present at all.

I walked back out to the living room.

What about pizza for dinner? Estelle, do you want to ring and order for me?

Goody. Vegetarian with extra cheese.

Naturally.

But I want Hawaiian, Daisy wailed.

Oh god.

Order both, I said quickly. Tonight I would have cut off my left tit – if I'd had one – to avert another of these tiresome scenes.

You mean one each? They couldn't believe it.

Whatever you want.

They looked at each other, calculating in nanoseconds how far they could exploit the advantage.

Can we get garlic bread too? And a bottle of Pepsi?

The entire deal, I said. Just ring them now, Stelly, and let's go and watch something stupid on TV.

The Simpsons isn't stupid, Daisy said.

All right, I said. The Simpsons is very, very clever. Anyway, she was right.

Dear Delia
I still can't find a recipe for cooking stingray flaps. I'd like one for dugong too, if you have it.
Fish lover.

Dear Fish lover

Have you ever considered cooking small native mammals? Recently I came across dishes like chargrilled possum (boned and skewered) and wallaby steaks in peppercorn sauce. I'm happy to pass on the recipes if you want.

Fifty-Eight

> Remember the most important thing of all: the funeral is for the living, not the dead.
>
> 'Funeral as Festival'
> *The Household Guide to Dying* (forthcoming)

The girls grew taller, moved up shoe sizes, decided that they loved spinach pie one month, hated it the next. Estelle dropped netball, Daisy took up jazz ballet. They continued to fight and cuddle each other in front of the television. For the next few months it was all a normal family life except I thought about dying, and wrote about dying. Organised coffins. Visited cemeteries and funeral parlours. I got on and did the research and wrote the chapters and kept the household chugging along as best as I could manage.

In between were weeks of lying in bed, of sleeping but always feeling tired. Then times when I could work and live as if nothing was wrong. There were visits to the oncology clinic and Dr Lee's rooms and there was the day that I walked out of the chemotherapy ward for good. I was happy that I'd been to Amethyst and seen Mitchell, Pearl and Tara, and collected the suitcase. Sad I never found Amber but glad I'd tried. In all those months while I made sure the girls were allowed to life a stable life I wondered what that was really. What was normal for kids?

Jean came to visit a lot more. Archie worked a bit less. I sat with the chickens every day. And in my spare time I went around the house quietly battening down the hatches. Taking unwanted stuff to the charity stores. Filling up the freezer. Getting to the bottom of the ironing pile. Making something special for the girls.

I'd already bought boxes: Daisy's with ducks all over it, Estelle's black with silver stars. Now I began to fill them. In one I placed the wedding list (well, she might find it funny in twenty years' time) and my wedding ring, which I'd not worn for a long time anyway, with all the weight loss. I added a plastic duck with a note around its neck saying, *Redeemable for a real live duck in two years' time. Remind Dad.* I had always promised Daisy a pet duck but couldn't see how to accommodate one with the chickens. I'd let Archie work that out. And I included a twenty-dollar note, so she'd know I meant it. I placed in there a copy of A.A. Milne's *Now We Are Six*. It had been Daisy's when she was younger, before that mine, and Jean's when she was a child, loved and treasured for decades. Perhaps Daisy would read it to a child of her own one day. Perhaps she'd just send it on to the Salvation Army store. But that didn't matter. She only needed to know that it was something coming from me. I put in Sonny's plastic magician set. It was mostly rubbish, but I thought she might like the wand which, with its concealed strings and magnets, really did work a bit like magic. And finally his fake, water-squirting daisy, of course.

For Estelle I had an old but perfectly good black silk camisole which I knew she would wear over rather than under her T-shirts. In her box, I placed a pair of crystal drop earrings which I had bought a long time ago at a second-hand store, and twenty dollars so she could go and get her ears pierced for her twelfth birthday, like I'd promised. She'd probably badger Archie into doing it sooner. I knew better than to suggest reading matter for Estelle, and I suspected she was the kind of girl who would be writing her own. So the book I selected for her was completely blank: creamy unlined pages bound in red fabric. I included my best fountain pen, and a bottle of scented ink which I'd hoarded for years. Estelle had coveted them both. From Sonny's things I chose the clown face paints and the red plastic nose. I thought she'd appreciate that.

I had considered getting them the electronic gadgets they so desired – a mobile phone, a hand-held game, a new digital camera, an iPod – until I realised the impracticality of that. Even if I died the next week such things would probably be obsolete. And I knew I would never have chosen the right brand, the right amount of megapixels or gigabytes or whatever it was that was so vital about these things. It didn't matter to me but it would matter to them. And that's what it was all about.

There'd be my books, my ornaments, my stationery, my clothes, my jewellery, my music, even my car. They could have the keys to the kingdom, and take whatever they wanted. The only thing that mattered was that I would have thought very carefully about what I most wanted to give them, since love, while it endured, could not be captured and contained in boxes like that.

Actually, when Estelle had turned eleven I'd already handed her the keys to the kingdom. Which is to say I passed on all responsibility for her bedroom, their room. As I entered it to hide their boxes I nearly tripped over Daisy's leopard-print backpack. I kicked it into her half of the room where it landed next to several homework sheets, a pencil case vomiting its contents over the floor, and about a thousand dolls in various states of undress. There was an invisible demarcation line in this room. Estelle's side with its posters of bands and singers or actors (I honestly didn't know) on the walls, and her clothes neatly arranged in the wire drawer set. Her books stacked on the bedside table, her CDs all in their cases and alphabetically arranged on the rack next to the player. Her bed was made and the pillows in place. Daisy's looked like it was inhabited by hyperactive meerkats. The pillows were always on the floor, the blankets concealing mystifying lumps, the cuddly toys wedged between the mattress and the wall. So many of their fights were territorial disputes. I was proud of how I'd let go about that. I'd hand them their piles of clean clothes and leave them to it. If the sheets hadn't been changed recently no one seemed to have contracted any particular disease.

I put Estelle's box on top of the wardrobe, where I knew she'd find it soon after I'd died. I put Daisy's in the wardrobe, on the floor of her half where, judging by the collection of food wrappers, dirty underwear, old fluffy slippers and other stuff I didn't even want to know about, it might lie undiscovered for years.

So, have you decided? Will it be Waverley or Rookwood? Archie took a long pull of his beer.

We were down by the chicken shed before dinnertime, sitting in the cane chairs that were so old they'd soon need to be thrown out. It was milder that evening than it normally was in September, but the chickens were already making moves towards bed. I was still holding Jane in my lap. If people knew just how soft and compliant hens like her were, they'd be more popular than rabbits as pets.

Wouldn't it be lovely to be buried here? I said. Just next to that laying box. Nice and deep where the best worms are. I'd be so content, under all the chicken shit and scraps.

Archie just looked at me.

It's okay, I said, I haven't any mad plans for that. Besides, it's against the law. Section 63 regarding the Disposal of Cadaverous Tissues, in the *Cemeteries Act* of 1908. I researched it for the guide.

Where, then? You're going to have to let me know sooner or later. Preferably not later.

Well, the two places are equidistant from where we live, so either is a practical option. That's if you're planning on visiting.

Of course we'll visit.

But the idea of Waverley is an attractive one. Arthur Stace is buried there.

Who?

You know, the Eternity guy.

Why's that relevant?

It just appeals to me. Don't worry, you'll understand soon.

Jane was fidgeting to get out of my arms so I put her over the fence and she trotted off to roost for the night.

So, you want it to be Waverley then. Do you think we should ... you know ... ?

Buy the plot now? I said. It's all right, Arch, you can say that. It makes it easier to say the real words, don't you think?

He stuck his nose deep into his beer glass. Of course, even by this stage, even after he'd risen to the challenge of my coffin, it wasn't easier for Archie to say the real words, it wasn't easier for anyone but me.

But no, I don't mean I've decided on Waverley, I said. A fantastic view, but it's pretty crowded out there, as you know. And Rookwood has such a wonderful poetic name. It has assonance. I love the idea of being buried in Rookwood.

You mean you'd choose a cemetery just because of its *name*?

Possibly. But the name Waverley has literary connotations, I said. And plenty of poets are buried there too.

He rolled his eyes. Well, you'd better make up your mind soon so we can start organising it. I'm getting another beer. Do you want anything?

Arch ... I held his arm as he got up. I'm not making up my mind. I haven't decided and I'm not going to.

You? Not deciding? Not planning? Bullshit.

That's right. I'm not.

Why not?

I've realised that I won't be visiting me when I'm dead, so I'm not going to do anything because I don't need to. You can do it.

Me?

Yep. You're the gardener. You'll make the right choice about where to plant me, I know it.

I sat back in the cane chair feeling possibly too smug but also that I was right. As he went off to get another beer I could almost see the cogs turning in his mind. Waverley or Rookwood. Rookwood or Waverley. Maybe he could just toss a coin.

Dear Desperate
In the circumstances, it was extremely generous of you to invite me to you and your girlfriend's commitment ceremony in Hyde Park. But I'm afraid I won't be well enough to attend. Otherwise I would love to be there. I'm sending you a little gift, which might match those towels.

Fifty-Nine

> You might, however, want to consider compiling a standby list. Even though the funeral is for the living, a great deal of bickering can take place amongst families over irrelevant details, like whether or not they should serve chicken sandwiches and smoked oysters at the wake, or if having a bagpipe player would be maudlin or wryly amusing.
>
> 'Funeral as Festival'
> *The Household Guide to Dying* (forthcoming)

I didn't plan the funeral either. I did at first, I'd written yet another list and named the place and the time. I wanted it to be a late afternoon, so everyone could kick on afterwards with plenty of drinking and fun – real drinking, too, with decent champagne and single malt whisky and cartons and cartons of boutique beer. Along with real food – generous platters of thickly sliced leg ham, fresh crusty rolls and gooey chocolate mudcakes. Plus party food for the kids:

they'd need Fanta and fairy bread and all that other disgusting glorious stuff.

It would not be like these anaemic funerals so popular now which were catered for by the one service, the package deal that took care of everything from the coffin through to the croissants. All clean and easy and soulless. Places in funeral parlours or crematoria that I'd encountered while researching the guide. Vast, empty secular temples with sterile music coming from hidden speakers, music that sounded like nothing on earth or in heaven. Where the bereaved were quietly ushered through the front door and out the side door in less than an hour, like they were on some slowly moving beige-carpeted walkway, and not meant to notice that someone had actually died. That there was a body in there. That the softly lit coffin (or casket) in front of those dove grey curtains didn't contain a note saying *Rest In Peace* or a joke saying *Sucked in!* But that this meant there was now a huge ragged hole in at least one person's life, right then, in that place.

I would have none of that. My daughters and their friends could sit around my coffin, eat their snacks on it if they wanted. Estelle could stick her CD player on the top. And Daisy could drip as much tomato sauce from her sausage rolls as she liked, while her mouse, China, ran around on it.

As for the order of the service, I stipulated the songs and the music. I wrote down the names of people I'd like to speak, or to read my favourite poems. I thought about making a recording of myself, smiling at all my family and friends, exhorting them not to be sad, telling them how much I loved them, reminding them to buy a copy of *The Household Guide to Dying* on their way out (but sorry, I wouldn't be able to sign it for them) and then saying goodbye, goodbye, goodbye. But then that struck even me as macabre. Plus I didn't have the technological skills to do it. Estelle may have been able to help me, but then it wouldn't have been a surprise. And after I'd worked it all out and decided the colour of the napkins they could use to mop up the food and drink, I realised I didn't need to do this. Not any of it. So I tossed the list away.

A short while later, as I knew she would, Jean said to me, Delia, we haven't discussed the funeral.

Yes, Archie said. What do you want to do? He went to the sideboard for a writing pad and pen and handed them to me. The girls were finishing off their homework and the house was quiet. I'll open a bottle of wine, he said, and we can sit down and work it through. You may as well tell us now what you want.

Nothing, I said, as he took the wine from the pantry.

Pardon? They spoke in unison.

You heard me. Nothing. I'm not planning a thing.

I don't get it, Archie said. You plan something like Daisy's wedding but not your own funeral? You were even thinking about making her wedding cake, for god's sake!

Yeah, I know.

But you said you want a good wake. What about writing a list of the music? Or of the food, at least? You're so particular about parties and things.

No, I'm not.

Oh, come off it, you *are*.

No, Archie, I *was*. Not any more. I've let go of that.

He and Jean looked at each other. She reached for the bottle of wine that he still hadn't opened.

I've worked something out, I said. In years to come, of course I want you and the girls to remember how much I cared. That's why I was mucking around with wedding lists and stuff. But the funeral isn't for me, it's for you. So you write the list. You choose the music. The poems. The hymns, if you want them. The food and drink. You can have party pies and sauce, cream soda and Foster's if you like. I don't care.

You really don't care?

No. It's amazing, isn't it? It'll be your event, not mine. I want you to do it your way.

I pushed the writing pad and pen over to them and got up.

Start writing it down now if you like, I said. There's something more important I have to do.

I still had one more empty box, but hadn't been able to decide what to leave in it. I went into the green room and shut the door and blew the computer into life. Then I typed the last list I would ever write.

Some months before, I'd tried to have the most difficult conversation of all with Archie, the one I thought needed to be had. Tried to tell him to think about himself. About sex. I'd even tried to say that, with my diminished – and then, in recent months, extinct – capacity, he should not think it wrong to think about a girlfriend. Of course it was a stupid conversation to attempt to have.

Isn't it sad for you? I said to him. We were lying on the bed together, cuddling. Don't you miss it?

I couldn't, at that stage, actually remember the last time we'd had sex. It seemed that I'd always been in pain, or vomiting, or in hospital, or recovering from surgery, or working, or asleep, or exhausted, and never interested or capable. It had only been two years since the mastectomy but by then it was hard to remember what it was like having breasts at all. But I did remember how much Archie loved them, how as we lay in bed he would cup and fondle them as gently as if they were baby birds.

Why should it be sad? he said.

I don't know. It's just that … we've had such great sex, haven't we? I don't want you to miss out on my account.

What do you mean, exactly?

I mean … you could, you know, go out with someone else. If you wanted.

(Of course by *go out* I meant *have sex,* but saying that was impossible.)

Like now?

Well, why not? I wouldn't mind. If it would help. Only if you wanted.

I was saying it in the wrong way. Archie was starting to look black in the face. Just saying it at all was wrong. But I couldn't stop. I had to tell him what I knew now, what even he didn't know, as closely as he was watching my life end: that you needed to embrace life and hold it as tightly as you could, all of it, before it slipped away like the armload of sand it was.

I mean, what about Charlotte?

(Wrong thing to say.)

You're just trying to control it all again!

Puzzled, offended, angry, everything. He would have felt guilty too, for the little flirtations, which he probably thought still upset me. He got off the bed and walked out of the room.

But hold it, Archie, I said. Seize it. Mr Lambert had got it right, even though it was too late for him. Carpe diem, I said as he was walking away, though I doubt he heard me.

So the conversation I'd tried to have, about the importance of sex and intimacy and other women, and maybe even Charlotte (I was sure they were fond of each other) never developed, but I'd not dropped the idea. I understood Archie, and I knew that eventually he'd want another woman, and also that he'd want validation from me, dead though I'd be. Whoever that woman was, whenever the time came, I'd still be able to finish the conversation we couldn't have. In fact, this way, he'd be listening, but I wouldn't be telling him a thing.

The other conversation we'd never had was one I'd run through my head countless times since I'd returned from Amethyst. Did you want me, Archie, because you knew I could bear children? Is that the real reason it didn't work out with Pearl? Is that why you broke up with her? I couldn't bring myself to speak the words. I didn't want to know. I didn't know if it even mattered or not. And I knew how hard that conversation would have been for Archie. He had enough to cope with now.

And so the last list I wrote was simple, neat, clear. It started with things like dried fruit, brown sugar, brandy and spices. It ended with plain white icing. And a real flower on the top. Frangipani, or gardenia, depending on the time of year. Maybe a sprig of orange blossom. For the first time, I wrote out the recipe for my wedding cake, the one I'd made for our own and for several others. The one I'd always conjured more than made, but which was always perfect, rich, moist, and able to last for years in the right conditions. I printed it out, put it in an envelope, wrote his name on it, sealed it with a kiss, and dropped it into the one remaining box that had been waiting for something from me, for Archie.

I had nothing special to leave for Jean. And yet I was leaving her everything. She would be with our daughters as they grew into women, and there could be no better gift than that. On one end of my desk, which was now tidied of all but the most necessary paperwork – the final drafts of the guide, the folder of medical letters, schedules, statements and bills – I placed the two photo albums documenting Estelle's and Daisy's lives, both with many spare pages. Jean could keep adding to them. On top of the albums I placed the box for Archie.

Mum, I said when I went back out to the kitchen, when I'm gone I'd like you to tidy my study, if you wouldn't mind. I've done most of it, but you might find stuff I've overlooked.

Of course I will, she said, holding her hand out and keeping her face focused on her glass of wine.

Dear Delia

You might have forgotten, but you were going to give me the details of that cake. I especially need to know how much brandy. The wedding is soon.

Thank you.

Mother of the Bride.

Sixty

> Preparations for the actual death should be simple. Most people desire to die peacefully in their own homes. It is tempting to romanticise the moment of death and introduce some classical music along with exotic herbal teas and readings from the Victorian poets. But the dying person might wish to lie in the back yard drinking Pimm's and listening to Mrs Mills. Or perhaps they might prefer an exit accompanied by the strains of Herb Alpert's Tijuana Brass band. Their last meal might be tinned tomato soup, or a lemonade iceblock. It does not matter.
>
> 'The Penultimate Moment'
> *The Household Guide to Dying* (forthcoming)

Daisy was sitting on the front fence post one Saturday afternoon waiting for a friend, and I was in the laundry folding towels, when I heard her yelling at me to come. I ignored her. She called me again and again, to come quickly. I went, slowly.

How many times have I told you? It's rude. If you want me, come and get me ...

But, Mum, look! Look at that. From the fence post she had a view across Mr Lambert's front lawn. There's writing there, she said. Writing in dark green flowers, or something.

She was right. Something was written right across his lawn. It looked lovely against the paler shade of the winter-green couch.

It's clover, I said. What does it say? She stood on the post, wobbling, trying to get a better look.

Be careful. I held her legs to steady her. What do you think it says?

She turned her head around, the better to read it. It's just one word. Enter-nity, I think. That doesn't make sense.

Come on, you can do better than that.

But it's running writing!

Read it again.

And so she did. Eternity, she said. *Eternity*.

And there it was, in huge dark green letters flowing right across the centre, spelling out so clearly you could read it from the deepest end of the heavens if you wanted: Arthur Stace's perfect word.

Just when I thought I'd finished the book, Nancy rang. She had an idea that it should contain a chapter on the afterlife, and had already lined up some interviews.

I've got you a priest and a Buddhist nun, she said.

I'm not sure about this, Nancy.

Plus a Muslim cleric.

Tempting, I said. But it's a guide to dying, not death.

What's the difference?

I had to think about this carefully. To me the distinction was a clear one and always had been, and I'd assumed that Nancy had understood this. I found the idea of the afterlife impractical, and having attended to practical matters in the guide I felt it would be out of place. But it was something more than that, something I'd only half known, until Nancy's question forced me to articulate it.

Death is a condition, but dying is an act, I said. It's a noun versus a verb. Death is later. I won't be here for that. And I hope you realise it's not just a matter of grammar. I can write about dying because I know about it, I'm doing it.

So what will the final chapter be?

I'm not sure yet. Someone else might have to write it.

Scrolling through the final draft to see if I could accommodate her, I discovered the book was in a reasonable state. Most of the chapters were there, and only a few were in need of a final revision. There was no index and no list of resources or references. If I didn't finish it, Nancy could always tidy it up. Maybe she could interview her priests and nuns. Whereas once I would have been ashamed not to complete a job, I wasn't fussy now. Besides, I'd agreed to deliver the manuscript by spring and spring hadn't ended. I finalised the contents list and clicked the Print icon to run out a final copy of the manuscript to leave in its folder on the desk. While it printed, I sorted through my notes and took out to the recycling bin all the drafts and papers that were no longer needed. I came across a picture Daisy had drawn, of a chicken roosting on top of a gravestone, of all things. I think it was inspired by our visit to the cemetery. Just for the heck of it, I wrote *The Household Guide to Dying* in thick black letters across the top, *Delia Bennet* underneath, and placed it on top of the manuscript. Nancy would enjoy the joke, if I didn't get the chance to deliver it to her personally.

Then I put some music on while I had a rest. It was playing rather loudly so it was a while before I realised there was knocking on the front door. It was late afternoon, Archie was still at the park with the girls. The knocks came again, sounding impatient or urgent. I made my way to the front door, which seemed such a long journey these days, turning down Elvis on the way, and wondered how long the person had been there.

When I opened the door she had her fist up, raised to knock again. Behind her the late afternoon light put her face in shadow. Tall, slender, long dark brown hair with bronze glimmers in it that could have been natural. So hard to tell with girls these days. About twenty. I had never seen her before. She was neither smiling nor stern. She was dressed in dark jeans and a black leather jacket, with a large bag over one shoulder. She did not look like a salesperson or a Jehovah's Witness. Her mouth was soft, twitching slightly, as if she were about to cry or laugh.

Are you Delia?

I noticed beyond her that Mr Lambert was out checking his mail. He turned around and stared at his lawn, as if seeing it for the first time. Then he looked directly at me, and I looked back. The first time our eyes had met for years.

Delia? she said again, louder, as if I were slightly deaf.

I dragged my eyes back to hers.

Yes.

I heard you were looking for me, she said. Grandma told me.

Grandma?

Yes, you asked her about me. And here I am.

For a few moments I had no idea what she meant, and then I remembered Margaret and the chickens, and how I thought she was keeping something from me. But how did I know it was her?

Who are you?

You know, she said, you know me.

How do I know you? This was too hard.

It's me. Amber Morgan.

Amber? There was so much doubt in my voice. I heard it tearing at the edges of that name.

Beyond her, beyond the verandah, the front fence, the day outside seemed an ordinary one. The cat over the road mincing up their front path. A silver car driving past, followed by a blue one. Mr Lambert still at his letterbox, staring at the lawn and scratching his head. It was warm despite the lateness of the day, yet there was also a chill to suggest the night would be cool. October was like that, shifting around, offering a taste of every season in the one day.

It was an October when Sonny died. When she got her new heart.

Amber Morgan? How do I know it's you?

Slowly, still staring at me, she unzipped her jacket and, grasping each side of her shirt, pulled it apart to reveal a long thick scar down the centre of her chest.

I'm so grateful to you, she said. I've been grateful all my life.

And the last age should show your heart.

She reached out for my hand and laid it on her chest, right over the place where I could feel my son's heart beating as steadily as a clock.

You wouldn't read about it. Life has stories wilder than any fiction. She followed me into the house after an eternity of hugging and crying, right on the front verandah. Mr Lambert regarded us benignly. He was possibly even smiling.

And then, when I didn't feel I could be given any more surprises, she did it again. We went to sit in my quiet green room, and as I paused to turn the music off, she stopped me.

I love that song, she said. Leave it on, please.

You like Elvis?

Oh yes. I sure do, ever since I was six. After I got better, I mean.

I had to laugh. Of course you do, it's in your heart. I paused for a moment, remembering. We were playing this song during the operation, I said.

So I left Elvis singing 'Always On My Mind' and we sat together while she told me how she was pursued by the media, always hungry for sensational medical stories featuring children. Her mother protected her by moving from house to house in Amethyst, finally staying, when she decided it was quiet enough, at the place in Nile Crescent with the long backyard. Her grandmother came to stay, and set up her chickens. Here they lived in peace when people forgot about the little girl who received a new heart a few days after a local boy was killed in a freak traffic accident. I *had* felt there was something about that place which connected to me, although I'd never been there before.

And then the Morgans left town, the parents divorcing and Amber and her mother moving south, where she attended university.

Before you visited her that day, Grandma had heard that you were looking for me.

It wasn't a secret, I said. I was asking around. But why did she lie to me?

She also heard you were working on a book. That you were a writer.

Now I understood. That would have meant the worst: a bereaved mother, a resentful mother, and now one with the means to turn it all into a book. She wasn't going to have her granddaughter's life exploited.

After she told me, I thought of looking you up, she said.

Not only did Nancy's website list all the titles in the guide series, but it featured *The Household Guide to Dying* as forthcoming for the summer list (Nancy was optimistic too) and boasted that it was being written by someone who had personal experience of the subject.

But dying. It made Amber think. What would this dying woman want as her last wish?

I rang a few times but hung up, she said. I just didn't know what to say. I thought about it for ages, then decided I should just come.

I'd been wrong. The season was not so cruel after all. Here, well before its end, came a gift to bring me solace. But then, I understood: I'd been granted my desire and now I knew what would come next.

By the time we had caught up on the past fourteen years, Jean arrived. She was dropping by every day now. Once again she astonished me by falling into tears.

You were there too? Amber asked.

Jean nodded. I remember we played his favourite songs, she said, sniffing. And I didn't cry then, I never cried, until now. Sorry, darling, she said to me.

I shook my head.

But look at you. Amber. You look so, so ...

Amber smiled. She was really tall, nearly six foot.

Big? she said. Healthy? Hearty?

Hearty, I repeated. That's it. Exactly the right word.

What I don't understand, Archie said, is why your family were so protective.

It was later that evening, after a dinner of Jean's ricotta cannelloni, and chicken broth for me. Estelle and Daisy had accepted the idea of their half-sister – for that's who she was in a way – with characteristic equanimity. Which is to say, what was momentous to Archie and me was ordinary and almost boring to them. I had finished reading to Daisy and returned to the living room, where Archie had dimmed the lights and opened a bottle of shiraz.

I didn't understand it myself either, Amber said, not until I grew up. I was only six at the time. But it's something to do with cellular memory. When I learned I had the heart of a boy who was two years older than me I was frightened at first. I thought it was too big for my chest. And then, after I recovered, my mother noticed changes in me. I refused to drink milk – in fact, hated dairy foods, they made me feel sick.

Sonny was allergic to dairy, I said.

Yes, that's what Mum assumed, or something like that. And my favourite colour had been pink. When I was sick I had my entire bedroom decked out in pink. Hot pink. After the transplant I couldn't stand it, complained so much that Mum had to redecorate.

Let me guess, I said. Red and blue? Royal blue.

Exactly. I also developed a taste for more adult music, hated all the kiddy stuff I used to listen to. I remember hearing Elvis singing 'Burning Love' on the radio one day and just starting to sing along. Somehow I knew the words.

One of his favourites.

And then as I grew up I became really sporty, adventurous. Less feminine. Wouldn't wear dresses, whereas before it was all frills and lace. I was the textbook girly girl. But afterwards I only wanted to dress like this. This is the real me now, jeans and stuff. I only feel comfortable dressed like this.

Mum had read about other cases, in America. One woman had gone on a talk show and explained how she'd received the heart of a grown man, and after the transplant started to crave spicy food, junk food, and admire blonde women. She thought she was becoming a lesbian. Then she met her donor's family and found out he'd been killed in a car accident, and his last meal had been at Taco Bell's. His favourite food was Mexican, burgers, spicy sausages, that sort of thing. And all his girlfriends had been blondes. There was a lot of controversy. She became a celebrity, then got depressed, suicidal. It was like she was living with two personalities. When Mum saw all the changes in me she was determined I was never going to suffer like that woman.

Cellular memory, Archie said. What's all that about?

Apparently individual cells can remember, it's why immunisation works. It's too complicated for me, and anyway I didn't have a clue about it when I was young. But Mum knows how different I became. My doctor ridiculed the idea, but I've read about it since. They say that our emotions and our personalities are stored in places in the body. The heart rules the brain as much as the brain rules the heart.

I took her hand and turned to Archie. It's funny, you know …

What?

Nancy rang earlier today, she wanted me to write a chapter on the afterlife, but here it is instead. The afterlife is with us now.

Dear Mother of the Bride
Use an entire bottle of brandy. One of whisky too. And plenty of eggs. You won't go wrong. It will be perfect, I know.

Sixty-One

> Of all the taboos surrounding the act of death, those regarding the intimate needs of the dying person are the worst. Death does not necessarily mean that the desire for sex evaporates. Indeed there is well-documented evidence of dying people developing a renewed interest in sex. It is as if the inevitability of mortality sparks the counter urge to live. Death is known to be erotic. Dying people and their partners are urged to embrace this. Remember the moment of climax is not called a *little death* for nothing.
>
> 'Sex and the Dying Person'
> *The Household Guide to Dying* (forthcoming)

Then it was as simple as waking one morning and knowing that one time had passed me by, and another had arrived. It was time to forget about cooking, to forget the domestic arts altogether. Instead it was time to prepare.

I told Nancy I was well enough and working away but that morning I also admitted to myself that I had done as much as I could. I wouldn't be seeing the guide through to completion.

This was the October morning that I woke to feel the cruelty, and decided to embrace the joy. The morning I stooped to collect damp mauve wisteria petals and hold them in my palm before the wind tossed them away. The morning I expected would be one of the last times to appreciate the beauty, the fresh clean smell after rainfall, the moist heat rising from the bricks beneath my bare feet as the day blossomed. The morning I went down earlier than usual to the chickens, calling them each by name – Jane, Elizabeth, Mary, Kitty and Lydia – all Mrs Bennet's daughters from the fussiest to the most foolish. The morning I realised that if time was running out then it was also time to let go of some things, seize others.

For a while, I'd forgotten about my other final gift. When words began to diminish, I listened more acutely. I had expected that my voice would be the first thing to go, but I hadn't realised how clearly I would hear. Conversations around me became musical; the household sounds were a chorus softly chanting. The oven door that still squeaked after five years, the tinny slam of the back screen door, the rumble of feet on floorboards, the urgent hiss of water in the bathtub, the tin-can chatter of cartoon television – all the sounds that had accompanied my life became harmonious. Outside, the metallic shrieking of the lorikeets in the flowering gums sounded tender. Inside, the girls' bickering was gentle, lyrical. Piercing through this chorus was the melody. The song.

Last as well as first, it was about the soundtrack. But it was the most unexpected thing, when it came. Not the songs I imagined, not the music of angels heralding me to some other place. Not some rousing chorus about chariots swinging low or my weary body being carried to its final sleep. Not music I might have selected for myself, like Pachelbel's Canon. Or something by Bach in the key of D minor. In more considered moments I had imagined some poetic Leonard Cohen song, full of muted charm and complex desire – 'Anthem', or 'Hallelujah'. Like the last book I thought I'd have in my hand, it was just as unexpected. No Faure, no Dylan. No Patsy going crazy, Aretha in full-throated voice, Hank confiding his weary, lonesome last.

As death approaches, hearing is the last of the senses to shut down.

Although there was music playing somewhere in the background – soft string chords of something folksy and restful, Archie's favourite Irish singers, I think – what I could hear clearest of all, as the evening approached, just outside the open window, from Mr Lambert's front garden, in fact, was a placid tock tock tock. The unmistakable call of frogs. Daisy's tadpoles, now grown up. The evening breeze brushed across me like a wing. *Tock tock.* The sound was an absolute miracle.

Estelle rushed into my room. Can you hear them?

I nodded and she raced off, calling out to Daisy. I understood about the strange alignments, the patterns that didn't make sense until the end. I'd been waiting to hear the frogs, or maybe they'd been waiting for me. A moment later, Archie entered holding something. He placed it in my hand, still warm, a wisp of featherdown attached.

Thought I might boil it for your supper, he said.

Not hungry, I whispered. And I smiled. For while I always assumed in the end I'd be holding a book, it was nothing like that. I was holding a fresh creamy white egg.

I had always been restless. Now while the household washed around me, I lay back and surrendered to my thoughts. I noticed some things for the first time, like how for all these years it was Daisy who was the one singing and playing her music, but Estelle only ever listening to hers. I focused on the odd and the unexpected. Like the heads of Archie, Estelle and Daisy as they moved back and forth around me. Archie's balding spot, which he denied existed. When he bent over to hug me I had a perfect view of it. (I didn't say to him, See, Arch, you *are* going a bit thin up there, though you deny it.) I saw Estelle's shiny brown head (soon, no doubt, to be a spiked and multicoloured statement indicating her cultural/musical/emotional credentials). And Daisy's straight part, dividing into neat plaits. That balding patch, that shine, that parting: I revered them now. The tops of the girls' heads became particularly tender, as I began to dwell on the possibility that I did not spend enough time, for all my devotion as a mother, on the contemplation and admiration of their perfect inviolate bodies. Things like the backs of their necks, the source of their unique scent, inspiring waves of joy in a mother.

I remembered their feet, the miraculous perfection at birth, right down to the last minuscule toenail, every tender wrinkle, the shape of each baby heel, as tiny and as soft as a single rosebud nestling in the palm of my enormous hand. I treasured those feet, after each baby was born and for months and years beyond. I knelt on the floor beside their cots at night, kissing the toes that had pushed their way through the bars, worshipping the miracle of babyhood, the gift of perfection that was the sleeping child. And feeling, as I kissed those sweet soles that motherhood was a palpable mystery, something to be seized and held and felt, if only for a few moments in the still of the night.

But I wondered if I marvelled long enough over their starfish hands, firm yet soft, and always, but always, warm? Appreciated for long enough the feel of a flaccid hand that mine could hold yet never contain? I wasn't so sure. I may have pushed their hands away sooner than I ought, sent them away to be washed too many times, or banished them from grabbing my breasts or twisting my hair, instead of accepting them, grubby, sticky, ticklish though they might have been. Now those same hands, larger and more capable, brought flowers from the garden, glasses of water, morsels of toast. Daisy's hands fluttered around my neck and stroked my arm. Estelle's pressed down on the green quilt. She was holding in check her reactions, for I knew she felt, as the older sister, a responsibility not to lose control, not to let Daisy see that everything, however much anticipated, discussed, planned, was now toppling into disorder, going awry.

I could see how vulnerable Archie's bald spot was, how protective I felt towards his head; I considered his earlobes, which I loved to kiss and nibble. Did I do that enough? Tell him how much I loved doing that? Or what about his glorious cock, its satiny folds when at rest, the smooth tip that remained like silken velvet despite years and years of friction? What a miracle, what a glory. What simple pleasure in licking it slowly again and again, tasting the thrill of its salty promises. I was too tired to tell him, so I hoped he knew how much I loved to wake and feel him hard against me, even if the feeling never led to the act, even if we had to leap from bed at the call of alarm clock or baby or the hundred other reasons a working parent has to rise, morning after morning, after never enough sleep, instead of being able to turn and face each other and welcome the day with slow sleepy sex. I hoped he knew I would have, if I could have.

Yet how ridiculous to have regrets when I'd not cared for sex for so long. How ironic and what a perfect joke – surely there must be a god after all, such wit could not be accidental – to be thinking of sex in your last moments when you are all but out the door, when you are barely there, when your body is lying inert and useless, but your soul is keen and almost alive. But death was like that, I understood now, surprising you with the regrets and the desires, as *thy willing soul transpires at every pore* to escape, to ascend.

I saw them, more distant, yet more clearly, as if I had strange new lenses reducing all beyond me to a pleasant greenish blur, but making them, the tight circle that was my family beside my bed, sharper, brighter. I even glimpsed Sonny there, a softer figure nestling under Archie's arm – or was that just the effect of these strange new lenses? – not eight as he was when I last saw him but not twenty-two either as he would be now. Just a sort of essential Sonny, a vision of who he was when he was killed and all he might have become. And standing behind them, tall and grave, an image of Amber, with that heart beating so strongly I could see each pulse as clearly as if her chest were made of glass.

How much I love them, and yet how much I desire to be free. How I can now adore every particle of them and yet for the first time want to leave, without a single stab of guilt.

That's a surprise too. I imagined dying to be similar to leaving them at the school gate on the first day, knowing you have to go, you want to go, but every muscle screaming as much as them to stay, every cell clawing you back. But no, now I'm feeling it for the first and last time in my life, I discover it isn't like that at all. I am calm. I feel no pain. I watch them coming and going and my heart could not be fuller with them, but I experience total freedom. My family. It seems to be an ending yet not a goodbye. I seem to be leaving them for something much better, though I can't have loved them more. Although I want them, I can let them go. Such splendid poetic ambiguity. I thought I was right before this and now I know it for certain. Death is a poetic moment.

Dear Mother of the Bride
One final tip, especially for you. Put Angostura bitters in the mixture, a couple of dessertspoons. It's been the one secret ingredient I've guarded for years. I won't be needing it any more.

Acknowledgements

My three children deserve the greatest thanks of all. Over the last few years they have had to hear the words, *Go away, I'm trying to write,* far more than they should. And they have all helped me in special ways. My oldest son, Joe, has always been so understanding and encouraging of my need to write. My daughter, Ellen, was an attentive reader of the manuscript and she created an inspiring image to help keep me focused. And my youngest son, Callan, when I was partway through the novel, faced and fought leukaemia with a courage I doubt I could ever have. He survived, and they all remind me, every day, what the most important things are in life.

Thanks to my dear friend and agent, Lyn Tranter, of Australian Literary Management, who over the years hardly ever said, *How's your next novel coming along?* even though it was a long time between this one and the last. As a reader she is always insightful, honest and good humoured, and as an agent she combines extraordinary instinct with utter professionalism. Thanks also to her assistant, Wenona Byrne, for dealing so cheerfully with the paperwork; and to Garry

Hogden who took over that paperwork when it became a total mystery.

Thanks to Ross Duncan for reading an early draft and making many helpful comments and suggestions; to Kirsten Tranter for a perceptive reader's report that made so much sense; to John Dale for yet more encouraging feedback; and to Margot Nash for correcting some details and for inspiring a few improvements.

Many thanks to my publisher Lynne Drew of HarperCollins for her great enthusiasm and support for this novel; she also provided me with much wise and helpful editorial feedback. In Australia, I also received invaluable editorial assistance from Rod Morrison and Sarina Rowell at Picador, and from freelance editor Ali Lavau; in the USA from Peternelle van Arsdale at Putnam; and in Canada from Nicole Winstanley at Penguin. They have all helped make this novel better in many ways.

Jane Palfreyman, now publisher at Allen & Unwin, deserves special thanks for her support. And thanks to Peter Doyle for advice on copyright matters.

Finally, I am grateful for the assistance of a small grant from the Faculty of Humanities and Social Sciences at the University of Technology, Sydney, which created time in the first half of 2007 to complete this novel.

Sources and references

The epigraph from John Forbes's 'Death, an Ode' is from his collection *The Stunned Mullet* (Hale & Iremonger 1988) and is reproduced with kind permission of Len Forbes. The references to a verb being brave (chapter 21) come from Don Watson's *Death Sentence* (Knopf 2003). The quotation from Dylan Thomas's 'Do not go gentle into that good night' (chapter 35) is from his *Collected Poems* (Dent 1952) and is used by permission. The idea for blood sausages made from one's own blood was inspired by Gay Bilson in an article she wrote in the *Sydney Morning Herald*'s *Good Weekend* magazine (14 May 1994) and again later in her book *Plenty* (Lantern–Penguin Books 2005). I incorporated this into my novel with her kind permission.

Mrs Beeton's Book of Household Management was first published in 1861, and I used the Oxford World's Classic edition (OUP 2000) for reference and quotation. The story of Arthur Stace, the 'Eternity Man', is well known, and has been memorialised in opera, song, story and film (and even on hats, T-shirts, brooches and mouse pads: thanks, Terry) but perhaps most famously in the culmination of the 2000 Sydney New Year's Eve fireworks.

And the secret ingredient for a fruit cake recipe was given to me by Joan Carey, mother of my dear friend Gabrielle. I'm not sure where Joan got it from, but I will always regard it as one of her many special gifts.